THE THIRD EYE

JENNA RAE

BELLA
BOOKS

2018

Bella Books, Inc.
P.O. Box 10543
Tallahassee, FL 32302

Printed in the United States of America on acid-free paper.

First Bella Books Edition 2018

Editor: Ann Roberts
Cover Designer: Judith Fellows

ISBN: 978-1-59493-604-3

Other Bella Books by Jenna Rae

Stumbling on the Sand
Turning on the Tide
The Writing on the Wall

Acknowledgments

I am very grateful for my beautiful children and my darling Lee. Thank you for offering your love and humor and patience. Maritza, Becca, Mary, Suzanne, Sarah, and Motsie—thank you for being your kind, loving, accomplished selves and for putting up with my neglect and distraction.

Ann Roberts, thank you for providing encouraging feedback along with direct, insightful suggestions for sculpting a book from my mess of a draft. As a reader, I have greatly enjoyed your books. As a writer, I have greatly benefited from your generosity, talent, and wisdom.

Thank you to the smart, dedicated, talented team at Bella Books and to our peerless leader Linda Hill.

To each reader I offer my humble thanks. Your time is valuable and your choices many. Thank you for investing irretrievable minutes and hours to this story.

CHAPTER ONE

Rookie patrol officer Tami Sheraton fell back when the bullet hit her chest.

A tiny video camera secured to the frame of Sheraton's eyeglasses watched tall, slender Sergeant Mark Donnelly saunter through the back exit of the liquor store with a paper sack in his left hand. His dark eyes widened and his fleshy mouth gaped in evident surprise. Donnelly drew his service weapon and spoke for six seconds. There was a blinding flash as he discharged his gun. The evening sky dropped and the audience gasped.

Captain Brenda Borelli blinked as the big screen went dark in the nearly silent auditorium. She swiveled ten degrees left to face her interrogator and answer his question.

"Yes, Commander, I did suggest Sheraton wear a hidden camera."

Briarwood Police Department Senior Commander Marty Banks raised an eyebrow. He cleared his fleshy throat, an action that generally presaged a long lecture, and Brenda decided to forestall it.

"Not a serious suggestion. Obviously. It was a sarcastic off-the-cuff remark, not something I expected Officer Sheraton to actually do. She understood it was a joke. We laughed about it."

Banks grunted and rolled his eyes. When no one seemed to respond to this, he cleared his throat again. He snatched up his dripping water bottle roughly enough to crinkle it.

While he chugged and choked, Brenda looked around the room as though gathering support. She chose her words with care. "I guess she thought about it and decided it wasn't such a silly idea after all."

"So you and Tami Sheraton were off alone somewhere, joking around, and you suggested something dangerous and thought nothing of it." Recovered now, Banks shook his jowls. "Did you often have private conversations with this female junior officer? And where was this personal conversation, Captain Borelli? Did it take place inside your home, a restaurant, a bar? This was at a time when you were off duty, wasn't it?"

Brenda kept her face blank, refusing to rise to the bait and wondering how Banks had advanced to the second-highest rank in the department. She watched the other members of the panel sit back, as though to distance themselves from Banks.

"As indicated in your briefing notes, Commander, I was walking into this building at approximately noon on Christmas Day. I wasn't scheduled for duty but had some paperwork to catch up on, and I wanted to support my officers who were working the holiday. I brought sandwiches and cookies, just like I have on every major holiday for the last several years."

Brenda waited a beat before continuing. None of the high-ranking bureaucrats ranged above her on their raised platform had been at work on Christmas Day, and everyone knew it.

"Sheraton approached me on the front steps to ask my advice on developing stronger observational skills and situational awareness. I suggested the usual things and warned it could take years to hone her craft. She was frustrated, so I kidded her, saying a camera might help. Sheraton laughed. It was obviously a joke."

"Captain—"

"I advised Sheraton to seek guidance from her training officer, Sergeant Mark Donnelly, and her station's commanding officer, Captain John Vallejo. She assured me she would do so, and I followed up with Captain Vallejo and Sergeant Donnelly within the week to ensure she had."

"And now Officer Sheraton is dead." The stark statement came from the only female officer in the Briarwood department whose rank was higher than Brenda's. Commander Victoria Paige Young widened her beautiful blue eyes and shook back her long golden hair. Brenda knew Tori had long been referred to as Commander Barbie by more than one senior officer, though no one dared say it in front of Brenda.

Elevated on the gleaming pecan dais with the other brass, Tori peered down at her ex with clear disdain. Brenda felt her spine stiffen. With what she hoped was invisible effort, she relaxed her shoulders and the muscles of her face.

"Yes, Commander." Brenda waited a beat. "Of course, a few things happened in between."

Tori blinked slowly and sat back, and Brenda sobered. Did Tori really think Brenda had misjudged the situation with Sheraton? Certainly she'd misjudged Tori.

Staring up at the glossy bureaucrat ensconced in a navy bespoke suit, Brenda had a hard time seeing the funny, smart, devoted lover with whom she'd shared nearly a decade. Brenda pushed her feelings aside to focus on the task at hand. She looked directly into the face of each of the big bosses one at a time.

"Tami Sheraton's family, this department, and this city have lost a good person and a good officer. But my joke didn't kill her. We only know the identity of her killer because she was wearing the hidden camera. The footage we just watched is from that camera."

She took a long sip from the glass of water in front of her and kept them waiting an extra few seconds. "Mark Donnelly is still at large. I request the allocation of additional resources to the search for Sheraton's killer, pursuant to the department's longstanding focus on officer safety and on ensuring the highest professional standards within the department."

Banks cleared his throat. "Captain Borelli, we are aware of our own policies. You're the subject of this hearing because your carelessness may have been a contributing factor in the death of Officer Sheraton." He caressed his tie, danced his stubby fingers through his thinning white hair and ran his gaze around the assembled officers who ringed the back of the large, plain chamber on the ground floor of the city's new five-story building. "You're hardly in a position to make requests of this department."

"Commander Young. Commander Banks. Commander Olivares. Commander Jones. Commander Fulton. I won't mention my twenty years of service to this department as a defense against your allegations of wrongdoing, though of course the only wrong I've done was to make a joke that the officer in question knew was a joke. Sheraton was a rookie who was focused on doing her most conscientious job. She took some initiative. In fact, she might have revisited the idea after she read this department's newsletters, two of the most recent of which detailed how many departments around the state and the country are requiring their officers to wear body cameras, a practice we can debate the relative merits of at a later date."

Based on the surprise painted on their faces, she guessed not one of the senior officers staring down at her had actually read any of the department's newsletters or was aware of current operational trends in law enforcement. Bringing up the newsletters' contents was her kill shot, and she could only hope she'd calculated its best use accurately.

As one, the brass section looked past her at the dozens of officers witnessing the hearing. Brenda noticed Tori's small, nearly invisible smirk and knew she'd scored big. She decided to build on the strength of her position.

"One of our own killed one of our own. That's the real issue here, the fact we allowed within our ranks a man who is corrupt, violent, dangerous, unethical, and a threat to our community and our department."

Brenda noted the way Tori shifted her shoulders. She knew the hearing was essentially over then and Brenda had won the rhetorical battle. What this would cost her in the long political campaign that was her career in law enforcement, she'd find out later.

There was more yammering. Each senior officer had to make a long-winded statement that could be quoted by the press and by the public-relations contractor. Then a few midlevel officers had to follow the bad examples of their bosses and express outrage and smug superiority. The onslaught went on for well over an hour.

This barrage of verbiage was finally punctuated by a brief, conciliatory statement from Chief Walton, who had positioned himself halfway between her and the elevated senior officers as though he were a neutral party.

She thought for the umpteenth time that Chief Walton was, if nothing else, a brilliant tactician. It was he who'd suggested she wear a suit instead of her dress uniform and insisted the hearing should be open to the public. She strongly suspected he'd also notified key officers to ensure a wall of blue stood behind her in the hearing.

She sat quietly through that last hour. She kept her face blank, her back straight, her hands relaxed on the table in front of her. Things turned out about like she'd expected, with no authorization for further investigative resources and no censure of Brenda or anyone else.

As she finally made her exit, exchanging quick greetings with dozens of officers on the way out, she noticed a woman staring at her with wide, unblinking eyes. Struck by the intensity of the stranger's gaze, Brenda returned the direct look for a long moment before the outsider turned away, disappearing in the crowd of officers and other onlookers.

The attractive newcomer—an elegant redhead with dark brown eyes—looked vaguely familiar, but Brenda couldn't place her. Was she an officer from a neighboring department? A journalist? A victim? A politician? Clear eyes and skin, very good haircut, tailored suit and erect posture were the only impressions Brenda had formed in her brief perusal. Who was the staring stranger?

Adrenaline engendered by the very public scolding she'd just experienced pushed her speculation away, and she plowed as gracefully as she could through the crowd. She shook hands and patted shoulders and smiled without letting anyone engage her for more than a few seconds.

She nodded at Dan Miller, CEO of Briarwood Watchdogs, wearing a bland expression despite the question that ran through her mind at seeing him: why would the head of a private security company show up for a hearing like this one?

As always, he sported a black polo shirt and gray pants, gleaming combat boots, a movie-style holster and a variety of mail-order badges and insignia. A civilian would take him for a police officer or a soldier, which she supposed was the idea. He shaved his thinning hair and always looked like he was about to head into some mysterious battle with unknown nefarious evildoers. The extra thirty or so pounds he sported in his midsection and the ever-present sheen of sweat on his pate blew the lie, but he didn't seem to know that.

Brenda eyed Miller as he approached, his mouth wide in a salesman's smile and his hand outstretched. She knew he'd squeeze her hand much too hard, so she summoned an iron grip to counter his. After a few tense seconds he broke the hold and smiled as if in concession.

"Congratulations. Ready to get out from under yet?"

She laughed. "You never quit, do you?"

"I'm a success because I surround myself with the best people. You're the best, so you bet I'm going to keep trying to get you on my team."

"Why don't you join us?" She countered with what she hoped was a friendly smile. "We could use someone with your leadership skills."

He pursed his lips and nodded before answering. "Don't think I haven't considered it. I have a lot to offer. I could shake things up. But I'm my own man, Captain. I'm on the winning team. I'm always on the winning team. Don't get left behind."

"If I change my mind you'll be the first to know."

"That's a maybe, and that's better than a no. I'll get you someday!"

He nodded as though they'd agreed to something, and she patted his arm as she murmured a goodbye and brushed past him.

"Thanks for coming, Padilla," she said to a recently retired officer, shaking his cold, dry hand and continuing to move through the crowd.

A reporter clutched her arm, and she extricated herself with a wry smile and a brief squeeze of his arm. "Come on, Cal, don't you guys at Channel Three have anything better to cover on a Friday night? It is football season, right?"

Tami Sheraton's captain, John Vallejo, stood in the swirling mass of officers and spectators, somehow apart from everyone while surrounded by the crowd. He was in Brenda's path, having apparently plotted her course and planted himself accordingly.

"John," she said, coming to a stop. Her Central Division counterpart was in his early fifties. His salt-and-pepper curls looked as droopy as his posture was erect, and she saw weariness in his dark, hooded eyes. His curt nod gave her pause, and she peered at his closed expression. "This couldn't have been any easier for you than it was for me."

He shrugged and looked away. "The sooner we can all put this behind us, the better."

"Agreed." She noted the strain in his voice, not certain whether he blamed her for Sheraton's death or whether he was feeling guilty himself. He was, after all, both Donnelly's commanding officer and Sheraton's.

As if reading her thoughts, he shook his head. "Donnelly—I still can't believe it. He seemed like a regular guy, a decent guy."

She murmured agreement and examined Vallejo more closely. He'd been smoking. She could smell it on him and knew how hard he'd worked fifteen years back to quit smoking when his second wife was pregnant with their first child. Or was it, she puzzled, his first wife and second child? It was getting harder to remember details like that.

She caught a whiff of booze in his sweat and was even more surprised by this. He had been sober for over twenty years. The strain of the situation was showing on her normally unflappable colleague, and she wasn't sure how to offer comfort without seeming patronizing or political.

"I never thought you were responsible," he offered, rubbing his chest as though it itched.

"Thanks. I never blamed you either, for what it's worth."

"Yeah. See you around."

Vallejo suddenly turned away and shouldered a path through the crowd. Brenda frowned at his retreating back, but another young officer was already approaching, and she offered a quick handshake and wooden smile before moving on.

It took nearly ten minutes to work her way past the crowd and across the street to the looming parking garage. Finally alone in her ancient Caprice, she took a deep breath, glad the evening was behind her.

What did she fail to see? What should she have done differently? She wasn't arrogant enough to think she should have been prescient, but she certainly wished she or someone had been able to see Donnelly was a bad apple.

She wondered whether the recent events showed as starkly on her as they did on her colleague. She'd seen Vallejo in a lot of ugly situations over the years and had never seen him look so brittle. Though she hoped otherwise, she knew she probably didn't look much better.

At this thought she snorted. The circus was over and no one would be at home when she got there. What did it matter what she looked like?

As she sat in the cocoon of her car, Brenda peered over the garage's perimeter wall and saw the crowd from the hearing was starting to spill out into the street. Loath to draw attention to herself by loitering in her assigned parking spot, she started home.

"Three hours completely wasted," she fumed by Bluetooth to her retired former partner Jonas Peterson.

"They have to put on a show, Borelli. Whaddya expect?"

"I notice my old partner didn't show up to support me."

He snorted. "It's not like you needed any help, Slick. And it sure as hell ain't like my presence woulda helped you."

She made a noncommittal sound. She'd never asked him to attend the hearing but had hoped he would show up. Sober, hopefully. But she couldn't pursue this without pushing him away and didn't want to give him a reason to disconnect.

Accept people as they are, she told herself. If she'd learned anything from the breakup with Tori, it was the necessity of accepting people as they were. She blew out hot air and tried to let go of her frustration and disappointment.

She tuned back in, and while Peterson shared his own stories of brass-coated misery, she wondered if she would end up like her old partner, with no life outside the department. She knew it would be easy to let that happen.

Like Peterson, she'd let the job swallow her hours and her years. Like Peterson, she'd lost the one person she'd expected to be with for the rest of her life. Like Peterson, she had failed to develop a support network outside the department. So far, she was batting a big, fat zero in work-life balance, just like her old partner. After setting up a lunchtime get-together for the following week, Brenda rang off feeling more alone rather than less.

If she and Tori hadn't broken up months ago, they'd have had dinner before the hearing, strategizing and anticipating what might happen, and afterward gone over the evening's events on the ride home. She'd have heard what Tori thought and could have talked about who said what, how it was said and why it mattered.

Of all the things she missed about Tori, it was their conversations she ached for most often. But there was no going back, and she knew she had to start really accepting the end of things between them.

"Acceptance," she said aloud in the bubble of privacy provided by her car. "Acceptance, acceptance, acceptance."

It was, as her best friend Andi kept insisting, time to move on. She would have to start dating again, she realized with a shudder. Later, she told herself. After Donnelly was caught, after Tami Sheraton's death wasn't hanging over her and staining every moment of each day. No matter what she did, no matter what punishment the judicial system ultimately doled out to Donnelly, Tami Sheraton was never going to be alive again.

"Let it go, Borelli," she told herself, determined to find the necessary detachment. She needed to put her grief, anger, and guilt aside. Maudlin mulling was, she knew too well, a waste of her time and energy.

She headed to the coastal road and drove home the long way, letting the cool and quiet of the late January evening soothe her. She passed one of the newer condo complexes and sighed. Briarwood had been her home for two decades, and she'd once known every road and just about every family in town.

But in the last five or six years there'd been a huge influx of new people, drawn from the various reaches of the San Francisco Bay Area to quiet little Briarwood by its good schools, low crime rate and reasonably priced homes Its proximity to the Pacific Ocean made the small northern California city a very attractive option, and its relative peacefulness made the long drive to Bay Area employment centers a worthwhile trade-off for many.

Waves of newcomers tipped the scales until everything they'd come to Briarwood in search of was spoiled. A population swell strained the resources of the small community, overloading the place with too many kids, too few jobs and a series of sharp rises in home prices just before the country's real estate bubble burst. Briarwood residents new and old lost their jobs and their homes.

Homeowners became renters as a wealthy few snapped up foreclosed homes at bargain prices, rented out the houses and charged tenants increasingly exorbitant rates. Crime increased, school test scores dropped and gang violence invaded the south side of town like disease in a weakened body.

Briarwood was still a nice place to live if you were middle class or upper class and had managed to keep your job or get a new one that paid several times more than minimum wage. But the shine had been scraped off the small city by poverty, uncertainty, and fear. Brenda felt guilty for her relative comfort. She also felt increasingly uneasy about the simmering unrest she sensed fomenting in the cauldron of widening economic disparity.

Where would it all end? How could a society survive with such weakness in its foundational elements? Brenda shook off the question and reminded herself she was not responsible for the fate of the world. All she could do was try to make Briarwood a little safer for a little longer. That would have to be enough.

Night hid Briarwood's grime and graffiti. The tips of the rooftops and the redwoods and the waves were painted otherworldly blue by moonlight. She caught glimpses of the Pacific between condominium towers and hotels and rows of identical beige minimansions. Boats dotted the small harbor that made Briarwood an attractive tourist destination, and she recalled the days when there were only a few dozen boats scattered around the shallow bay.

She breathed in the cool, clean, salt-washed air and felt scrubbed. The sweet apple scent of the briar rosebushes that dotted nearly every yard and shopping center in the city balanced the crispness of the sea air and mostly covered the industrial and automotive smells.

She sniffed deeply as she drove along, drawn by the perfume of Briarwood to memories of her early days here, when she'd found this mix of clean, sweet air so irresistible. In the dark she could still be a young newcomer and Briarwood could still be a charming little village. It could still be the sweet small town named after a rose.

Over and over she saw the ugly, ubiquitous signs of Briarwood Watchdogs. Dan Miller's private security company was the most successful venture in town. Its numerous signs, resplendent with fluorescent renditions of the city's namesake flower, glowed proudly in front of at least half the homes she passed. They seemed to reflect a newer, more cynical world that thought a plastic flower was better than a real one and neighbors couldn't trust each other.

Brenda wished she could always see Briarwood through the softening veil of obscurity and found herself wanting to do the same with regard to Tori. She pushed away this whimsical thought with a snort not unlike Peterson's.

Her tension dropped as she unlocked the front door of the foursquare cottage she'd bought back when the northern part of Briarwood was still affordable. Like most of the older homes, it was surrounded by the sweet briar roses whose foliage perfumed the air with their apple scent.

Brenda yanked off the charcoal gray suit she hated, the one she used only for court, meetings, and hearings. She left a trail of sweat- and coffee-scented clothing on the way to the bedroom, the one part of the house she'd tried to strip of Tori's presence, albeit half-heartedly.

In a fit of pique, she'd bagged up the bedding, a sumptuous suite of gold and silver threads and bold geometric shapes, and dropped it in a donation bin. She'd replaced it with a plain gray comforter and scratchy white sheets that would have been right at home in a detention center.

But the unlovely bedding was still surrounded by antique furniture, beautiful fixtures and warm gold paint a shade or two lighter than the gold Tori had picked for the living room and hall. The bedroom still glowed with the hominess Tori had brought with her, and Brenda wasn't quite ready to ditch all of that.

Tori's mark was all over her as well, Brenda realized as she sighted her reflection in her dresser's mirror. Her short, dark curls were cut to look carelessly flattering by in-demand stylist Logan, to whom Tori had brought her a decade back. Though she couldn't have said how he achieved simple elegance with her formerly unruly mop, she had to admit it looked more professional and a lot more attractive than when Brenda used to hack at it herself.

Her mascara and tinted lotion, now worn daily, had felt strange back when Tori had first suggested she wear them when testifying. After a while it had been a natural transition to putting on the minimal makeup every day, because the same strategy also worked when Brenda was interviewing victims and witnesses. Wearing the makeup made her seem more approachable, according to Tori. More importantly from Brenda's point of view, doing so had made Tori coo about how beautiful her brown eyes were.

She was also in the habit of wearing the fancy Breitling watch Tori presented to her on their fifth anniversary, along with the diamond earrings Tori gave her several Christmas mornings back.

Upscale clothes, accessories, lingerie, and sundries had become the norm during her years with Tori, and she hadn't let go of those luxuries. Nor did she particularly want to. The things Tori had given her had become part of Brenda.

Of course, Brenda had given gifts too, hadn't she? Last week and again at the hearing, she'd noticed Tori wearing the vintage sapphire pendant and earrings Brenda had given her on their second anniversary. The Dior perfume, the Philippe watch, the Carven scarf—every time Brenda saw her, Tori was still sporting at least one of her gifts.

What did it mean that they both continued to don these presents? Was it simple pragmatism, or was there some unconscious desire on both their parts to retain the good pieces of the relationship? Did Tori want to get back together? Or was Brenda imagining things? If Tori ever did want to get back together what would Brenda say? She bit her lip.

Speculating about what she'd do if Tori wanted to rekindle their relationship when Tori had never indicated she wanted to do so was the height of ridiculousness. She knew that, but she'd caught herself indulging in such musing more and more. The phone rang, and she knew even before she looked that it was Tori.

"I know you think I went after you," Tori blurted, jumping in without preamble as usual.

"Was that you being gentle?"

"Oh, come on, Bren, you know I couldn't be seen as going soft on you or those vultures would've eaten you alive. Use your head for once. You could thank me, you know."

"Don't do me any more favors, huh?" Brenda snapped her mouth shut. She knew that Tori was right.

Everyone in that room seemed to know about their relationship, and the only reason she'd walked away relatively unscathed was that the other brass saw Tori as a vengeful dyke bitch out to screw her former lover. They'd let Brenda off out of spite for their barely tolerated only female commander. Tori had played them at least as well as she had, but Brenda wasn't quite ready to acknowledge that.

She called me Bren, she thought. Tori hadn't done that since their breakup, or rather several months before it. What could it mean that she did so now?

"Sorry," she said. "You're right."

Tori inhaled sharply. "Oh." She breathed in and out audibly. "Listen, I don't know how to say this."

Brenda heard a sound she recognized: Tori tapping her tongue on the roof of her mouth the way she always did when she was uncertain or distressed and briefly regretful about having given up smoking. Brenda had given her a flower every day for nearly six years as thanks for quitting. She'd only stopped after Tori had told her the daily flower had become less a gift and more a painful reminder of her having taken up smoking in the first place.

"Whatever it is, it's probably best to just spit it out." She spoke more sharply than she'd intended and grunted as if in apology.

"Yes. Of course. Spitting it out. A few hours ago Mark Donnelly's body was found in a motel in West Sacramento, gunshot wound to the head. Could be suicide. Yolo County says it's likely to be processed quickly. You weren't going to be allowed into the investigation, obviously, but I imagine you were planning to look into it on your own. No need to any more. I just thought you should know."

"Yeah, thanks." Brenda sank onto the bed they'd once shared. "Any word on his co-conspirators?"

"Well, the department's position is—or will be, as of five minutes after Yolo County's statement tomorrow—Donnelly was working alone."

Brenda scoffed.

"I know you think differently." Tori made an indistinct, wordless sound. "I wish I could convince you to drop this. But I don't think you will. You feel guilty about Tami's death. You hold yourself responsible, even though you clearly weren't. I imagine you think I shouldn't ask you for any favors, Bren, but I want you to just walk away from this. Please."

"Walk away?" She fought a rising note in her voice. She stilled herself, refusing to argue with Tori yet again.

"Listen." Tori sighed heavily. "It's late and I'm tired and so are you. This isn't exactly the way I wanted to spend my Friday night either, you know? I just wanted to tell you about Donnelly."

"Thanks."

"Who was she?"

The question was an echo of the one Brenda had asked six months before, and she held her breath, unable to speak.

Tori jumped back in. "That woman you were making eyes at. After the hearing. You know who I'm talking about."

"I don't know. I-I mean," Brenda stammered, "I know which woman you're talking about, but I don't know who she is. I just saw her staring at me and looked back. And what do you care anyway? You left, remember? You—whatever."

"Yeah." Tori huffed quietly. "Whatever." And she was gone.

Brenda hated not getting the chance to go after Donnelly, but while the department might think the case was closed, she knew better. And if Tori thought Brenda was walking away from the case that had left young Tami Sheraton shot through the chest and bleeding to death in a rat-infested alley, she was crazy.

CHAPTER TWO

By the following Monday, the department had moved on and so had the media. Brenda barricaded herself in her office all morning, which served only to provoke curiosity and unease in her officers.

Belatedly she realized that in doing this one thing, sitting alone in her office instead of taking calls and circulating among the women and men who looked to her for leadership, she'd already started changing course.

She had taken most of the weekend to carefully consider her course of action, one that would hopefully, but not necessarily mean she'd still have a career to come back to afterward. She'd worked hard to build her reputation in this department, but something was rotten in Briarwood, and she intended to root out that something.

Hamlet had been driven to pieces by his desire to make things right, just like Ahab had been by his pursuit of his white whale. Was she following in their ill-fated footsteps? Would it be better to just let the disruption and uncertainty of the last weeks die with Donnelly?

Certainly it was tempting. Brenda had a good life. She had supportive friends and a successful career and a nice home. She would be able to find another girlfriend if and when she wanted to do so. She was lucky enough to have made it this far with her health, her retirement and her good name intact.

Why risk all of that to pursue a case against some mysterious, possibly imaginary evil in her upstanding little department in her idyllic little city? There had been, according to everyone else, a terrible, inexplicable, isolated tragedy. Tami Sheraton was dead. By some miracle, the bad guy, Mark Donnelly, was also dead. The matter was resolved. Case closed.

The department was prepared to seal the files on the sordid little matters of extortion and murder as if the crimes had nothing to do with anyone but Donnelly. Everyone was acting like he appeared one day out of nowhere, did his dirty deeds and then conveniently killed himself outside of city and county limits, where no one from Briarwood had to deal with him.

As the clock ticked toward noon, Brenda answered her cell phone and smiled when she heard Andi's low voice. After two decades, her contralto tones were as familiar as the waves on the nearby shore.

"Did I hear right? The thieving, murdering scumbag's dead?"

"So it would seem."

"What's the deal? I'd have thought you'd be happier."

"Yeah, I don't know. It feels unfinished. Too easy."

"What's that like, too easy?" Andi sighed loudly. The owner of Briarwood Café had no doubt already been at work since four that morning, baking cakes, scones, muffins, cookies, and bread.

The very sound of Andi's voice put the scents of vanilla and cinnamon in Brenda's nose. Of course, Andi had also probably been doing payroll and inventory and other such prosaic things since before dawn too.

"Oh, come on, you must have gotten a good three or four hours of sleep last night, slacker."

Andi's laugh was more polite than amused, but Brenda appreciated the effort.

"I know I should drop it, Andi, but it's all too neat, don't you think? Donnelly kills Sheraton. Then, before anyone has to do anything crazy like track him down or investigate the extortion, he conveniently turns up dead? What're the odds it's that simple?"

"Yeah," Andi said, sounding distracted. "Listen, maybe you're right. But why don't you give it five minutes before you make up your mind about what happened?"

"Maybe." Brenda sighed and then grinned. She could always count on Andi to cut through her nonsense and tell her the truth, whether she wanted to hear it or not.

"I gotta go. There's a crowd and my new cashier is falling apart. Call me later."

Brenda set down the phone with a fond smile at the image of Andi swooping in to rescue the cashier who was probably doing fine. Self-appointed rescuer of the lesbian, gay, transgender and just plain lost kids in Briarwood's increasingly fragmented society, Andi had a tendency to hover over her informally adopted charges long after they were ready to take wing.

Her smile died as she let her thoughts drift away from Andi and back to the convenient death of Mark Donnelly. She smelled resolute complacency in the station's recirculated air, and she eyed the men and women under her command. Not one face was turned to look at her. Not one officer had cocked an ear in her direction when she'd picked up her ringing cell phone. But somehow they all seemed attuned to her.

On a normal Monday morning she would have asked about Sergeant Abbott's new car and congratulated Gonzalvo and Johnson on Friday afternoon's successful conviction of a rapist they'd worked tirelessly to build a case against.

Normally she'd have gone through the paperwork accrued over the weekend, checked in with Thompson about his team's ongoing investigation into gang-recruitment activities, and had a friendly chat with the two training officers who'd recently been assigned rookies to groom. Today she'd done none of it, but no one had questioned this or commented on the omissions. So, she concluded, they already knew or sensed what was going to happen.

She glanced at the clock and noted that her self-imposed deadline had arrived. She took a deep breath and called in her two most senior lieutenants to explain what was going to happen in the coming weeks.

Abe Johnson seemed less than enthused about doing the management work, but she assured him he'd be back investigating before long. Sean Miller had a glint in his eye that told her he relished the opportunity to demonstrate leadership, and she wondered how long it would be until the man started bucking for her position.

"And of course, I'll be reachable, day or night."

Johnson nodded and examined the breakdown of duties. "How long, Captain?"

"A couple of weeks, I suspect. Not long." She forced a smile. "Just pretend I'm on vacation like a normal person."

Miller's phony laugh was an awkward braying, and she smiled to hide her distaste.

"Don't you worry, Captain, we can steer this ship until you're back at the helm."

"Thanks. Complete change of topic, here, but I've been meaning to ask for months: are you related to Dan Miller?"

"He's my cousin. Why do you ask?" Miller crossed his legs and plucked at his perfect crease with manicured fingers.

"No reason, just wondered."

"Ah." Miller smoothed back his wavy blond hair. "We're all very proud of his success."

The canned answer made Brenda blink. She suspected Miller had political ambitions, and it sounded like there was some competition between the cousins. Sean Miller was not her favorite person. She considered him self-absorbed and self-serving, but in her evaluations, she indicated the truth, that he was capable and sufficiently personable to do his job. Funny, she thought, I don't like his cousin either. She pushed the idle thought away and asked if either of her lieutenants had any questions.

After a few clarifications, she thought she'd prepared them as well as possible. Leaving the pair to sort through her carefully considered framework of instructions and schedules, she strode away from her unusually well-organized office without a backward glance. If she hesitated, she'd give up on her quixotic mission and go right back to her desk. Knowing this, she didn't let herself perseverate any longer. It was time to do the thing or not, and she was determined to do it.

As she passed Maggie, her assistant jumped up as though she'd been waiting. Petite, middle-aged Maggie Gomez, her dark curls bouncing as she tap-tapped in high heels alongside Brenda, was breathless with curiosity and asthmatic tension. She peppered her boss with questions about upcoming meetings, appointments, and paperwork that needed signing.

An astute and organized administrator, Maggie was the heart of the station, which Brenda made a point of verbalizing both privately and in front of others on a regular basis. This simple acknowledgment had earned her Maggie's unflagging loyalty, a valuable commodity in the increasingly politicized Briarwood Police Department.

Since this particular station was housed at the department's headquarters, it could have felt like an ancillary segment of the administrative division. In the months since her promotion to captain, Brenda had worked hard to make sure it didn't. Though it policed the more complex crimes in the increasingly restive southern part of Briarwood's burgeoning downtown, South Central Station had a high solve rate, low turnover, and relatively few interpersonal problems.

She was proud of her team and felt a tug of reluctance to walk away from it. Looking into Maggie's clouded brown eyes and knowing she refused to question her boss because she didn't want to appear mutinous, Brenda pushed away her last internal resistance. She answered the administrative questions she could, handed Maggie a pile of signed paperwork, and then stopped midstride. She raised her voice just a little so she could be overheard.

"I know things have been a little weird around here, Maggie, and I'm sorry. This morning has been especially strange. Talk to Lieutenants Miller and Johnson. I'll probably be taking a little time off starting today, and they'll split my duties while

I'm out. I know they can handle it, but they'll need your help. If something comes up and you really need me, of course, just call."

Maggie nodded. "I figured something like that. What do you think, a week? Maybe two?"

"Hopefully no longer than that." Brenda gazed into Maggie's dark eyes. "I appreciate your being so understanding. This is a good team, and I know you'll take good care of them for me until I'm back."

"And you are coming back, right, Captain?"

"Absolutely, assuming they'll have me." Brenda smiled and let her gaze drift around the large room. "I care a lot about this place and everyone in it."

The station went mostly quiet then, and she felt dozens of eyes on her as she made her way to the elevator. There'd been a strange tension in the air in the days since Sheraton's murder, and Brenda had tried to dispel it by focusing on open cases and compelling her officers to do so as well. It had worked about as well as she could have hoped.

Upstairs, she cooled her heels outside Chief Daniel Walton's office, knowing he was at lunch until one. She took the chance to figure out how she was going to deliver her message. When Walton came in, Tori was with him, and Brenda fought the lurching sputter of her emotions that always accompanied Tori's presence.

"Captain Borelli, what a wonderful surprise!"

She ignored the lie and mirrored the chief's wide, warm grin, pretending she didn't know Walton's secretary had texted him the minute Brenda walked onto the fifth floor and requested a meeting. She stood and gave both superior officers a firm handshake, noting that Tori wore the sapphires again and that Walton's hand was tacky.

"Chief, Commander, nice to see you both. How was Dave's Bistro?"

Tori rolled her eyes, but Donny Walton goggled obligingly. He loved to play the magnanimous leader, and today Brenda was willing to go along with the game.

"Did someone tell you where we were?"

"No sir," she responded, smiling widely. "You're both sucking on those blue mints, and your tie's picked up a tiny spot of that special sauce Dave mixes up for his favorite customers."

"Wow, nicely done, Captain!" He gave Brenda a careful pat on the arm before looking down at his brightly patterned silk tie. Both women waited a good thirty seconds while he stood with his head bent nearly double and fingered the edges of the overpriced accessory.

When he finally found the miniscule brown dot, he crowed in what seemed like genuine delight. He would, she knew, change ties as soon as he was alone again. Beaming at him, Brenda felt Tori stiffen with obvious impatience at the prolonged exchange.

"You're not just here to do parlor tricks, I hope, Captain Borelli." Tori's tone was hard. Her ice-blue eyes narrowed, and her hair fairly crackled in its low, perfect ponytail.

"Oh, come on now, Commander, let's give the captain her due." Walton's affable manner was a key component of his success in the department and, if the rumors were true, would soon be of use to him in the political arena as well. "She's sharp as a tack, our own Sherlock Holmes. Brenda, why don't you come in and have a seat, hmm? Do you prefer Commander Young join us or not?"

"As you like, Chief."

Walton looked at Tori, who gave a wry chuckle.

"Oh, I wouldn't miss this for the world." Tori led the way into the chief's office, and Brenda smiled as she followed the familiar hourglass figure.

Tori had always known how to present as exactly what she was: perfectly professional, highly intelligent, tightly controlled and a veritable fountain of sexual energy. Behind her, Walton's subtle intake of breath announced he was as appreciative of Tori's retreating figure as Brenda was.

There was silence as the three settled into their places: Walton behind his oversized desk, Brenda at one of the low chairs in front of it, and Tori off to the side, leaning against the walnut credenza and tapping her pocket.

"You, ah, you knew Dave, didn't you?"

She nodded, swallowing hard. "He was a friend of the department for a long time. Michael too."

"He's done a fine job picking up the reins at Dave's."

"I agree." She didn't want to think about the sudden heart attack that had made Michael a widower at fifty, but she kept her expression neutral.

"They were somehow connected to that terrible case, years ago, what was it?"

"Child trafficking. Dave's was still a fish-and-chips shack back then, if you can believe it. The guys lived across the street from the house we believed was being used to keep the victims. Dave let us use his house for surveillance. Darius Brown and I spent practically every night staring out of his living room for weeks. Michael and Dave had just gotten together, and poor Michael didn't know what to think at first, but he went along with it. The guys would bring us sandwiches and coffee."

"If the rumors are true, you didn't exactly have authorization for all of that."

"You're right. On paper, there wasn't enough to go on. But Brown and I were convinced all we needed was a little leeway. In the end, the department was too pleased by the convictions to censure us. And back then we were usually given more leash to follow our instincts. Anyway, that was a long time ago. Dave Morgan heard us out and never hesitated. He was instrumental in our success, but he insisted we never reveal his role in helping us."

"I believe he passed away last year, right before I moved here."

Tori jumped in. "And Michael took over several years before that. Dave's heart had gone a little weak. He had a quadruple bypass, a couple of stents. He was mostly retired the last few years."

"I wish I'd met him. Michael seems like a nice enough fellow."

"I agree."

She nodded to offer appreciation of his easy acknowledgment of the men's marriage. Dave had been the dreamer, Michael the businessman. It was Michael who'd insisted on the renovations and revamping of the menu, but it would always be Dave's Bistro, and she understood why.

Tori blinked several times, a sign of impatience and irritation, and Brenda wondered if she had as many tells as her former girlfriend.

"Well, Commander Young, you seem to have some idea of what this is about, but I'm in the dark." He gave a self-deprecating laugh and the two women smiled, but Brenda wasn't fooled. He was savvy enough to make her spell out what she wanted.

"Chief, I won't waste your time or Commander Young's. As you know, the last couple of weeks have been pretty trying for all of us. To be perfectly frank, I'm struggling with it. Sheraton wasn't one of mine. She was under Vallejo's command, as you know. But she was part of our family. I thought of her as a protégé and to be honest, I'm pretty shaken up by her murder, especially at the hands of one of our own."

"It's hard to believe this could happen here to one of ours, isn't it? I understand why you're upset; I'm upset too. And I'm glad you know you can talk to me. I really do understand." Walton's soulful brown eyes widened. "Her death was a tragic loss for all of us."

"I know I'm not actually at fault for her death—"

"Of course not," he agreed. "The commanders determined that. There shouldn't even have been a hearing. It was necessary for form's sake. No one actually felt you had done anything wrong. Captain Borelli, Brenda, I want you to put it out of your mind."

"Thank you, sir, I appreciate your support. Logically I get that I'm not at fault. But the thing is, I sort of developed a bit of a maternal feeling toward the kid." Brenda avoided Tori's cold stare. "And her death has hit me pretty hard."

"Oh, come on!" Tori snorted, shifting against the low cabinet.

"Chief." Brenda let her voice break a little. "I'm really shaken up."

"Of course you are." Walton oozed warmth and sympathy through his fake tan and expensively tailored brown suit.

She lowered her gaze, blinking several times so her eyes would be moist. She reached out an imploring hand, which he grasped between warm fingers that were still slightly sticky from Dave's secret sauce. She'd noticed this during their handshake but hadn't thought about what it meant.

Walton had used the sanitizing wipes instead of washing his hands, and Brenda was surprised. His stock-in-trade was his likability, and sticky fingers reflected poorly on the chief of police. She was relieved when he released her.

"I'm a good cop, Chief. Never let things get to me before, even some pretty bad stuff." Brenda felt Tori's effort to rein in her nonetheless visible irritation. "But I'm having trouble concentrating. I can't sleep. I just keep hearing myself making that stupid joke and then seeing that horrible video. I keep imagining Sheraton, putting herself in danger because she thought the camera would protect her."

"Captain Borelli, no." Walton squeezed his eyes shut before popping them open. "That hearing couldn't have helped much."

"The commanders were just doing their jobs. I know that. I was drowning in guilt before the hearing. Why didn't I follow up? Why didn't I take five minutes to check on Sheraton one more time?"

He regarded her gravely, his lips pursed. He reminded her suddenly of the fathers in early television shows. Those wise, loving characters had worked to teach viewers both good manners and social responsibility. Even as a youngster, she'd noted they were all male. But at least someone had been trying to impart values back then. Now who was there to provide a moral compass?

"I should just shake it off," she continued. "But I can't seem to. I hate being weak like this, especially as one of only two women above the rank of lieutenant. I hate showing this weakness."

"Caring about our officers is hardly a sign of weakness, Captain Borelli!" Walton shook his head. "Tell you what. I have an idea. You're one of our longtimers who never takes vacation, right? You have, what, eight or nine months' worth of paid time off on the books, don't you?"

She nodded, holding her breath.

"Why don't you take leave?"

She looked at him curiously, as if the thought had never occurred to her.

"Take a few weeks. Go on a cruise, sleep in, practice yoga, whatever. See Dr. Hill, hmm? He'll sign you off and away you go. Come back, see how you feel. If you need more time after that, we'll talk about it."

"I don't know, Chief, it seems kind of—"

"Nonsense." Walton was at his most charming. "Captain Borelli, this department values you. I value you. We all know what you've given up for this job. One of our own betrayed us, and you're shaken by that. Who wouldn't be? You feel a special sense of responsibility for Tami Sheraton's death and so do I. Take the time, please. Nobody will think any less of you for it. In fact, I'll think more of you for being honest. It's setting a good example for junior officers. Isn't that right, Commander Young? Tori?"

"If that's what Captain Borelli needs." Tori's words escaped through her gritted teeth, and Brenda assiduously avoided her hard stare.

"Excellent!" He stood and took both of her hands in his slightly tacky ones, offering her a warm smile. "Captain Borelli. Brenda. I want to commend you for your honesty and for leading the department to a healthy resolution of this ugly chapter. Go see Hill this afternoon, hmm?"

"Yes, sir." She smiled with real gratitude. "Thank you, Chief, I really appreciate your understanding and support. In terms of my duties, I'm thinking Lieutenant Miller could handle personnel and paperwork compliance, and Lieutenant Johnson could oversee new and open cases." She shrugged. "If Commander Young is willing to be a lifeline for them, we should be okay."

"Sure, Captain." Tori beamed at Walton. "Always happy to support one of our own."

She pulled out her badge and ran her fingers over the seven points of its star. In the center was the briar rose, the symbol of their city.

The badge had always meant something to her, of course. Carrying it was an act of faith in their department, in their system, in the law, in the triumph of good over evil, order over chaos. *Bono malum superate.*

"Do you want me to turn this in until I'm back?"

Walton shook his head before the words were out of her mouth. "Of course not. You're on leave, that's all. We aren't quite done with you yet, Captain. You have many more years of service to offer this city, don't you?"

"Yes, sir, I do."

With the lovefest over, she spent fifteen minutes on the fourth floor getting messy, affable Dr. Benjamin Hill to sign off on her leave, after he extracted from her a promise to see him once a week. She rode the elevator down to earth with a patient, humble expression painted on her face. Eager though she was to get started, it wouldn't do to look like a kid let out of school on the video cameras.

After a quick escape from the lobby, she bounded outside to find Tori standing on the front steps, tapping a patent leather Jimmy Choo. Brenda paused, wishing she could just once see her ex and not lose her breath.

"Hey, slow down," Tori demanded. "What do you think you're doing?"

"You know exactly what I'm doing. Donnelly didn't just conveniently off himself. He was murdered, and whoever killed him is also at least partly responsible for Sheraton's death. I'm going to solve Donnelly's murder. And if you had a shred of decency, you'd be helping me."

"You're making a lot of assumptions, Bren. For one thing, I am helping you, more than you know."

She kept going as though she hadn't heard, and Tori followed her, her stiletto heels assaulting the concrete with each step.

"Walton might've fallen for that helpless-female routine, but it was bullshit. You know it and I know it. By the way, he's not as stupid as you think."

"You're the one who showed me the ends justify the means," Brenda retorted over her shoulder. "So you can climb off your high horse."

Tori's smacking pace faltered for a second or so before Brenda heard Tori's breath at her back.

"Brenda, wait! I'm not blaming you for playing Walton, or letting him let you think you did. Get over yourself. You're not exactly *la femme fatale*, my brogan-wearing darling, whatever you may think. But you're being an idiot. What do you expect to accomplish? You think you're going to investigate the department from the outside? If you think I'm going to stand by while you commit career suicide—"

"Tori!" Brenda whirled to a stop and stood an inch away from the most beautiful woman she'd ever seen. Facing her former lover's blazing baby blues, she was unbalanced and unable to get enough air. Even now she couldn't ignore Tori's perfectly proportioned features, her smooth skin, her flashing eyes, her soft natural scent beneath her light floral perfume. "You forfeited any right to an opinion about my career or my anything six months ago."

"Fine." Tori's composure slipped and she took a step back. She'd touched up her lipstick while Brenda was in with Dr. Hill, and Brenda wondered what that was about: a natural thing to do after lunch, or a calculated attempt to soften her? Either way, it was working.

Staring at Tori's lush, full lips, Brenda could picture herself kissing them until Tori made the tiny moaning sound that meant she wanted more than a few kisses. It had been months, but she still thought of Tori as hers, still thought of Tori's mouth as the mouth of her lover, and Tori's eyes as the eyes of her darling.

She took a deliberate step away. Tori never did anything without careful consideration. She'd put on the lipstick for a reason. The perfectly flattering shade of Coral Dawn made her seem naturally pretty and not carefully made up. It was all a show.

Tori's gaze hardened. "Fine," she repeated. "Ruin your career. But don't drag me down with you."

"Of course," she hissed. "All you ever think about is yourself."

She fled to her car and veered wildly out of the parking garage. She spent the drive home working not to call Tori and rage at her. She pulled into the driveway and was blinded by the reflection of the afternoon sun off the living room window.

She remembered then and was wrenched by pain. Her hands shook, rattling her keys. It had been bright like this the last day she got home early. It had been autumn but had felt like summer then.

She'd been surprised to see Tori's red Mustang in the driveway. There'd been another car, a white Lexus, parked in front of the house. The Silvermans across the street had just acquired a new son-in-law from San Diego, and Brenda had assumed it was his. She'd noted the plate number out of habit, but she hadn't been alarmed.

She hadn't considered the possibility that the owner of the luxury vehicle was in her house. Why would she? It was a weekday. Tori was at work. Everyone they knew was at work.

Brenda knew there wasn't a vehicle parked in front of her house now, but she swiveled her head to look anyway. She turned back to face the house before she stalked to the front door, jammed the key in the lock with unnecessary force and shoved her way inside.

Standing in the entry in the same bright afternoon light, she was raw. Was it now, she wondered for a lost moment, or seven months ago? She was falling down a hole in time and felt helpless to stop her descent into the past.

Tori was supposed to have been at a meeting until seven, and Brenda had decided to go home early and make a romantic dinner. She felt the remembered surge of excited anticipation. She scrambled to finish her paperwork, went by the marina to check on a surprise for Tori's upcoming birthday, then stopped to buy flowers and steaks and petit fours, Tori's favorites. She raced home, delighted to see Tori's car. She thought maybe she and Tori had the same idea.

She snuck in, set the groceries on the kitchen counter and strode to the bedroom, planning to surprise Tori. They'd been drifting apart, spending less and less time together. She'd forgotten their anniversary just weeks earlier, and Tori had complained about her lack of romantic overtures. For whatever reason, that day, the one day she should have just stayed at work as usual, Brenda had an impulse to offer Tori some of the romance she'd been missing.

Now, seven months later, Brenda could still smell the mingled perfumes and see the tangled limbs and Tori's stricken face and the languid smile of the woman—a stranger with short, bed-mussed blond hair—as Brenda interrupted their lovemaking.

Now, in the silence of the empty house, she staggered to the master bedroom and saw nothing and no one. Still, she felt seasick. She shook her head, backed away from the bedroom and gulped for air.

Kicking off her shoes, she sank into the beautiful couch Tori had chosen. She curled up, knees in front of her, and sobbed into her clawed hands. How could it still hurt so much after all these months? How could something as simple as coming home at the same time of day pull her back so completely?

She could smell the flowers she'd brought home, could feel her left hand, cold from holding the package of steaks. Brenda hiccupped and swallowed, fighting her tearful self-indulgence until she could breathe.

"This is ridiculous," she scolded herself when she could talk again. "Forget your stupid, adolescent, poor-me crap. She cheated. People cheat. Happens all the time. Get over it."

She pushed herself off the couch, made coffee and washed the ruined makeup off her stinging eyes. Enough was enough. She hadn't taken the trouble to walk away from her job so she could sit around nursing a broken heart.

She'd put her career on the line so she could make things right. What if she found out someone she knew was involved in Donnelly's scheme? She shook off the thought. She'd figure out who had done what and then decide what to do about it.

She would work the case like the murders she'd solved back when she'd been what she privately thought of as a real police officer, before she'd gotten the promotion to captain and become a project manager and babysitter. It was time to get back to being an investigator again.

Before meeting with her lieutenants and then heading to Walton's office, she had made copies of the relevant files. Now she sat at the dining room table and went over each recorded detail with painstaking care, hoping she'd come across some random bit of information or evidence that had been overlooked thus far.

She set her badge down in front of her and again examined its seven-pointed star. She took seriously the vow to safeguard the people around her, and she wasn't about to give that up now. The briar rose represented the promise she'd made to safeguard the city's most vulnerable and most essential resource, her citizens.

Bono malum superate.

The words were more than a slogan. They were a creed. She would do everything in her power to overcome evil with good.

She pushed the badge to the side to focus on the work ahead. Starting a fresh, spiral-bound and sunny yellow notebook, she developed and wrote out dozens of theories, feeling after a while that none of these were based on anything meaningful. This strategy usually helped her home in on the most likely scenarios. This time, however, nothing came together.

At eight thirty that night she answered Andi's phone call with a guilty start.

"A leave of absence? Why didn't you call me? Why didn't you tell me?"

"You already heard?"

"Oh, sugar." Andi laughed, a dry, raspy sound Brenda loved. "You know my place is the gossip center of this town. You should have told me. I shouldn't have heard from strangers."

"I'm sorry, Andi. You're right. I'm not really falling apart. I just want to look into Donnelly's death. I want to know who else was involved."

"Duh, I get that. But you should have told me."

"You're right." She grimaced. "I'm really sorry. I guess I got a little caught up."

"No kidding, Bren. What else is new? Listen, I get it—you don't like a dirty cop in your house, especially one who murders sweet young kids with damp ears." Andi huffed loudly. "But, honey, you get to the point of obsession. Especially when you feel like you're all that stands between Briarwood and Satan. I don't want to see you tear up your life again. When can I see you? I wanna make sure you stay level."

"No, I know."

Funny, she thought, Walton just brought up that old case too. The traffickers operated out of a house dubbed "Satan's Lair" by local rag *The Briarwood Sentinel*. Brenda and her partner Darius Brown had grown obsessed with shutting down at least one tentacle of that monster. They had sat in Dave and Michael's living room night after night for weeks, staring across the street at the plain ranch home that housed the monsters and their young victims.

As if reading Brenda's mind, Andi asked, "Do you ever hear from Darius?"

"Once in a while. He came down to see his uncle last summer, and we hung out."

"Don't turn this into another crusade."

"I won't. This isn't like that."

"Isn't it? Innocent gets slaughtered, cop obsesses over making things right? That sounds awfully familiar to me."

"That was different. Those were little kids. Sheraton was young but she wasn't a child. She should have—ah, well." She made a face at herself. "You're right. Listen, I'm pretty wide-open right now. You're the busy lady. When are you available?"

There was a loud exhalation, and Brenda waited while Andi sorted through her various schedules. Her café was not only the busiest bakery and coffeeshop in town, but one of the primary venues for local bands, artists, poets, and writers. Opening her doors to the offbeat and the unknown made Andi's business a mainstay of the creative community. It also made her café a twenty-hour-a-day project.

"I don't know. I'll get back to you on that tomorrow. Listen," Andi muttered in a gruff tone that made Brenda swallow hard, "don't be an idiot, okay? If someone out there killed the guy who killed Tami Sheraton, he's dangerous. I don't want anything to happen to you."

"Hey, now." Brenda grimaced, hearing what Andi wasn't saying about having already lost her wife. "After twenty years, you're not getting rid of me that easy."

"Has it really been? God, we're old." Andi gave a wheezy laugh. "Well, you are anyway. You were so damn young. I still see you, wearing a buzz cut and acid-washed jeans. All I could think was, 'So much ugly on such a pretty girl.'"

"The jeans or the buzz cut?"

"Both."

Brenda smirked. "Before you get too high and mighty, please recall you were still wearing harem pants and a high-top fade. Or don't you remember?"

"I wish I didn't. Lauren always said—" Saying the name of her late wife seemed to take the breath from Andi.

Brenda bit her lip. After three years, she still didn't know what to say to console her best friend. Lauren only lived for two months after her cancer diagnosis, and she spent her brief, precious last weeks ravaged both by the evil disease and by the toxic treatments designed to slow its progress.

Brenda had done what little she could to help. She'd brought food and picked up prescriptions and cleaned their house and managed visitors. She'd held Andi's hand. She'd hugged and rocked and consoled her. She'd called Lauren's parents and begged them to come first to visit and later for the funeral, and she'd kept secret from Andi their refusal to do either.

She'd also convinced Andi to go back to the café after only a few weeks, knowing her connections to the community were the only lifelines Andi could grasp. Since losing Lauren, Andi had thrown herself even more fervently into the role of savior for one lost soul after another, and Brenda could only hope at some point her friend would be able to slow down and stop running from her grief.

Andi cleared her throat. "Anyway, it's not our fault we came up in the eighties, is it? We can be forgiven for our fashion choices. What can't be forgiven is it's all coming back. Kris, the new cashier, is wearing neon green one day, fluorescent orange the next. Looks like a highlighter. Good kid, though. Sweet. Not like you. You were a pain in the ass and you still are."

She swallowed tears. "I was so happy to meet you. I couldn't believe I'd found another dyke in such a hick town. You and Lauren—I thought I'd be all alone out here in the boonies."

"Well, it's not the boonies anymore, for better or worse. Listen, I gotta set up tomorrow's dough. Love ya, Bren."

"Love you too."

After a grim, sleepless night of thinking and note-taking, Brenda stretched her stiff muscles and made a fresh pot of coffee. She took a quick shower and spent Tuesday morning theorizing and eliminating options. Unfortunately, after several hours, she had come up with a plethora of theories and a dearth of clarity. She'd given herself two weeks, and a whole day was already gone.

Every crime had a true narrative, and usually she could sift through the evidence and eliminate most of the options to isolate the most likely scenarios. In this case, there was very little of which she could be sure.

She ended up leaving at the last possible minute to meet Jonas Peterson at his favorite pub for their prearranged lunch. She sped past police headquarters, where she would've been had she been on the clock.

The top floors were reserved for the mayor, various city managers and department brass, while its ground floor housed city council meetings and events like Friday night's hearing. The undistinguished second floor housed the South Central Station that had, until the day before, been her dominion.

South of the city building by just enough to be slightly seedy, sat The Hole, a cop bar opened decades earlier by a trio of beat cops and purchased six years back by a retired detective named Richie Simpson.

She had only worked with Simpson for a few weeks on a case some years back and remembered him as reasonably intelligent but lazy, willing to cut corners and ride his assumptions rather than examine evidence with rigorous attention to detail.

They had not been good partners, not least because old-fashioned Simpson had been convinced Brenda's job responsibilities included providing him with both secretarial support and sexual favors. It had taken a sharp elbow to his solar plexus to clarify her position on the latter and a convincing show of clerical incompetence to avoid the former.

After regaining his breath and stammering out a reluctant, insincere apology, he had treated her with grudging respect that only occasionally sagged into pouting petulance. Now that he was finally on the other side of the golden handshake, he played magnanimous lord of the manor in his rundown bar and sulked whenever he saw Brenda.

She was only willing to tolerate Simpson's sullen attitude and the pub's cocktail of testosterone-laced bravado and despair out of affection for Peterson. Her former partner was seated at the long, pitted counter to the right of the door when she came in. Judging by his reddened eyes and sallow skin, he had been there more than a few minutes. She slid onto the green vinyl stool next to his, sipping the still-cold beer he'd ordered for her. His bottle was half-empty and stood in a nest of empty highball glasses. She pretended to ignore the evidence of a morning spent drinking, but she examined her old partner closely.

Peterson wore his customary white shirt, navy trousers, black loafers and red tie, but his shoes were dull and his shirt rumpled. She noted with dismay his shaking hands and bloodshot eyes. She summoned a teasing tone and a sardonic smile, pointing at the evidence of his heavy alcohol consumption.

"Breakfast of champ—"

"Shut it," he snapped.

"Whoa, what the hell?"

He took off his trifocals and rubbed his overgrown eyebrows. He shook his head and gave her a baleful sideways look. "You're an idiot, Borelli."

"So you've said." She eyed Peterson speculatively. "Any particular idiocy you're focused on today?"

"Are the rumors true? You're taking compassionate leave? You're a girl and you might cry, so the department should give you paid time off?"

He gestured at The Hole's owner and bartender, Simpson, who stared meaningfully at Brenda before sliding over what looked to be Peterson's sixth scotch.

"The gossips didn't waste any time, huh? It's only so I can work Sheraton's murder, obviously. You need me to connect any other dots?"

He grunted and looked away.

"How are you, partner? You're looking a little rough around the edges." She adopted an amused expression, shaking her head at his pique, hoping she hid her concern over his disheveled appearance and surly manner. The last thing he would want was some kind of intervention.

"Drop it." He hoisted the shot, drained it and slapped down the glass. An unsteady landing meant the small vessel toppled and rolled a few inches. With exaggerated care and a grunt of irritation, he set it upright.

She watched this with affected disinterest and ignored Simpson's attempts to catch her gaze. Obviously, Peterson was cut off and Simpson wanted her to handle it. Great, she thought with heavy disgust, now I can do the bartender's job too.

"You want me to ignore the fact that you look about two steps past okay, or do you want me to ignore the fact that one of our sergeants murdered one of our rookies because she caught on to his criminal activities? I mean, really, Peterson, which is it?"

He shook his head and looked straight ahead. She'd shamed him, and she blinked hard. She'd focus on the latter of her two concerns for now.

"Don't investigate the murder of one of our officers?" She took another sip of beer and considered how to proceed. "Is your casual attitude the result of advanced alcoholism or impending dementia?"

"I knew you were wet behind the ears six years ago, Borelli, but I figured I musta taught you a few things. Now I know how much I failed you."

"What's that supposed to mean?" She masked her hurt, wondering if Peterson knew he'd crossed the line from their usual teasing banter into mean-spiritedness. Was he trying to provoke her? Or was he becoming a mean drunk? Was she missing something?

"You're planning to look at Donnelly's death and work backward?"

"Yeah, so?"

"Who're you looking at, his mom, his girlfriend? His neighbors, maybe his priest? Christ, Borelli, you think this is some big, bad conspiracy and you're gonna crack it wide open? Are you completely fucking paranoid?"

"No." She took a deep breath, finally aware that some part of his touchiness came out of his concern for her well-being. Though warmed by his caring, she had to fight annoyance at having to face her own worries about where the investigation might lead. "I know there could be some awkwardness, might mess up my future as a suave, hotshot politico."

Peterson stood, bracing himself on the bar. Simpson gave Brenda another warning look, which she acknowledged with a nod as she slid off her own stool, standing by in case her old partner needed extra steadying. Peterson turned slowly to face her, and she was struck by how much he'd aged in the couple of weeks since she'd last seen him.

"Come on, Peterson," she said in as light a tone as she could muster, working to quash her rising alarm. "I can take care of myself."

"You're a guppy, Borelli, and these waters are chock-full of sharks. This is a stupid mistake and you're bound and determined to make it."

He turned too quickly and had to brace himself with a hand on the barstool. "You made up your mind without telling me a damn thing. That shows me exactly how useless I really am to you. Just like with my girls. I'm useless." He tottered with remarkable speed across the mostly empty bar to the restroom.

"He's cut off, Borelli," said Simpson.

"Got it. How much?" She reached for her wallet.

"He keeps a tab, pays it off at the end of the month like most of the old guys. A tip for the girl might be nice."

She handed Simpson a ten-dollar bill, which he accepted with an absent nod. She was just turning away from the bar when she sensed someone behind her. She turned slowly, figuring it had to be another cop.

"Where'd you come from?"

Retired captain Harry Trimble ignored her question. He had retired about the same time as Peterson but looked a decade younger than his contemporary. He was trim, with a full head of glossy white hair that was frosted with an artificial layer of lemon yellow.

She noted toned muscles under his Arnold Palmer golf togs, the same light blue polyester outfit she'd seen him wearing dozens of times, back when Tori had coerced her into joining the Briarwood Fitness Club so they could casually run into their superiors on the course and in the clubhouse. Tori turned out to be a natural, effortless golfer, of course, and eventually stopped making hopeless duffer Brenda come along.

She wondered if Tori and Trimble still competed as fiercely as they used to. Trimble was sizing Brenda up as much as she was him, and she wondered what the man saw when he looked at her. She had to give him credit: he'd apparently been wearing the same clothing size for thirty years and had both a full head of hair and an enviable swing.

"You driving our friend home, Borelli?"

"It's that or let him float home on his own." She crinkled her eyes and widened her mouth in a poor showing of a fake smile. She had only vague memories of Trimble's work on the force. She knew there was no love lost between him and Peterson and that Trimble's contemporaries didn't have much to say about him.

In her experience, silence so complete was usually indicative of some problem. She assumed Trimble had spent more of his career kissing brass than doing actual police work, but she'd always wondered if there was more to it than that. Was he someone she should look at for Donnelly's murder, if murder it was?

"You enjoy The Hole, Borelli?" Trimble leered and winked at Simpson, who turned away but continued to eavesdrop with little attempt at concealing his nosiness.

"I'm meeting up with my old partner for lunch. How about you, Captain? You spend a lot of daylight hours in here?"

His mouth tightened before he forced a wide smile and followed it with a hearty laugh. "No, I spend most of my time on the golf course and following my wife around the mall, trying to explain what a limited income is." He chucked his chin in the general direction of the bathrooms. "He's looking a little rough."

"Misses me, I guess."

His laugh seemed to catch him by surprise. "Do you see him much these days?"

"Now and then," she said with a vacuous expression. "You?"

"Oh, now and then." He ran his fingers through his thick white hair. "He and I worked together years ago. Early days for both of us, still in uniform. He was a pain, always too smart for his own good. One of those who can't walk away from the job. These guys don't know how to live as civilians, and they don't last long. Drink, drugs, women or gambling. Hope your old partner doesn't fall into those traps. We've both been off the clock for nearly a year now, and the strain is starting to show on your buddy there. Time he let it go."

"And you have?" Brenda offered a smile to soften her arch question.

"Yes, Captain Borelli, I have. In part because things never change, do they?"

She made a noncommittal noise and inclined her head.

"Oh, sure, the girls can play with the boys now, and even the gays, the coloreds, whatever. But it's still the same old game. The big guys run the show and the little guys shove themselves in harm's way and never get any thanks."

She decided to ignore the casual bigotry. "You sound pretty bitter."

"Ah, don't listen to me. I guess I'm a little bored, that's all. Still talking shop, so I guess I'm just as bad as Peterson."

"He's not so—"

"Funny," Trimble continued, smoothing down his pastel shirt, "none of my old partners stay in touch with me, but here you are visiting Peterson at his home away from home. Nice. Maybe that's one of the benefits of letting the girls join the club. I hear there are lots of fringe benefits."

"Peterson was a good cop, Trimble. And a good friend. I'm not sure what else you're suggesting."

She considered the slight man in front of her. Was Trimble trying to unsettle her for some specific reason? Maybe Peterson had been right. Maybe she was a guppy in a shark tank. Thinking of how hard Tori had fought to move up in the department, she offered Trimble her blankest pleasant expression as she waited for his response.

"I'm just joking around, Borelli. I know Peterson's a good man. Uh, listen, you handled yourself pretty well at that hearing."

She raised an eyebrow. "I didn't know you were there."

"I hear things." He waved an airy hand. "You know how it is. Funny, the other thing going around is how the department's gotten so top-heavy the last few years. Five commanders and seven captains for a department this small? Doesn't that seem odd to you?"

She didn't respond. Of course it had occurred to her. But a police department had to spend every dollar of its annual budget to get its allocation the next, and Briarwood had grown very quickly and not in a particularly healthy way. At least that's what she'd been telling herself for the last couple of years.

She wondered why Trimble was bringing up the issue with her. He was, if she recalled correctly, part of the group that pushed to expand the brass section. He certainly seemed interested in rattling her cage.

"Oh, well," he muttered, turning away, "everybody gets a nice, fat pension. At least, that's what they tell us. Doesn't feel so fat to me. Take care, Captain."

She waited until the door swung shut, closing out the brightness that flared when it opened, the glare she recalled not noticing just before Trimble showed up behind her. She waited three beats before easing over to peek through a gap in the thick plastic blinds that blocked most of the sunlight from coming through the bar's big front window.

She watched Trimble climb into his beige, four-door sedan and ease out into midday traffic. It was the same car he'd been driving when she'd moved to Briarwood in the eighties. He lived in the same house, wore the same watch, the same shoes, the same clothes. Same wife too, which meant that unlike most officers she knew, he actually got to hold on to his money.

He probably had a million dollars sitting in the bank and still kept complaining about how broke he was. She pondered his repeated references to his limited financial resources. Was he shamming, or did he have some weird paranoia about running out of money? Between his membership at the country club, his big old boat, and his membership in Wharf Rats, the marina's most exclusive yacht club, Trimble had a pretty nice lifestyle.

She checked her watch. Peterson had been gone four minutes. She gave it another sixty seconds before ambling toward the head. Was he so drunk he'd passed out or taken a fall in the john? Or had he been the victim of some health crisis? He was only in his late sixties, but he'd lived a hard life. He'd also spent what looked like much of the morning tying one on at the bar. Maybe that was how he spent most of his mornings.

"Hey, I know you've got a huge prostate, but I don't have all day," she called through the door. No response. The doorknob yielded to gentle pressure, and she walked into the surprisingly clean men's room to find it empty. She dashed out and checked the alley beyond the emergency exit, but it was occupied only by a startled cat and an overflowing Dumpster.

Jonas Peterson had disappeared.

CHAPTER THREE

"What do you mean, he disappeared?"

Tori's voice was too loud, and Brenda held the phone a few inches from her ear.

"He went to the john and out the back, that's all I can figure. I called his cell phone but he hasn't called me back. I can't imagine why he'd just take off like that."

"Maybe he didn't want to get sucked into one of your crusades. He's retired. Some people actually stop working when they retire. Maybe he went home."

"No, I looked. His car's still here."

Tori exhaled loudly. "Hasn't he been drinking? He was a drunk on the job, even more so after he retired. The fact he knows better than to drive after spending all morning in a bar means he isn't entirely pickled."

"Listen, forget I said anything. I wouldn't have, except you called just as I was looking for him." She bit her lip and shook a stray curl out of her eyes.

Yes, Peterson liked a drink, but so did most of the people she knew. She couldn't get the image out of her mind: Peterson sitting in front of a collection of empty glasses, his shoes dull and his shirt wrinkled.

"Well," Tori said with a huff. "Sorry I bothered you."

"Wait, why did you call? What's up?"

"Not on the phone. Meet me at home. At your house. Ten minutes."

She sketched a wave at Simpson and tried not to race to her Caprice parked around the corner from the bar. She and Tori hadn't been alone in the house since Tori moved out. For the first time, she realized she'd never asked Tori to give her back the key to the front door. Would she let herself in?

She didn't. When Brenda pulled into her driveway, Tori was sitting in her red Mustang convertible, parked on the street. Was Tori aware, Brenda wondered, that she was parked right where the Lexus—the vehicle belonging to Tori's fling—had sat seven months before?

She doubted Tori allowed herself to think about that. Tori's choice was a matter of stating the obvious: her presence here was that of a guest and not a resident in Brenda's life or in her house. While this was accurate, it was another painful reminder of what should have been and wasn't.

She and Tori should have spent the rest of their lives together. They should have taken the trips to Spain, Egypt, Japan, Australia, and everywhere else they'd planned to visit. They should have gone through with the adoption they'd talked about for years. One child, they'd said, and then we'll see. But they never did it. They should have bought one of those cabins they'd gone to view that second summer and saved up for.

Tori had wanted a boat and to join the yacht club. The boat, bought to surprise Tori for her birthday, still sat in its expensive berth. She didn't even know Brenda had bought it for her. If she'd known about it, would she still have cheated? How much of her cheating was Brenda's fault?

The question hung around her as she walked past her former lover with only a curt nod. She unlocked the door and left it open for Tori to follow. She put on the kettle, knowing Tori would want a cup of tea. Brenda fought defensiveness because she didn't have any of the fancy loose-leaf kinds Tori liked, but she refrained from making excuses as she pulled out the tin of ready-made teabags and set it gently on the counter next to the gas stove Tori had chosen.

She heard Tori come in and ease the door closed. Maybe Tori was as shaken by their meeting here as she was. Why, then, had she insisted on meeting at home? Was Tori playing some kind of game? Was her information so secret that she couldn't risk someone overhearing it, or did she only want Brenda to think it was?

"I wanted to talk to you alone."

Brenda nearly dropped the yellow caneware sugar bowl, part of the set they'd found at an antique shop near San Francisco. For ten years, she'd joked that Tori could read her mind. She'd seen it as a sign of their closeness. Now that they were disconnected in all the important ways, she wondered if she was just predictable.

She made a face. "About Donnelly."

"Obviously. Listen, I need a minute."

Tori gestured toward the hall bathroom, and Brenda nodded like Tori might have forgotten where it was. She got out a box of stale cookies, realizing how much of the food in the house had been purchased by Tori when she still lived here. She put the box back in the pantry. She heard Tori come back from the bathroom but ignored her entrance until she heard Tori's brusque voice.

"Any suspects?"

She shook her head. Over the years, she'd gotten used to Tori's abrupt conversational style. Tori could schmooze when it benefited her to do so, and it felt intimate, the way Tori didn't feel compelled to put on her company manners with Brenda. Was that self-deception? Was Tori's casual curtness more a matter of indifference than of familiarity?

"You need to look outside the department, Bren." Tori headed for the stove when the kettle whistled. At the last second she backed off and watched Brenda pour into the lovely teapot that was part of the set she'd left behind because she said Brenda didn't have the taste to pick anything decent for herself. Brenda wobbled the kettle a moment, wondering if Tori remembered all the horrible things she'd said to her.

"Because?"

She sat at the red, Formica-and-chrome table Tori had picked out, gesturing so Tori would sit, wondering at the strange formality of their manners.

"Because I'm already looking inside the department." Tori sat across from her, not in her old chair but the other one, the one with the gimpy back leg they'd talked about fixing but which still wobbled on its shorter fourth foot. Tori leaned forward, elbows on the table, breasts resting on the tablecloth, glorious cleavage on display. Brenda leaned back.

"Do you have any suspects?"

Tori shook her head, and they sat in silence for a long moment.

"Since you're here, I've been meaning to ask… You said you didn't want anything else when you left. Have you changed your mind? Is there anything here you decided you want? It would be okay. It would be fair. We got pretty much everything in this house together. You picked almost everything, since you were always the one with taste."

Tori eyed Brenda, her expression unreadable. She sat back, letting the chair wobble.

After a beat she persisted. "Just so I know. So there isn't some resentment between us because you want the silver salad tongs or the Bing or whatever."

"I love her work. Remember when we—" Tori looked toward the living room, where the huge Bernice Bing painting had pride of place on the wall facing the front door.

"Of course. How could I forget? That's one of my favorite memories."

They'd talked endlessly about it ahead of time, making sure they could afford to invest in one original piece by their favorite artist before they went to the Berkeley gallery auction. They'd both loved the same colorful abstract and simply smiled at each other when bidding started for the large painting. It had been both their hands on the paddle.

This had been during the golden period of their relationship, when their intimacy was still unspoiled by hurt feelings and disappointment and misunderstandings. Brenda swallowed hard. She'd never imagined the impossible distance that stretched between them now.

"Mine too. Thanks for offering. Amazing, wasn't she? And gone far too soon. But no." Tori shook her head slowly. "I left it for you. It doesn't matter about the money. We both make enough to buy what we need and want."

"Thanks."

Tori seemed to have to force her gaze back to Brenda's face. "This is hard, and I want it to stay professional, okay? I don't want us to get personal. It's too raw still. For both of us."

"Sure." Stung, Brenda nodded crisply. "Okay."

"Don't." Tori rolled her eyes. "You always act like I'm being cold or unreasonable or something, but I'm not. I just don't want to open our wounds again in mutually masochistic emotional masturbation."

"No, I get it." She swallowed hard. She'd once suggested Tori join a support group for individuals addicted to alliteration, and she still remembered Tori's surprised laugh.

"I'm sorry Peterson ghosted. I know he means a lot to you."

"Thanks. He does. It's funny. I saw Trimble. Remember him? He was talking about how top-heavy the department has gotten, and I hadn't really thought too much about it in a while, but he's right. Briarwood wasn't even incorporated as a city thirty years ago. Law enforcement fell to the county sheriff's department."

"Why are you bringing this up now? Who cares about Trimble? He was useless." Tori waved him away like his very existence was a pesky fly. "Briarwood's more than doubled in size since then, mostly in the last five years. You know that."

"Yeah, true. But it's not balanced the same way. Do you realize we have the same number of patrol officers as Winston, but we have double their number in ranks above lieutenant?"

"And Winston still runs its department using an abacus and papyrus. It also doesn't deal with the huge gang problems we have or the tech companies. Our tax base, even after the bubbles burst, is a lot bigger than theirs. And distributed less evenly. Which means—why are we even talking about this? Trimble was taking a dig at you and me. You know, the only reason we got our promotions is because we're women. They had to make a bunch of office jobs to keep the women busy. That's one of his favorite little passive-aggressive games. You know better than to get sidetracked by him."

Exhaling to dispel defensiveness, Brenda nodded. "True."

Tori sat back. She fussed with her hair, pulling it out of its low ponytail and finger-combing until it was a mass of cascading waves. Brenda blinked. Playing with her hair was a nervous habit Tori displayed when she wasn't sure of her footing. She only resorted to it when tapping her tongue wasn't enough.

"What do all of you do?" Brenda poured tea into their respective cups, trying not to drip the spout. She was surprised to be so shaken by her nostalgia-induced nerves. She'd put out their special cups without even noticing: the delicate green Shelley for Tori, the more prosaic Wedgwood for her. Lemon and honey for Tori, just lemon for herself.

How many times had they sat at this table and drunk out of these particular teacups? How often while doing so had she said or done something that made Tori bristle the way she was doing now?

"Are you kidding?" Tori ignored the steaming brew in front of her. "What do we do? I get it, Brenda. You think everybody above you isn't a real cop. What we do is work our asses off, trying to make sure the rank-and-file have what they need to do their jobs and don't get sued. And, lest you forget, you parked your trim little ass behind a desk months ago and haven't come out from behind it since. What do you do all day? It's not that different for me, only I swim with the barracudas."

Brenda couldn't help but wonder if Tori was trying to wind her up. Hadn't she just wondered that about Trimble? Struck by the fact both Peterson and Tori had talked about swimming with dangerous predators, she went to the sink, pretending to rinse her hands as though she'd spilled tea on her fingers.

"Why do we need so many commanders?" She spoke softly, looking out the garden window to the neglected backyard, her back to Tori. The sea of rosebushes had gone wild, and blackberry brambles were overtaking the fence. "Why did I get promoted to captain? I was happy as a lieutenant."

"Oh, come on!" Tori stood abruptly, knocking her hip into the corner of the table, and Brenda whirled to face her. They both looked down and watched as tea sloshed out of their footed cups and into the saucers. "You worked for that promotion like your life depended on it, and now you want to act like I made you go into management? No way you're pinning that on me, sweetheart."

She was gone in a flash, slamming the front door behind her and pulling her gleaming Mustang away so quickly the tires squealed. Brenda didn't bother to follow her. Even during the good years, Tori had made a regular habit of storming out anytime they disagreed. The best strategy had always been to give her some space.

Or, she wondered now, had it? Maybe if she'd been better at communicating they'd have managed to work through their problems. Maybe she should have chased after Tori and made her finish the difficult conversations they never seemed to get past.

She shook her head and sighed. She'd wound Tori up and pushed her away, which was a mistake she'd made hundreds of times in their decade together. Now they were apart and she was still poking at Tori's tender spots for no good reason. Over the years she'd gotten very good at making Tori defensive, and that thought pained her.

They'd joked, once upon a time, about the briar roses in the backyard, how they looked so delicate and pretty but had particularly vicious thorns. Back then, both of them had been willing to admit they could be thorny themselves. But too many sharp barbs between them had left them both reluctant to admit to anything.

The uncomfortable truth was that Tori was right. Brenda fought to get the promotion because she thought newly minted

Commander Tori Young might feel she was slumming, being with a mere lieutenant.

Shortly after Brenda's promotion, though, they were broken up and it didn't matter, and she had given up the parts of the job she loved for nothing. Months later, she was still trying to reconcile herself to playing a role she wasn't sure she liked.

She might not really have that job ever again, she realized with a pang. She might have just maneuvered her way out of it. Would they offer her early retirement? She had her twenty years. Maybe she was already done and just didn't know it yet. She couldn't imagine not being a member of the department. It was part of her. Would she end up an alcoholic like Peterson, unable to walk away from the job?

She snorted. She could always go work for Dan Miller, who'd been trying to woo her to his private security company for the last several years. If she ended up getting pushed out of the department at the end of this thing, she might have to consider it. A shudder ran through her, and she tasted bitterness.

He was everything she hated, a slick, self-serving huckster who genuinely saw himself as superior to other people. His money had come from his family, she knew, and the only reason he was still solvent was that he'd somehow managed not to squander it all. He reeked of privilege and its inevitable byproduct, sanctimony.

She drifted toward the front window, wallowing in a nauseating mix of self-loathing and self-pity. On the way to the living room, she heard a car start, noting absently the unfamiliar engine. She'd lived on the same street for years and knew the neighbors' cars as much by sound as by sight, and this one was new to her.

Feeling her pulse quicken as she hotfooted it toward the door, she thought maybe Mrs. Johnson finally got a new sedan after fifteen years. Maybe someone got lost. Maybe the Silvermans had a visitor.

She heard the mystery car pull out, noting that it was only seconds behind Tori's. Funny, Tori's was the only car parked on the street when I got here, she thought. She yanked open the front door and peered out, but Tori's Mustang and the other car were already out of sight.

A vague feeling of unease kept her looking outside for a few minutes. She wasn't sure if she was being paranoid. She'd been in a funk for months. One of the neighbors could have bought a new car without her noticing. She was almost always the first person to head out in the morning and the last to head home at night. A neighbor could have had a visitor. There could have been a salesperson or a caregiver or someone who'd just moved in and was exploring.

There were a hundred reasons for a new car to arrive on the street during Tori's brief visit. The last new car Brenda remembered noticing on the street had belonged to the woman Tori cheated with, though surely there'd been others since then. Maybe, she thought, she was too awash in her memories of that day, seeing ghosts where there were none.

But two decades in law enforcement, preceded by a childhood spent trailing her mom around the least civilized parts of the Western states, had taught her to be suspicious of coincidences. Frustrated by the lingering thought that had she been ten years younger, she'd have been able to reach the front door quickly enough to see the mystery car, Brenda pondered the possibilities.

Was someone following Brenda or Tori? And what happened to Peterson? Did he get frustrated with Brenda and take off? Or did he suddenly realize he was too drunk, the way someone will upon getting up to use the restroom? Or did someone take him? He could have gone out back for a smoke. He'd quit smoking years earlier but still snuck the odd cigarette now and then, especially after a drink or two. Or, Brenda reminded herself, six or seven. He didn't go out to get his car, which would be towed if left where it was parked for a couple of days.

She tried to recall the sounds of the bar: the traffic, the humming of the air conditioner and refrigerators, the murmurs of the few patrons lounging on the bench that served as seating behind a series of small round tables along the south wall. There were three retired cops sitting with their backs to that wall when Peterson went down the narrow hallway to the bathrooms and the same three when Brenda went to look for him. Trimble stayed near the door.

She remembered thinking there was something odd about his entrance but couldn't recall what that something was. Had he come into The Hole looking for someone? He'd left right after talking with her. Had he been there to distract her while someone lured or forced Peterson out the back door?

Brenda closed her eyes. Trimble had stood behind her, and she had turned to face him. Would she have heard a struggle taking place in the alley? She wasn't sure and decided to table the question for the moment. She needed to think about it without being clouded by emotion. After cleaning up the tea-soaked mess on the kitchen table, she dialed Tori's number.

"What did you want to talk to me about, specifically? Did you just want to tell me you were investigating inside the department?"

"Pretty much."

"Sorry I sandbagged you."

"Old habits. On both our parts, I guess."

"Can you do me a favor? Look into Trimble?"

"Yeah. On it. I'll get back to you." And she was gone.

Brenda smiled. One of the things she'd always appreciated was Tori's quick mind. She missed their best conversations, the ones that made sense to no one else because so few of the words were spoken aloud while the ideas flowed seamlessly over and around and through each other. It was dizzying, those first years together, when she was still getting used to someone understanding her thoughts.

Her smile died. She couldn't imagine sharing that connection with anyone else. She reminded herself she'd had other relationships before Tori and would find someone else when she was ready to do so. She'd been telling herself that same thing for months. And just like every other time, it sounded like a lie.

She shook her head to clear it. She had to figure out what had happened to her old partner, and standing around moaning over her personal problems wasn't going to accomplish that. Tori was right. They should have kept things professional between them. But she'd been unable or unwilling to listen to Tori, as usual.

She drove down to The Hole and saw Peterson's car still parked where he'd left it that morning. Then she went to his house, noting the perfectly manicured lawn, the sparkling windows, the polished door handle. Peterson had been a Marine once upon a time, and he still lived like one, with everything shipshape and all potential emergencies anticipated and prepared for. His desk at work had been the same, perfectly organized and so neat she had teased him about it.

At the bar she'd noticed some decline in his personal grooming. He looked fine, by most people's standards, but not his. His hair had grown out just a little and his shirt was creased. Most unlikely of all, his shoes were not shined. In the years she'd known her former partner, she'd never seen him looking so disheveled. Maybe Tori was right. Maybe Peterson was finally losing his ability to function, either because of the alcohol or some age-related decline. For all she knew, he could be dealing with Alzheimer's.

She peeked in Peterson's living room window, noting the green, healthy plants and recently polished furniture. The place looked like an ad for conventional suburban living: one sofa, two side chairs, the requisite walnut coffee and side tables. Matching brass lamps adorned the side tables, and two small houseplants sat atop a brass stand in the middle of the front window. It could have been a stage set, meant to represent middle-class orderliness and propriety.

There was a large seascape over the fireplace, whose mantel featured six framed photographs. Five of these she knew from memory: his black-and-white wedding photo, the high school graduation pictures of both of his daughters, a Marine Corps portrait of nineteen-year-old Peterson, a formal photo taken at his graduation from the police academy.

In the center of the grouping stood the newest addition, a large framed snapshot from his retirement dinner. In it Peterson's arm was slung over Brenda's shoulder and a wide smile brightened his normally somber features.

She stood staring into his front window. Even with the sun hot on her shoulders, she shivered, gripped by the need to make sense of his sudden, unexplained departure. Maybe he had the flu. Maybe it was the anniversary of his mom's death. Maybe he had a brain tumor. Maybe he got his heart broken by some smooth-talking lady. Maybe he was, as Tori suggested, reluctant to get involved in the informal investigation she was conducting. Maybe he blamed her for Sheraton's death and didn't want to say so.

She shook her head. His demeanor had been decidedly different. And it must have taken more than a few hours for his normally spit-and-polish appearance to reflect global carelessness. His decline was recent. It must have occurred within the last week, she decided. Long enough for the man to visibly neglect his personal appearance but not yet house and car—she'd noted the vehicle's characteristic gleam.

She wondered if he'd had a stroke and wandered home. No one answered her knocking or ringing the doorbell. She peered through the gap in the gate that led to his backyard, but there was a lock on the latch and it was engaged. She called his cell phone and left her third message. Then she called The Hole.

"Hey, Simpson, this is Borelli."

"Yeah, you ever find your partner?"

"Negative, that's why I'm calling. Anything there?"

"Not a whisper. Some of the guys, you know, they can't hack retirement."

"Yeah." She thought for a moment. "Is that why you bought the bar?"

"That and taxes. Listen, if you track down the runaway, let me know?"

"You bet. Hey, Simpson, does Captain Trimble come in a lot?"

"Trimble? Nah, he's a Boy Scout, remember?"

"Yes, I do." She pressed her lips together. "Listen, I'm not asking this to get personal. I'm worried about him just taking off like that. You mentioned Peterson keeps a tab. Does he come into your place a lot?"

"What's a lot?" Simpson put his hand over the receiver and spoke sharply to someone. He sighed heavily into the phone. "Shit. Gotta go. Take it easy, Borelli."

"You do the same."

She wondered why Simpson was willing to say Trimble didn't usually come in the bar but unwilling to say how often Peterson did. She was rarely so uncertain about what she should do. As far as she knew, her inebriated former partner had walked out of the bar's backdoor because he was annoyed with her, too drunk to drive home and too embarrassed to admit it.

She could report him missing and specify he was an at-risk individual, but if he'd just taken off in a fit of pique, he'd be humiliated by her filing. If she did nothing and he was lying in a gutter or creek, hoping for help, her inaction could cost him his life.

She groaned in frustration and scanned the neighborhood as though some visual cue might guide her. All she saw were small, carefully maintained ranch homes surrounded by lovingly tended gardens and cheapened by ugly security system signs from Briarwood Watchdog.

She could break into his house. Peterson had invested in good locks and doors, but any of the windows would provide easy access. She could get a window replaced if need be. She tapped on the front window and debated. Obviously it would be better to get into the backyard and access a smaller window in the guest bedroom, which was not an insurmountable task. She just wasn't sure she was ready to tread on his privacy.

He'd accepted and eventually embraced her as a partner in some measure because she was respectful of his boundaries. Now that he was retired, he seemed touchier and more in need of that respect than ever before. She wasn't prepared to step on his dignity any more than absolutely necessary, and she wasn't a hundred percent sure it was necessary. With some reluctance, she left Peterson's silent, orderly house in peace.

She drove back downtown to canvass the area around the bar. She was hoping someone had seen him. If he went to The Hole as often as she suspected he did, the local merchants probably knew him by sight if not by name. With a shrug, she fell back on the old investigative standby: pounding the pavement. Two hours of shaking hands and showing store clerks and local residents Peterson's digital likeness on her cell phone rendered her nothing but hungry, thirsty, and tired.

She called him yet again and left a message. "Listen, either call me back or I start breaking into your house and car to find out where you are. Unless you want broken windows and me digging around in your stuff, call me." She lowered her voice. "Seriously, Peterson, I need to know you're alive and well. You're important to me. Okay?"

Then she left a much longer message for Andi, knowing her old friend would spread the word through Briarwood faster than any police report could. She detailed the odd disappearance of her retired buddy and emailed Andi a photo of Peterson, requesting that she ask one of her charges to make a poster and blanket the city with copies. Then she let it go, knowing Andi would get it done.

As she trudged back to her car, she noted two of Dan Miller's guards strolling toward her. To her they always looked oddly out of place on the relatively peaceful streets of Briarwood. With their black tactical shirts, pants and boots, festooned with badges and holsters and cryptic insignia, their shaved heads and stern expressions and bunched fists, they looked like contemporary Gestapo. Even from a block away the guards appeared more menacing than protective. The pair stomping in her direction looked like clumsy clones of their boss.

Dan Miller went to a military academy after he was expelled from a dozen prep schools. He flunked out of six different colleges until his father bought a new library for a private university somewhere. After several years, Miller finally got a degree.

He borrowed money from his father and lost it. Then he borrowed more money from his father and started buying small companies, liquidating their assets and firing their employees. Then he tried his hand at a variety of sales jobs: real estate, gold futures, financial instruments of various shady kinds, real estate again. He won and lost too many fortunes to count.

Then he ran into legal trouble and was very nearly convicted as a slumlord. He lost what was rumored to be nearly five million dollars in payouts and attorney fees to secure a settlement that meant he didn't have to admit wrongdoing.

Since then he'd ballooned his private security empire. She knew he was making money, but she wasn't sure he was earning it. Miller and his employees seemed less like guards and more like arrogant teenage boys playing soldiers.

The few passersby shot wary glances at the guards, who took up the whole sidewalk and clearly expected pedestrians to scurry out of their way. She stared down the one she guessed was the dominant member of the approaching duo, the one who made sure his foot hit the ground an inch ahead of where his partner's did. Predictably, when she held his gaze, he bristled and actually puffed out his chest. His arms edged slowly away from his body as he sped up his pace.

He looked like he would try to barrel right through her, and she thought he resembled a ridiculous rooster. She was annoyed enough not to move out of the idiot's way. She would force him to go around her. She squared her shoulders and blew out a slow breath. Relaxing her face and slowing her heart rate, she felt like a kid playing red rover. Just like when she was a kid, she guessed, the opponents saw her slim shape and calm expression and underestimated her.

Big Guard and Little Guard, as she'd come to think of them in the seconds since she'd first noticed them, tensed and exchanged a quick look. The shorter guy placed his hand on his waistband as though planning to reach for his weapon. Wondering what happened when Dan Miller's guards encountered puffed-up teens and grumpy grandparents, she decided to see how far the pair of meatheads would go. She was awash in the rush of adrenaline she hadn't felt for almost a year, the ecstasy of anticipation she always experienced when someone wanted to play chicken with her.

As the macho guards drew closer, nearly running as they closed in on her, she maintained her gaze on the big guy. He was flushed, his blue eyes flashing, his nostrils flared. His black polyester uniform shirt was too thick and obviously didn't breathe. Sweat ringed his underarms and the center of his chest and the collar of his polo shirt. Dried salt from previous shifts frosted the unforgiving fabric in unflattering places. The guard looked like he was roasting. He was an overheated bull in a too-small ring, his unpolished boots dull hooves that pawed toward her with the fury of insecurity.

Then the little guy recognized her. She saw it in an instant, the flash of memory. He muttered something unintelligible to his partner, whose eyes flew wide open. The men stopped so quickly they almost toppled. Then they spun around and stomped away from her without a word. Both of them had huge sweat stains spread through the middle third of the backs of their shirts. Whatever Dan Miller was spending to market his company's services, he should be spending on training and better uniforms.

She stood on the sidewalk and watched them retreat, her expression troubled. What would they have done if the little guy hadn't recognized her as a decorated police officer? What did they do when they encountered civilians who challenged their authority? Their badges were decorative, their training quasi military, their bearing far too cocky to be effective in dealing with civilians.

Miller only paid his armed guards a pittance more than they could earn slinging burgers at a fast-food joint. If they could get jobs as police officers or prison guards, they would earn several times more than the salary Briarwood Watchdogs paid them.

They'd barreled toward her like the street belonged to them. They'd been willing to engage a woman, who as far as they could tell, was unarmed and alone and simply walking down the street. Was it hubris? Or had they been trained by Miller to treat everyone like a suspect?

Brenda had known more than a few private security guards over the years, and each of the best worked on finesse and watchfulness and de-escalation rather than macho posturing and bullying. If the pair she'd just seen gave an indication of how Miller's guards presented themselves, the company was going to be in trouble soon.

Still heady with the rush of adrenaline her near-encounter had engendered, she pushed away her concerns about Watchdogs and its training methodology. At some point, maybe she'd bring it up with someone. For now she had bigger things to worry about.

Frustrated and unsure of the best course of further action regarding her missing partner, she decided to focus on Donnelly and Sheraton for a while. The file on Donnelly's death, which had already been ruled a suicide, was shamefully thin. It was easier to close the whole embarrassing episode than to deal with the mess his actions had created. It was also politically expedient for Yolo County, in whose jurisdiction Donnelly had died, to keep things discreet and friendly with the Briarwood Police Department. Yolo County was, she had no doubt, doing its best to offer professional courtesy to a fellow law enforcement agency.

Sergeant Mark Donnelly shot Tami Sheraton and left her to die in a trash-strewn alley behind a low-rent liquor store in the most run-down part of Briarwood. Between the video footage from Sheraton's hidden camera and the forensic evidence, there was no real room for doubt about that.

She pulled up the video on her laptop. She'd already seen it dozens of times but had to brace herself nonetheless.

Donnelly had been extorting several low-rent businesses in the southeastern part of the city, most of them within a block or two of Sam's Discount Liquor Store. Sheraton had apparently become suspicious enough to don a hidden camera.

Brenda wondered: why hadn't Sheraton gone to anyone for help? Why hadn't she come to Brenda for help? There had been rumors Vallejo was out to lunch in some way. She'd heard the rumors but hadn't reached out to her fellow captain. Now she wasn't sure why. Maybe Sheraton tried to talk to Vallejo. Maybe she tried to talk to someone else in the department. If so, her confidant was keeping mum about it. How many people had dropped the ball?

"I did," she muttered to herself.

It would have been easy for a manipulative mentor to send Sheraton to the alley behind Sam's at just the right time and set up Donnelly so he felt he had no choice but to shoot the rookie. The theoretical puppet master wouldn't have had to do more than put the crooked cop and the eager kid in the same place at the same time. She made a face. She again reminded herself to focus on the facts. She played the video again, peering intently at the screen.

Donnelly's face reflected shock. He blinked twice. His left hand held a paper bag of what the liquor store owner later stated was cash. The merchant had been paying him protection money for months.

His eyes flew wide open. He started toward Sheraton. He was talking, his expression serious but friendly. Sheraton jumped, startled. Before she could do more, he took out his service weapon, the same Glock 22 issued to everyone on the force in Briarwood before the recent switch to its cousin the Glock 23. He shot Sheraton from a distance of about four feet. Muzzle flash translated into momentary nothing—white, undifferentiated blankness.

Then there was movement as she fell backward against the Dumpster and onto the filthy ground, her head tilted at an awkward angle that showed nothing but velvety night sky. How long had Donnelly stayed to make sure she was dead? Would he have called for help if she had still been alive? Would he have shot her again as needed to avoid leaving her behind to report him?

Brenda rubbed her eyes and watched the video three more times. She'd have loved to listen to what Donnelly said, but she was glad not to hear the shot and Sheraton's death. Sheraton's arterial spray had been phenomenal. She must have died relatively quickly.

Still, Brenda wondered whether for some period of seconds or possibly minutes Sheraton had time to process what happened. Was she scared? In pain? Did she imagine someone might come to her rescue? Did she hope to survive? Did she think the tape would get Donnelly convicted? Did she lie there drowning in regret because she hadn't brought someone in to help or had asked the wrong person for help?

Brenda remembered the first time she met the freckled rookie, how Sheraton approached her like a kid on a dare, introducing herself with the bravado of the very young. She eyed the uniformed youngster, taking a moment to notice she was not, as Brenda had thought at first, barely old enough to buy a beer, but rather she was closer to thirty than twenty. No matter, she'd still seemed more like a kid than an adult to Brenda.

Sheraton was smart, conscientious, insightful, and engaging. With her baby face and open smile, she was disarming, and the intelligence in her eyes would be missed by the less astute.

Since Brenda's station served as the department's violent crime clearinghouse, junior officers from other stations could often find excuses to liaise with the only station housed at headquarters. Sheraton found her way into Brenda's lair on a regular basis in her short stint in the department, and she always came armed with questions.

"Why aren't there more women, especially in leadership positions?" Sheraton had asked this only three months before Donnelly shot her, and Brenda recalled launching into some vague nonsense about change being incremental at first and then gathering speed later. She thought she was saying something meaningful, but Sheraton shook her head in the middle of the speech.

"No, I mean here in Briarwood." Sheraton frowned, leaning over Brenda's desk and poking it with her long finger to emphasize her words. "This department is ninety-six percent male. Ninety-six! That's ridiculous! Wilton has twice as many women on the force as we do, and a lot of places are doing better than that. We make up fifty-three percent of Briarwood's adult population. Why are we so underrepresented here in the police department? And why are you and Commander Young the only women who've made it above lieutenant?"

Brenda admired Sheraton's fire but admonished the rookie to keep her cool. She was distracted, as she recalled. She thought herself too busy to seriously address Sheraton's concerns. She thought Sheraton didn't appreciate how much easier it was for female police officers in her generation than it had been for their predecessors.

Now she wished she could go back and listen more closely. Sheraton's isolation must have been painful and frightening. She must have felt no one had her back. Brenda rubbed her eyes. She should have been the mentor Sheraton sought instead of just another busy bureaucrat who hadn't bothered to listen.

If she'd paid more attention maybe Sheraton would have approached her with her concerns about Donnelly. Then Brenda could have helped her. She could have set up a meeting with Vallejo so they could go through the narrative. They could have gotten approval to set up an actionable plan. Sheraton wouldn't have been alone in an alley with Donnelly.

She rolled her head and listened to the popcorn in her neck and shoulders. Had the kid shared anything, however vague, with anyone, maybe someone in her personal life? Sheraton was survived by her mother and a sister, both of whom lived nearby. There was a brother too, but he lived in Southern California and was nearly twenty years older than his baby sister.

Maybe Sheraton confided in her mom or her big sister. She must have divulged her plans to someone, if only out of caution. Brenda made a note to follow up on Sheraton's family and friends. Then she put that aside and moved her focus back on Donnelly.

When Chief Walton relayed the family's emphatic desire for distance from those on the force, Brenda wondered whether this was because the family blamed the department for the death, or because the rapacious media had descended on the scandal like Briarwood's tragedy was theirs for the feasting. Either way, the department was left with a pair of scars: the loss of a potentially valuable junior officer and a shameful breach of public trust by one of its sergeants. She wished they'd been allowed to organize a ceremony to honor their fallen officer. The powerful, moneyed family objected strenuously to such public fanfare. The funeral was private, closed to both the public and members of the police department, and they had no chance to unite in grief over their shared loss.

The most they could do was line the street when the funeral procession passed. Hundreds of uniformed women and men pressed shoulder to shoulder, expressions closed and spines rigid, watching a series of cars roll past. Overhead, helicopters swarmed, and behind the blue line on either side was a teeming crowd of photographers. It was too remote. It was too impersonal.

Brenda was one of several captains who organized family picnics to allow their squads a chance to grieve, to distract themselves with the laughter of children and the chatter of the spouses and the ribbing of their fellows. Donnelly left Sheraton dead or dying in the alley and went on the run, turning up two hours later at a no-tell motel in Fairfield, about eighty miles east of Briarwood. She watched video footage of his checking in and paying cash, using the name Mike Guzman.

He stayed in the Denton Motel until nine the following morning. He ate pancakes and drank a large coffee at a fast-food restaurant with poor-quality cameras in the dining room, and by then he was wearing a plain black sweatshirt and jeans he likely kept in the trunk of his car.

Many officers kept a coat and a change of clothes for emergencies, but as far as she knew, no one had followed up on the possibility this wasn't the case here. What if Donnelly bought those clothes or retrieved them from a gym locker or a girlfriend or relative after killing Sheraton? Brenda made another note to herself.

Their second sighting of Donnelly was the next morning at another no-name motel, this time only twelve miles farther east, in Vacaville. She wondered what he'd done with himself between the two sightings. Twelve miles, even in heavy traffic, was nowhere near a day's worth of travel. In Vacaville he used cash and the name Donald Mills.

They had no record of his withdrawing money from his bank accounts to that point. Of course, he'd been extorting small businesses for months, maybe years, so cash probably wasn't an issue—though it was bulky.

She made a note to look for storage units under his name, the name of one of his girlfriends and any possible aliases. Donnelly ate at the diner attached to the Vacaville motel, waffles and bacon and coffee. He tipped well, smiled, joked with the waitress.

He looked completely relaxed, not at all like a man on the run after murdering a fellow police officer. He wore the same shirt and jeans. Though his face was all over the news by then, no one recognized him.

Continuing east on Interstate 80, he checked into a motel in West Sacramento at five minutes past four that afternoon. She noted the long gap between his breakfast in Vacaville and his check-in at four in West Sacramento, only thirty-odd miles away. What had he done for all those hours?

She'd need to check for rented storage units and possible co-conspirators in the areas around and between the relevant cities. At a small motel in West Sacramento he paid for two nights and used the name Don Gonzalez.

Ten minutes later he was on camera buying hair dye, tanning spray and new clothes at a discount superstore, where he also picked up junk food and sundries. In the video from the store, there were a few California Highway Patrol officers in line behind him. None of the three uniformed officers seemed to give him a second look.

He paid cash at the superstore and again a few hours later when he went to one of the many fast-food restaurants near his motel, ordering five burgers and a large soda to go. By then he looked marginally disguised, wearing a gray baseball cap and a bulky hooded jacket in navy blue. His dyed black hair and an orange-tinted tan changed his appearance as much as the new clothing did.

She examined his behavior in the burger-joint footage. He'd changed more than his appearance as he'd moved away from Briarwood. In West Sacramento he'd finally started looking like the fugitive he was. However belatedly, he began lying low. She made a note to figure out who might have contacted him and scared him. Or had dyeing his hair made him realize the gravity of his situation and thus present himself differently?

Video from an exterior security camera showed a motel housekeeper approach the open door to Donnelly's rented room the next morning. She looked in before backing away and then turning tail and running. The housekeeper's frantic departure caught the eye of the manager, who found the body only seconds later and called for help. Yolo County deputies and crime scene personnel showed up within minutes. He was identified and pronounced dead within the hour.

She perused the list of items found in his motel room. His duty weapon, the Glock he used to kill Sheraton. A spent shell. His wallet, containing seven hundred dollars. A trio of large manila envelopes under the motel's mattress bulged with a combined total of nearly nine thousand dollars, most of it in carefully bundled twenties. His laptop and cell phone were at the bottom of the bathtub, which was half-filled with water.

The room's furniture and floor were littered with clothes and trash. On the bathroom counter and the low dresser sat the predictable detritus left behind by a fugitive: sundries, antacids, coins, a pocketknife, breath mints, extra ammunition, and snack food. He had two key rings, both jammed with dozens of keys, multiple vehicle fobs, and several unnamed items. She made a note to follow up on what those items were and what exactly the keys and fobs opened.

In the motel Dumpster nearest his room, Yolo County investigators found a notebook detailing his extortion activities and victims, including not only several small businesses but a host of pimps, prostitutes, and drug dealers. All victims were identified by name, location, occupation, and scheduled pickups.

In the same Dumpster, investigators also found his old clothes and the packaging from his hair dye and tanning spray. He tested positive for marijuana, cocaine, methamphetamines and a mélange of prescription antidepressants and painkillers. In his stomach were the remains of two burgers, snack cakes, and antacids.

The other three burgers and a bag of potato chips sat unopened on the nightstand alongside a second bottle of antacids. She thought about that. If he'd been planning to eat five burgers, why were three still sitting there? Would a suicidal man buy a bunch of food, hair dye, and tanning spray? Why bother with a disguise if he was going to kill himself? Had he changed his mind, become too anxious to continue?

Why buy two bottles of antacids? She wanted to check the receipt from the superstore. Maybe he'd already had one bottle, almost empty, and he'd bought a second for when that one ran out. Maybe there was a sale on antacids that made buying two bottles just too tempting a deal to pass up, and a lifetime's frugality had kicked in. Either way, it was odd behavior for a man planning to kill himself.

Maybe in his last minutes or hours he'd learned something that caused him to panic or lose hope. Had he felt guilty? He surely hadn't planned on Sheraton's presence in the alley. Maybe the guilt caught up with him. Maybe he started to panic as his cash reserves ran to what he considered low.

While nine thousand dollars was a lot of money, it was hardly a nest egg. Maybe Donnelly's real nest egg ended up beyond his reach somehow. Maybe his co-conspirators left him in the wind. She rubbed her forehead, trying to figure out why he'd made the choices he did.

Certainly, his escape path didn't seem well planned. He drove out of town, looping south toward San Francisco and then northeast toward the central valley. He stopped after eighty miles. Then after a single night in Fairfield, he took a whole day to show up a mere twelve miles east in Vacaville.

Where was he that day? Was he waiting for someone or had he already connected with a co-conspirator? Why bother moving only one medium-sized city farther east? The long gap between his sighting in Vacaville and his appearance in West Sacramento intrigued her. Where was he? Was he with someone?

He'd spent three days going only a hundred and twenty miles. Within those three days he could have traveled several states away from Sheraton's murder. He could have gone to Mexico. Even going the same distance toward San Francisco would have been a smarter choice—he could have blended in with the crowds of Oakland or Berkeley, San Francisco or San Jose, and been rendered almost invisible. Instead, he went to the relatively small city of West Sacramento.

The report noted the presence of an abrasion ring under his chin. The abrasion ring was described as "presumptively" having been left by his service weapon. She was surprised there were no pictures and no measurements. There was no support documentation. Her experience with Yolo County had led her to expect an extremely detailed, carefully accurate report. This report was none of those things.

She examined the possibilities with care. Had Yolo County's normally meticulous detectives glossed over the uglier details because Donnelly was both a cop and a cop's killer? It wasn't hard to imagine even the best officer falling under the shadow of such difficult conflicts. She wrote herself a lengthy message detailing how to conduct the needed follow-up without making the Yolo County investigators defensive.

A single bullet was positively identified as having come from Donnelly's service weapon—though the report included no evidentiary support or reference thereto. The bullet entered his mouth through the lower jaw, traveled upward and blew out a section of the top of his skull. There was no notation to indicate the recovery location of the pieces of his skull.

His prints were the only ones on the weapon and the bullet. He was right-handed, and the report specified that the angles of entry and exit were consistent with a self-inflected gunshot by a right-handed victim of his height seated on the edge of the bed. There were no other injuries noted.

She closed the thin file with a sigh, knowing she didn't have enough information to develop any meaningful insight. Yolo County's reports did not draw definitive conclusions about Donnelly's death. It could have been a murder or a suicide.

She couldn't shake the notion that someone had murdered Sergeant Mark Donnelly. Someone soaked his phone and laptop. Someone either staged a suicide or somehow compelled him to kill himself. She considered this possibility carefully. Under what circumstances could someone convince a cop—one brazen enough to extort money from small businesses and murder a nosy rookie—to kill himself?

"Am I just too invested in thinking the guy wasn't doing this on his own?" She again rolled her head from side to side, feeling and hearing the cracks and snaps this caused.

She made another note to herself: get video footage from the outside of his last motel, the one he died in.

She examined her to-do list and sighed. She had a lot of unanswered questions. One question in particular dogged her as she sat staring at her pages of notes: who was at Donnelly's door in the hours before his death?

CHAPTER FOUR

When she was still solving crimes instead of attending meetings and badgering people about paperwork, Brenda often imagined she wanted to commit whatever crime she was investigating. She would develop detailed plans for how to do so and choose the safest and most effective one.

If evidence suggested the perpetrator's plan was very different from her own, she tried to imagine why they might have chosen that methodology instead of one of the more obviously efficacious ones.

It was the seemingly illogical choices in the commission of and attempts to get away with a crime that often served to help identify the perpetrators. Sometimes it was odd little quirks or habits that tripped up criminals too, she recalled with a shake of her head.

A few years back, Peterson and Brenda stood watching grainy, black-and-white video footage of an armed robbery, one of a series in various neighborhoods in south Briarwood. Because the robber was becoming more violent and abusive toward store personnel with each robbery, the cases were kicked over to their unit.

Peterson was grousing over the pettiness of the crime—usually they worked murders and higher-profile cases—and complaining about the poor quality of the cameras in the all-night convenience stores. As usual, she ignored his muttered commentary and squinted at the screen.

She noticed the robber repeatedly pushing up his balaclava and pulling a great wad of tissues from the left front pocket of his jeans. Each time, he blew his nose, pulled the mask back down and continued to menace the store clerk.

She went back over the video from prior robberies and noticed an escalation in the perpetrator's sinus problem. She idly wondered if the escalation in violence correlated more closely with the increase in his congestion or his building confidence as he continued to commit robberies without getting caught.

Guessing the robber had allergies, she scouted local drugstores for customers buying decongestants that contained pseudoephedrine, the purchase of which in California requires the presentation and recording of identification.

Despite their years of successful investigative collaboration, Peterson thought her theorizing a waste of time, especially since the recovery of records for such purchases required tedious paperwork and negotiation in the name of interagency cooperation. Then they had to look through hundreds of hours of footage to find the man who'd cased each store by purchasing decongestants in the week before each robbery.

It wasn't until her theorizing worked and the nose-blowing robber was identified, investigated, arrested and convicted that Peterson grudgingly acknowledged the fruitfulness of her line of inquiry.

"Not bad," he'd said with a grudging smile, "for a girl."

Both of them got better at the job and worse at life—a cop's inverse proportion of happiness—working seventy-hour weeks and ruining both his marriage and her relationship with Tori. But as absent as they'd been with their respective romantic partners, they'd become increasingly effective as an investigative team.

Now all of that was in the past. Brenda was a paper pusher and Peterson a binge-drinking retiree who haunted cop bars and, it seemed, disappeared at the first sign of potential fuss.

She shook her head out of the past. She imagined she was Sergeant Mark Donnelly. She pictured herself extorting money from small-business owners and low-level criminals, keeping careful track of the schedule and amounts in a small notebook. She wouldn't trust an electronic tracking system to be impermeable. She imagined feeling secretive and gleeful, powerful and frightened at the same time.

She paced the room, trying to walk like Donnelly, think like Donnelly. He'd had what she thought of as a skunk walk, hips forward and head back a little, like there wasn't anything that could touch him. It was bravado, of course, but her Donnelly self didn't realize that, not consciously.

She found the posture as she paced, slowing down and tipping up her chin. She pulled her center of gravity up, stiffened her hips, swung her shoulders with each step. She held her arms slightly out from her sides as if to suggest she had massive muscles that made this necessary. She puffed up her chest and breathed in self-satisfaction.

She saw herself as Sergeant Donnelly, strolling into the liquor store and smirking at the wary foreigner behind the counter, knowing that the store owner was afraid and would hand over the money quickly. She saw herself as the corrupt cop, opening the bag and pretending to count the bills and probably swiping a candy bar or beef jerky or whatever, just to remind the counterman of how powerless he was to stop the extortion and the thievery.

As Donnelly she gloated over the power as much as over the money, the way bullies everywhere do. And like most bullies, her Donnelly self was covering for overwhelming fear and insecurity.

She saw her Donnelly self panic and shoot Sheraton, feeling she had no choice. Shooting Sheraton was not something she'd wanted to do. As Donnelly, she had to give up the extortion game and her life as a sergeant and her home and everything she valued except whatever money she'd managed to squirrel away. The hard part about escaping into the ether was losing the people in your real life. As Donnelly, who would she love? Who would she not want to give up? Donnelly had two girlfriends. Did he want to take one of the women with him? As Donnelly, involved in a high-risk criminal endeavor, she'd have avoided developing significant personal relationships. She would want to be able to extract from her life relatively painlessly.

Somehow Sheraton ended up in the alley. Her Donnelly self panicked and shot her. So what would she do? She would gather as much cash as possible and flee the country. She would have long before set up an escape route and a backup plan or two or three. There was no way she'd have left herself vulnerable to capture and prosecution in the event of discovery. She'd have slid down the rabbit hole within thirty minutes of shooting Sheraton, and she would have never again set foot in the United States or in any of its extradition partners.

But Donnelly didn't do that. He spent days drifting slowly eastward across Northern California, casually heading from Briarwood to West Sacramento, staying in no-tell motels and eating junk food. Why? She asked the question of herself though she already knew the answer: he had a partner or a boss, someone he answered to or was counting on for something. He was waiting for help or instructions from something or someone.

If she were Donnelly, hanging around, she would be desperate to contact that someone. What if they hung her out to dry? Would she go after them? What if they came after her? Until the night before his death, Donnelly hadn't acted like a man on the run, and he hadn't acted like a man hiding from a co-conspirator. He hadn't seemed afraid until somewhere between Vacaville and West Sacramento.

Brenda wondered about a few things. If his cohort or cohorts lived and worked in Briarwood, why did he flee to West Sacramento? Why, if he'd decided to kill himself, did he bother to hide his notebook and disguise tools, and so half-hartedly?

If she had been on the run, she'd have burned the notebook, wiped the tech and her chargers clean, smashed the hard drives and flushed the crumbs of them away. She wouldn't have counted on water to destroy the laptop and cell phone. Both were in a lab somewhere near Sacramento, being dried out so information could be harvested from them.

She'd have covered her tracks. She'd have been a lot more careful than Donnelly. She certainly wouldn't have driven her own car or shopped at a store near a CHP administrative office. She wouldn't have used her service weapon to kill herself or another cop. She would have tried harder to get away.

Any thinking person would come up with a plan for discovery. She didn't know Donnelly well, but he had managed to garner decent performance reviews and a promotion to sergeant in his five years on the force. Both his lieutenant and his captain thought well of him. So what were the odds he'd failed to even consider the possibility of things going awry? He'd almost certainly had some kind of plan.

Did his plan fall apart, or did he not prepare some escape hatch for himself? Why didn't he bug out to the Sierras, where only hours away from Briarwood loomed huge mountains of largely unpopulated forest?

Why didn't he just go to Mexico? He was proficient in Spanish and had wads of cash. Briarwood was a port. If Brenda had been running some criminal venture, she'd have had a boat at the marina and would have sailed to Mexico while the world chased her on land. But she'd checked, and he didn't have a boat. If he had a partner, she wondered, did the partner have a boat? If so, why didn't he use it?

He was dating two different blondes: one an exotic dancer at a bar down the street from The Hole, and the other a lingerie saleswoman at the mall. Both were in their twenties and well over a decade younger than he was. He'd taken dozens of selfies with both women, and Brenda scrolled through his social media pages, noting that entries only covered the previous year or so. Big smiles, big breasts, big hair. Lots of cleavage and spangles surrounded smug, self-satisfied Donnelly in photo after photo.

She considered the few interactions they'd had. He hadn't seemed like either an idiot or a genius. He'd seemed a little immature but decently competent. She'd never picked up on any criminal component to his personality. If anything, she'd thought of him as a plodder whose greatest skill was filling out forms. She'd dismissed him as part of what Peterson called the new breed of police officer, too myopic and too willing to be micromanaged to ever become what her old partner had referred to as real cops. She admitted to herself that she'd shared some of his disdain for guys like Donnelly, officers who were good at doing what they were told but lacked the intellectual rigor and bandwidth to really think through a problem logically.

Donnelly's shooting Sheraton must have been a knee-jerk reaction, like that of a kid lying to cover up some minor infraction. It was less an indication of his capacity for crime than of panic. Brenda couldn't imagine Donnelly taking the initiative to shake down a score of small-business owners, not only organizing the necessary muscle to intimidate them but keeping the whole thing going, even after being assigned a curious, wide-eyed rookie to train.

She decided to operate for the time being as though she knew he'd been working for someone. But for whom? And was he the only cop this theoretical crime boss had been running? That seemed doubtful. The big boss was willing and able to run one or more shakedown rings, involve at least one cop, then murder a cop, all while managing to completely cover his tracks.

She examined the behavior of every cop she'd encountered since Sheraton's death. No one stood out. Not one of her fellow officers had been shifty or nervous or off. They'd all behaved exactly the way she'd have expected them to. Of course, if Donnelly's big boss was in the department, he'd managed to fool every officer in the city.

If she were a dirty cop running other dirty cops, she'd stay out of her own house. While it would be more convenient to run a crime ring using officers under her command, it would be safer to use officers nobody would connect to her.

How would she do it, logistically? Burner phones, obviously, and a coded communication system. She'd only use a couple of people she really trusted and keep them in the dark about each other as much as possible. She'd do as the larger crimes rings did: assign a lieutenant to manage each crew and keep them apart. Isolated cells were harder to track back to their capos. She'd discourage them from doing all the things Donnelly had done: keeping an account of the extortion, living high on social media, even having two girlfriends. Spurned lovers and those who formed the pointy ends of love triangles were great sources of actionable evidence in many criminal cases.

As the boss of the crime ring, she'd have kept a tight leash on Donnelly, and she'd have done everything in her power to keep him from letting a rookie trainee discover his nefarious deeds. With enough juice, she'd have ensured he never got a rookie trainee.

She made a list of individuals to investigate further, starting at the top of the department roster: Walton, the commanders and Vallejo were the obvious possibilities. She thought about retirees too, those who still had strong contacts on the force and the freedom of movement to do what they wanted. She had less to go on with them, but she decided she'd poke around to find out what she could.

She was startled out of her thoughts by her phone.

"You can't do that," Tori blurted.

"Do what?"

"Get personal when we're working."

She struggled to remember their conversation. She'd been blaming Tori for her own insecurities again, as she recalled. She'd implied Tori's ambition was the real reason they'd broken up, a thing she'd been indirectly alluding to for months.

Unable to apologize or to defend her sullenness, she pushed the topic aside. "We are not working this case, Tori. You're just—"

"Donnelly had two extra cell phones."

"One extra, I get. Two extra is weird." She thought about this. "There weren't any in the room other than the one in the tub, according to the report. Yolo County told you about the phones?"

"The girlfriends both had the number for his real phone, which is still not accessible. The stripper had the number for the second, and neither knew about the third. We found phones two and three in his car."

"The car. There was nothing in the report about the car." Tori said.

"Because it wasn't parked at the motel where he died. One of our guys found it twenty minutes ago when he was driving to his mother's house in West Sacramento." Tori laughed. "Guess where it was. Never mind. It was parked on the street in front of another no-tell motel down the block from the death site."

"Anything from the forensics on the car? Or are they even working the car? Can we get hold of it?"

Tori tapped her tongue, and Brenda listened to the sound. She'd get an answer to her questions when Tori was good and ready. First, she'd spit out what she'd called to say. That was how she'd always been. Brenda counted to twenty while she waited.

"We have his call records for the real number from the provider, and there's nothing particularly interesting. He called the girlfriends, some department buddies, a few workout buddies, Vallejo's office line once in a while. Sheraton's a few times. Nothing."

"So how do you know the second and third phones are his?"

Tori laughed. "I looked up his credit card usage. He bought the phones with cash but used his Visa to add minutes to both."

"Brilliant. Great work. You were always good at finding those odd little details and figuring out what they meant."

Tori made a scoffing sound. "Was that you, acknowledging I know what I'm doing?"

"I always thought you were a good investigator, even if I never said it. I should have said it." She pursed her lips. "You figure the third phone was for the big boss? It could be for a third girlfriend, a dealer, his bookie, whatever. But it's a good lead."

"Too bad we can't access call records for the burners."

She listened to Tori's tapping. "Amen to that. Any chance of a warrant?"

"Bren, the car's already been towed to impound. They didn't send along any real info on it, but I'll follow up. Remember Jim from Yolo County? We played a round with him and his wife at the club last year. Penny? Jenny? Wendy, maybe. She had the horrible choke swing, worse than yours, until her second drink. Then she was smooth as silk, remember? They kicked our butts from the eighth hole on. Wendy. Red hair and plaid skirt. In the car going home, you called her Sloe Gin Wendy. Jim and Wendy. I'll call him. Maybe he'll help grease the skids for us."

"Yeah, good." She cleared her throat. "What about his keys? There were two key rings. Do we have anything on what those keys opened?"

"Not yet. You know that'll take some time. And it's not surprising he had two key rings. He was living two lives."

"There's a reason for those extra phones. A lot of potential reasons, none of them particularly good."

Tori laughed again. "I always could count on you to anticipate all the bad possibilities. I guess nothing's changed. Okay, call me if you get anything."

"Wait," she said to the dead line.

Tabling Tori's comment and its implications, she called Donnelly's girlfriends, leaving a message for the lingerie saleswoman and catching the exotic dancer.

"Hi, Miss Smith. This is Brenda Borelli." She pursed her lips and decided to stretch the truth. "I worked with your boyfriend."

"Oh, gawd, not another one. Listen, I can't really stay on the line. My daughter's sick and I need to get her some cough medicine."

Brenda looked out at the late afternoon sun and made a face. Time was rushing past her. She'd spent most of the day accomplishing nothing but going over the same ground endlessly. She didn't want to wait another day or two to meet this woman. "I'll bring you whatever your daughter needs if you allow me to stop by for a few moments. Just tell me what brand and what kind."

A little persuasion and a trip to the drugstore later, she was knocking on one of a hundred brown doors in a newish apartment complex halfway between her house and where Donnelly had shot Sheraton. Evening was falling. In this neighborhood that was less a golden time of softening light than the coming of gloom and all its hazards.

Here, where there were no lawns on which to post Briarwood Watchdogs signs, nearly every window sported one of the fluorescent pink flower stickers that proclaimed the humble domicile a haven of safety due to the private security company's attentions.

The woman who opened the door looked more like the president of the PTA than a stripper. Clad in a pink polo shirt and faded jeans, she held a little girl maybe two or three years old. The kid was glassy-eyed and flushed with fever, nested in a thick pink sleeper and carrying a stuffed elephant. Brenda held out the bag of medicine with what she hoped was a warm smile.

"You brought it. Thank you so much! Come in, give me a sec." Staci Smith took the bag to the adjacent kitchen, murmuring soothing words at the kid. Brenda looked around. The small living room was furnished with a battered sofa, ancient television, and dozens of toys. She stepped across cardboard bricks and stuffed animals and picture books, almost tripping over the pieces of a large wooden train puzzle.

Listening to Smith sweet-talk the toddler into taking her medicine, Brenda tried to picture Mark Donnelly sitting on the sofa chatting with Smith while the little girl played with her toys. Whatever he spent his money on, it wasn't furniture. Even the toys, while numerous, weren't high-value items. So where did the money go?

When Smith came back from putting her daughter to bed, she came to stand next to Brenda, who was examining an array of photos on the wall. The pictures formed a chronicle of the baby's life. There was a single photo of several young women in what looked like club wear, and she recognized the signage for Bubbly, a strip club only blocks away. There were several shots of the happy couple, and Donnelly looked like a completely different man from the one Brenda had been investigating.

"I can't believe he's gone."

Brenda turned to see Smith wiping her reddened eyes.

"I'm sorry for your loss, Ms. Smith."

"Thanks. Call me Staci. Seriously. Miss Smith sounds like somebody's old aunt." The blonde seemed to gather herself. "Listen, can I get you a soda or a beer or something?" '

"I'm good, thanks. I would like to talk with you, if that's all right."

They settled on opposite ends of the sofa, and Brenda smiled. "You have the best living room décor I've ever seen."

Smith laughed. Suddenly her face fell and she grimaced. Brenda watched emotions play across the younger woman's delicate features. It had startled her, laughing, and she felt guilty about it, and then she defiantly decided to let the laugh live.

It was strange to see such a naked display of feelings on someone Brenda had assumed would be hard and manipulative. Of course, the woman could simply be a more skillful manipulator than most. Donnelly appeared to have been, so maybe they were two of a kind.

Smith picked up a stuffed monkey and flicked at its worn tail. "I guess she's kinda spoiled. I just want her to have everything. A perfect life, if I can pull one together for her. That's what me and Mark were working on. A nice house and good schools, dance lessons, college, the whole thing. Does that sound crazy coming from a nobody like me? I must sound like a nut."

"Sounds like a mom to me." She shrugged. "Why wouldn't you want the world for your child?"

"I bet you seen plenty of people that don't."

She mirrored her grim expression. "True. But maybe if they weren't too scared to hope, they could shoot higher."

"What do you mean?"

"I think if the world has mostly disappointed you, it can be hard to want a lot for your kids, because it's even more painful to be disappointed for them than for yourself."

Smith stared at her for a long minute. The gravity reflected in her light blue eyes belied her youthful good looks. "You have kids?"

She shook her head.

"I never planned on it, but Jess is the best thing in my life. Mark came along and once we got serious, I let him meet her. He wanted to be the father she never had. We talked about giving her a little brother or sister in a few years. He didn't care, boy or girl. The important thing was to get ourselves all set up to give them a good life. Buy a house in a good neighborhood, save money, all that. We had a plan. It's all gone now."

"I'm sorry." She sighed. "He had an eye toward the future. Sounds like that was something you shared."

"Mark didn't kill himself. I don't care what they say."

"What makes you think he didn't?"

"I don't know." Smith stood. She moved around the room, tossing toys into a plastic toy chest with surprising accuracy. "Like you said, he had a lot of plans for the future. He made reservations for dinner at Dave's Bistro on my next night off. I scheduled a babysitter. We just bought plane tickets to go see my sister for Thanksgiving. Mark wanted to get married so he could adopt Jess. He was studying for his lieutenant's exam. We were talking about looking at houses."

"So this whole thing was a shock."

"He wouldn't do this to me!" Smith waved a hand in the direction of the bedrooms. "He wouldn't do this to us."

"I'm so sorry."

"You all think he was this asshole. I know how you guys see us. I'm a lowlife stripper and he's a crook. Was a crook."

Abashed, she shook her head.

"Mark loved me. He loved my daughter. We've been together for almost her whole life. He was there for her first words, her first steps, the first time she used a spoon by herself. When she has a nightmare, she wants him to pick her up and tell her it's all right. He's the best thing that ever happened to us. Now he's dead and I don't know what I'm going to do."

"I can't begin to say how sorry I am."

"Yeah."

"Listen, I'm not sure if you know about—"

"The other women? Yeah. I know. Gawd, he didn't lie to me. I mean, not about that. I never knew about the other stuff he was supposed to be doing. I didn't like it when he suddenly wanted an open relationship, I can tell you that. But, well, Mark changed. I figured eventually he'd get back to being himself, but there wasn't time. I thought it might be 'cause of my job. You know, like he wanted me to quit but knew we needed the money, so he kind of wanted revenge. I been through that before. People do weird stuff like that sometimes. It doesn't mean they're bad people."

"I agree. Sometimes we do ridiculous stuff, and we don't know until later why we did it. Or we never figure it out."

Smith looked around the room and straightened a pillow before rejoining Brenda on the couch.

"Gawd, they questioned me a bunch of times. Like I might know something about it all. The money. They showed me all this proof. I think they wanted me to say I knew all about it, but I didn't know anything. I still can't think of Mark doing all that." Smith swiped at her eyes again.

Brenda held steady. Smith was obviously aching to talk to someone.

"We had them over for dinner, Tami and Mason. Nice kids. I didn't know she was suspicious of Mark. I didn't see that at all."

"Mason, that's her boyfriend?"

"He works for Dan. Small world, huh?"

"Dan? Dan Miller?"

"Yeah. Now, he could be a little shady."

"Oh?"

"Not, like, a criminal or whatever. He always has to be right, the smartest person in the room. Lies to everybody, says whatever people want to hear, flexes his muscles. He's my boss, and when he asked me out, I didn't really feel like I had a choice. He didn't say that, but that's what I figured."

"He's your boss?"

"Yeah, he owns like half the gentlemen's clubs in town. He's a pig, to tell the truth. Don't tell anybody I said that, okay? I really need this job."

She wanted to ask more about Miller but didn't want to burn through all of Smith's willingness to answer her questions. "Some guys are like that, I guess."

"Yeah, for sure. And where do I meet guys? At work, where they basically see me as just my body. So it's not like I'm stupid. I know all the tricks guys can pull. I know all the lies, all the games, I've known since fifth grade what men are like. But Mark wasn't like that. He wasn't a crook or a liar. He was a good man."

Smith twisted in her seat to look at Brenda and her eyes widened.

"You think he was murdered too."

"I don't know. I just want to understand what happened." She bit her lip. "You said he changed."

"About the time he got to be a sergeant. Maybe a year and a half back. He was always such a nice guy, really sweet. Then things changed. It was little stuff at first. He was quiet. Even before he got his promotion, he was weird, like, always really tense. I thought he was nervous about the sergeant's exam, but it didn't get better even after he passed. He started saying maybe he didn't want to settle down. He wanted to see other people. All this stuff about a last hurrah before we walked down the aisle. What could I do? I figured he just needed a little understanding. I'd stand by him, let him sow his wild oats or what have you, and it would be over."

"But it wasn't."

"I don't know. He was, like, usually the old Mark. Sweet and nice and funny. Then I'd look at his Facebook—he barely even knew what Facebook was before me—and I'd see all these pictures of girls with big boobs and him being all rude and weird, and suddenly he'd be busy all the time. But then when he was with me and Jess, he was still a total sweetheart."

"Sounds confusing." She thought about how Tori had changed as she'd ramped up her career ambitions. Brenda had been mystified by the sudden shifts in Tori's focus and had, like Smith, tried to wait out the mysterious storms in her lover's personality.

Unlike Staci Smith, though, Brenda had not been willing to accept her partner's infidelity. Of course, unlike Donnelly, Tori didn't announce her intention to sleep with someone else. "Did you confront him?"

"I tried to talk to him, but I didn't want to give him a reason to leave us. I wasn't sure what to think about it all. Now, I have some ideas. But they sound paranoid."

"Try me."

"Gawd. Ohhh!" Smith covered her face with her hands, then dragged them down, pulling her skin momentarily. Brenda blinked at the preview of what Smith would look like in ten years. After several seconds, Smith released her cheeks and nodded.

"I sound like an idiot. But Mark loved us. He started a college-savings plan for Jess. He took me ring shopping, and we looked at houses near good schools. He said we have to get in the right enrollment boundaries at least ten months before she starts kindergarten. He said we had to look at where she'd go to middle school and high school too, because that's where it all falls apart for kids, especially girls. He really wanted a good life for her. He woulda done anything for us." Smith hugged herself. "Mark was a good man. I keep hearing about the stuff they say he did, but he cared about doing the right thing."

"You—"

"I think he did it because someone made him. Maybe they threatened me and Jess. Maybe they tricked him the first time and they threatened to turn him in, so he had to work for them. But he didn't just go out there and commit a bunch of crimes on his own."

"You think someone made him do all this stuff?" She sighed. "I saw the video. He shot Tami Sheraton."

"I know. I saw it too." Smith covered her face with her hands. "Someone sent it to me."

"Why would anyone do that? That must have been awful for you."

"He didn't want to train a new cop, did you know that? He's not experienced enough. I don't know why they made him when he'd only been a sergeant for a little while. He wouldn't have killed her, but he had no choice. I'm not saying it was okay. Gawd, he killed her. But he was trapped, I know it. The people that made him do all that stuff are the ones that really killed her. They made him be in that place doing all those things, otherwise he wouldn't have done any of it."

"You sound pretty sure. Any thoughts about who could have compelled him to do all this stuff?"

"No idea." There was a wail from a bedroom and Smith rose with a frown. "Listen, I got a feeling Jess is gonna be up all night. Thanks for the medicine. And thanks for being so nice to me. The other cops mostly think I'm pretty much a hooker."

"Thanks for talking to me." She stood. "I'll let myself out. You take care of yourself and Jess. If it's okay with you, I'll check in with you in a few days. If you think of anything, if you need anything, please let me know. And please lock this door behind me as soon as you can."

Placing one of her cards on the end table, Brenda exited the apartment. As she closed the door behind her, she noted the locks were standard-issue apartment models, easily bypassed. She'd have replaced the knob and deadbolt with better-quality models and wondered briefly why Donnelly hadn't done so. She hoped, useless as the locks were, Smith would engage them before too long.

Driving home in the nighttime chill, she thought about Donnelly and the way Smith talked about him. Was she deluding herself? Had the guy been putting on an act? If Smith was right he was only involved in extortion because someone threatened his girlfriend or her child. Of course, there was every possibility the young woman preferred thinking her dead boyfriend had been a good guy in a bad spot and that she was just kidding herself.

The tidbit about Dan Miller was interesting, though it seemed unrelated to the situation at hand. She didn't think much of the guy, with his macho posturing and slick salesmanship. Her recent encounter with two of his uniformed thugs had made her think even less of their boss. She hadn't realized he owned any strip clubs, and she wanted to find out more about that. He hired men for their brutish muscle and women for their willingness to become sex objects.

Staci Smith had hinted at distasteful aspects of his personality, and Brenda wanted to take a closer look at the man and his security company after she'd found Peterson, apprehended Donnelly's killer and figured out who else, if anyone, should be held responsible for the murder of Tami Sheraton.

She grunted, irritated by the plethora of unknown aspects to this case. She'd always been more comfortable with the quantifiable and verified than with the nebulous world of perceptions and misperceptions, though she'd worked hard to develop skills with both.

Back at home, Brenda made herself a cup of tea and ate a frozen burrito. The house was eerily quiet, and she turned on the stereo. But when Aretha Franklin's evocative mezzo tones came out of the speakers, she turned it off. The CD was one of Tori's favorites, an early gift from Brenda. She'd bought two copies so Tori could keep one in her car.

"I should take that out and mail it to Tori right now."

But she didn't. She got on her laptop and looked at Donnelly's social media profile again. His pages on each site were barely over a year old. She wondered if she was letting Smith convince her of a delusion. She'd have to ask Tori to pull Smith's cell phone records, as well as those of the other girlfriend, Teresa Fortune. Brenda looked at Donnelly's publicly posted pictures again.

All of the many women looked the same, and she had to peer at each blank-eyed smile to determine which buxom blondes were Smith and which were Fortune and which were other, unidentified women. They were tagged with stage names: Staci, Bambi, Champagne, Cinnamon, Amber, Chichi.

A club manager had posted a photo on Donnelly's page and asked if Donnelly knew his history. In the photo were eight very young blondes in skimpy outfits. Brenda was reasonably sure the one on the end was a teenaged Teresa Fortune. She ran her hand through her hair, feeling the low thrumming that signaled the beginning of pain.

She was losing focus. Her headache coalesced until a vise squeezed her tender skull. Closing her eyes against the light, she recalled how Tori used to rub her temples and massage her neck when her head hurt.

She couldn't resist picking at the emotional scabs tickled by Tori's words. Was Tori right? Did Brenda always think of the worst options? Or was her disaster anticipation merely a natural result of two decades on the job?

She left another message for Peterson and again watched all of the video footage of Donnelly. She took notes remarkably like the notes she'd taken earlier that day. She kept hoping to run across something new, some clue to the identity of any person or persons who could've driven a cop to become a criminal and a killer. No matter how many times she watched, though, nothing new jumped out at her.

She spent a few hours doing background research on Chief Walton and on each of the commanders, treating Tori just like the rest, as a potential suspect. She found plenty of cronyism and infidelity and mutual back-scratching, but not a whiff of verifiable corruption of a significant nature. She found herself spending more time and energy examining Banks than his fellows. His lifestyle was more lavish than most, with his social life focused on the yacht club and the country-club golf course and a habit of dining out for most meals.

"You don't like the guy," she said. "You're seeing what you want to see."

Banks's wife had family money, as she and everyone else knew. Banks had for some years referred to himself as a trophy husband, and no one laughed. His photographs from earlier years told the tale of a tall, muscular lad with dimples and a wide, toothy smile. His current decline notwithstanding, Banks had once been good-looking enough to be arm candy to a wealthy spinster eight years his senior. His upscale world was paid for by his wife's inherited fortune. Grimacing, she put aside the subject of Commander Banks and his rich man's life.

It occurred to Brenda that she might be too close to the situation to see the dynamics in her department clearly. She shot an email to her old partner, Darius Brown, asking for guidance in doing a forensic analysis of the financial and political profiles of the subjects. Brown shot right back, asking if her question had anything to do with the recent murder.

Snorting at her own transparency, she wrote back that recent events had made her cast a more cynical eye on everyone. When her phone rang, she laughed.

"Guess I don't have to say, 'Hope I didn't wake you.'" Brown's deep rumble sounded the same as it had twenty years earlier, and Brenda fought a wave of nostalgia.

"When did I ever get a good night's sleep?"

"About the same time I did, twenty years ago. Nice to hear from you, Borelli."

"I thought you moved to Oregon to get some rest?"

"Turns out, they have crime here too."

"No, really? Bummer. How have you been? How's Janelle?"

Brown sighed. "She just found her first gray hair, so now we have to go on a cruise."

"Give her my love."

"You decide you want a new start, and I'd be happy to have you on my team."

"I'll keep it in mind."

"You reached out to me because you know I'm the best." Brown laughed at himself. "And I have access you don't have. I won't break any laws, obviously, but I'll see what I can find. I assume there's a clock on this."

"And it's ticking loudly. Thanks, Brown."

They made plans for Easter and rang off, and Brenda felt better than she had in a while. She had for the last seventeen years blamed Brown's decampment on herself and on the poisonous Satan's Lair case. They'd both run their lives into the ground and both nearly lost their badges over their shared obsession with shutting down the child-trafficking ring.

She still missed his sharp mind and quick humor. His move to Oregon had felt a little like abandonment at the time, but she had understood it too. Satan's Lair left its stain on Briarwood and on the officers who investigated its heinous crimes.

Sheraton's murder felt somehow like a full-circle event, bringing Briarwood back to its lowest point and exposing ugliness beneath the thin veneer of civility that kept the city functional.

She shut down the computer and sat in the dark for a few minutes. She sighed and rubbed her aching head. Without thinking, she called Tori.

"You call me a lot more now than you ever did when we were together," Tori complained by way of greeting. "What's your plan?"

"Follow the yellow brick roads, I guess. If someone was running Donnelly, I want to know who that someone is. They're responsible for Sheraton's death too."

"You're making a lot of assumptions, Bren."

"No, I'm just looking at all the possibilities."

Tori sighed again. "Let's think on it and talk during a civilized hour."

"Okay."

"Try chamomile tea, take a nap."

"Huh?"

"For your headache." Tori snorted. "I can always tell by your voice, you know that."

"I'd forgotten. Thanks, I will try the tea." She took a deep breath. "Tori? One more thing. I—"

"Yeah?"

"Take care of yourself, okay?"

"You bet. Hey, Brenda?"

"Yeah?"

"You too."

CHAPTER FIVE

"Captain Borelli?"

"Who is this?"

"Listen, I thought of something."

Brenda opened one eye and looked at the clock. Was it really after seven? She'd grabbed the phone off the nightstand without even really waking up, and she couldn't remember falling asleep a couple of hours earlier. She smelled the chamomile tea Tori had recommended. Her headache was less excruciating.

"Staci Smith?" Brenda sat up, startled by the brightness creeping in around the blinds and curtains. "Is Jessica okay?"

"Yeah, yeah, thanks for asking." There was a silence, and Smith coughed. "Still sick, but she'll be fine. I caught her cold, I guess. I was up with her all night, and I was thinking about what you said. Crap! Hold on a minute."

"Everything okay?" Brenda ran her fingertips over the rough edge of the gray blanket pooling in her lap. Why had she bought such an unappealing bedcover?

"Yeah, it's Jess. She threw up again. If you don't mind the germs, can you come by? I think I have some information, if you really, actually want to find out who mighta wanted to hurt Mark—"

"Sure, what time?"

"Ten?"

"Perfect. Need anything from the store?"

"Gawd, you're so sweet. No, we're good."

She rushed through her shower so she could get a few things done before ten o'clock. First, she went to Peterson's house. There was still no sign of her former partner, so she picked up a leaflet that had been placed on his porch and left him another voice mail.

She checked her email while trying to decide what she wanted to do about Peterson. Darius Brown had already written her a message with Chief Walton's name in the subject line. She skimmed the attachment, a breakdown of Walton's life as prepared by a federal contractor with nearly unfettered access to a multitude of databases. Brown's note also promised more later.

She skimmed the topics: Walton's conservatively managed finances, his unremarkable Internet usage patterns, his educational and professional record and his personal relationships. Brown had also written a series of questions and conjectures that focused on Walton's willingness to glad-hand whoever could be useful to him politically.

The man apparently had ambitions that led to the governor's mansion but no farther. While Brown thought Walton lacked intellectual rigor and was too fond of the camera, he concluded Walton was unlikely to be involved in something as potentially high-risk as extortion or murder.

She made a face. Did she want Walton to be fishy? Was that why she resisted her most trusted old partner's conclusions? He'd put this report together in a relatively short time, and she wondered if he made a habit of keeping tabs on the folks in his old department and therefore had already compiled a dossier on Walton and the commanders.

It would be comforting to blame Briarwood's ills on the new guy from out of town. He'd been chief for a year, but he would be the new guy in the Briarwood Police Department for a long time. Yes, she concluded, she was biased against Walton because she preferred to think it wasn't someone she'd known for years who'd put Donnelly on the path of corruption and ultimately to murder.

So, if it wasn't Walton, it had to be someone near the top of the department, with the freedom of movement and lack of accountability to run a criminal enterprise without being detected. No one under the rank of captain, she thought. She closed her eyes for a moment. She was assuming there was one man, one big boss who'd run Donnelly. What if it was a whole network? What if half the department was in on the extortion and untold other crimes? Was she picking the lock on Pandora's box?

They'd broken Satan's Lair open, she and Darius Brown, and she would never forget he was the person willing to listen to her. Together, they discerned the obscure behavioral patterns that suggested her theory about the human traffickers might just be the truth. Nothing had been the same after that, and she believed Brown moved away because Briarwood was forever tainted by the stench of complacency that had allowed a nightmare to flourish undetected in their little burg. Yes, she could believe he kept tabs on the leadership of his old department.

She and Brown had lost something they'd never discussed missing. In hindsight, she thought maybe she'd lost her faith in the basic decency of humanity. Night after night, the two officers had sat in Dave Morgan's living room spying on the child traffickers across the street. Night after night, they'd skipped sleep and sat silent, grim and desperate, accepting cups of coffee and sandwiches from Dave and Michael.

She remembered the first time she and Brown had approached Dave Morgan. A handsome, thirtysomething former surfer with a bad knee, he'd invited them into his sparsely furnished front room to hear them out. Michael had brought coffee and had sat next to Dave, stiff and uncomfortable, and painfully polite.

"What is it you're investigating, Officers?"

She had heard the fear in Dave's question. Being gay in a small town was a delicate balance, especially back then. For all the men knew, they themselves could be the subjects of a witch hunt.

"We can't say much," she'd told him. "But it would be a great service to the community. We're not playing a game, I promise you."

Then Michael had sucked in his breath. "She's family."

The men had exchanged a look, and Brown had said something about child abuse.

And that had been that. The couple had opened their home to the two strangers after a glance at their badges and a five-minute conversation. Dave had gone to the kitchen and come back with a pair of house keys.

"In case we go out of town."

When the case broke open, she and Brown were sucked into the maelstrom of interviews, paperwork, and trial preparation. They effused to their superiors about the generosity of their vigil hosts, but no one was interested in publicly honoring the gay civilians whose accommodation had made the investigation possible. And certainly neither Dave nor Michael had sought attention or accolades.

No keys to the city were issued to Dave or Michael. Still, when a prime piece of real estate was about to become available at the waterfront, someone in the mayor's office called Dave to tell him about it. And someone mentioned to Bill Halloran at Briarwood Credit Union that Dave Morgan was a good guy who wanted to expand his food shack into a full-service restaurant, one the city's leaders would be interested in patronizing.

Without much fuss, Dave's Bistro became the centerpiece of the upper end of the waterfront commercial district, and everyone essential to the city's administrative and enforcement agencies ate there regularly. The food was good, the location magnificent and the service top-drawer. She still believed Dave's Bistro was the city's thank-you gift to the men who'd quietly facilitated the salvation of so many of the town's children.

Now she couldn't think of Brown without recalling that time and the overwhelming emotional toll it had taken. She and Brown couldn't talk, email, or text without her feeling the rage, frustration, hope, despair, and exhaustion of that time. Nor could she think of it without feeling immense gratitude to the Morgans and grief over Dave's passing.

She sent Brown a reply effusive with thanks and a few follow-up questions on Walton. If Brown believed, as he so clearly did, that Walton was clean in this matter, she should move forward on the assumption that was probably accurate.

The final request—a workup on Dan Miller—she had mixed feelings about. She definitely had concerns about violating the privacy of a private citizen, but she kept running into his name. If Briarwood had, as it seemed, outgrown its folksy days when everyone knew everyone, how was it she kept finding Miller under every rock? She typed his name slowly, erased it and typed it in again, asking Brown to see if there was anything of interest about Miller's background or financials.

At some point she'd scanned one of the many business cards Miller had given her. She pulled up his information and left him a voice mail and emailed him. She'd figure out what she wanted to ask him once she'd set up the meeting. She was more than willing to bait him with the possibility she was retiring and looking for a second career in the private sector.

While she had her phone out, she called the station and spoke with Lieutenants Johnson and Miller, who gave her brief updates on several cases and a few minor administrative matters. While neither expressed irritation or impatience, she didn't want them to feel she was hovering, so she didn't press either for too many details.

She emailed Maggie a few requests on behalf of the lieutenants and inquired after the progress of some items that had been delayed due to Sheraton's murder. She felt adrift from her station and more maudlin about being absent than she thought she should, given it had only been a few days.

She also emailed Peterson, in case he was ignoring his phone and was checking email. She also left messages for a couple of his old buddies from the force. She called Peterson's cell phone again before she went to Joe's Place, his favorite diner, for breakfast.

Chiefly, she was hoping her old partner would be there. If not, he might have some buddies there who knew where he was or might be. There was another, more nebulous thought behind this. She hoped somehow going to his favorite place might help her feel more connected to him. This was pretty crunchy-granola for her, but she still headed for the diner with that thought in mind.

The outside of the stolidly square restaurant was decorated with giant aluminum circus animals in faded primary colors, and the windows wore looming neon ads promising five-dollar steaks and three-dollar biscuits with gravy. A narrow strip of dirt between the bright barn and its parking lot was replete with the town's namesake rosebushes and was dotted every ten feet or so with a Briarwood Watchdogs sign.

She ambled through the glass door of the eatery wondering why Peterson loved Joe's Place so much. Both gaudy and shabby, it seemed antithetical to the world her old partner worked to fashion for himself.

Inside, Joe's Place was just as colorfully dilapidated. The worn carpet sported red sailboats cavorting on a sea of blinding turquoise, while the yellow-paneled walls were adorned with bright, many-hued movie posters, most of them from decades earlier. She slid into a red vinyl booth wrapped around an electric-blue Formica table and looked at her fellow diners, none of whom were Jonas Peterson.

A tired blond waitress in her thirties chomped on bright green gum as she filled Brenda's mug without being asked.

"What can I get you, hon?"

"Joe's Special any good?"

The waitress shrugged.

"I'll take it, wheat toast."

"Yeah, got it. You a cop?"

She peered at the scarred nametag. "Interesting question, Dottie. I have one of my own: do you know a customer named Jonas Peterson?"

"Old cop?"

"Yes, ma'am." She turned on her most charming smile, but the hollow-eyed server only shrugged again.

"Reason I ask is, they been looking for you." Dottie chucked her chin back over her shoulder.

"They?"

"There's a whole crew of counter critters comes in here every day. He was in here the other morning like usual. Seven on the dot, he always says. Cuz of my name, you know?" The sun-seared waitress waved a surprisingly graceful hand around the dining room. "A lot of these old guys like their corny little jokes. He okay? He isn't here today."

"Well, he's probably fine, but he took off yesterday."

"You should talk to those guys." Dottie waved her hand toward the long, L-shaped counter and pointed to six men clustered along the shorter side. "They been looking for you, like I said."

"Thanks, Dottie."

"Go ahead over. I'll bring your food."

Brenda snagged the coffee and tried to look casual, heading toward the back counter. Dottie had been sure she'd want to stay and talk to them, which likely meant she was concerned for Peterson, which likely meant he really did come here every day. She eyed his buddies, who'd turned as one and watched her approach. They looked like they belonged in the diner as much as the red stools on which they perched.

"You looking for Jonas?" asked the apparent leader, peering at Brenda with keen eyes. His freckled head was shiny, bald and pink, his waist trim, his oxblood loafers gleaming. Not a cop, she guessed. Maybe military, once upon a time.

"Yes, sir. I'm Brenda Borelli. He and I used to work together. I understand he's usually here for breakfast."

"Hasn't missed a weekday, in what? At least eight months."

"Seven," another retiree, a little thicker in the waist and round-shouldered, corrected the first. "He had that appointment, remember?"

"But we knew about that," a third man, dark-skinned and trim, chimed in with an emphatic nod. "His being gone is unexpected this time. That's what she needs to know, isn't it, miss?"

"Yes, sir." She mirrored his nod and slid into the empty stool closest to the corner. "Mind if I join you?"

As one they all scanned the restaurant.

"He's working a case for you, that's what we figure," the leader confided. "I'm Stan. This is Bill, Andy, Mike, and those guys are Big Henry and Just Henry."

"Just Henry?" She grinned. "Nice to meet you all. So—"

"What'd you order?"

"Uh, Joe's Special. Is it any good?"

"Not bad. Kinda fattening for a skinny little girl like you."

"Stan, you're a terrible liar and I like you for it."

The guys all laughed heartily at that and seemed to relax. She had been worried about Peterson when he retired. She'd pictured him sitting home alone and drinking himself to death or eating his weapon on a sunny Sunday afternoon.

But he had pals. He had a routine. He had people who waited to see him every morning and worried when he didn't show up. He was part of the gang here. They had their coffee and their jokes and a place to hang out and belong. She sipped her cooling java and wished she'd come by before Peterson went missing. She'd noticed the flock of glasses in front of her old partner at The Hole and thought he spent the whole morning there. But he'd come here first.

She eyed the abandoned breakfasts of his usual companions. Based on the remnants, she inferred they'd ordered eggs, bacon and fried potatoes with rye toast, every single one of them. So Peterson probably had the same thing. It should have slowed down the booze. A daily drinker like Peterson should have had a very high tolerance and needed a lot of alcohol to feel drunk.

"Dottie said you've been expecting me?"

"Something happen to Jonas?"

She shrugged. "He's probably fine, but he left suddenly yesterday."

"You were meeting for lunch at The Hole." Mike nodded, and the others followed suit. "You get together with him regular, every couple, three weeks."

"He was a good partner, I miss working with him." She frowned. "I'm a little worried. I was hoping he'd be here this morning. You said he's been working a case? Can you tell me a little bit about that?"

It was Big Henry who responded, and he, Brenda surmised by his tone and burned-out eyes, was a retired police officer.

"Not officially, obviously. But he's had some concerns about the rookie who got popped. He figured you were gonna be looking into it."

"He's smart."

"Listen, there's something else." Big Henry looked at the others one at a time, and the group seemed to reach consensus. "Peterson didn't exactly have the easiest time with retirement."

The others laughed like this was an understatement, and she watched them closely. To cover her scrutiny, she took a swallow of coffee.

Big Henry visibly handed the conversational ball to Stan, and she swung her gaze toward the smaller man she now pegged as a Marine, a twenty-year man. His spine was iron, his eyes rimmed by squint lines so deep they looked drawn on his skin with a Sharpie.

"Sir?"

"He drank some." Stan ducked her gaze and stared at the neon orange wall behind the line cook, a burly man with a bulbous nose and a surprisingly spotless apron. "But he still had it under control. Mostly."

"He started looking kinda tired." This came from Just Henry.

"Hungover is what you mean." Bill spoke for the first time. "Every day."

Andy cleared his throat. "We were trying to decide if we should just let him work it out or say something. When he started to get a little more pep in his step, we figured it helped him, having a reason to stay sober. He wanted to be there for you."

She nodded.

Bill piped up. "He never called me back."

She looked a question at Bill, who pointed at his watch. "I called him at sixteen hundred yesterday. Basic message. He has caller ID, and he never called me back."

"Which he usually would?"

Bill nodded and a chorus of low, urgent voices sounded from the men.

"Now he's disappeared."

"Out of the blue."

"He didn't show up or call any of us."

"And you're here."

"Looking for him."

"Which means you're worried about him too."

They all started arguing about what this might mean and what they should do. She listened to the babble while Dottie slid an overflowing plate in front of her and filled up all the mugs. She dug in, noticing that each of the retired men paused long enough to thank Dottie politely before going back to arguing.

They seemed to forget her presence while they debated the merits of telling her about Jonas's drinking and the possible implications of their buddy's absence. The hot, cheese-smothered pile of meat, eggs, and potatoes filled her stomach while the words filled her ears.

At some point, she realized the guys had stopped arguing and were quietly sipping coffee and watching her eat. Once she'd put down her fork and blotted her mouth, they all straightened up as if on cue.

"Young lady?"

"Yes, sir? Stan?"

"We think something may have happened to Jonas. We'd like to help you investigate."

She considered Stan's words and said, "I hope you're wrong, but I'm a little worried you may be right." She checked her watch. "But I'm not even officially investigating, and he may have just decided to run off with some hottie nobody knows. Obviously I can hardly endorse a posse, but I could use some help. I just need to figure some things out. Listen, I need to get to a meeting. Can I come by, check in with you tomorrow morning?"

"No good," said Just Henry. "Stan finally got an appointment with the good proctologist. He shouldn't cancel it, and we all stick together." He held Brenda's gaze to underscore his secondary meaning, and she nodded.

"Lunchtime, then? Here's my card." She took the time to hand one of her business cards to each of them. "Please don't do anything until we've met tomorrow, except call him. My hope is that one of you will hear from him, we'll all give him heck for scaring us, and I'll be back here to see you all for a regular visit sometime soon."

From a chest pocket, Big Henry produced a carefully hand-lettered list of names, along with contact information for each member of the counter crew. They'd been here since six or seven a.m. and not seen Peterson. They'd discussed the lack of a callback from their old buddy. They'd decided something was wrong and she'd probably come here looking for her old partner at some point, and they'd planned to give her this list. She smiled and thanked them, dropping enough cash on the counter to include a generous tip.

"Thanks, Dottie," she called on her way out. She'd learned enough on her field trip to be really worried about Peterson and to feel guilty about neglecting her former partner. She'd met him for lunch or dinner every few weeks, but that was it. She'd been so caught up in her own nonsense that she hadn't paid enough attention to him.

He was unsentimental and gruff as usual when she'd told him she and Tori were splitting up, telling her no self-respecting police officer retired without at least one ex-wife to split the pension with. But he'd watched her in that speculative way of his, assessing her state of mind. Did he start drinking heavily again in part because of the stress of worrying about her?

As the daughter of an unrepentant alcoholic mother and unknown father, she knew better than to take responsibility for his alcohol abuse. He'd been a heavy drinker for years before she'd even met him. But he'd been able to confine his tippling to his few off-duty hours during the part of his career she'd witnessed, and he had rarely been more than slightly tipsy around her even after his retirement, at least until yesterday.

She knew he had long seen her as a protégé or daughter figure. She sighed. Peterson's diner pals seemed pretty astute. One had been a cop in a former life, and at least half of the rest had been military at some point.

She figured this meant their buddy's drinking had to get pretty out of hand before they would be concerned enough to talk about it with her. Like Peterson, they'd assessed her and decided she was worth confiding in—to a point. She'd assessed them and decided they were worth confiding in—to a point.

She thought about this on her short drive to Staci Smith's apartment. She couldn't remember a time when she hadn't sized up everyone she encountered. Part of that was the result of growing up with her boozy mother and her mom's motley collection of mostly drunk, occasionally abusive boyfriends.

Certainly she'd learned to stand up for herself. She'd learned how to dodge a blow and deliver one without breaking her hand. She'd learned how to pick a lock, survive without help, and maintain normalcy under abnormal circumstances.

She'd learned, during her turbulent early years, how to shoot, how to sail, how to escape a fire, how to climb a tree and ride a bike and drive and disarm a lunatic. And she'd learned to assess people for hidden motives and dangers. Without ever intending to do so, her mom had helped train her to be a police officer.

But Brenda thought part of it was inborn. There were cops who learned on the job to assess everyone. Maybe people who chose law-enforcement careers were more likely to have been born to wariness and hyperawareness and an innate need to perform ongoing threat assessments wherever they went.

For years she'd automatically sorted people into cops, bad guys and regular people. While she'd worked hard to recognize the blurring of those lines, there was still a series of litmus tests her mind seemed to run on everyone she met. She couldn't help but notice things like posture, eye movements, breathing and speaking patterns, the tiny tells people weren't even aware of. She knew she had big blind spots, especially when it came to people she cared about, but with strangers, she often saw far more than she wanted.

Dottie the waitress was in an abusive relationship, the current boyfriend the latest in a long series of losers who made her a punching bag. How did Brenda know that? She'd come to the conclusion so quickly she had to think back to recall what led her to it.

Dottie wore a long-sleeved gray sweatshirt under her polyester uniform, though it was warm in the diner. She shifted her gaze down to the floor when annoyed or uncertain. Her pancake makeup aged her but was necessary to cover the remnants of a black eye and finger marks on her cheek and neck. She stayed on the balls of her feet like she might need to dodge a blow at any given moment. Her seemingly saucy attitude notwithstanding, she slipped by tables like a cat in a room full of dogs.

He had sacrificed his wife and his two daughters to the job and to the drinking. He'd worked too much, gotten drunk and loud too many times, and now the ex-wife and the girls who'd once been his world wouldn't even talk to him.

He'd stumbled along, depressed and lonely, just doing the job and counting time. Then he'd been forced to accept Brenda as a partner. Before long she had realized she was becoming a kind of emotional surrogate for his family. She'd allowed this because it was clear the man was emotionally tattered and needed to feel something for someone.

She gripped the steering wheel, numb with dread and guilt. She should have read Peterson more clearly. She should have realized he was in trouble. His buddies from the diner were aware of his drinking as a problem, while she'd seen it as normal behavior for a newly retired cop. What else had she failed to see? She clenched her jaw and unclenched it to blow out a slow breath. Maybe it was egocentric to think he'd disappeared because of her.

She parked in one of the narrow spaces in the lot outside Staci Smith's apartment complex, wishing she could hear her old partner's voice and know he was alive. She was drawn out of her thoughts by a dawning awareness of stink.

She eyeballed the area around her. Here in the southern part of Briarwood, the mingled scents of the city's eponymous roses and their perfumed leaves were barely discernible. The stench of overflowing Dumpsters was everywhere. The foul smells of rotting food, automotive exhaust, marijuana, cheap beer, cigarettes, dirty diapers and unwashed clothing stained the air and permeated her senses. It all added up to the not-unfamiliar stench of poverty.

Whatever money Donnelly had made, he hadn't spent much of it on housing. He'd lived in this apartment with Staci Smith. Even if he only lived on his salary and not on the profits from his extortion activities, he should have been able to afford a better place. Defensible space was one of the most important components of a home for everyone Brenda knew. So why had he lived in this cheap, ugly, smelly, unsafe environment? Smith said they wanted to buy a house in a good neighborhood with good schools. Why not take his would-be family to a safer place in the meantime? Bad neighborhoods were hazardous for children, especially when both adults in the home worked second shift.

Her phone rang. "Mr. Miller, thank you for returning my call."

"I was surprised to hear from you, Captain Borelli. Glad, but surprised. Have you reconsidered my offer?"

"Well, I'm still thinking about it. Actually, I called for a couple of reasons. Is now a good time? Can we meet in person?"

"I'm on my way to the airport. I'll be in India for a cyber-security conference and some meetings for a couple of weeks. Is it something quick? I have a good twenty minutes before I get to the airfield."

"No, it's nothing that can't wait until tomorrow. And I'd like to have more than twenty minutes of your time."

"Intriguing as always, Captain Borelli. I'll call you."

Curious, she searched online and found there was indeed a big cyber-security conference about to start in India. It was advertised as the venue that introduced the most advanced technological equipment in the world. She wondered why the CEO of a relatively small home-security company and a handful of strip clubs needed to fly all the way to India to such a conference.

She'd learned a long time ago that people lied to police without even thinking about it. Asking questions was a game, like everything in an investigation. Sometimes the lies and evasions were more revealing than the honest answers.

She dragged herself up the stairs toward Staci Smith's apartment, suddenly overwhelmed by aloneness. Having walked away from the department and having let Peterson ghost on her, she was lost. She was relying on a bunch of old men, her old partner from twenty years ago, and her ex-girlfriend to help her investigate. She pushed away her self-pity and cleared her throat.

There was no response when she knocked on Smith's door. She called but got no answer, and a frisson of alarm went through her. She'd talked to the woman a few hours earlier, and Smith had been under the weather but hardly on her deathbed. Had she taken her daughter to see a doctor? Had she slipped out to the drugstore for something? Brenda spent ten minutes banging on the door and calling Smith's cell phone.

She considered her options. She could pick the worthless lock on Smith's front door. Brenda eyed it askance and frowned. She recalled the deadbolt was useless too. She'd have replaced the whole thing if she'd been forced to live in this run-down apartment complex.

She shook off the distracting question of Donnelly's failure to secure his home and returned to the question at hand. She could call the apartment's property manager, flash her badge and say she was concerned about the sick mom and kid. She could call the department and ask for a welfare check. She could leave and come back later.

All of those choices had unfavorable consequences. If Donnelly's killer worked in the department, calling for help could bring the bad guy's attention to Staci Smith. Picking the lock was illegal and could damage the cheap thing, which would mean she would have to pay to replace it, and, given the fact she didn't actually know anything was wrong, would be inappropriate. Someone should replace the useless lock, but she was reluctant to trespass on what was not her business.

Leaving the apartment complex and ignoring the fact Smith was missing could imperil both Staci Smith and her young daughter, if there was some problem that needed attention. Had there not been a child involved, and had that child not been ill, maybe Brenda could have just chalked up Smith's absence to flakiness and walked away. But there was a child involved and that child was ill. And the dead boyfriend of the mother was a crooked cop, a cop killer and dead from a gunshot wound. That boyfriend might have been working for someone even worse.

She couldn't pretend there was no potential risk to the kid. She thought maybe Smith actually cared about being a good mom. Then again, Brenda reminded herself, people don't walk around talking about what lousy parents they are. Every abusive parent she'd encountered in her twenty years on the force vehemently proclaimed his or her devotion to their bruised, molested, filthy, half-starved children.

She checked her notes and saw Smith's only vehicle was a 2007 Chrysler minivan. She eyeballed the parking lot and saw the silver van with the right license plate in less than a minute. So Smith hadn't bailed at the last second, not in her minivan. She hadn't taken the child to the emergency room. She hadn't managed a last-minute doctor's appointment and taken her daughter there.

Throughout Brenda's childhood, she and her mother had wandered up and down coastal California, staying for varying amounts of time in one apartment or trailer or duplex or motel after another. They'd even lived on a boat for almost a year, drifting up and down the coast, evading the ex-boyfriend who owned the boat. Eventually they abandoned it in a port she no longer recalled.

And in each situation she developed survival tactics. She knew how to pack in under an hour, how to fix broken appliances and toilets, how to handle a boat and a motorcycle, how to read strangers' moods and intentions, and how to escape through a window. And her mother had survival tactics too. She knew how to game the system, how to manipulate men into paying her bills, and how to get a low-wage job in an afternoon.

Her mom had always had at least one friend nearby, a drinking buddy or babysitter or a random someone with a spare key for when Mom was working late or passed out. Brenda was too young to be left alone for hours or days without some neighbor calling the cops. That newly minted bosom buddy usually had a kid too, so the two moms could bail each other out of the dozens of crises a marginally employed single parent with no family and too little money might face.

Thus, she started knocking on neighbors' doors. It was late morning on a weekday, and the parking lot was at least three-quarters empty. No one answered the first seven doors. Number eight was an older lady with a highball glass in her hand and a cigarette dangling from the corner of her sloppily painted mouth. In answer to Brenda's query, the tipsy septuagenarian wordlessly pointed at a door three down from her own. After a few minutes of knocking and pressing the button for what she suspected was a defunct doorbell, she heard someone struggle with the doorknob. She let her hand rest near her weapon until the door inched open.

She gaped down at Jessica. Staci Smith's little girl was wearing a purple fleece sleeper and clutching her grinning green elephant. She looked feverish and was in urgent need of nose blowing, face washing and hair combing. If the smell was any indication, the child was also in need of a clean diaper. Topping it off was the acrid odor of vomit. Brenda recalled that Smith had interrupted their call, saying Jessica had thrown up.

"Hi, Jess, remember me?"

The kid wandered away from the door, mewling plaintively, and she peered inside. Two little boys, maybe three and four years old, sat on the couch staring at a cartoon on the blaring television. The place was littered with toys, dirty clothes, and half-eaten snacks.

While she waited for an adult, Jessica clambered onto the sofa next to the other kids and started sucking her thumb. Based on the odor in the room, more than one kid needed a diaper change. She watched the kids fix their gazes on the fast-moving animation before them and waited a full two minutes to call out for an adult.

"Hello? Hi, is someone there?"

"Dammit, Tyler, how many times I hafta tell you not to answer the fuckin' door?" A very young woman in worn-out sweats and an oversized undershirt finally came out and frowned at Brenda. "Who are you? What the fuck you want?"

"I'm looking for Staci Smith."

"Ain't we all? She was supposed to take my fuckin' kids today."

"I—"

"You find her, tell her I get it, okay? She's been through a lot and all that. But she was supposed to babysit for me. It's her turn. I had to call in sick. How the fuck I'm supposed to pay the rent if I don't work?"

Despite or maybe because of her teased black hair, heavy Goth makeup and shapeless outfit, the woman looked more like a disaffected middle schooler than a grown woman with two kids.

"When was the last time you saw Staci, ma'am? How did Jessica end up here?"

"Ma'am? You a cop or something?" The woman narrowed her eyes at Brenda. "Yeah, fuck. Fine, I got nothing to hide. She was supposed to take my boys for a couple hours, but then she wasn't there. The kid was all by herself, and my asshole boyfriend didn't show up either. So here I am. I got my kids, her kid, no babysitter, a useless man, and no money for the day. What the fuck I'm supposed to do? So I brought her here."

"Leaving Jessica alone, that's pretty unusual for Ms. Smith?"

"Well, yeah!" The woman rolled her eyes. "She one of them stuck-up bitches. No sugar, organic, and all that bullshit. Thinks she's better than me, but who the fuck's here with her fuckin' kid? Me, that's who! Her place was a damn mess too. If she thinks I'm gonna keep her sick kid here forever, she's fuckin' nuts! I got two kids of my own, and now they gonna get sick too, so I'm a miss more work. What the fuck?"

"I'm sorry this happened to you. I used to work with her boyfriend. Did you know him?"

"That makes you a fuckin' dirty cop too, and I don't talk to no dirty cops. Don't worry about the kid. I'll watch her until

Staci shows. Get the fuck outta my house. I don't want you here, cop."

"I'm not trying to intrude. But I'm worried about your friend. Don't you think it's strange, her taking off like that and leaving her daughter alone? I'm worried something might've happened to her. If you know anything that might help me figure out what's going on, I'd really appreciate your help. Please."

"Whaddya want from me? That cop was a crook, right? So how I know you're not a crook too?"

"Oh." She grimaced. "You have a point." She eyed the three glassy-eyed kids lolling on the sofa. "I'd be suspicious too. But all I can tell you is, I want to make sure Staci and Jessica are all right."

"Typical. Girls like Staci always get the attention. Me and my kids could die right in front of you and you'd say it was our own fault, but that hot little piece goes prancing by, every guy—and every dyke—in town breaks into a sweat. And don't think you're above it all, because I know what the fuck you are. You can kiss my ass, cop, and get yourself and your 'lifestyle' out of my fuckin' house!"

Brenda backed away, hands up, noting that Jessica looked alarmed by the rising voice, while the two boys didn't seem to register it. She'd been like those boys as a kid, pretending to ignore screaming and things being thrown around the room. It took some time to develop the skill of covert watchfulness, and these little kids, still too young for kindergarten, already had it down pat.

The ringing of her cell phone startled her, and she nearly dropped it when she yanked it out of her pocket.

"Any word on Peterson?" Tori's voice was brusque.

"No, nothing. I swung by his house, talked to some of his friends, all that. But nothing. Listen, I went by Donnelly's girlfriend's place, and she thinks someone forced him into the whole scheme. I—"

"She's a hooker, Bren. She's used to letting men tell her the sky is green."

"A stripper. Listen to me. She asked to see me this morning, and then she was gone. She left her little girl all alone, and—"

"Oh, what a shock. The hooker—excuse me, stripper—is a bad mom."

"When did you turn into such a snob?" She shook her head. "Maybe you should spend a little more time on the streets and less time kissing the city council's ass. Then you'd get it that people don't always have a lot of options."

"Okay, Gandhi. Let me guess. She's gorgeous and she cried big crocodile tears and waved her cute little kid in front of you, along with her big, fake tits. You feel sorry for the poor wee stripper and can't imagine she was playing you."

Brenda sputtered and held the phone away from her head while Tori railed at her. Eventually the squawking stopped, and Tori hung up. Brenda considered Tori's suggestion. She went back to the neighbor's apartment and pounded on the door.

The young mom yanked the door open. "What now? Coming back to plant some drugs in here, cop? Maybe you can call CPS and get my fuckin' kids taken away? Huh?"

"Do you have a key to Smith's place?"

"Why, you planning to wait in her bedroom?"

"Ma'am—"

The door slammed in her face, and she stood staring blankly at it for a moment before it flew back open and something shiny hit her in the chest.

"Take it, cop," the teen screeched. "Get the fuck away from me!"

She managed to grab the key before it fell. Still pondering what she should do about Jessica, she went down the row of identical front doors until she reached Smith's, let herself in and looked around at utter chaos.

She cleared the rooms, weapon in one hand and cell phone in the other. Only when she was sure no one was in the apartment with her did she holster her weapon and pull on gloves and booties. Then she took her time looking around at the mess.

The place was torn apart: couch cushions slashed, dishes broken, toys and clothes and ruined stuff strewn about the rooms. The fridge, the kitchen cupboards, the dresser drawers—every corner of the apartment had been tossed. This had taken time. Smith had called Brenda at seven fourteen, and the neighbor had found Jessica alone about two hours later. Brenda figured at least ninety minutes, if there was more than one person searching, given the fairly narrow window of opportunity.

She went methodically through Smith's apartment. She saw the scattered remains of Mark Donnelly and Staci Smith's life together. The toys and clothes could have reflected lackadaisical housekeeping, but the ravaged furniture belied such a fantasy. The bedrooms appeared to have borne the brunt of ransacking rage.

In the larger of the two bedrooms, birthday cards and love notes and photo albums surrounded chunks of a jewelry box that had been smashed open and discarded in pieces on the carpeted floor. The jewelry was scattered around the master bedroom.

She studied the most valuable pieces: a diamond tennis bracelet, a large ruby pendant and an elegant emerald stud earring whose mate was likely somewhere under the mess. After a careful examination of an overturned drawer, she saw the other emerald earring twinkling under the edge of a pair of tightly rolled men's black socks. The intruders left behind a small fortune's worth of gold, silver, and gems, so whatever they came looking for was of greater value, financial or otherwise, than the jewelry. At least, she noted grimly, there was no blood.

Maybe Staci Smith struggled with an assailant and then left the apartment, either under her own steam or not. What were the odds she'd left her young daughter behind willingly? Or maybe Smith left and someone tossed the apartment after her departure. Was Jessica home while someone went through the place? It was tossed before the neighbor came by to drop off her kids; she'd said it was a mess, with a note of real surprise in her cynical voice. How long was Jessica here on her own?

Suddenly it occurred to Brenda that there was no vomit smell. Smith had said Jessica threw up. The child still smelled of it, though her sleeper didn't. What happened when a small child threw up? A wipe down, a diaper change, clean clothes for the kid and maybe clean clothes for the mom too.

She checked the trash cans. In contrast to the wild disarray of the rest of the apartment, the three trash cans were pristine, with new plastic bags stretched over their top corners. There was what appeared to be only adult-sized laundry dumped out of hampers in the master bedroom, but no dirty laundry in the baby's room. Nothing smelled like vomit. The bathtub still smelled vaguely of baby shampoo.

Brenda pictured it. The young mom has been up much of the night with her sick child. The baby throws up and the mom cleans her up, changes her clothes, throws the dirties in the hamper, tosses the diaper and maybe wipes or paper towels in the trash.

She has someone she doesn't know well coming over in a few hours. She thinks she might be catching the baby's bug, and the odor may be triggering her own nausea. Maybe she puts together a load of sick-baby laundry and takes out the trash along with it, trying to get rid of the smell.

Brenda checked out the laundry room on the ground floor at the end of the building. In one washer was a load of what looked like Jessica's clothes: the right size, pastels, still wet, smelling strongly of fabric softener and stain remover.

The nearest Dumpster was overflowing, and right on top of the edge was a trio of garbage bags of Smith's brand, each stuffed with the distinctively odiferous detritus produced by a child's illness: dirty diapers, vomit, and standard kitchen garbage.

A possible version of the narrative took shape. The young mom cleaned up the baby. Then she ran downstairs to throw in a load of laundry and take out the trash. She thought she'd be just a moment and didn't want to take the sick child down all the stairs in the early-morning chill. She'd just run down, she told herself, and be right back. Three minutes, no more. That's when someone took her.

Would whoever tossed Smith's place come back for Jessica? Brenda wasn't sure she felt comfortable questioning the little girl, especially since she was not on duty. She'd already wasted time with her dithering. Decision made, she called Child Protective Services. She also called her office. Lieutenant Johnson answered, and she filled him in on what she'd found at Smith's apartment.

"We'll get a forensic analysis as soon as possible," he promised. "Anything else?"

After several minutes of discussion over some mundane administrative matters, she signed off and let Johnson get started. She thought through what she'd done and what she knew. She'd reached out to Peterson, who'd gone missing after talking to her. She'd reached out to Staci Smith, who appeared to have gone missing after talking to her. Tori wasn't missing, but someone appeared to have followed her away from Brenda's house.

Was Tori in danger? Unlike a retired, alcoholic cop and a low-rent stripper, Tori was a medium-profile, semipublic figure. She couldn't just get disappeared without fallout. Would Tori's career success insulate her from danger? Brenda knew she was skirting one possibility.

Tori had largely ignored, rebuffed, and insulted Brenda for months until Donnelly's murder. Now she was showing up at the house, calling, offering to help. Was she just playing Brenda? Would it be dangerous to ignore the possibility that Tori was one of the bad guys?

CHAPTER SIX

"I'm just ready for a change."

"Well, young lady, that's wonderful!" The cologne-soaked salesman leaned close and attempted a flirtatious leer. "I'm sure we can find something that works for you." He eyed Brenda's ancient Chevy Caprice with skepticism and a wide, soulless smile. After all, a commission was a commission.

She turned away from the neon ribbons and red balloons that festooned the front of the low-end dealership. She chucked her chin at the less festive rear of the car lot. "Show me the cheapest used model you have that actually runs."

"Are you sure you don't want to look at one of our more affordable newer options? We have special financing and incentives for some very fine sedans. No credit is too bad for Swann's Fine Autos!"

"No thanks. I'll be paying with cash." She rattled the paper bag she was holding under one arm. She'd stopped by the credit union on her way to the second-rate auto row that lit up the southern end of Briarwood, and already she had misgivings. But she was here now, and she might as well go through with it.

The salesman nodded as though lugging a lunch sack full of money to the used car lot was a perfectly normal thing to do. She recalled the array of fast-food restaurants, check-cashing shops and liquor stores she'd passed on her way to the dealership. Now that she considered it, she thought maybe more than a few of Swann's customers bought vehicles with bags of cash.

She looked across the street at Dan Miller's Watchdogs headquarters. The black cube looked like something from a science-fiction movie. She turned away from Watchdogs and eyeballed her choices.

Twenty minutes later, she was driving a battered 2007 Dodge Caliber. The diminutive Dodge wouldn't have been her first choice under normal circumstances, but for now it suited her needs. It was black, careworn and unobtrusive. Fiddling with the creaky controls of the wheezing car stereo, she reminded herself she needed to replace the shuddering old Caprice anyway, and she could always trade in the Caliber on something else later.

Suddenly it seemed ridiculous, changing vehicles in the middle of all this. Donnelly's death might have been a suicide. He might have been working alone. His girlfriend might just not want to admit he'd been a crook. Brenda might be assuaging her guilt over Tami Sheraton's death by pursuing a fantasy investigation.

But. She talked to Jonas Peterson and he disappeared. She talked to Staci Smith and she disappeared. For all she knew, Smith was a flaky and neglectful mother who made a regular thing of taking off. But that didn't jibe with what she'd seen or what the neighbor had said.

And she knew Peterson. They'd been partners for years and had been together fifty or sixty hours a week for most of that time. He was moody, stubborn, rigid and more than a little self-righteous, but even on his worst day he was not flaky.

After a moment's thought, she nodded in sudden decision. She called Chief Walton's office. After a brief exchange of pleasantries with his assistant and then with him, she explained her call to CPS. Walton murmured vaguely as she told him Donnelly's girlfriend was missing and that she needed him to file a report. He asked few questions and promised to get it done.

She took a jaunt several miles inland to a large discount store in relatively well-developed Santa Rosa, where she bought hair dye, colorful makeup and clothes too flashy for a professional woman in her forties.

Stopping at home, she emerged two hours later a redhead with slightly shorter, much spikier and more odiferous hair. She also sported bright magenta lips, heavily made-up eyes, and spangled earrings. The look was completed by neon sneakers, a colorful, low-cut top and tight, stretchy black jeans. Her holster rode a tad lower in the new pants, and she found herself chafing not only at the unfamiliar positioning of her weapon, but also the discomfort of walking in the world as a different person. In her early years on the force, she had spent more than a few hours undercover as a prostitute, and she felt now much as she had then, like an imposter.

She spent much of the night researching Dan Miller and the early part of the morning awaiting his call. Given the time difference, she'd expected to hear from him before daybreak. When his call didn't come, she finally left him a message and sent an email. Ten minutes later she got a response to her digital missive. Miller was having trouble with his phone and would call her in a day or two. If something was urgent, could she call his office tomorrow to leave a message with his assistant?

She grunted. Why was Miller suddenly giving her the runaround? She speculated about this for some time before looking at the clock and realizing it was too early to do anything meaningful. After a short, broken nap, she dove into Thursday ready to start moving into the shadows of Donnelly's troubled life.

She called Peterson's house and left yet another message on each of his phones. She talked to bar owner Simpson at The Hole, but there was no news. Restless, she drove south and walked through all of the little shops Donnelly had been extorting money from, but no one would talk to her. They acted like they didn't know what she was talking about, and she couldn't get anything out of them.

Of course, she was just wandering into the stores and not identifying herself as a police officer, and she wondered if their response was more or less guarded because of this. One tobacco shop owner finally admitted, in the most indirect way possible, that the business owners had received a financial settlement from the city and had signed a nondisclosure agreement as a condition of the settlement. Then he shut down and asked her to leave.

Nodding, she went to the business next door. At Sam's Discount Liquor Store she met the owner, Narek. There she explained she already knew about the settlement and was not asking anyone to violate that agreement. "I'm not trying to cause trouble, really. My dad and my brother-in-law are partners, and they're thinking of opening a candy store down where the old salon used to be. My dad wants me to find out about the deal because he doesn't quite trust that this ugly business is over. I just want to make sure they're not walking into a bad situation, you see how it is."

"Hmm. We signed the paper and they gave us the money. A settlement." Narek presented each syllable with care. His wide mouth curled with distaste, and Brenda felt a sudden affinity for the owner of the store behind which Tami Sheraton had died. The short, thin Armenian shrugged, and his dark, troubled eyes darted to the street as though he expected ruffians to appear in the store's doorway. "Now we cannot talk about it. You see?"

His wry look suggested that if he was going to break that rule, it wouldn't be by talking to some crazy lady who looked like she was headed to the local bingo hall to smoke Pall Malls and gossip about celebrities. Brenda doubted he believed her lie about the brother-in-law, but he was too polite to call her on it.

Nodding, she caught a glimpse of herself in a small mirror hung behind the counter and realized her altered appearance was familiar. Was she imagining that? No, she realized with a start, she wasn't. From a distance she looked exactly like her mom at forty. How strange. Was that some passive-aggressive nonsense sneaking up out of her subconscious? She'd spent hours making herself look like her late mother and not realized she was doing so. She pushed the thought aside.

If the victims of Donnelly's scheme had signed nondisclosure agreements with the city as part of the payoff designed to prevent lawsuits, how was she going to investigate?

"Okay," she said to Narek, "what if we talked about theoretical stuff? Like if, for example, some random business was getting shaken down by some random dirty cop, when might that have started?"

"Who are you? Why are you asking these questions? The truth, please." He slipped out from behind the counter and walked down the middle aisle of the small store. He fussed, adjusting a bag of chips, a carton of crackers, a whip of jerky. She wondered if he realized he was promising himself the store was still there, still his, still real. Or was she projecting her own insecurities on the shop owner?

"I knew Tami Sheraton." She saw recognition and fear on his face. "I want to know why she died. I want to make sure her death wasn't in vain."

"I do not want any more trouble. I had no doings with this murder of lady police Tami Sheraton."

"And I have no desire to cause you any." She made a wry face. "Listen. The theoretical cop who was threatening theoretical business owners like yourself? Maybe he was on his own, but I don't know for sure. I wonder if maybe someone else was running the show, which would mean that someone else could still be shaking down business owners like you, or is likely to do so again soon."

This was not a revelation to him, judging by the resignation in his expression.

"I would like to prevent that so you can stop forking over your hard-earned dollars to some bully. Even if the money comes out of the settlement for a while, that payout won't last forever, and then you're still on the hook for the extortion fees."

"Ah." He looked down at the candy in the endcap display, needlessly straightening and rearranging colorfully wrapped items on the spotless metal shelves. "The theoretical extortionist, his cohort, would have to be someone the victims did not fear, you see? For them to say a single word. It would have to be someone whom the shop owners did not think was dangerous to them also."

She nodded slowly and sighed. He was scared. She took in his shallow breathing, flared nostrils, lowered gaze. She noted how his mouth was a tight line bracketed by tension lines. His body language—tight and restless at the same time—was that of a prisoner under surveillance and trying to look casual.

Her gut lurched, and she was sickened by the fact that right under her nose, in her town, folks were being terrorized by the very people who'd promised to protect them. "This has been terrible for you, I'm sure."

He carefully nudged a candy bar into alignment with its fellows and turned to face her.

"I have lived in seven countries since I left my home. Everywhere I had to pay bribes to corrupt officials. Then we came to America. My cousins, they said it was different here. They said we do not have to bribe any officials. It is the criminals who must hide because they do not control police. But my cousins, forgive me, they were wrong. It is the same here as everywhere else."

"No, sir, it's not." She leaned forward and stared into his eyes. "It's not. That's why I'm here. I want—"

"She used to come here for shopping."

She was taken aback. "What?"

"Lady police Tami Sheraton. She always bought some special thing—dessert wine from Spain or Irish whiskey or some special thing. She would come to the back door because I asked it of her. People are worried if police come always to the store. Maybe she will ask for money also, you see? So she came to the back of the door as my favor. She would come to ask me, 'What is a good sake? What is a decent Australian shiraz?' Not like most people who are shopping in here. A lady. I liked her."

Her mind raced. "I didn't know that."

"But that is all I can say. I am sorry she is died. May God forgive us all for the wrong men do. But I cannot help you. I have a family to take care of. I cannot be foolish."

"I don't want to cause trouble for you. I just want—"

"You are not only a friend of lady police Tami Sheraton. You are also the police, but you are pretending not to be. You are bad like— No. No. You are hiding from your own people, because you do not trust them also. You cannot help us."

She opened her mouth and shut it again. He'd read the situation as clearly as if it were a menu. She shrugged helplessly. "Please talk to me."

He spoke over his shoulder as he strode away from her on stiff legs. "They will kill me if I talk to you, and they will kill you also if you keep doing this thing. Please go away. You will make them angry and they will punish us. Do you not see? Go away from here. Do not come to this store anytime. Please go now. Please."

"Narek—"

But the man was gone, having escaped into the storeroom. Brenda drifted out to the parking lot, wishing she'd found a better way to handle things with the liquor-store owner. She'd frightened a man who was already scared, a refugee who'd fled his home in hopes of a better life and found here only the same corruption and scare tactics he'd found elsewhere. Wasn't America supposed to be better than that? Wasn't Briarwood supposed to be better than that?

She chose Briarwood because it seemed like the idyllic American town, safe, prosperous, and hospitable. She was shaken by a sudden awareness that she might have lost touch with the reality of life for most of the people who lived in the city she loved. She was at sea.

At sea, she thought, repeating it like a mantra, over and over, as she trudged back to the Caliber. Andi is my anchor, she thought wildly. She grabbed her cell phone.

"What? You're actually calling me? Did NATO dissolve? Is everything okay?"

"Ha-ha. I'm a little freaked, actually." She updated Andi on what she'd been up to and what she'd found out, hoping she wasn't oversharing. By the time she'd finished giving voice to it all, she was breathless. She waited a few seconds before Andi responded with a low grunt.

"What?"

"That's a lot to process. Send me a picture of your hair."

She complied and listened to Andi's hoot of laughter.

"Sugar, that is a truly terrible color on you. You look like a middle-aged hooker with a personality disorder."

"Thanks, pal. Real charming. Supportive too. I'm supposed to look different."

"Well, mission accomplished. I'm all for a good midlife crisis, you've earned it, but this is just sad." Andi's tone dropped. "Bren, I'm not sure this is a good idea. I'm not even sure what you're trying to do."

"It's temporary. It'll wash out."

"Not the hair color, though, yeah, thank God that's not permanent." Andi paused and Brenda listened as she apparently went into a quieter room, probably her office in back of the café. "You know what I'm talking about."

She made a noncommittal sound. "Hey, what do you know about Dan Miller?"

"Watchdogs Dan Miller? Lots of money, obviously. A little off. Thinks he's smarter than everyone. Thinks he says all the right things, but he doesn't manage to sound sincere. His guards are Neanderthals. We had to demand they change personnel here at the boardwalk five times, because the first four crews were drooling, jackbooted thugs. Why do you ask?"

"I don't know. Just chasing every random idea, really."

"Stay away from him, kiddo. I wouldn't trust that man with an empty wallet."

She gave an abbreviated laugh. "Miller's playing rabbit with me, which is weird because he's been persistently offering me a job for the last several years."

"Well, maybe he's not too thrilled about how this Donnelly thing makes him look."

"What would it have to do with him?"

"His whole shtick is that Briarwood is safer because of him and his company, so how does it look when a cop gets murdered by another one? Half the businesses down at that end of town pay his company a lot of money they can't afford for electronic surveillance. Why didn't his guys see something was wrong? Why didn't their computer geniuses notice there was a cop walking around with literal bags of cash every time he left these small businesses?"

"Well, we didn't, and they were ours to protect."

"Yeah, but you don't have cameras set up all over town and practically unlimited access to the footage. You know how the whole trend now is to privatize government programs, so we lose all accountability and transparency while taxpayers line the pockets of the greedy few?"

Andi's late wife, Lauren, had been passionately opposed to the unholy marriage of politicians and profiteers. It had been one of her most constant themes, and Brenda bit her lip at the way Andi phrased the concept the way Lauren used to. She swallowed hard, missing the sound of Lauren's voice.

"Yeah?"

"The politicians can make more money, the private corporations can make more money, they can destroy the unions and our infrastructure, making us finance the whole debacle with our taxes. It's a game, and Dan Miller, idiot though he is, knows how to play it."

"I know, but it's not like the security guards are going to replace the police department, Andi."

"Oh, no? Why not? It'd be cheaper. No pensions, no health care, no raises, no equal-opportunity requirements. Law enforcement could be a few dozen guys making minimum wage looking at cameras and playing with their guns. The only people you have to pay a decent wage are the tech guys, and you only need a few of those once you've got all the cameras in place. It's a perfect nightmare: secretly held, privately owned, taxpayer-funded invasion of privacy. They even call themselves Watchdogs!"

Brenda absorbed that. "Right now all I'm looking at is who got Donnelly to run this extortion thing. Then I'll know who besides that rabbiting lowlife is responsible for the death of Tami Sheraton."

"Listen, either you're completely paranoid and overreacting, or you're stirring up something dangerous. Either way, I'm not happy about it."

"Yeah, well." She bit her lip as she listened to diminutive Andi sink heavily into her creaky office chair. It was falling apart and needed to be repaired or donated, but Brenda knew that Lauren had bought the chair, so Andi would never replace it. Maybe for Andi's birthday she could hire somebody to fix the chair so at least it wasn't a safety hazard.

"I had the kids put up the posters like you asked. They made a Facebook and Twitter thing too. Do you think Jonas is really missing, like dead or kidnapped? And the girl, the stripper? Or do you think they're both kind of fragile people who can't handle weirdness?"

"Oh, Andi." Brenda exhaled loudly. "I don't know. Honestly. I mean, I can't say about the woman. I met her one time. Peterson? It's hard to say. He has a drinking problem, and I've been worried about him. He hasn't seemed like himself lately. But I can't picture him taking off like that."

"I don't want you to disappear. Don't end up like Tami Sheraton. I can't lose you too."

She closed her eyes and swallowed hard. "Oh, Andi."

"I mean it, Bren. I love you. I need you to be careful."

"I love you too. I promise to be careful. If things seem hinky, I'll call in for help. Really, I have no interest in playing with fire."

"Speaking of, have you talked to Tori about all this stuff?"

"Yeah, funny. We're talking more now than we did back when."

"That wouldn't take much. What does she say?"

"Well—"

"Let me guess, she wants you to avoid following the white bunny down the hole, and you're not listening to her either. Right? She and I can agree on that much at least. Oh, gotta go. I have a delivery driver trying to get my attention. Call me tomorrow?"

Before she could respond, Andi was gone. She snorted at herself. She couldn't believe she was still obsessing over Tori. She would close her eyes at night and smell Tori's perfume. She would see something funny and think of telling Tori about it.

The sweetbriar rosebushes that filled their little city with cheery color and sweet scent had somehow become tied up in her feelings about Tori and the life and sweetness she'd brought into Brenda's world. Now, nearly everywhere she went were painful reminders of what she'd lost.

She'd built her whole life around the job and around Tori, and now the job was tainted by corruption, and Tori was the ex who'd cheated on her with some random woman. How had she let both things slip through her fingers like that?

Cancer had robbed Andi of Lauren, and there hadn't been anything she could do to stop it. Heart disease had robbed Michael of Dave. But some enemy hadn't taken Tori, not even the woman she'd cheated with. Brenda knew she'd blown it with Tori. She'd known they were off course, and she'd failed to do what she could to stop it.

The day before Lauren died, Andi stood staring at her unconscious wife from the doorway of their bedroom, her face as blank and smooth as a wall. Then it twisted into a mask of pain and horror. Brenda had known what Andi was thinking before she whispered it.

"How did I let this happen?"

Brenda knew exactly what she meant. You were supposed to protect the people you loved. You weren't supposed to let bad things happen to them.

What if the bad thing that happened to Tori was me?

When her phone vibrated and interrupted her thoughts, she knew without looking it was Tori. She bit her lip and grunted in greeting.

"Why did you have Walton report the stripper missing?"

"Because she left her three-year-old alone, which I already told you."

"And it's Super Brenda to the rescue, right?"

"She asked me to come see her, and then she took off and left her kid alone. And her place was torn apart."

"So she knew a police officer was coming over soon. She read you like a book, Bren. She knew you would make sure the kid was okay."

This thought hadn't occurred to her, and she took a moment to process it. "You're right, that might have been what happened. But I don't know. Just like every other weird thing, we check it out. We don't just tell ourselves a story and leave it at that."

"Don't we?" Tori blew out air, and the sound filled Brenda's ear. She knew that meant something but she didn't know what.

"I met with Peterson and he vanished. Then I met with Staci Smith and she disappeared. Her apartment was ransacked, but a bunch of expensive jewelry and the electronics were left behind. Doesn't any of this seem odd to you?"

Tori snorted. "Jonas Peterson's a depressed, lonely drunk who was barely functional before he got pushed out to pasture and decided to drink himself to death. Staci Smith is a high school dropout whose boyfriend just killed himself because he was a crooked cop. Odds are, she's off doing whatever drugs she takes to deal with her soul-killing job."

"If you suddenly disappeared, what would you want me to do? Or do we only care about certain people?"

There was silence, and Brenda gave Tori a minute to process her thoughts. Either she'd hang up in rage or she'd restart the conversation with a cooler head. There was a moment of tongue tapping before Tori's voice came across at cucumber temperature.

"Who're your main suspects?"

"The entire department. Everyone above lieutenant." She had spoken without thinking and bit her lip, glad Tori couldn't see her face. Except you, she knew she should add, but she didn't. There was another long pause. Then Tori muttered a curse and rang off.

Talking with liquor-store owner Narek about Tami Sheraton's murder had reminded her to call Sheraton's family members again. She'd already left messages on their phones, not expecting to hear back. She'd hoped to see them at the funeral to offer her inadequate condolences, but the family had kept that private. Still, she wanted to follow up again. Maybe Sheraton had confided in her mom or sister or cousin.

If twenty years on the job had taught her anything, it was that people always talked to someone. Good guys, bad guys, witnesses—everyone needed a friendly ear sooner or later.

A slew of phone calls later, she had again left messages for Sheraton's mother, sister, brother and aunt. Hopefully one or more of them would get back to her. Families of slain officers tended to either enthusiastically seek interaction with members of the force or shun it entirely.

If the shuttered funeral was any indication, the Sheraton family was leaning toward the latter. But that might have been the mother's doing. When her child was murdered by a fellow officer, Mrs. Sheraton might have been understandably angry at and distrustful of the department.

There was a boyfriend listed in Sheraton's phone only as "Mason" with a heart emoji. She left a message for him too.

She headed back to Joe's Place, where the décor was no less appalling at second glance. She found her old partner's friends at their counter, nursing cooling cups of coffee and wearing anxious expressions. At her arrival, Peterson's friends took in her new look with disarming nonchalance and a few significant glances between them. She smothered a wan smile.

"Good idea," put in Andy, raising his eyebrows, "going undercover. We'll call you Sharona."

She made a sound like chuckling but didn't follow up on this.

Big Henry offered her a small smile, which she returned by half.

Just Henry leaned forward. "So what've you learned?"

"Well, things are weird." She debated how much she wanted to share with these men she barely knew. "Listen, you guys are civilians, and I'm not even officially—"

"We're not fools," Stan said softly, holding her gaze. "We look like a bunch of daffy old geezers, I know, but we're not about to do anything stupid or dangerous. We're certainly not about to do something that'll get you into trouble. Captain

Borelli, I've known Jonas Peterson for thirty years. And you mean more to him than you realize. The girls—well, you know. You kinda took their place."

She nodded, trying not to choke on the sudden lump in her throat.

Stan offered her a pained expression that almost approximated a smile. "Our friend is in some kind of trouble. No one's seen him for twenty-four hours. He's a senior citizen, which means we can call him an at-risk missing person. Right, Big Henry?"

"Affirmative."

"So we can make that call instead of you. If Jonas is off in Vegas with a coochie-coo and comes back to find himself on the news, fine, he can throw a fit about it. But we don't think that's how it is. Somebody was working with that little weasel, that's what Jonas thought. He said Donnelly wasn't competent enough to tear wet paper. So what do we need to do? Who do we need to talk to?"

When she hesitated, Big Henry held up a hand. "Let's do this, Borelli, I'm gonna make a guess and you don't even have to confirm or deny, okay?"

She nodded. The interaction was an uncomfortable echo of her conversation with Narek.

Big Henry turned his large body slightly so he was facing the group. "Donnelly killed the rookie, Sheraton, behind Sam's Liquor, which, like many of the small businesses in that neighborhood, is owned by an immigrant."

She kept her expression blank and receptive, wondering where this was going. She noticed the others were listening as intently as she, so Big Henry was sharing his theory for the first time.

"Folks from other countries are often used to having to pay to be in business. Bribes, extortion, whatever. And they're usually pretty easily dissuaded from trying to get help. They're used to the police being as crooked as everybody else in power. So I figure Donnelly was shaking down the easiest marks. Then he got stuck with the rookie, and the kid found out what he was doing. He ended up shooting Sheraton in a panic because she caught him in the act. It wasn't premeditated, that's obvious. We've all seen that video. Hell, it's been on the Internet for days."

Brenda saw the other guys eyeing her for some reaction, but she gave none.

Big Henry nodded at her. "Borelli and Peterson—Jonas—both think Donnelly was working for somebody bigger and smarter than him. So Borelli's in a delicate position. Jonas is retired, and she's on vacation or compassionate leave. How else could you go after somebody in the department without clueing them in on what you're investigating? So you could use some men to do legwork for you."

"Hmm."

"Victimology," said Stan. "Big Henry told us, that's one of the things you look at."

She jumped in. "Donnelly had a girlfriend. Two, actually. One of them hasn't returned any of my three calls. I saw the other one yesterday, and I was supposed to see her this morning again. Now she's missing. Left her sick three-year-old alone and upped and left. Her place was tossed. No jewelry or electronics missing, except her cell phone."

Big Henry and Stan exchanged glances.

Stan nodded slowly. "So you met with Jonas to talk about Donnelly and he went missing. You met with Donnelly's girlfriend and she went missing. You file a report on the girlfriend because of the kid?"

"I had someone else do it. And I would appreciate your filing on Peterson like you offered. Also, are any of you familiar with Briarwood Watchdogs?"

"Mike Miller's boy started that." Stan made a dismissive gesture. "We call 'em the Meathead Patrol."

"Wannabes." Big Henry scowled. "Too many steroids, not enough brains."

"Are they dumb but clean, or dumb but dirty?"

Just Henry blinked at her. "Dirty how?"

She shook her head. "I'm fishing. Anything?"

Bill plucked at his ear. "We could nose around a little. I know the guy who patrols around this place acts like he was trained by the Gestapo."

There was a chorus of dismayed agreement.

"Well, keep it under the radar. Just keep your eyes and ears open on that one. I don't want anyone's guard up, so to speak. Do not engage under any circumstances. Listen, there's other stuff I'd like to ask you to do, but it's scut work."

She eyed each of the men in turn, noting their resolve. There was no way she'd involve them in anything that could either endanger them or jeopardize some future prosecution of perpetrators.

She was equally aware that, having jumped in the puddle of their concern for Peterson, she couldn't just walk away and risk their hatching some hazardous plan to find their buddy. What she could do with a relatively clear conscience was give them tasks that would not only actually help her but also make them feel useful and keep them out of trouble. They could do surveillance from a distance, check public records at the library, write a narrative of events that didn't face the limitations of her own assumptions and perceptions. She wanted to know more about each of the commanders, about each of the captains, about Walton, about Miller. Brown could look in the digital universe for her, but these men had lived in Briarwood for decades and knew things she did not, things that had never been recorded digitally.

She held up a hand and sat staring into space for a few seconds. Then she snapped her fingers and wrote a list of specific tasks and names, leaving it to Stan and Big Henry to divvy up the chores. After agreeing to meet up with her recruits again in a couple of days, she looked around at Peterson's friends. They were scared for her old partner and that worried her.

She tried to shake off her anxiety before it became too apparent to the diner gang. It wouldn't do Peterson any good for her to wring her hands and weep into her pillow, or for her to get the guys more worked up than they already were.

Ten minutes later she left the diner feeling like a character in a cut-rate television show. She'd just recruited a bunch of senior citizens she barely knew to help her solve a crime. She'd even assumed a disguise. All she needed now, she thought wryly as she sank down in the Caliber that didn't yet feel like her car, was a tagline and a sidekick. At that her phone vibrated, and her smile deepened.

"You are a pain in my ass."

And there's the tagline, she thought, hearing Tori's sardonic voice. She burst into laughter and held the phone away for a few seconds to collect herself.

"Tori," she managed to spit out between chortles, "how's my favorite sidekick?"

"Sidekick? If anything—whatever. What have you learned? Any sign of Peterson?"

"Nothing. His buddies are going to file a report. I think there may be some link between—"

"There's no link, Brenda. You're chasing this phantom case like it'll exonerate you for a crime you didn't commit. Sheraton wasn't even your officer. She should have gone to her superior above Donnelly with her concerns and didn't, not really. Did Vallejo tell you? She had every opportunity to talk to him about Donnelly, but she didn't."

"Vallejo hasn't been himself lately, you know that."

"I thought it was under wraps, but I guess half the department figured out he was in the drunk tank. Banks and Walton and I are the only ones who were supposed to know about it."

"Oh."

"The latest wife made him go to addiction camp or whatever twelve-step is covered by our insurance. He went three times in the last six months."

"Tori—"

"So he's been distracted, and she didn't have anyone else to turn to. Hey, she's a rookie. Was a rookie. What did she know? Maybe Vallejo could have pulled his head out of his ass in between trips to rehab, but he didn't. Hell, maybe none of us would've seen it. I sure didn't. It's not anybody's fault, including yours. Donnelly was a crook, and he acted like one. Sheraton was a rookie, and she acted like one. Vallejo is a burnout, and he acted like one."

"I—"

"You did all you could do to help Sheraton, given she made up some vague thing about wanting to be more observant, instead of talking to you about how she thought Donnelly was crooked. She played Nancy Drew and walked into a situation she was unprepared to handle. Donnelly panicked. He figured he'd been caught and he killed the officer who caught him. He went on the run. He freaked out, realizing he'd burned his life to the ground. Now he's dead. End of story. Banks was right, the sooner we put this all behind us, the better."

"Banks? Since when is he your best buddy?"

"Don't do that, Bren. It was his call and mine, keeping Vallejo in place despite everything he's been going through. Walton agreed. Maybe we shoulda pulled him. I wanted to, but Banks said we owed him after all he's done for the department, and he was right."

"What happened? Last time we talked, you were on my side. You thought there was something going on. Now all of a sudden—"

"All of a sudden, nothing." Tori started tapping her pocket. "And it's not a question of being on your side or not. I got caught up in your predictable, self-serving hysteria. I know it's based on misplaced guilt, but I let myself get tangled up in it and shouldn't have. Let it go, Bren. Please. Listen, I have to go. We have a meeting. I'll call later."

Brenda leaned back against the headrest, trying to figure out what was really going on with Tori. Had Banks talked Tori into keeping Vallejo in his role as captain because he was somehow involved in the extortion ring? She sighed. She didn't like Banks, but that was no reason to believe he was some master criminal. She had begun to count on Tori as her eyes and ears in the department, but now it felt like Tori was abandoning her all over again.

CHAPTER SEVEN

Teresa Fortune, Donnelly's other girlfriend, worked at a lingerie shop in the older of Briarwood's two shopping malls. Brenda looked around the mostly empty parking lot and wondered how the stores in the weathered concrete block stayed in business.

There were a few wan saplings sagging in small squares of weed-dotted dirt every twenty or thirty feet, and they did little to dispel the air of neglect and despair that permeated the mall's lot. At the base of each of the struggling evergreens stood a bright pink Briarwood Watchdogs sign, and their vividness made the little trees seem even more pathetic.

As in much of the southern end of town, the lower elevation and slightly increased distance from the Pacific meant staler air than in the better parts of Briarwood. There were none of the city's namesake roses, other than those depicted on the security company's ubiquitous signs. As in the area around Mark Donnelly and Staci Smith's apartment, the stench of poverty was given free rein.

In contrast to the barrenness of its outdoor space, the inside of the shopping center was a riot of sensory input. Brenda developed an immediate headache from its garish colors, invasive lighting and echoing noisiness. She couldn't imagine having to spend forty hours a week in such a crummy place.

Teresa Fortune had a juvenile record and as an adult had been arrested for shoplifting, solicitation, petty theft, vandalism, and simple assault. She'd only been prosecuted twice as an adult, sentenced to rehab the first time, and spent a few months in county lockup for the second. She'd been on probation for the last two years.

Brenda wondered who'd hired Teresa Fortune to work in a retail shop, where she had constant access to credit card numbers and other identifying information.

She found a pretzel shop across from Teresa Fortune's workplace and spent five dollars providing herself with a stale, salted excuse to linger at a stained plastic table. She noticed neon pink Briarwood Watchdogs stickers in nearly every storefront's window and wondered if would-be shoplifters were deterred by the cheerful image of a fluorescent flower.

With little enthusiasm she gnawed on her overpriced snack and watched three blondes at the Silky Stuff lingerie shop fold panties, hang up bras, and argue with each other for a good ten minutes. Why did such a small store need three sales clerks in the middle of a weekday in a nearly deserted mall? As she'd found herself doing so often the last few days, she filed the question away for later.

She recognized the blonde in the highest heels and shortest skirt as Donnelly's second girlfriend. She waited until the other two workers were in the back of the store and Fortune was halfway through setting up a busy, sloppy window display. Then she sauntered across the mall's faded tile passageway, wondering whom the cheap, garish underwear was supposed to entice.

Teresa Fortune spoke without turning around or looking up. "Welcome to Silky, what fantasy can I help you with?"

She accepted the lifeless greeting with a bland smile at Fortune's back. "Good morning. Teresa Fortune?"

"Oh, goodie, another cop." Fortune glared at Brenda over her shoulder. Without waiting for confirmation, she rolled her heavily outlined eyes and grabbed her phone from somewhere within her red lace tank top. She jabbed at the screen with her long red fingernails. Then she snagged a crowded keyring from a nearby counter and clipped it to the waistband of her skirt. It was comically heavy, dragging the skirt perilously low and setting it askew on Fortune's insubstantial frame. After a moment one of the other clerks, a tiny teenager with pink highlights in her long blond hair, tip-tapped onto the sales floor.

"Try not to break anything while I take my ten. And remember to push the white lace thongs. We got six boxes of the stupid things."

Fortune scurried out of the store and into the mall, jangling the keys with every quick step. Brenda trailed after her until they were outside, following her into a heavily littered concrete cove that clearly served as a smoking area for mall employees. She watched Teresa Fortune light a menthol cigarette with shaking hands and a frown of concentration.

"What're you hassling me for, cop?"

She didn't react but watched Donnelly's girlfriend suck in smoke and awkwardly shift her insubstantial weight from high-heeled foot to high-heeled foot. Each lurch was accompanied by the sound of keys sliding past one another on her key ring.

"You wanna know if I knew Mark was doing all that stuff. If I was in on it."

She shrugged. With her emaciated body and nervous gestures, Fortune looked like a relatively functional junkie. She would talk to fill silence.

"Yeah, well, if I was in on something like that, I sure as shit wouldn't be working at the panty shack, would I?"

She shrugged again. Fortune shook her head and groaned, pressing a thin, pale hand against the side of her head. She launched into sudden, hysterical laughter that died as quickly as it sprang to life. "Fuck me. I see where you're going with this. You think I been using the store to launder money."

"And?" Masking her surprise at Fortune's comment, Brenda waited to see what else she might reveal. Was Fortune's panicked conjecture based on some actual money-laundering activities or was the addict trying to misdirect her?

Fear flashed across Fortune's face, but she shook her head and offered a wry grin. "This place don't make enough money to be any good for that. It'll be outta business in six months."

"And then what happens to you and the other employees?"

Fortune shrugged as though the question was moot. She rubbed her bony hip as though it hurt. "There are plenty of places that need experienced shift managers. I'll just find someplace else to pay me like shit and work me a million hours a week with no overtime. Like, twenty feet away. Hell, it might be a different store in the same damn spot!" Another burst of wild laughter shook her narrow frame, and Fortune nearly lost her balance. She steadied with grave care and pursed her lips.

Brenda nodded, a sympathetic expression drawing down her features. "Why are you working here if your boyfriend was making a bunch of money? Didn't he share the wealth?"

Fortune rolled her eyes. "They're saying he made a whole pile of cash, but he didn't spend it on me, that's for damn sure!"

The brittle woman shot an assessing glance at Brenda, who kept her face blank. She wondered how much Donnelly and any possible partners had made in the extortion scheme and what Teresa Fortune considered a lot of money.

Meth offered a relatively cheap high, but the cost of maintaining a habit could escalate astronomically, depending on how much an addict was using. Fortune wore gaudy costume jewelry, knock-off PVC stilettos and drugstore makeup. She drove a twelve-year-old Buick and had no kids to support. If she had any money at all, it was probably funneled directly to her dealer.

"Fuck it, 'cause like I said, don't look at me. Whatever he was pulling down, he wasn't spending it on me. Sure as shit he was spending it on that titty dancer, Staci or whatever. The bitch with the kid."

"Oh?" Brenda wondered if the woman was fishing for Staci Smith's name or testing to see if Brenda knew it. She also wondered if Fortune's jewelry box—or the pawn shop nearest her apartment, or the pawn shop nearest her dealer's apartment—featured high-value gems like the ones Brenda had found in Smith's place.

"So he didn't buy you a lot of gifts?"

She launched into a tirade of complaints about Mark Donnelly, to which Brenda half listened. Fortune's tone turned whining, and her words rode out on a cloud of sour smoke and spittle.

"He wasn't like the love of my life. The cheapskate took me out maybe once or twice a month, threw me a few bucks now and then when I was running low. Me and him were mostly just fuck buddies, you know? He was a laugh or whatever, and, honey, he had a great big dick. I liked to fuck him, and he liked to fuck me. That's it. So don't look at me for nothing."

"How did you meet?"

She dropped her cigarette and used her red stiletto's pointed toe to grind it into the rough cement with more force than was required. She'd touched up a crack in the shoe's vinyl with a red marker in almost the right shade, and Brenda felt a stab of pity. Fortune pulled out another cigarette from the pack in her bra. Brenda took the lighter and lit the cigarette for her, taking the opportunity to get a closer look at Donnelly's second girlfriend. Her eyes were bloodshot, her skin rough under heavy pancake makeup. The last yellowing of a black eye showed through layers of concealer, and several fingertip bruises in various stages of healing dotted her neck and arms. One cheekbone sported a greenish contusion poorly disguised by bright pink rouge. An angry-looking rash on her chest and neck was only highlighted by the body glitter she'd applied like spackle.

She also displayed wide horizontal scars on the insides of both wrists, each festooned with an illegible tattoo. The mass of keys had dragged down her skirt to expose several inches of bare skin, displaying a rose tattoo and the yellow-and-green edge of what looked like a large bruise. Had Donnelly been the author of these injuries, or was Fortune seeing more than one man?

Just looking at Teresa Fortune made Brenda depressed and angry. As she saw it, Fortune was the product of a sick society that undervalued its children, especially its little girls, and let them get twisted into receptacles for men's anger, lust, selfishness, and indifference.

What had become of the child Teresa Fortune? Had there even been a time when the little girl dared to dream of being anything but pleasing? How long had it taken for her to turn into the brittle, bitter shell of a woman who stood shaking and twitching before Brenda now?

"How'd we meet? Mark just came into Silky one time, and we clicked, you know? He was nice. He came in to buy some shit for some girl, and he asked me what my bra size was. Guys do that all the time, you know that? They think 'cause I sell panties I'm like a hooker or something. I'm not, by the way."

She nodded her understanding, wondering if Fortune was lying about how she'd met Donnelly. Had he busted her? "You work ten to six?"

"Why? You looking for a discount?"

She ignored this. "He worked evenings. I figure he came on his day off or before shift."

"You figure, huh? You think you're smart?"

"I wasn't smart enough to see what he was doing."

Fortune acknowledged this with a raspy chuckle.

"That looks like it hurt. Did he do that?" Brenda lightly tapped her own cheekbone.

"Nah. Don't start thinkin' that. He was a lot of things, but he wasn't like that."

Brenda murmured as though in agreement. "Miss Fortune—"

"Fuck that fake nice bullshit and get the fuck off my back. Listen, it's not like we had some big love affair, okay? He was cute. I was horny. I was hooked on him, you know how it is with some guys." Fortune gave Brenda a sly, sidelong glance. "Or maybe you don't. No skin off my dick. Anyhow. Mark was classy, that's all. Polite. He dropped like five hundred bucks on panties and shit. A guy spends money like that, you figure he'll treat you right."

She hoped her skepticism didn't show on her face.

"Was I wrong! Asshole never spent more than fifty bucks on me! Believe me, sister, I know what I'm doing in the bedroom.

It didn't matter for shit. He was willing to buy me a burger, fuck me, whatever, but that's it. Now he's dead. I'm still stuck in this shithole, and that stripper bitch is sitting pretty. Whatever. It's not like we were in love or anything."

"Still, I'm sorry for your loss."

At Brenda's words, Fortune began crying, thick black tears streaming down either side of her narrow scarlet mouth.

"You know what? Fuck you!" Fortune dropped her lit cigarette at Brenda's feet. "Stuck-up bitch, coming in here talking like we're best fuckin' friends! I been worked by a hundred damn cops and you motherfuckers are all the same. I didn't do nothing wrong and you can't pin shit on me. Fuck off! Don't bother me again!"

She spun awkwardly on her high heel, strode back to the mall entrance, yanked on the heavy door, and disappeared into the depressing shopping center without a backward glance.

A Watchdog guard came out from where Fortune had just stormed in, and he stalked toward Brenda. She hid a smile. The man had the red face, bandy legs and puffed chest of a rooster. He ruffled his arms as if they were wings, and she had to force herself not to focus on his appearance.

"Is there a problem here?"

"What kind of problem?" She kept her tone cool and her expression mild. She wanted to see what the guy would do.

"Teri's crying! What'd you do to her?"

By now the guard was within a yard of her and he sneered. His breath smelled like candy, and his cheeks were flushed. His uniform was too tight and displayed sweat rings and dried salt from sweat that had dried in the uniform. The fabric clearly didn't stretch or breathe, and she wondered why the company didn't get better uniforms.

She also wondered if the guard was diabetic, given the dark, sweet scent of his breath. She felt suddenly sorry for him. He was trying to stick up for his friend, and he didn't have the bandwidth to do so effectively.

She didn't look much better herself, and she was supposed to be lying low. She faked nervousness and hugged herself. "I didn't do nothin' wrong. Her boyfriend's dead, of course she's crying.

What do you want?" She employed a wheedling, ingratiating tone, and the guard practically laughed with satisfaction.

"That better be it." He looked her up and down with disdain, and she wondered for the thousandth time at how easy it was to play a part and elicit the desired response from people.

"Leave me alone."

"Why don't you move along, lady? Unless you're shopping, you're loitering."

"Yeah, I'm goin'." She slunk away, wondering if there were any Watchdogs employees who knew how to interact professionally with the public. She'd never seen security guards behave like Dan Miller's overheated 'roid patrol.

Tami Sheraton's boyfriend, Mason, worked for the company, and she found it hard to believe Sheraton would be interested in a macho bully. With a moment's reflection on the myriad women she had watched return to abusive boyfriends and husbands, though, she let go of the assumption. All kinds of people chose all kinds of people for reasons they seemed mostly not to understand or even examine.

Having met Teresa Fortune, she couldn't help but compare her to Donnelly's other girlfriend. She'd assumed it was Donnelly who'd bought the high-end jewelry for Staci Smith, and realized she should follow up on other possibilities. For all she knew, Smith's family had money. Or she'd invested her income in jewelry. Or the pieces had been bought by some ex-boyfriend or admirer of Smith's.

She was young and pretty and personable, and strip-club customers often liked to imagine they had relationships with the dancers. More than one young woman in tassels had received marriage proposals, cars and flashy baubles, real and fake. The pricey jewelry could have come from Dan Miller, who had apparently dated Smith at some point and was presumably amassing a fortune with his growing security business. Brenda wondered: who was Jessica's father? Had the jewelry come from him?

Why did Donnelly and Smith stay in that cheap apartment in that terrible neighborhood instead of selling off some of the jewelry to finance a nicer, safer place? They'd been saving for a house, Smith said, but few cops would feel comfortable living in a Cracker Jack box in a crime-ridden neighborhood, even during the saving-up period.

She pulled out her cell phone while trudging back to her car through the parking lot. She called Dan Miller again and left a brief message following up on her earlier request for contact. She let her tone harden a little to prompt him to actually respond. She'd barely disconnected after leaving that message when her phone vibrated in her hand.

"Hey, Tori."

"Yeah, I think I owe you an apology," Tori said, her voice low and indistinct. "I'm a little worried about you."

She made a noncommittal noise and got into the driver's seat of the Caliber that still felt like a stranger's car.

"I do think there's something off about the whole thing. But hold on." Tori put her hand over the phone and spoke with someone. She heard voices and wind and some faraway music, sounds that made her think of Green Rock Marina, where members of the exclusive yacht club Wharf Rats kept their overpriced vessels. Tori had always wanted to join, and apparently she'd finally gained access to the lofty circles. For a second Brenda thought about telling her the number of the slip that housed Tori's boat. Tori must have seen it in passing and wondered whose it was. She clearly had no idea it had been purchased as a gift for her birthday months before.

"Listen, about earlier—"

"You want to dig up dirt on my friends." Tori barked a laugh. "You were always jealous when I spent time with anybody but you."

"That's not true. And that's not what this is about. Any one of the people you're playing golf with or sailing with or drinking with could be involved in this."

"Who, exactly, do you imagine is the mobster? Walton? Banks? Johnson? Trimble? The mayor? Maybe you figure the guys on the city council are on the take?"

"You've done a one-eighty, and I don't get why."

"We don't live in some Hollywood movie where the perfect little town turns out to be a nest of vipers, Bren. Briarwood isn't that mysterious a place. Walton spends too much on his haircuts, Banks plays millionaire playboy, I spend too much on shoes. You hoard cash like Ebenezer Scrooge. That's all. Nothing more nefarious than acting like entitled Americans. I have to go. I'll call you later. Be careful, okay?"

She swallowed a pang of pain and regret. When Tori started eyeing the upper reaches of the department's ranks, she developed a strategic plan. She presented her case to Brenda and insisted they join the country club and take up golf. She demanded they start dining several nights a week at the half dozen restaurants on the waterfront, where a limp Caesar salad could cost twenty dollars and a mediocre glass of wine ten.

Tori also wanted to join Wharf Rats because "everyone who mattered" belonged to the pricey, exclusive yachting-and-sailing club. It was the sort of place that either excluded or exploited the people Brenda liked best. None of the officers under her command would ever be allowed in such a place, unless they were moonlighting as security guards. Maggie's husband, Jorge, worked as a handyman at The Nest, the club's lounge, and Brenda thought more than once that she'd rather have a beer with Jorge than hundred-dollar whiskey with anyone who belonged to the sailing club.

Tori wanted to be one of the fancy people. She craved access to the rarified air enjoyed by those in the upper echelons. She clawed and fought and charmed and invested and maneuvered her way to what she wanted. Whatever the price, it never seemed too high, and it worked. Tori was one of them now, and Brenda was exactly what she'd feared becoming, an ex on the periphery of Tori's life.

Did Tori think of their relationship as a mistake? Sometimes it felt like that. She recalled all too clearly the months she'd spent feeling left behind. She remembered taking calls like the one she'd just gotten: Tori on a boat or golf course or in a bar somewhere, saying she was busy.

Every time it sounded like Tori was at sea, of course, it hurt all over again. The cruiser she'd fixed up for a birthday surprise sat berthed at Green Hand Marina, probably only yards away from where Tori had just embarked. Brenda was a terrible golfer, but she knew how to handle a boat, whether cruiser or sailing craft, and she'd hoped part of the surprise would be her ability to skillfully maneuver Tori's birthday present, a beautiful thirty-four-foot cruiser.

More and more over the last months they were together, Tori drank overpriced wine and made small talk with the Briarwood power brokers and their wives on the west side of town while Brenda played den mother to investigators who chased down leads on domestic-violence assaults and rapes and murders in moribund neighborhoods on the south side.

Tori became enthused about all things expensively nautical. She began pricing luxury cabin cruisers and striped designer shirts, practicing knots and memorizing sailing protocols. She talked endlessly about Green Hand, the exclusive marina named for an algae-slimed rock.

"You know I want to learn how to sail. Why don't we get a little boat?"

By the time Tori brought it up, Brenda had already bought the thirty-four-foot Seahorse Europa that was too old, too worn and too small to impress anyone. But she bought a newish replacement engine and hired a crew of restorers to work on the cruiser for her.

After months of expensive repairs and updates, the craft was deemed seaworthy. While smaller and less luxurious than her berth neighbors, she was a classic and just nice enough to make them the poor pier neighbors who nonetheless belonged. Brenda dipped into her long-accrued savings and spent far more than she should have to get one of the few small berths in Green Hand Marina. Nearly all of the berths were for boats in the fifty-to-seventy-foot range. The Sheratons had a slip, as did most of the commanders, Walton, the mayor, several dozen millionaire entrepreneurs including Dan Miller, and the richest ten or fifteen families in Briarwood. There was one row in Green Hand that held smaller, thirty- to forty-foot craft, and a ten-thousand-dollar deposit netted her a slip there, only one row away from Green Hand's best.

Two weeks before Tori's birthday, the harbormaster called Brenda to tell her *Bernice* was ready and berthed. She left work early and stopped by to check on it. She grinned, seeing the dark, beautiful mahogany and crisp white paint and cheery Moroccan bedding and curtains she'd chosen to suit Tori's tastes. She made sure everything was perfect for the coming surprise. Then she went to the grocery store for steaks, flowers, and dessert before she headed home for the smaller surprise of a special dinner.

That was when she walked in and caught Tori cheating.

She had yet to go back to Green Hand Marina. Though she knew it was unreasonable to do so, she still tied the two things together. Boating and cheating, cheating and boating. Would they always feel inextricably linked in her mind? She hoped not. That particular conflation could make living in a coastal town miserable.

After she caught Tori *en flagrante*, she sank into despair and self-pity. Andi offered support and kindness and dragged her to a grief-group meeting, where they listened to participants talk about the deaths of their loved ones. Within minutes Brenda was restless and wanted to leave.

"Stay. It might help you get some perspective," said Andi, her voice gentle. Ashamed, Brenda agreed.

The group's facilitator, an earnest woman in her twenties, tapped her forehead and nodded sagely as she looked around the room. As she moved, her cluster of necklaces clinked and tinkled. "Open your third eye," she said, her voice high and thin. "Move beyond your emotions, your physicality, your grounding in the now. Transcend. Journey above what you can see and feel. Close your lower eyes and open up as a spiritual seer. Go on, close your eyes and access truth. Don't judge, don't try to control what is, just accept it. Acceptance, my friends, acceptance."

Brenda had shot a sardonic glance at Andi, who glared at her and then lowered her lids. Finally, to avoid being called out, she closed her eyes. She felt foolish and resentful and silly, but she tapped her forehead. A wave of dizziness came over her.

Without perseverating about it, she decided to actually follow instructions. Within seconds, she felt her breathing deepen and her shoulders relax. The decade she'd spent with Tori came rushing back to her, a diaspora of memories. She felt lifted and weightless and, for the first time in weeks, calm. She felt her body as a thing separate from her mind, had a moment of formlessness, panicked and snapped her eyes open. The facilitator—Penny? Patty? Perri?—had been watching with a placid but attentive expression, so Brenda blinked them closed. The weight of her bitterness and hurt and guilt and anger felt like outsiders instead of elemental components of her being, and the relief of this was so great she sank into it and sighed in surprising, fleeting joy.

Then she was back inside her normal self and again felt heavy with feelings. She worked to regain that moment of peace but could only feel the slightest easing. It was still an improvement, she noted. After a minute or two, the young group leader had summoned them back into the real world in the gray little room in the community-center basement. As Andi and Brenda walked out, she felt Andi's gaze on her.

"What?"

Andi shrugged and smiled. "You look…I don't know, more like yourself than you did an hour ago."

"Thank you," Brenda said. "I only went to humor you, but it was a gift. You've given me countless gifts. I don't even think you realize how many. You are the truest friend I've ever had. Thank you."

Andi had nodded and turned away, trying to hide her tears, before elbowing Brenda and suggesting they go out for burgers.

Though Brenda never went back to the group, feeling like an intruder because her loved one had left her but was very much alive and well, the moment stayed with her. She knew it was possible to step outside her feelings and perceptions, and that felt like a safety valve she could at least try to rediscover. That was exactly what she needed to do now.

"Acceptance." She took a deep breath and opened her eyes. She felt more clearheaded but nowhere near as detached from her emotions as she wanted to be. Maybe she needed to accept not always being able to achieve peace.

She went by Peterson's house again, debating the advisability of breaking in to check his place for clues. It suddenly struck her as odd that they'd never exchanged house keys. After some vigorous knocking and bell ringing, she decided to try another approach.

"Okay, Peterson, if you have an emergency key, where do you keep it? Hmm?"

She looked up first because Peterson knew that most people would check low before high. There were a few obvious places. She found nothing in the homemade birdhouse tucked into one of the eaves. The rough box was a gift given to him long ago by his younger daughter, years before his girls stopped speaking to him. She retrieved a screwdriver from her glove box and took off the large number plate near the garage door, but that was a bust too. Down low were several potted plants, the requisite briar roses in a neatly trimmed hedge, a series of solar-powered path lights, and a small stone frog. She checked each of these, though they seemed too obvious for his tastes.

She closed her eyes. He was fastidious, detail-oriented, and smart. He'd been a cop for thirty years and like so many police officers, a budding juvenile delinquent before that. He was very good at outthinking criminals. So where, if at all, would he hide a key?

If he had an emergency key, he didn't hide it right by the front door. She walked around the accessible front half of the house, searching along the fence line under his neatly trimmed boxwoods and carefully pruned briar roses and Japanese maples. She found nothing but a few ladybugs and a praying mantis. Finally she gave up. She would give it a little more time. Back at the car, she sat and rubbed her tight forehead.

Something nagged at her and she wasn't sure how to determine what that something was. The department's brass, the powerful elite, the humble extortion victims, Briarwood

Watchdogs, Dan Miller... There was something there, right behind the veil of unknowns. Everywhere she went in Briarwood, she saw Miller's fingerprints. She felt there must be some insight, some critical piece of information she should have seen already and had somehow missed.

She tapped out an email to Darius Brown, apologizing for making yet another request of him and asking him if he'd had a chance to take a peek at Dan Miller and Briarwood Watchdogs. What exactly she was asking, she wasn't even sure, but the security company and its CEO seemed to have a finger in every pie in town.

She kept thinking of what Andi said, something about how Watchdogs had cameras all over the city but they had never noticed Donnelly walking around with bags of cash after leaving the small businesses on the south end of town.

She slid her phone into her pocket and sat in her car in front of Peterson's empty house. She wished she could rewind the last several years. There were many, many things she would do differently. Would she start up with Tori all over again, knowing how it would turn out? She rubbed her forehead again. Yes, she would. Given a second chance, she'd try to do a better job of making sure Tori actually felt that love instead of looking elsewhere for it. The ugly end of their relationship didn't erase the things she valued about Tori or about what they'd shared.

However much Briarwood had changed in the last twenty years, she wouldn't give up on her swollen little city either. It was, for those who could afford its safer sections, a nice place to live. People worked and paid their taxes and raised their kids and took care of their yards and went to dance recitals and soccer games and gave money to charity and did all the stuff decent people everywhere did. Sure, Briarwood had growing pains, but didn't every expanding city?

"Nobody's all angel, kid, and nobody's all asshole."

She heard herself mutter the words in a startlingly good imitation of her mom's voice. She flipped down the visor and stared at her reflection in the small mirror. The sun, dropping slowly behind her, made her distorted image impossible to see, and she raised the visor again. Where inside Brenda had her mother's voice come from? Was it all the weird costuming that made her feel haunted today?

She tried to push her personal feelings aside. For all her posturing, her mom had been an idealist, ever disappointed in the vagaries of the people around her. Over time, she'd traded her pie-eyed optimism for at least the posture of cynicism but had been constitutionally incapable of actually addressing reality.

When Brenda had leaned in to light Teresa Fortune's cigarette and smelled the combination of smoke and raunchy perfume and cheap makeup, she'd felt a wave of déjà vu. Now she understood why. She'd felt stiff, courtly, a little embarrassed and a little put off.

It was a familiar cocktail of reactions. She was around five when her mom taught her to light cigarettes and mix drinks. For months, her mom joked to everyone in the Oroville trailer park about how great it was, having her own personal bartender.

Her mom's then-boyfriend, Mike something, laughed at her mom's little joke in the less-than-nice tone that characterized most of his utterances. Then he snapped his fingers at Brenda and pointed at the fridge, explaining he wanted her to fetch him a beer whenever he snapped his fingers. She looked at her mother, who shrugged and averted her gaze with a nervous laugh. Brenda bristled but obeyed. When she brought Mike the cold, sweating can, he grabbed her lower lip and told her to stop pouting. She took a deep breath and waited for him to lose interest, but her cheeks burned and she was hot with anger.

Once the beer wasn't cold enough because the electricity had been turned off that morning. Mike had already been upset about not being able to watch television. When she brought him a lukewarm beer, he grabbed her arm and wrenched it behind her back.

"You fuckin' with me, baby bitch? Huh?"

"The power's out," she said through clenched teeth. "The fridge runs on power."

Her mom cackled, "You need my little girl to explain any other shit, Mikey? She knows how to tell time and tie her shoes too. Maybe she could tutor you."

Then the two adults went at it, screaming and throwing things. She didn't stick around to see how it all turned out, because she knew how it all turned out and didn't need to see any more of that. She lit out for the woods and stayed there until almost dawn the next morning, when she was sure they'd both be asleep.

Weeks later, just after her forgotten sixth birthday and a truckload of fetched beers, she figured out what to do about Mike.

She snuck out early in the morning with a garbage bag full of necessities that she hid under a bush in the heavily wooded hillside behind the trailer park. She unlocked the front door and screen, cleared a path through the piles of junk in the living room and waited. When it was time, she got ready and went to school as usual. That afternoon, she came home and again waited.

When at sundown Mike's snapping fingers summoned her for the third time, she obediently got the beer from the refrigerator. She carried it over, stood behind the sofa and opened the beer.

The adults were watching television, paying her little mind. Her mom's Southern Comfort on the rocks dripped condensation onto the worn corduroy of the sofa. Mike was fondling her mom's upper thigh, pushing up her short shorts and orating about the stupidity of the people on the news. Brenda stood behind the couch and stared down at Mike's lank, greasy, thinning hair. She took a deep breath and poured the entire beer on his head.

Then she ran as fast as her skinny legs could take her out of the trailer's front door, up the hill and into the woods, far past where a wet, clumsy, overweight trucker could easily climb. She hunkered down in a remote spot fifty yards up, and there she camped for three days. She didn't dare show her face until she saw Mike's pickup truck, weighed down by his broken motorcycle and the plastic garbage bags that served as his luggage, jounce out of the trailer park's entrance on the dusty dirt road while her mother screamed curses at him from the front door.

Even at that age she wasn't naïve enough to think her mom kicked Mike out over her, but by then she already knew the signs of an impending breakup and had chosen her timing carefully. Her mom got very quiet right before she picked a fight with the latest loser to darken her door and stink up her sheets. Later, Brenda thought Mike hadn't even been that bad. He'd never tried to get in her pants or really beaten her. He'd been a jerk, but hardly the worst jerk. It was only as an adult she'd realized the thing that had gotten her riled up about Mike was his need to humiliate her.

Just as Mike had, her mom's boyfriends invariably failed to realize she was tired of them and continued to bumble along in blissful ignorance until the day she picked a fight and threw them out or fled with her daughter in tow. Mike had been on his way out for weeks, and Brenda's decampment had only been a useful excuse to throw out the tiresome paramour.

Her mom had been wrong about a lot, but about one thing she'd been right: things were almost never a simple matter of good versus bad. Mike was a Vietnam veteran, a hero with a few medals stored carefully in a shoebox that ended up in a plastic bag in the back of his truck. Peterson was an alcoholic who served his community with dedication and skill. Tori was a lying cheat and a crusader for justice. Briarwood was a complicated ecosystem, just like anywhere else. A lot of people made a lot of mistakes, often because they didn't know any better or because they'd been squeezed on too much to think clearly. That didn't make them bad people. The folks in Briarwood were her people, for better or worse, and she wouldn't give them up even if she could.

And Tori? She rested her head against the back of the seat. She felt her mouth smiling even as tears pushed against the corners of her tightly closed eyes and made her cheap mascara even slimier and stickier.

She was snapped from her musing by a sound she'd heard before: that engine, that unfamiliar car engine she'd heard in front of her house. She whipped around and forced her streaming, burning eyes open so she could see the mystery vehicle, but in the sunset glare she saw nothing.

Banging awkwardly out of the low-slung Caliber, she darted on foot toward the nearest intersection, six houses away. Traffic was light even on the more traveled thoroughfare of Elmhurst Avenue, but of the seven cars heading south and the five heading north, four were light sedans.

Any one of them could have been the car in question, which could have turned off Elmhurst in the frustratingly long time it had taken Brenda to run to the intersection. She turned around and glanced down Peterson's street, struck by the fact his house was the only one with no Briarwood Watchdogs sign in front of it. Shaking off the irrelevant detail, she snorted in irritation.

"I'm an idiot."

Stalking back to the Caliber, she shook her head. She'd been blinded by her sentimental attachments for too long. She'd been treating the department and the city like old friends who deserved the benefit of the doubt. Wasn't that exactly the kind of cronyism that led to soft corruption, which led to hard corruption? She was disgusted by her inadequacy and let her screeching tires communicate that disgust to the disinterested universe.

She drove home and paced the living room for several minutes before settling in at the kitchen table to write down her new plan of action. An hour later, she put down the pen and took a deep breath. Examining her strategy, she was struck by how much cooler her head was now she'd detached from the situation emotionally. How long since she'd been clearheaded like this? How long since she'd looked at things through her third eye? The grief group? She'd become sloppy, careless, arrogant in the way of her early years and too caught up in her own perceptions and assumptions to see the real edges and shapes of things.

She was yanked out of her self-castigation by a call from a number she didn't immediately recognize. Her internal hard drive whirred as she tried to make the connection.

She shook her head, unable at first to conjure an image to put with the name. Shay Sheraton. Tami Sheraton's sister. She wanted to meet with Brenda in person to talk about something. Not sure what she was walking into but unwilling to rebuff the only Sheraton who'd called her back, Brenda agreed to meet the sister for dinner.

An Internet search of Shay Sheraton gave her a preview of what face to scan for, and she studied the digitized image. The pretty, lightly freckled woman in a black suit was apparently some kind of attorney. She had red hair with lighter blond highlights. Staring down at the screen, Brenda studied the bright, dark eyes and smiling mouth of Tami Sheraton's sister with some surprise at how she both resembled her late sibling and did not.

Brenda showered and changed into a pair of sedate gray slacks, sleek loafers and silver-blue blouse. Her garish hair made her roll her eyes, but she slicked on tinted lip balm and her simplest jewelry. She eyed her reflection in her bronze-framed bathroom mirror with some dismay. She looked old, tired, and pale. She grimaced at her image, wondering why she even cared what she looked like. As long as she presented as professional and appropriate, that was all that mattered, she reminded herself.

She strapped on her weapon and squared her shoulders. Meeting Shay Sheraton for dinner was about paying her respects and finding out if the slain officer had confided in her big sister about Donnelly or any other suspicions she might have had. But the flash of attraction she'd felt seeing the woman's photo had unsettled her. It had made her feel for a moment as though she was heading out for a date.

She rolled her eyes at herself and strode out to the parking lot, queasy as a first-year deckhand. She'd find out soon enough whether this dinner would be an informal wake, a trial by verbal fire, or a potentially deadly shootout.

CHAPTER EIGHT

Dave's Bistro was crowded despite the early hour, and Brenda scanned the crowd. She smiled to see that, and though she'd shown up fifteen minutes ahead of their five o'clock dinner, she wasn't first to arrive.

Shay Sheraton was already seated at the center table in what locals referred to as the crow's nest, a five-table enclave up a short flight of stairs. It was a little quieter, a bit away from the fray. Each cosseted diner had a perfectly framed view of the sun's evening rays as they frosted picturesque Briarwood Harbor. To the south sat the boardwalk, to the north Green Hand, and ahead was the huge, city-run marina that housed most of the sailboats and smaller cruisers enjoyed by both locals and tourists.

Shay sat gazing out of the window, her glossy, burnished hair the most visible thing about her. Usually this section was reserved for bigwigs like the mayor, Chief Walton, commanders, judges, visiting movie producers and high-powered executives. As the head waiter led her through the mass of customers, tables, and servers to the crow's nest, Brenda wished she'd taken another minute or two to read more about Shay. That good table wasn't for Brenda, of that she was sure. So who exactly was Tami Sheraton's sister?

In person and up close, Shay was even more gorgeous than her picture had suggested. Her strawberry-blond hair and whiskey eyes made for a striking combination, and her wide, warm smile was dazzling. Brenda had to work to concentrate on the banalities of polite greeting when Shay stood and offered a firm handshake. Her skin was cool and soft, her gaze clear and direct.

The pair made the usual introductions and exchanged pleasantries while they examined one another. Shay's eyes were a deep, rich brown flecked with gold. Blinking away sudden nerves, Brenda told herself the light she saw in those dark orbs was nothing more than a phantasm born of sudden, surprising attraction.

Shaken by her physical response to Shay, Brenda was relieved to take her seat. She let her talk, offering little more than a polite smile and nods of encouragement until she could speak in a steady tone.

"Thank you for calling me back. How are you doing?"

The redhead smiled, dimpling prettily, and answered with words Brenda barely registered. She again let Shay's voice flow over her agitation, in hopes the time would allow her to regain some equilibrium. But tension and awareness flowed through her, enervating her from the inside out.

She let herself acknowledge it: Shay was stunning. Her skin was smooth and unblemished, her hair a halo of glowing good health. Even her ears were pretty, delicate and pink. She had a slight overbite and perfectly white teeth. She had small hands with short nails and tapered fingers. Brenda took in the minutiae of her beauty with painfully tender attention.

Of course she'd been attracted to many women. She'd known she was lesbian since long before her high school years, and she'd always reveled in the myriad ways in which women could be beautiful.

But for the last decade she had hardly noticed—noticed in the way that was now making her body quiver and her heart pound—anyone but Tori. She silently chided herself, dismayed the woman who'd struck such a deep chord in her was the sister of Tami Sheraton.

Or was it the family connection that resonated with her? Was her guilt somehow making her respond to Sheraton's sister? She made a conscious decision to separate her mind from the way her body responded to Shay, who was, after all, nothing but a stranger. Brenda shook herself. This was Tami Sheraton's sister, here only because the kid was dead.

Tami and Shay had the same coloring, but that was the end of the resemblance. This was more apparent in person than when Brenda had looked at Shay's picture online. Tami had been tall and solidly built, with strong features and coarse, straight hair. She'd still looked like a coed, one who played lacrosse or field hockey. Shay was shorter and smaller-framed than her sister. She had fine features and wavy hair and was at least a decade older than Tami.

She also seemed different in other ways Brenda worked to identify. Tami's watch had been a Timex, while Shay's was a Patek Philippe. Tami's haircut had been a blunt Supercuts special, and Shay probably went to an exclusive salon in Berkeley or San Francisco for her perfectly balanced custom coif.

Brenda knew she was intellectualizing, focusing away from her physical response to Shay in order to regain functionality. Noting this didn't make it any less challenging, though, and she felt like she'd retreated behind a sort of emotional glass wall like a frightened child hiding behind her mother's skirts.

From behind her clear curtain she saw Shay and heard her voice. She responded to her appropriately. She heard her own voice and watched herself play the part of someone whose world had not been knocked off-kilter.

They ordered iced teas from the fawning waiter. They commented on the spectacular view, the crowded bistro, the good weather, the brilliant sunset, and Dave's updated menu. Brenda offered her condolences and Shay thanked her for providing her sister with a valued mentor. They ordered dinner, salmon for Brenda and something the waiter already knew Shay wanted, which Brenda noted and wondered about. Just how early had Shay arrived? Had she called from the restaurant? Or did she dine here so regularly that the waitstaff knew her on sight?

"Do you come here often?"

Shay smiled, her cheeks pinking prettily above her perfect dimples. "Too often," she said, rolling her dark eyes. The unguarded gesture humanized the beauty and made her even more attractive.

"Is that possible?" The smile that rewarded her silly joke warmed Brenda unduly.

"This is where I do half my job."

"Oh?" She took a slow, deep breath and smiled. "Tell me about your work."

The answer went on for several minutes, something about corporate law, and she was glad for the respite it provided. It had been Shay's idea to meet at Dave's for dinner to talk rather than to meet somewhere quieter and more private. What did that mean? Was she simply accustomed to suggesting it as a meeting place, or was she looking for home turf because she was uncomfortable?

Brenda was unsettled and intrigued in equal measure. She smiled at a little self-deprecating joke Shay made and drank iced tea so she wouldn't gawk at her dark eyes, full lips, and sumptuous curves, the last evident despite the perfectly tailored, slightly severe slate suit she sported.

"Sounds like you love your work," she ventured.

"Sometimes." A little laugh accompanied a rueful smile. "Sometimes not."

Something about the redhead was familiar, and from more than just the Internet photo and a passing resemblance to her sister. The Pacific reflected the golden-pink setting sun with glaring intensity, and she finally gave in and looked back at Shay rather than at the blinding light. Where had she seen her before? And then it came to her.

"You were at the hearing," she said, her voice subdued. "Last Friday night."

"I'm sorry you had to go through that. It was ridiculous." Shay made a rueful face. "I wanted to thank you but you seemed pretty done with people after that circus. You handled the clowns brilliantly, if my unsolicited opinion counts for anything."

"Thanks," she murmured. "It must have been terrible for you, seeing the video and listening to all of that."

"Yes." Shay nodded crisply. "Not as terrible as going to her funeral. After that, everything awful is just another echo."

She simply held eye contact. There was nothing meaningful she could offer beyond a bland apology.

Death was always the enemy, wasn't it? It took Lauren. It took Dave. It took Tami Sheraton. It even took helpless children and innocent families. Brenda had spent much of her life fighting that foe. She'd disarmed assailants, convinced potential suicides to at least postpone their self-destruction, escorted victims to safety and testified against men who, left free, would have continued to wreak destruction on others. Sometimes she'd saved people. Sometimes she'd only delayed the inevitable. Death was ever victorious, in the end.

"Ms. Sheraton, I appreciate your being willing to meet with me." She made an aborted gesture, a useless flap of her hand that seemed to speak more eloquently than her words conveyed how helpless she felt in the face of death.

"Back at you. I want to thank you, Captain Borelli."

"For what? Letting your little sister get murdered?"

"You don't hold yourself responsible? That's—no." Shay sat back, and Brenda saw past the smooth perfection of the woman across from her. Relaxed, with her composure allowed to slip, Shay looked much more human. Brenda could more clearly see now the faint dark circles and tension lines around her expressive mouth and eyes.

"Ms. Sheraton, I appreciate—"

"Shay, please. If it doesn't seem too strange, let me say, I feel oddly intimate, sitting here talking about Tami with you. I guess because she thought so highly of you. She…She was hard to impress. You impressed her a great deal. She saw you as a role model."

To this Brenda could only give a vague nod. She didn't want their conversation to be about her, but about the young woman who had been murdered.

Shay seemed to see this and shared a brief, amused smile before sobering. "If anyone is responsible for her death, it's me. I was supposed to take care of her."

Brenda held her gaze, willing her to open up.

"I tried to control her. I told myself it was to protect her, which boiled down to the same thing. I knew I pushed too hard, but I couldn't stop myself. I let her down and now she's dead. So climb down off the cross, Captain, I'm already there."

Brenda gave a rueful smile and let her words hang between them for a moment. Finally she shrugged. "I don't know how to have this conversation with you. I should, I guess, but this is pretty surreal. I think we're both drowning in guilt and pretty shocked by what happened to Sheraton—to Tami. You're her family, and—"

"Let's cut through the bull, okay?"

Brenda blinked. "Okay."

"I met Mark Donnelly. Well, more than met him."

"Oh?"

"Of course. He was my little sister's training officer. I wanted to check him out." She shrugged. "Tami and I were fifteen years apart. Our folks were pretty distracted by the time their little 'oops,' as they called her, came along. They divorced when she was two. Tami had a nanny, so it's not like she was neglected, but she was less their child than a little pet they would forget about and then bring out once in a while to show off to their friends."

"So you filled in."

"It was fine when she was still a little girl. I could distract her with a hug or a game. But she started to resent our parents once she was old enough to wonder why they weren't interested in her. I tried to compensate, and maybe I overcompensated. I lavished attention on her." She winced. "When she got older, I had to learn to let go."

The grieving sister stared out at the light-spangled Pacific Ocean. Her shoulders slumped ever so slightly. She looked tired and defeated. Brenda nodded, trying to convey sympathy and encouragement.

"I had a hard time with that. Smothered her. Daddy died of a heart attack, and Mom has never been as dialed in as Daddy. Tami became distant when I tried to steer her away from police work and toward something safer. I almost wondered if she became a police officer to defy me. I know, *hubris, hubris*, but I still find it—found it—hard to remember she wasn't my kid sister anymore. She was a grown woman, a fully functional, capable adult, etcetera, etcetera, etcetera."

They shared a smile at the old-fashioned reference and suspended their conversation when the waiter brought their food along with his solicitous attentions. Watching the waiter fuss over Shay, Brenda was struck by how hard the staff worked to please her.

There was family money. Was that a factor in Tami Sheraton's death? For all she knew, Shay hired Mark Donnelly to murder her little sister. Plenty of people were murdered over money by people who claimed to love them and who cried big crocodile tears at the funeral.

She grinned when Shay flashed the waiter a brilliant smile to go with the thanks she offered, and he nearly tripped on his own feet.

After a minute, she prompted her. "You were saying?"

"It was wrong of me to try to discourage Tami. I know that now. But I was afraid for her. I tried to bribe her to leave the police academy and go to law school. Did you know that? Oh, it was gross, crass. God, it was despicable. I offered her money!"

She mirrored Shay's rueful expression and nodded at her to continue.

"Of course she was offended. Understandably. She wouldn't talk to me for months. When she—I still can't believe I'm saying this—when she was killed, we were just getting close again.

"Just when I'd come to terms with her decision, it happened, the thing I would have given anything to prevent."

"I'm so sorry."

"God, I miss her. She was such a stinker." Shay laughed and shook her head. Her mouth twisted like she was trying not to cry. "She was so smart and always in trouble, always asking a million questions. I'm sorry, I don't mean to be mawkish. I don't want to reminisce about my sister's life. I'd like to talk about her death." She stared down at her untouched dinner.

"You didn't know she was investigating Donnelly?"

"No, of course not. But that's the problem, isn't it? If I'd been more supportive instead of making her feel defensive, maybe she would've confided in me. Maybe she would have let me help her. I could've hired an army of investigators to help her, and she would still be alive." She took a deep breath, redirecting her gaze and staring out at the sunset-painted marina and expansive Pacific.

Briefly Brenda wondered if Shay could have arranged Donnelly's death. If she really had the money and power she seemed to possess, why not? In her shoes, Brenda would have been sorely tempted to avenge the death of a beloved younger sister. In her shoes, she would have fantasized about killing her sister's murderer. She might perhaps have done more than fantasize.

"I have something to tell you."

She offered a quick, encouraging nod.

"It's funny, well, no, not funny at all. It's haunting. I hired a private detective to investigate him, but I stopped the investigation. I was worried Tami would find out."

She took a tiny bite of her salmon to force a break and cover her keen interest. "Tell me about that."

"Right. Well, this is my baby sister we're talking about. She tells me all about how great it is to finally be in uniform and on the job, how her training officer is so supportive and encouraging and helpful." Shay stared at her. "I'm cynical."

She nodded, her expression receptive.

"She's beautiful. She was always more beautiful than she realized, and of course she had her trust fund. I always worried she was vulnerable to manipulation by men, and she resented that. She thought it meant I didn't trust her judgment. Which I understand. Understood. Yes, she was smart. But she was a young, rather naïve and a decidedly heterosexual woman enthralled with her male boss." Shay shrugged, her gesture and expression each a mix of embarrassment and defiance.

"Oh," Brenda said, working to hide her surprise.

"All I could think was, this man could put my sister in a really bad situation, and I've made her too defensive to come to me for help if she needs it. I didn't see anything that made me suspicious. I just didn't like some man I didn't know having such profound power over her. If I couldn't stop her from putting herself in danger, at least I could try to minimize that danger."

"So you hired a private detective?"

"Through an attorney, Jim Belafonte. Kind of an outsider. I'd just paid the retainer. I hadn't even checked in with him when I got cold feet two days later and told him never mind. Frankly, after Tami was killed, I was afraid to check in with him."

"Afraid?"

"That's not quite the right word." Shay took a long drink of her iced tea. "I didn't want to know if there was information that could have saved her. Do you see what I mean?"

Brenda nodded

"I'd hired this person to find out about the man who ended up murdering my sister just a few short weeks after I canceled the investigation. If he, if I—please excuse me."

Rising suddenly, Shay fled to the restroom. Brenda considered following her but decided to wait at the table. This was a hard call. Shay was vulnerable, shaken, ready to spill. By the time she got cleaned up and back to the table, she may very well have shut down. But the poised attorney was moneyed, professional, and careful about her public image.

Brenda wanted to be someone Shay felt safe with, and the woman would not feel safe with someone who violated her need for privacy when handling strong emotions. Allowing her a minute alone to compose herself would endear Brenda to her, and she'd be more likely to open up and reveal whatever else she was hiding.

Was Brenda trying to ingratiate herself to Shay because she was investigating the murder or because she found Shay attractive? She couldn't have said.

She sighed heavily and took a sip of iced tea. Reassuring the hovering waiter that Ms. Sheraton was fine and there was nothing wrong with the food, she considered the implications of what Shay had said. Rising tension and excitement fought with her desire to stay cool and objective. She replayed each time she'd brushed off Tami's overtures because she was caught up in her own worries and those of her own officers. And she was reluctant to step on Vallejo's toes.

Guilt and regret dampened the fire in her belly, and she breathed deeply and slowly to clear her mind. In some Pavlovian response, she could hear the jangling of the grief group leader's many necklaces, and she felt herself smile.

Tall, handsome Michael Morgan approached the table, a blithe expression smoothed over his nonetheless evident curiosity. She rose and they hugged.

"You've lost weight," she said softly. "Not very good advertising for a restaurant owner."

His low chuckle drew a few glances. "I'm too busy running this place to actually eat the food. I had no idea how much Dave was still doing."

His thick, dark hair fell over his forehead, and she grinned. "You look like Clark Kent."

His smile faltered. "That's what he used to say." He pushed up his glasses. "How are you doing?"

She shrugged. "Let's get together for coffee one morning next week. Text me?"

"That'd be great. Probably Tuesday, does that work?"

They chatted about mutual friends for a couple of minutes before he glanced at the restroom. "She okay?"

"Yeah. It's a tough time."

He nodded. "Shay's a nice lady. So are you. Hmmm."

With a wicked grin, he turned away and strode toward the next table in the crow's nest. For a moment she was struck by the fact Andi's wife had died, Michael's husband had died,

Peterson's marriage had ended and her relationship had ended. Did anyone manage to live happily ever after? She swallowed hard to push down her personal feelings. She wasn't here to socialize or to work through her feelings.

By the time Shay returned from the restroom, Brenda had stilled her emotions and was sitting back, calmly examining the view.

"I'm sorry, Captain Borelli, that was—"

"Perfectly understandable." She shifted forward in her seat and held Shay's gaze, aware again of the distraction caused by prolonged eye contact with the beautiful woman across from her.

"Thank you. You're very kind."

"I'd like access to anything Belafonte and the investigator might have put together, even if it's just raw data. They may have collected nothing at all, but let's find out. Can you talk to Belafonte and arrange that?"

"Yes, of course."

"I might not be able to tell you what I find out right away."

Shay sat back, pressing her lips together. She obviously didn't agree with this but seemed to accept it. Brenda made a mental note to clarify her position with the attorney and the private investigator. Even so, she realized, they'd been hired by Shay and would likely disclose to her any information they gave Brenda.

"We don't even know if any leg of the investigation was underway when you canceled the contract."

"True." Shay rubbed her forefinger and thumb against each other, a nervous gesture she didn't seem to be aware of. "But one of the things I was paying for was expedited service."

"Can you give me any details on that?"

"I think the retainer was ten thousand." She pulled out her cell phone and opened an app. "Mr. Belafonte gave me a choice of three men. I picked the one I did because Mr. Belafonte said Dan's company sometimes hires the same guy, and I went with that one. Chang, I think. Mike Chang."

"Dan Miller? So Mr. Chang does investigations for Watchdogs?"

"I guess so. Is that important?"

"Probably not. Do you know Dan Miller well?"

"Not well, but he never misses a chance to rub elbows." Shay made a face. "Daddy used to call guys like Dan hustlers. You know the type, always on the make. Dan always seems to have a purpose in everything he does. Just the sort of person Tami hated, always looking to get over. Anyway, sorry, that's off topic and probably a little harsh. He's never been anything but perfectly nice to me."

"You said Jim Belafonte was an outsider? Can you tell me what you mean by that?"

"You must think I'm obnoxious." Shay rolled her eyes at Brenda's murmured demurral. She rubbed her thumb and forefinger together again, a silent digital cricket. "I work in my father's old firm, and there's a whole circle. Not just lawyers. Doctors, politicians, various professions, you know what I'm saying. We all know each other. We all went to private school together. We all belong to the same country club. I've seen you there, by the way. We all lunch at the same places, like here, and we all go to the same parties. It's an incestuous little group."

"Ah."

"I asked a junior associate in our firm to quietly find information on someone who wasn't a client." Shay shook her head. "It was awkward. She'd asked me out, but I couldn't— it would have been inappropriate. She worked for me. If she worked anywhere else, sure, but I don't like to get sloppy with that sort of thing. Anyway, she gave me Jim Belafonte's name and I hired him. He told me about Mike Chang."

Brenda nodded and watched Shay wait for some response to her personal revelation. When none was forthcoming, she pulled a pair of business cards from her pocketbook. She'd prepared for this disclosure but delayed making it. Belafonte's office was on the southern end of town, two blocks south of the car dealership from which Brenda had bought the Caliber.

Why did Shay want her to know she dated women and was too ethical to date a junior employee? Was it even true, any of it? Masking her curiosity, Brenda watched her pull out a printed list of four names.

"These are her three closest friends, at least the ones I know about. And she was seeing this guy, Mason. I think he works for Dan Miller as a computer consultant or something. I'm afraid I didn't bother getting to know him, mostly because I didn't want to be intrusive again. He seemed nice enough. Quiet, smart, and he seemed agog over her."

"Mason, the boyfriend, do you think she might have talked to him?"

Shay shrugged. "She spoke about him like you might about a favorite puppy, like he was this brilliant, innocent child. I doubt she'd have wanted him to know she was doing something reckless. She liked to be…unfettered when she knew she was crossing a line into unwise behavior, and she was always drawn to people who were more cautious than she."

"Is there anything else you think I should know? Anything else I should look into?"

Shay sat back wincing. "This whole thing is too much. I can't process it. Tami was just starting her life. Childhood, college, the police academy, a few months of working, and now she's gone."

She waited.

Shay fiddled with one of her modestly-sized diamond earrings. "I got these from Grandmother for my thirteenth birthday. I've been wearing them longer than Tami lived."

She shook her head in sympathy.

Shay reached out, her cold fingers gripping Brenda's. "It's so wrong! She shouldn't have died. It's a total waste of this amazing woman who just happened to be my favorite person in the world. I can't accept that this wasn't preventable. I just can't. It's ridiculous! How in the world did this happen?"

She held Shay's searching gaze. "I'm going to do everything I can to answer that question."

CHAPTER NINE

Watching Shay start up her late-model green Subaru in the golden light of the setting sun, Brenda's breathing went short and fast. Could Peterson see the sunset, wherever he was? And was Smith with him? She'd immersed herself in the interaction with Shay and compartmentalized her feelings about everything else. This was what she always did. She put her feelings aside and focused on the puzzle before her. Now that she wasn't sitting across the table from Sheraton's sister, she felt the anxiety and guilt and frustration rushing back into her consciousness.

Back in the bad old days when she was sitting next to Brown in Dave's living room, watching Satan's Lair, she would feel this same weight fill the space around her until she was gasping for air. Brown pretended not to notice when she started gulping air, just like she pretended not to notice how he sometimes needed to stand up and walk around, clenching and unclenching his fists and shuddering like a horse after a strenuous race.

They were both fighting the same self-imposed pressure to save the victims and keep the bad guys from creating yet more victims. She did now what she eventually learned to do then: breathe more slowly and deeply until the vise squeezing her chest loosened its hold bit by bit. After several long, slow breaths, she stood in the parking lot of Dave's Bistro and watched the last of the day's light fade. She listened to the song of the surf until her breathing returned to normal.

She left messages for attorney Jim Belafonte and private investigator Mike Chang. Then, hesitating only a moment, she called Laurie Standings, the associate who'd given Belafonte's name to Shay. Again she left a message. Then she left another round of messages for Tami's friends and her boyfriend Mason.

The phone signaled an incoming call just as she finished sending Brown a request to look into Shay Sheraton and her family and firm. She was going to owe him the price of that cruise Janelle wanted him to take her on, and she had no illusions he'd allow her to pay him back in money. She would need to make up for the many unreasonable requests she was suddenly making of him.

She smiled, grateful for the friendships she'd managed to hold on to despite her obsessive work ethic and the years apart. She glanced at the screen of her phone and saw Tori's name.

"Why'd you have dinner with Shay? How do you know her? Why didn't you tell me?"

"What's with the twenty questions? Who told you? And why do you care?"

"Oh, come off it, Brenda. This is a very small town. Okay, you were at Dave's. You had salmon, and she had paella, but neither of you ate. You made her cry, you—oh, no, that's right. Shay was Tami's sister! Sorry, never mind, talk to you later."

"No, wait, tell me about the Sheratons. You know everything about everyone."

"Hardly." Tori snorted. "Rich, of course. Daddy did wills and very big divorces, Mummy lunched and ran the family foundation. One son, investment banker in Mummy's family's firm in Boston or New York or somewhere back there. Maybe he opened a branch in LA. I can't remember."

"And?"

"And Shay and Tami were very close. Shay wandered around in a couple of different specialties at Daddy's firm and is now a senior partner. I think she does corporate law, I'm not sure, something terribly lucrative and politically important. Walton kisses her ass, and so does everyone else. Daddy's dead. Mummy's a cougar and drunk in the Caribbean most of the time. Brother's an absentee and Tami was the rebellious youngest. Shay's a dyke. You probably sniffed that out."

Brenda grunted noncommittally.

"Speaking of small worlds, she used to date Moira. You remember her, the psychiatrist who dated Kami a million years ago. Remember? We used to go to their potlucks, way back when. Moira drank a little too much. Kami would get passive aggressive, and Moira would humiliate her."

"Oh, God, I remember. We haven't seen them in forever."

"You refused to go to their parties after one particularly nasty night. You don't remember, do you? Lauren couldn't stand Moira, so Andi wouldn't hang out with them. You know how Lauren was. She could get along with anyone. But she thought Moira was mean, which I think she sort of is. Anyway, the lovely Shay is seriously old money. Sailing, lacrosse, tennis, horseback riding, the whole nine. Lived in London for several years. I think Tami lived with her off and on. Shay had adventures when she was young, sailed around Australia or something. Amazing golfer. Smart. A cool customer. Pretty too."

"You're jealous of Shay," Brenda said without thinking, wincing as soon as the words were out of her mouth.

"What?" Oh. Huh. Yeah, I guess I am."

Nonplussed, she made some small exhalation for her only answer.

"Well, she's had everything handed to her. No," Tori amended, "that's not fair. Crap, I hate how I feel about her. She seems like a really decent person despite being everything I wish I was. Maybe that's what bothers me the most. I'd like to hate her, but she makes it impossible. She—did you know her before?"

"No." Brenda was still processing Tori's unexpected disclosures. "You did, though. You knew Shay. Know Shay."

"We met at the club. I like her. Hell of a golfer. Kicked Trimble's ass and Walton's. Mine too. She even beat Miller, which is saying something."

"Miller? Watchdogs Miller?"

"Yup. Dan's a hell of a golfer. He almost made it to the professional circuit, has an amazing short game. Chokes sometimes. Drinks too much."

"His ugly signs are everywhere."

Tori laughed. "And his dollars are multiplying like fat little rabbits. Shay kicked his ass, and it was a beautiful sight. Cool as a cucumber, sweet as pie. Closest thing I've ever seen to a black widow in plaid shorts. She and Walton and Miller and I played a pickup round just three or four weeks ago. Before her sister was killed, obviously. They both mooned around after her for eighteen holes while she casually flirted with all of us."

"What do you think of him, Miller?"

"Slick, or imagines he is. Rougher around the edges than he realizes. Not as smart as he thinks he is. All ego. Always working the angles. Distasteful. A pig. Why?"

"Sean Miller is his cousin, which I somehow never knew until recently. And he dated Donnelly's girlfriend, Staci Smith, at some point, or so she said."

"It's a small town, Bren. She's a badge bunny, worked her way up, or down, depending on how you look at it, from a guy starting a security company to a sergeant on the force."

"So, are the Millers our anti-Kennedys?"

"What do you mean?" Tori sounded irritated.

"Well, Sean's moving up in the department, ambitious as all get-out, hungry for my job, Walton's, yours. And Dan's spread his tentacles all over the city. Those ugly signs, his cameras, those thugs he calls guards. He always offers me the same sales pitch: get rid of unions and regulations and let his company take over for the department. The horrifying thought is, they may get their way."

"Oh, come on, Bren, don't be an alarmist." Tori tapped her pocket several times. "Not that I like the idea, but it's ridiculous. People would never go for it."

"Miller's approached just about everyone with a few stripes, I guess."

"Oh, yeah. He's always in sales-pitch mode."

"Who's taken the bait?"

"Who hasn't? Some of the retirees consult with him. He pays generously to be able to say he has a lot of former police officers on the payroll as consultants."

"Trimble? Simpson? Peterson? Anyone I know?"

"You think your old partner would sell his soul for money? That's how Peterson would see it." Tori huffed. "Why don't you ask Dan? I'm not on his payroll, and I don't keep track of who is. Trimble? Maybe. That man always has an agenda, that's for sure."

"Why do you care who I have dinner with?"

"What?" Tori sucked her teeth for a moment. "Oh, I was just surprised. It's not really any of my business, is it? No," she continued, answering her own question, "it's not. Okay. Anything come up about Donnelly?"

"Hmm." She kept her tone casual. "I just felt like I owed the family something. I wasn't actually investigating, I just figured—"

"Bullshit. You wanted to know if Tami confided in her."

"Well, yeah." She smiled.

"Big sister didn't want little sister to put herself in danger by joining the force, and little Tami wouldn't have wanted Shay to know there was a problem."

"Exactly. She didn't tell me anything useful. She told me lots of stuff that had nothing to do with anything." She bit her lip, unwilling to show Tori all of her cards.

Tori tapped her pocket slowly this time. "Tami must've been so lonely. Did she have a lover? A best friend?"

"I left messages for the friends and the boyfriend, who works for Miller. Mason. Mason Harding. Computer guy. Do you know him?"

"Afraid not. Any word from Peterson yet?"

"Nothing. Any word on Staci Smith?"

"No, nothing. Could she have just taken off?" She again sucked in air through her teeth. "Meaning, her boyfriend just died and she freaked out because he turned out to be a crook. Maybe she just bailed."

"It's possible." Brenda sighed. "I don't know what to think. She seemed pretty levelheaded to me and focused on her daughter, but I can't be sure she wasn't just snowing me. When it comes to Sheraton's death, I don't have the objectivity I should."

"Well—"

"It's just that I had this picture of Briarwood, you know? This sweet little place where bad stuff happened, bad stuff happens everywhere, but nothing really corrupt, nothing the good guys couldn't handle. At least since the traffickers got busted back when. Now I don't know what to think."

"Briarwood grew too fast. You know that. There was one bad officer and he got caught. Sheraton's death was tragic, but I have yet to see the Four Horsemen galloping down the off-ramp. This is still a good place. It's just having growing pains. It's still the same place you fell in love with twenty years ago."

Brenda swallowed hard to stifle sudden tears and couldn't speak.

"Anyway, Bren, I gotta go."

"Hey, Tori? Thanks."

"What for?"

She sighed. "I don't know. Caring how I feel."

Tori grunted. "Okay."

She watched the lights on the phone fade after Tori signed off. After a long moment of silence, she spoke into the darkness gathering thick around her.

"I miss you," she said. "I miss you. Oh, man. I'm talking to myself again!"

Checking her watch, she headed south to Teresa Fortune's apartment. A mile into the drive, she flexed her fingers. They'd gotten tight on the steering wheel as she'd gotten closer to the gray monolith that was Briarwood Arms.

She had been to this particular complex dozens of times over the last two decades, for every kind of call, from simple burglary to homicide. As she had done every other time she'd approached the repository for discarded people, she thought, if I had to live here I'd kill myself.

Arms—as it was referred to by the residents and by the public servants who wrangled, arrested, and tried to protect them—was a long, narrow, five-story building surrounded by parking lots. Arms was, she noted with a pained twinge, strikingly similar to the mall where Teresa Fortune worked. Most of the windows in the apartments featured the garish pink stickers that advertised Briarwood Watchdogs.

What must it be like to work in that mall and come home to this place? No wonder Fortune took drugs. Maybe it was the only way to survive the unlucky life the woman found herself living.

Each apartment was six- or nine-hundred square feet of watered-down whitish paint, moldy beige carpeting and smoke-stained popcorn ceilings. She had seen few places more depressing than Briarwood Arms and had to force herself to leave the humble Caliber's relative luxury for the stale corridors that reminded her of a prison's hallways.

As she pulled into the parking lot, a dozen young men conferred among themselves. They dispersed like a cloud of smoke, fading back and easing into the shadows, a band of soldiers blending into the background. They both terrorized and protected the residents of the building, and they recognized her as a "government type" before she'd made it into the lot.

Police, social worker, schoolteacher—the marginalized often had a well-developed distrust of people who showed up claiming they wanted to help. Brenda couldn't blame them. More than once she'd seen a well-intentioned public servant worsen an already bad situation by interfering without having the power to make things meaningfully better.

A few loitering kids slipped inside the block of a building when she got out of the car, and she knew she was unlikely to see anyone else once the little lookouts gave residents word of her arrival. The kids had been charged with finding out whether she was going to come inside, she thought. Sometimes social workers and therapists got as far as the parking lot and decided they didn't really need to follow up on their charges after all. Even with her newly garish hair color, she was apparently still recognized as an outsider. More importantly, she had probably arrested a two-digit percentage of the residents. She yanked open the entrance door and gritted her teeth at its groaning, squealing protest.

Briarwood Arms' flickering fluorescent lights gave her the usual headache. The musty, poorly deodorized air didn't help her feel any better. She and her mom had stayed in an apartment much like those in Briarwood Arms for most of her third-grade school year and she'd smelled the place on herself long after they'd moved to yet another subsidized-housing block in yet another dying city. She and her mom had moved into still another place dismayingly like it for her eighth-grade year, and by then she had been looking for a way out of her mother's chaotic, dreary life.

Working to shrug off her bad, old memories, she listened to the unnatural silence of the block building. Her only relief came from Fortune's location on the first floor, because it meant she could avoid the hazards of both elevator and stairwell. Odd numbers were on the right, evens on the left, and her only company was a chorus of buzzing flies that darted frantically around the musty hallway.

There were always flies in the hallways at Arms, though there never seemed to be much food for them. The occasional body was usually removed in short order. Nonetheless, she had never come to this desolate place without hearing the symphony of flies as the theme song of the apartment building.

Sixteen doors from the front entrance was the apartment designated by the number 131. It was near the emergency exit that was again chained shut, which was both a violation of the fire code and a practical measure against break-ins.

She called Fortune's cell phone before knocking but got no response to either overture. There was no scrambling sound from inside either. Fortune had been wrecked by their short conversation and might have visited her dealer for some chemical consolation, but she had expected her to burrow in at home as soon after work as possible.

Some addicts liked to explore their world and share their high with friends. From what Brenda saw, Fortune was brittle, depressed, solitary and both physically and emotionally exhausted. Despite her flinty protestations to the contrary, Teresa Fortune was obviously deep in mourning for Mark Donnelly.

More for form's sake than anything else, she tested Fortune's doorknob and was shocked when it turned. Her breathing went hot and fast, and she took a moment before deciding to go in. This was stupid, of course.

She knew she should call Tori or Walton or any of a score of fellow officers who would show up, no questions asked, to assist her. She knew she should tell someone where she was and why. But after a moment's silent rumination, she eased the apartment door open and examined the darkness inside.

The hallway light went dark momentarily, and she reminded herself that was what outdated fluorescent bulbs in poorly maintained buildings always did. Still, her heart jumped and she hesitated in the doorway. She reached to her waistband and drew her weapon, pointing it and her small, powerful flashlight, still turned off, at the gloom in front of her. When the hallway light flickered back on, she automatically scanned for a shadow, but there was no one behind her.

She began to make out dim shapes inside the apartment: sofa, chair, television, table. Stepping over piles of debris, she cleared the few rooms. The place was obviously a mess, but it was hard to know in the dark whether that was the result of a junkie's prototypically poor housekeeping or a home invasion. Finally she flicked on the light switch in the central kitchen and blinked at what she saw.

Peterson had disappeared. Staci Smith had disappeared and her apartment had been searched. Had Teresa Fortune disappeared?

The furniture was a mélange of old cast-offs and cheap mass-market bits. There were dirty dishes in the sink and on the floor and tables. There was an excess of detritus everywhere and a thick gray ring around the tub, so Fortune wasn't going to win any housekeeping awards. But the place was more than dirty. It had been tossed.

The overturned drawers, slashed couch cushions and scattered belongings were obviously the work of whoever had been looking for whatever he'd been looking for. There were no overt signs of a struggle, but in the chaos of the clothes, makeup, food and garbage it was hard to tell for sure.

She played with the notion that Fortune had ruined her own things. Junkies could get delusional and paranoid, thinking someone had hidden extra drugs or money or cameras in their sofa cushions, appliances or walls.

But Fortune was still a working addict. She had the wherewithal to go to work, run a cash register, put makeup on her bruises, style her hair, match her fingernail and toenail polish, touch up her worn shoe with a marker, shower and wash her clothes. Someone else had torn her place apart, and recently.

Brenda forced herself to take copious notes on the conversation she'd had with Fortune only hours before. Then she detailed why she'd come to Fortune's place and how she'd found it. She called the department to report a burglary and decided to leave it at that.

Only then did she start trying to canvass the neighbors, none of whom opened their doors to the police officer who did not identify herself as a police officer. Two hours later she was back in the Caliber, having learned nothing of use and having called Walton to let him know Donnelly's other girlfriend was now a possible missing person.

"Captain Borelli," he said, "I appreciate your letting me know about this, but really—"

"Chief, please hear me out," she cut in. "I get that Yolo County said Donnelly might have killed himself, and I get that I can't investigate any of this. But something is really off. My asking questions of people is not the problem here; the problem is that three people I talked to about this have disappeared shortly after I talked to them. Fortune's apartment was ransacked, just like Smith's."

There was a long silence. She sat in her new little car and wished she had never heard the name Mark Donnelly. Suddenly a thought occurred to her. "Chief, I should mention, I had dinner with Tami Sheraton's sister Shay. I think you know her, she's a lawyer—"

"I'll send patrol to her house and call her myself." He heaved a great sigh. "I'm sure nothing's really going on, but we can't take a chance. The last thing we need is the eldest Sheraton daughter going missing after her little sister gets killed by one of ours. Call me tomorrow, okay? I'll have someone get in touch with you if anything comes up. And Borelli?"

"I know," she croaked, "don't talk to anybody else."

"Please." He cleared his throat. "One other thing, and I know this is awkward. I don't quite know how to ask it."

"No, sir," she said, her tone neutral. "I do not have a personal relationship with Shay Sheraton. I just wanted to give her my condolences on the loss of her sister."

"Of course." He gave a hollow laugh, the edges of which were ragged with obvious relief. "I wasn't going to suggest otherwise. Heh, heh, heh. Well, good night."

She left a message for Tori. Then she drove home as quickly as she could. She opened her own front door with a relieved smile. Here, in her lovely little house, she could breathe without having to filter out the despair, filth and chaos of poverty. Here she was safe.

The first thing she saw after her customary visual sweep of the room was the beautiful Bernice Bing painting she and Tori had exclaimed over and showed to their friends with the joy of a restaurateur basking in the culinary glow of a brilliant new chef.

She smiled over the lovely landscape they'd both fallen in love with, then over the books they'd read together and talked about, and the beautifully detailed candlestick holders they'd put first on the mantel, then on one bookshelf, then another, giggling at their own silliness.

The things they'd surrounded themselves with had been imbued with some glow of romantic hopefulness, once upon a time, and the items still held some of that magic for her. She knew she should either let the stuff go or at least stop seeing it as evidence their love was real, but she wasn't ready to do that yet.

She called Dan Miller yet again. This time she indicated she would need to hear from him or there would be unnamed consequences. She felt ridiculous, leaving yet another message for someone who was not beholden to respond to her while she was on leave.

After a long, hot shower to wash off the grime she imagined was left by Briarwood Arms, she lay on the scratchy new sheets she regretted purchasing. What kind of penance did they represent?

Even with the lights off, the ambient glow of the moon and various electronics—her laptop and phone, both charging, the clock radio, the stereo—made her head ache and her eyes sting. She curled up on her side with her hands over her face, feeling cold and lost and alone. Everything suddenly felt like too much. As if unleashed, the pressure that had squeezed her chest in the parking lot of Dave's threatened to come back. She measured her breathing until she felt back in control.

She could see the faces and hear the voices of everyone she had spoken with through the last few days, and she couldn't push them away. Where was Peterson? Where was Staci Smith? Where was Teresa Fortune? Had she endangered them? How about Shay Sheraton? Had meeting her for dinner put Shay in danger?

And Tori? She'd been talking to her every day. What if Tori disappeared too? Of course, Tori had disappeared long ago, in her own way. The last few years had been difficult between them, and they had soured the sweetness they'd once shared so gleefully and squandered so recklessly. She watched her hand reach out for her phone.

"If I called you, would you come to me?"

She could picture it. She could call Tori and let her hear the despair, frustration, and guilt in her voice, and maybe Tori would even be willing to come over. Just as a friend, of course, because that's all they had left. Maybe she would even lie next to Brenda and hold her hand or even cuddle a little, if Brenda begged her. For the first time, she could picture Tori in their room without being flooded by rage and hurt at the memory of the other woman in this very bed with her.

"What did I do to make you cheat on me?"

But there was no anger left, not at that moment. There was plenty of guilt and a lot of hurt and confusion, but finally she could truly see the ways she'd let Tori down, and the distance and resentment she'd allowed to grow between them. Maybe she'd left Tori so lonely she'd become desperate.

She hugged herself, racked by cold. She'd cried so much over Tori she barely noticed she was crying over Tori again. She'd let her world shrink to the job and Tori, and now Tori was gone and maybe the job was too. It seemed a pretty poor bargain.

"Stop feeling sorry for yourself." Her voice was hoarse with tears, and she sat up and swiped at her eyes.

She ran through the long list of ways in which she'd failed on the job and in her marriage—and, legal or not, it had been a marriage—and she knew she'd taken the good things in her life for granted. She'd gotten complacent, self-centered and smug.

Even acquiring the boat, which had cost more than she should have spent to buy, repair, and berth in Green Hand Marina, had been a late-stage move made out of fear, not a generous gift of thoughtfulness and love. If she could go back—but it was no use wishing for a time machine. All she had was now.

"How do I go on from here?"

Her long, lonely future stretched out in front of her like a prison sentence. She couldn't picture herself walking back into the station and sitting at her desk, meeting with the brass to justify expenses and convening her detectives to go over their new cases.

She couldn't imagine going on first dates with new potential girlfriends, trying to look for red flags without sending up any of her own. She couldn't fathom calling up all the friends she'd mostly ignored for the last several years, asking them to lunch or inviting them over to watch a movie. Andi would always be there for her, but she was dealing with her own pain.

Brenda and Tori had built a quiet, insulated little life for themselves with no room in it for anyone else. Then Tori had chafed at the isolation and pushed for ways out of their bubble built for two. Maybe, she thought, if I hadn't made her feel so trapped, she wouldn't have chewed off her own foot to get out.

"Just stop! You messed it up. She messed it up. Stop going in circles!"

But she couldn't seem to do that. She chewed on how she'd driven Tori to betray their promises to each other, unable to let it go... It was hours later she imagined Tori was just in the bathroom or getting a drink of water and would be back any second.

She could almost see Tori's shape in the bunched blankets, her hair in the filtered moonlight. She could almost smell Tori's scent in the cool nighttime air. With a sigh she finally let herself succumb to sleep.

CHAPTER TEN

"She's hot. I'll give you that."

Brenda looked up from her steaming mug. "What are you talking about?"

Andi slid a plate in front of her. "Shay Sheraton, of course. Now eat your breakfast."

"Don't have to tell me twice." She eyed the fresh, sweet-smelling pastry and grinned. "Which one of us is the detective?"

"You forget, I know everything that happens in this town." Andi was wearing one of the necklaces Lauren had made for her, and the reddish jasper beads drew Brenda's gaze. She was glad to see them. Andi hadn't worn any of the handmade jewelry since Lauren's funeral.

"I've always loved that necklace. She was incredibly talented."

Andi ignored this. "You're losing weight. Stop yakking and eat."

"It wasn't a date, you know." She peeled off a strip of croissant and chewed thoughtfully on the buttery layers. "Wow, this is amazing!"

"She's one of the hottest dykes in Briarwood. So are you, and you're both single."

"It doesn't matter, Andi."

"It matters. And it really matters with a hottie like that."

She rolled her eyes.

"You could take her on that boat."

"I don't know. That seems kind of weird."

"Because you got it for Tori but never gave it to her?" Andi raised an eyebrow. "She was fucking somebody else in your bed. You're free to have drinks with someone else on your boat—and it is your boat, after all that money you spent. And it's time. You'll spend the rest of your life mooning after Tori if I let you."

"Does that mean you're ready to start looking around?"

Andi pursed her lips. "What else is eating at you?"

"Peterson, of course. And two women who might be missing too."

"Do you think this is related to that sergeant shooting Tami Sheraton?"

"I don't really believe in coincidences, but I don't have a whole lot of actual information. I'm shooting blind, if you want to know the truth."

"Always. I've got some stuff to do. Be right back. Eat up."

She watched Andi escape to the back room, wishing she'd found a gentler way to respond to her best friend. In the crowded café, paintings and sculptures by local artists adorned the warm yellow walls. Sun shone through the wide windows that looked out on the wharf and the biggest of three piers that drew visitors to Briarwood. A symphony of laughter, conversation and movement enlivened the bright, beautiful space with vitality and warmth. The café was a little nest on the edge of the wide, unknowable sea.

Behind the counter was a large photo of Lauren. Brenda couldn't tear her gaze from the black-and-white presentation of Andi's late wife. Even in the gray tones of the portrait, Lauren's vitality and humor shone through. Brenda's vision blurred with unexpected tears. She felt Andi's hand on her shoulder and swallowed hard.

"Sorry."

"You okay, Bren?"

"Just—the picture."

Andi slid into the chair across from her. "I know. It gets me at the oddest moments. Just yesterday, I was going over the timesheets and looked up. I saw her eyes, and it just hit me."

She grabbed her oldest friend's hand. "Are you okay?"

"Didn't I just ask you that?"

She shook her head. "You're the one who—"

"Don't say it." Andi shook her burgundy hair out of her eyes. She was nearing fifty, but when Brenda looked at her, she saw the twentysomething dreamer who still had her whole life in front of her. Then, as now, she was a tiny powerhouse with big, dark eyes and boundless energy. "I know you're dealing with more urgent things, but I don't know anything about police work. I want to talk about this Shay Sheraton thing."

"What thing? There's no *thing* to talk about." She laughed, feeling her cheeks grow warm.

"Oh, really, sugar? Because that little blush tells me there is a thing, and no words you say will convince me otherwise."

"She's—"

"Yes, her sister was murdered, and that's terrible, but it has nothing to do with the fact you get this puppy-dog face when I mention her." Andi eyed her speculatively. "You haven't looked like that since you first met Tori."

She shrugged. "I'm not ready to even think about getting back out there. And certainly not with Tami Sheraton's big sister."

Andi made a face. "When you say it like that—"

"While we're talking about getting out there again, I'm sorry to be so rough about it, but—"

"No." Andi sat back and crossed her arms. She looked shrunken and drawn all of a sudden. "I absolutely will not talk about it."

"Lauren wouldn't want you to be alone for the rest of your life."

"Don't. Just don't."

"You still have her shampoo in the shower. You still bake her carrot muffins. You still drink her chicory coffee, even though it was never your favorite. You haven't cleaned out her closet. You haven't taken her name off the deed to the house or the mortgage or this place. Andi, it's been almost three years. Let me help you."

She leaned forward. "Why, Bren? What exactly is the purpose of taking away what little I have left of her? She was my wife. She was my whole world, and she was stolen from me. Seeing her stuff makes me feel better. It makes it possible for me to get through the day. What's wrong with that?"

Brenda shook her head. "I'm not saying there's anything wrong with it. I'm just worried you put a strong face on because you want to be here for everybody else, but you didn't really get a chance to deal with her death at all."

"Why should I?" Andi shrugged. "What's the point of sitting around feeling sorry for myself?"

"You know that's not what I'm saying. Are you okay? Whatever you need, I'm here."

"I know, thanks, but I'm okay. Focusing on this place is the only thing keeps me upright."

"Are you going to grief group?"

"I am." Andi bit her lip. Brenda thought she might say something more, but then a skinny young kid of indeterminate gender skidded to a stop at the small corner table they occupied. Bright blue hair covered most of the teen's face.

"Kris, slow down!" Andi shook her head.

"Sorry, boss, I'm totally late. My roommate—"

"No excuses, kiddo. Just go wash up and put that hair back before you start. And Kris?"

"Yeah?"

"Breathe, huh?"

She nodded and fled to the back of the store. Andi watched the departure and smiled as she shook her head.

"Another one of your foundlings?"

"All they need is a little help. These kids are on their own, no safety net at all."

"Except for you." Brenda looked around at the three young employees busily helping customers. One had spent months in jail after aging out of the foster system and before coming under Andi's protection. The other two had been homeless before Andi's intervention. The fourth, just coming out from the back room, still tying on a black apron, was new to her.

Andi smiled. "I think I need these kids as much as they need me. But you've changed the subject very nicely, and I'd like to get back to it."

She looked at her watch and slid out of her chair. "Oops! Look at the time, I've gotta go!" She hugged her best friend. "Thanks for everything."

"Coward!"

She strode out of the coffee shop with Andi's rich laughter surrounding her like a shield. If losing Tori had taught her anything, it was that she needed to give more to the important people in her life. She'd let Tori slip away without realizing she was doing so. She'd let Peterson literally disappear.

She didn't want Andi to slip away too. The last three years had eaten away at her friend in ways she didn't know how to quantify. Andi was still warm and energetic and kind, but there seemed to be a wall up around her innermost thoughts and feelings, and she seemed less than eager to let that wall down for a single moment, even to Brenda.

"I have to do a better job," she muttered. "I have to be a better friend."

In what had become habit in the last few days, she dialed Dan Miller's number. When he actually answered, she was caught off guard.

"I'm so sorry, Captain Borelli. I had some trouble with my phone, but I got a new one this evening. I gotta make sure I'm using the best technology so I can be the best in the business."

She wondered what time it was in India and if Miller was still there. "I need to ask you a few questions." She waited for him to make some vague murmur of agreement. "Staci Smith—"

"Captain, I'd like to jump in there, if that's okay. I dated Staci, if you can call it that, for about five minutes four years ago. I—"

"Is Jessica your daughter?"

"What? Is that her child? No. God, no. I barely know that woman. As you can imagine, I never have a hard time finding a date. Women are drawn to power, and I have a lot of power. I knew Mark Donnelly, of course. I make a point of trying to meet all of the officers in your department. But I'd only met him a half dozen times and didn't know him well."

"You have a finger in every pie in town."

"It's not easy juggling it all, I'll tell you that, and no one appreciates it." He sighed heavily. "I keep people safe. What I do is as much a public service as what you do."

"You seem a little defensive, Mr. Miller."

He laughed. "I guess I am. I love my company. I think we're good for this town and doing great work. I believe in what we're doing. I want other people to like it too. What else can I answer for you?"

"I've seen a few of your guards around town. Pretty macho fellas. A little jackbooted, maybe."

"I know. I know. I'm working on that. I'm training them. Once I get this next contract, I'll raise their pay. It'll be amazing, believe me. I know how to make this company do great work. A lot of people tell me they know I'm the man who can do it."

"Sounds admirable." She wondered how long he'd been telling himself that story. "Do you know Teresa Fortune?"

The four seconds of silence at the other end sounded far away, as if the distance were a third participant in their conversation. "I've never heard of her. Who is she?"

"How about Mason Harding?"

The relief in his voice when he sounded the affirmative was a striking contrast to his tension at her previous question. She smiled as he told some vague story about computers and geniuses. She'd figure out how he knew Fortune as soon as possible.

"I know you like to recruit from the department. Do you know John Vallejo?"

"Oh, yes, your counterpart who is not your equal. Of course."

"Commander Banks?"

"Of course. I know all the commanders, Chief Walton, and most of the senior members of the department. My cousin Sean is under your command, says you're a good boss. I'm a partner with the department, and I provide an essential service to this city. My people do amazing work."

"Why didn't you join the department when you moved back to Briarwood?"

"Listen, Captain Borelli, I'm thirteen hours ahead of you. If you're fishing, could we do this by email? I'm a good citizen, trust me. I support law enforcement, and I want to cooperate. I have cooperated, but—"

"Since this is a bad time for you, why don't you call me back in twelve hours? That will be daytime for you, right?"

"Well, I don't think you realize just how important a man I am, Captain. I'm pretty booked. I have—"

"Say, sometime in the next twelve to eighteen hours? That's a pretty big window and should make it feasible for you to continue to cooperate with me. I look forward to your call. Thanks for your help, Mr. Miller."

She hung up and shook off the tension engendered by the call. The more she talked to Dan Miller, the less she liked him, but she wasn't sure that made him anything but annoyingly cagey and manipulative.

Her phone rang just as she reached her car, and she veered away from the parking lot and toward the beach, trudging toward the shoreline until the sand was damp enough to be firm.

"Damn it, Brenda!"

"Good morning, Tori. No, I am not trying to be a pain in your ass. It's just a side benefit of being myself."

Tori's grudging laughter warmed her.

"We laughed so much at the beginning."

"Yeah, we did, didn't we? Then we got very serious about everything." Tori sighed. "I miss the fun we used to have."

"I wish I'd made you laugh more as we went along," she said without thinking. "Made more of an effort to show you I loved you. I wish I'd told you how much it meant to me that you were my lover and my friend."

"Oh, Brenda."

"I'm sorry I let you down. You were so loving, and I took you for granted. I should have proposed. I should have given you the ring I bought three years ago."

"You bought a ring? You wanted to get married? Three years ago?"

"Yes."

Tori clucked her tongue. "Then Lauren got sick."

She swallowed regret. "It seemed wrong, proposing to you when Lauren and Andi were going through so much, like dancing on Lauren's grave before she was even in it. Then time went by, and I chickened out. I thought you were leaving me behind. I sabotaged what we had by being an ass. When you cheated, I got to play victim without really looking at my own behavior. I'm sorry, Tori. I really am. You there?"

"Yeah." Tori sighed. "I would have given anything to hear you say those things, not so long ago. I still—but we're past that, aren't we?"

She pressed her lips together to stop herself from denying it. "I think we are. Even though I feel like I've learned so much."

"You weren't all bad."

"Neither were you."

"Well." Tori exhaled loudly. "I don't even remember what I was going to yell at you about. You totally knocked me for a loop."

"In a good way, I hope."

She held her breath until Tori coughed a laugh and answered. "Yeah. In a good way. I keep thinking—never mind."

"What?"

"I keep thinking we had it all. That what we had was the best I'll ever have. And I'll always end up comparing anyone else I meet to you, and they'll always fall short."

She choked up, surprised by sudden tears. "I think the same thing about you," she whispered. "Who the hell can measure up to you?"

"Could you ever let it go, Bren? And just start over?"

"I don't know. Could you?"

Tori offered a shaky laugh. "I still love you."

"And I still love you."

"Where does that leave us?"

"I don't know." She grunted. "It's hard to focus on this with Sheraton's death and the disappearances, especially Peterson's."

Tori cleared her throat. "Let's get this business resolved, and then we'll figure out the personal stuff, okay?"

"Yeah, okay. That's a good idea."

"Are you at the beach? I hear waves and wind."

"Yeah. By Andi's."

"How is she?"

"Meh. Still kind of on hold, you know what I mean?"

"I do. Lauren's death...I don't think I'm over it yet, so I can't imagine how she must feel. It was just so wrong, so unfair." There was a long silence. "So, what's the plan as of now?"

"I don't know." She huffed out air. "Any ideas?"

"Kidnapping people is a giant pain in the ass. You and I both know it's hard to kidnap and keep one person, much less three people."

"That's what has me so worried. Frankly, it'd be easier to kill all three of them than to keep them alive somewhere. And if someone is keeping the three of them somewhere, that takes manpower. Who has that kind of manpower? Who has a crew of people who can be trusted with that sort of secret? There are only so many options, Tori."

"Is there any possibility they haven't been taken? That they got spooked and took off?"

"Peterson? He'd rather eat his gun than let somebody scare him off. And he was worried about me. He wouldn't abandon me. Maybe Staci Smith would abandon her little girl. That wasn't the vibe I got, but I only met the woman once. Teresa Fortune, who knows? As far as I can tell, her most important relationship is with her dealer."

"Hmm."

"Her situation may have nothing to do with Donnelly. She could owe her dealer money or have a lousy boyfriend. She had bruises. Someone was beating on her. She's not enthused about police, and my showing up could have spooked her or whoever's putting hands on her. Peterson's place didn't look ransacked, but both Smith's and Fortune's apartments did. Of course, they both live in crap apartments. Maybe each of them took off and their places got broken into by neighbors. They both had Watchdogs stickers, everybody does. Dan Miller's still stonewalling me, which makes me wonder what he's hiding, and whether it has anything to do with this or not."

"Why would he do that? Oh, yeah, because you despise him and he knows it. Listen, I'll talk to Dan."

"Hmm."

"So, here's the deal. I read the report on Donnelly. It's pretty lightweight, missing a lot of details. I'm not sure it's actually indicative of something other than suicide, but I can tell you I'd never have signed off on it from one of my officers. And it's not up to Yolo's usual standards, not by a long shot."

She made a vaguely inviting sound, knowing this was all a warm-up to what Tori wanted to say.

"Let's just pretend for a second that I think Donnelly might not have killed himself."

Again she only murmured, knowing Tori would drive the conversation for now if given free rein.

"Donnelly just bought the stripper an engagement ring. Used a credit card that gets miles. Already paid it off, four big payments. It's worth more than my car. Princess cut, a full carat, very close to flawless. He made reservations at Dave's. He called his old parish priest to ask about pre-wedding counseling and available dates next summer. He talked to a lawyer about adopting her daughter. He also looked at a house not far from ours—yours—and toured the elementary school, the one on Kenneth."

"The good one," she murmured. She remembered Tori's enthusiasm for the school with good test scores. If they'd adopted like Tori wanted, they might have a child there now. Would they have stayed together for a child?

Tori huffed. "Listen, you and I both know somebody can be a good guy in one part of his life and a monster in another. We've seen it plenty of times."

"True."

"But. It all makes him sound like such a choirboy, doesn't it? I don't know. I'm glad we have the video, so we know for sure Donnelly killed Sheraton."

"He wouldn't be the first person to justify bad actions by saying he was taking care of his family."

"Yeah. I need to think."

Tori hung up without a goodbye, and she suppressed a groan of frustration. She turned to face the morning surf and closed her eyes, though it meant leaving herself vulnerable out here in the open. She breathed the brined air and listened to the gentle music of the waves and the sharp calls of the birds swooping overhead. For her, in moments like this, Briarwood was still a sacred place, made newly profane by violence and corruption.

"I'll fix this," she vowed, opening her eyes to stare out onto the light-dappled reaches of the Pacific. "I will fix this."

CHAPTER ELEVEN

The next morning, Brenda's ringing phone woke her, and she shook her head to clear it. How many times in the last twenty years had she been awakened by one phone or another?

"Andi? What's up?"

"I waited until five, are you up?"

"Yeah," she lied. "Are you okay?"

"Not so much. Can you come to the shop?"

"On my way. Should I bring anything in particular?"

"Booze. Booze would be good."

She forced a shaky laugh and promised to rush. Seven minutes later she'd brushed her teeth, sucked down a microwaved cup of leftover coffee, and thrown on jeans and a blue sweater. She snagged the dusty bottle of whiskey she'd gotten several years back for when Andi and Lauren came over for dinner.

Whatever had happened to put Andi in such a state, it had to be bad. She tried not to speculate as she drove the still-cold Caliber through peaceful early-morning streets, past houses where people were just getting up, starting the coffee, taking their showers and waking up their kids. The only thing she'd ever seen knock Andi on her butt was Lauren's death, and after three years, it was still probably the only thing that could make her falter.

Brenda parked in the nearly empty lot next to the boardwalk and jogged toward the only lit storefront. The café glowed like a beacon in the late-dawn gloom, and she found the door unlocked. With the whiskey in her left hand, she reached for her waistband, noticing only then that she'd strapped on her service weapon while dressing. It was a habit of so many years she hadn't even noticed she still wore it everywhere she went.

What did it mean when she found an unlocked door at her best friend's restaurant—where Andi was awaiting her arrival and had probably just unlocked the door for her? Her first response was to reach for her weapon. Putting the question aside for later perusal, she eased open the door and crouched low. The inside of the café looked empty and spotless, a blank canvas for the customers to paint with conversation and movement and laughter.

She edged around behind the counter and crept toward the door to the large space that served as an office, breakroom and storage area. There she found Andi hunched over in the worn office chair Lauren had given her years back. Andi's normally animated face was drawn and streaked with tears. She flicked her dampened gaze toward Brenda and shook her head.

Without a word, Brenda put away her weapon and set down the bottle of whiskey. She pulled Andi into a tight hug and held her. At first, she resisted, but then she relaxed into Brenda's embrace and wept. Her body shook as she sobbed, mumbling incoherently.

"It's okay," she crooned. She let her cry for several minutes.

Finally, Andi took a deep, shuddering breath and pushed her away with small, cold hands. "Thanks, I needed that."

She merely nodded. "I love you, you know."

"Yeah, me too." Andi blew her nose and dried her swollen eyes. "Coffee?"

"Only if you really, really do love me."

They shared a quiet breakfast of yesterday's banana nut bread and strong, hot coffee while Andi talked about the upcoming spoken-word festival she was organizing for queer college students. She enthused about the students' talents and griped about the minutiae involved in the project and the many people who wanted a say in how things were done but didn't want to do any of the work involved in getting them done.

Brenda let her talk. She'd work her way around to whatever had set her off in her own time. And if she needed to prattle on about her latest project first, so be it. People rarely started talking first about the thing that was actually on their minds, and she'd learned not to press them.

For the first time, it occurred to her that maybe Tami Sheraton had tried to talk to her about something other than what she'd brought up. Maybe she'd been sounding Brenda out before getting to what she really wanted to say. The thought was appalling, because it meant she really had let the kid down. She pushed this aside for the time being to focus again on what Andi was saying.

"So, anyway, I feel like I need to confess something."

She hid her surprise. She smiled and waited, unable to imagine Andi had ever in her life done anything truly wrong.

"I loved Lauren. With my whole heart. As you know."

"I do know. She loved you too."

"I was lucky to have almost twenty years with her." Andi sat back and pressed her lips together. She teared up again and had to wipe her eyes and swallow coffee before she could speak again.

"Something happened?" Brenda prompted, struck by an idea of what that something might be. She kept her face carefully blank.

"I could never love anyone like I loved my wife."

She offered a noncommittal sound and made sure her expression was receptive.

"I was at the grief group—it's funny, you just asked me about it."

She nodded.

"There's this woman there, Diane. She and I didn't really hit it off at first. I don't know why, but after a while I got to know her."

"I remember when you first started going. She started just before you. You thought she was pushy."

Andi laughed, and her suspicion was confirmed.

"I still think she's pushy. But—anyway, Diane lost her wife in Afghanistan. Marie died two months and three days before Lauren."

She made a sympathetic sound. She didn't want to do anything that gave Andi an excuse to stifle her impending disclosure or to talk herself out of what she was feeling.

"So we've been through a lot of the same stuff. Di—Diane—is a doctor. She works at the new hospital downtown. In the ER."

"High-stress job."

"It is. But she loves it. When she talks about it, you can see how much it means to her to be able to help people."

"Sounds a lot like my best friend."

Andi laughed. "What I do is different. I just give them a little community nest so they can fly when they're ready. She saves lives."

She smiled. "So you and Diane like each other. A lot. And you feel guilty."

"I know it's ridiculous. My wife has been gone for three years. So has Diane's. We're adults and don't owe anybody anything."

"But."

"But I feel disloyal to Lauren. I feel cheap. I feel like it means what I had with Lauren is over for good, and it was just one part of my life, which it obviously is and was, but it's hard to accept that."

"She'd want you to be happy. You know that, Andi. She loved you and she wanted you to move on. She told you not to spend the rest of your life sitting in the corner grieving for her."

Andi sat back. Tears streamed down her face, but she nodded.

"You don't need anyone's go-ahead to let yourself be happy again, but if you want mine, I'm giving it. I love you. I was there when Lauren told you to be happy. I was there when she told you to be open to new love. I know this is what she wanted for you."

Andi nodded again.

"What can I do to make it easier for you?"

"You just did." Andi smiled through her tears. "I know you're right. She'd want me to be happy. She'd want me to find love where I could, with somebody who's good to me."

"Yes, she would. And if Diane isn't good to you, I will kill her and we'll find you somebody better."

Andi laughed a release. She would be able to move forward with Diane. Whether they found happily-ever-after or not, trying to do so would be an important first step in her healing and living the rest of her life fully engaged.

The twinge of sorrow Brenda felt was hers to deal with privately. What Andi needed was unconditional support and love, and she would give that.

"She's a good person."

"So are you."

"I'd like to clean out some of Lauren's things, but I can't do it by myself."

"That's what I'm here for."

Andi's smile was brilliant, her eyes shining with tears. "Not now. Not today. I don't know when. Soon, maybe."

"When you're ready, you'll tell me. Today, next week, April, whenever. I'll do what you need when you need me to do it."

"I know. Thanks, Bren. I really needed to see you today. You're the only one who understands how it was."

"I'm here for you forever."

"Right back at you. Now get out of here. I have to get ready for the morning rush."

"Aye-aye."

"Finish this thing with your rookie's killer, Bren. You're losing weight and looking tired. I'm worried about you."

"You don't have to be. This is almost over, love. I promise. And then I'm going to gain twenty pounds sitting behind my desk again."

"Good, you could use a little junk in that abbreviated trunk."

"If only I had a best friend with unlimited access to baked goods!"

Andi laughed. "Message delivered, message received."

After a long hug and promises to get together again soon, Brenda strode back to her car with a lighter heart and hands burdened with a huge box of day-old pastries Andi had pressed her to take. She would, she decided, stop by the station and drop them off. She wanted to check in with her people anyway, and this gave her a good excuse.

She drove downtown with a fluttering feeling in her chest. She knew it was good Andi was moving forward. It was healthy. It was appropriate. It was for the best. But it meant the closing of one chapter to make room for the next, and she could only try to understand how hard that was for Andi. It was hard to hear about it.

Like Andi, she, too, had been suspended in grief and held on to the vain wish that Lauren would come back. Lauren would not be coming back. She was gone for good. They'd lost that magical time when the four of them made a family of their own and shared the little ups and downs of their days and weeks and months and years. It was all gone forever.

She parked in the garage, and, bracing herself, jogged up the stairs to the lobby of the big new city building, greeting folks she knew. It was only seven in the morning, but there were plenty of people scurrying around. Shift change always meant a crowd. Plus, the city had many workers on a seven-to-four shift, trying to alleviate some of the traffic from downtown Briarwood to the surrounding neighborhoods.

"Welcome back, Captain," called one of the city managers from a distant hallway. She threw a wave of thanks and headed toward the stairwell. She didn't want to give people the impression she was back at work, and she didn't want to get caught up in a lot of idle chatter, so she took the opportunity to reclaim some lost muscle tone by avoiding the elevator and the inevitable gossip it would engender. Holding the giant box of pastries on the trot up the stairs practically made it exercise, she told herself with a silly smile.

Ducking into the back corner of her station's floor, she finally felt like she was coming home. The smell of the place was reassuringly the same. She was heartened by the way her dominion's gray walls were brightened by posters and plaques, photographs of her officers, the Briarwood children's sports teams, various fundraising events, picnics, barbecues, and the other events that made their team more than a bunch of coworkers.

By the time she reached the breakroom, she was surrounded by officers and staff who wanted to know how she was, whether she was back for good and what treats she'd brought them. She let herself revel in their warmth and enthusiasm for a little while, knowing she was indulging herself and not caring.

They needed to see her as much as she needed to see them. Because of her timing, she was able to see almost half of her officers. The night-shift folks stuck around for a little while and the day-shift folks hung around the break table scarfing pastries and guzzling coffee.

She made sure she connected with everyone, asking about their cases, their families. She noted their mixture of gladness at seeing her and wariness at her stopping by. None of the officers questioned her about what she was doing or when she was coming back, and she didn't know what to make of that. It was Maggie who finally beckoned her away.

"How's it going? Any word on who was really behind it all?"

She laughed. "No fooling you, is there?"

"We all know what you're doing."

"How's that playing in Poughkeepsie?"

"Some worry you'll get sacrificed on the altar of public relations or politics."

"Anything I should know about here?"

Maggie pursed her lips, shaking her wild curls. "The usual. Gonzalvo's wife is due next week. You sent them a lovely hand-sewn quilt from their registry. You're welcome. Abbott's getting divorced."

"Again?"

"Again." Maggie rolled her eyes. "Would you stay married to him?"

She gave her assistant's rounded forearm a gentle squeeze. "Thanks for getting the quilt, Maggie. You're the best."

"Yes, I am. On that note, you wrote me a glowing performance review, which is on your desk in the red file full of papers I need you to sign."

"I'll look at it now. Why aren't Miller and Johnson signing?"

"They are, but some stuff needs you. You're not that easily replaced, Captain Borelli."

The shift to formality made her raise an eyebrow. Then she saw Maggie's gaze flit to the side, and she turned around.

She blinked. "Commander Young."

Tori, resplendent in a tailored black suit, shifted her weight to rest on one pointy-toed black leather boot. "Captain Borelli. I imagine Maggie has plenty for you to catch up on here, but when you're done could you stop by my office?"

She nodded. "Grapevine works fast. I just got here."

"That it does. You barely hit the stairs when I heard you were here bearing gifts. From Andi's place, I'm guessing. Maggie, good to see you."

"And you, Commander."

As Tori strode away, Maggie plucked at Brenda's sleeve. "I'm glad you came today. The whole station's been holding its breath since you left."

She thanked her and went in to find her office cold and still and disturbingly neat. Johnson and Miller had labeled their respective inboxes and outboxes and crisis boxes, and there was an empty disposable coffee cup in the wastebasket. At least one of the lieutenants had worked late the night before. A second glance told her it was Johnson, who took his coffee black. Miller took his with four sugars and an abundance of soy milk.

With Maggie standing over her, she perused the stack of paperwork in the red file. Within ten minutes she'd signed everything that needed signing and made changes on a few documents.

"The boys want your attention now," said Maggie with a grin.

Johnson and Miller were wandering around the squad room. Johnson was talking to the officers, joking and catching up by the looks of it. He was clearly trying not to encroach on her. Miller moved about the space as if everyone in it were invisible. His gaze was locked on her, and she shivered slightly. He had the eyes of a vulture, avid and soulless at the same time. While the officers engaged with Johnson, they all avoided looking at Miller.

She waved in the two men and spent a couple of hours troubleshooting cases that were clogging the system. Johnson and Miller were both stiffly formal with her for the first several minutes, but she was able to warm them up after a while. She got updates on the progress of their pending investigations, offered suggestions for a thorny interpersonal issue and commended both men on filling in for her.

"I'll be back soon," she promised as they wrapped up their briefing.

Miller escaped as quickly as he could, claiming he had a meeting with somebody whose name he mumbled. She let him off the hook, wondering if her investigation was putting him in an awkward spot with his cousin. She'd never really considered whether Sean Miller might be embroiled in a mess because of Dan Miller, but she needed to dig into that. She chatted briefly with Johnson, trying to gauge how he really felt about his new, temporary role.

"Are you interested in at some point moving into this office or one like it permanently?"

He raised his eyebrows. "That was direct." He laughed. "I've been thinking about it, naturally. But I already feel removed from investigations more than I'd like. And I'm certainly not interested in playing in the viper league upstairs."

"I can understand that."

"You made the move from my job to yours. Captain, are you glad you did?"

She made a face. "Sometimes. I can do a little more to represent our officers in this chair than in that one. It's pretty removed from the work, as you said. That's not much of an answer, I know."

She watched him decide not to ask her when she would be back at her desk. Instead, he thanked her and let her close their chat. He would be a good leader, she thought. He didn't say everything he thought but was nonetheless sincere. He had integrity.

Would it be a favor to encourage him to move up? It would be a favor to the officers under him, but she really wasn't sure moving up was such a great thing for someone who cared about the job and the people who did it. His ambivalence let her off the hook for now, but at some point, assuming she was allowed to step back into her role at this station, she'd have to either encourage Johnson to move up or let Miller claw his way higher. She sighed, knowing the decision wouldn't get easier with time.

Like his cousin, Dan, Sean Miller was good at one thing—looking out for himself. Whatever damage he did to others he would forget or dismiss. He was part of what she thought of as the new breed of crook. They were all slick liars who manipulated the system as needed, to swindle, deceive, and manipulate people into doing their bidding.

She took a deep breath and pushed the disturbing thought away. Just because she didn't like some people, didn't make them sociopaths.

She handed the file of signed documents to Maggie on her way to the stairwell and thanked her, grateful for her insight and warmth. The glowing review she'd just signed really did reflect the value Maggie brought to the group, and one of the things Brenda wanted to do, once all of the current nonsense was resolved, was raise the profile of the support staff in the department. In such a macho environment, the office staff sometimes got treated like second-class citizens, and it was time for that to change.

Trotting up the stairs to see Tori, she realized how much she was looking past the current situation. Not so long ago, she'd have had trouble doing that. As Andi and Tori had both pointed out, she had a tendency to develop rather singular focus on her caseload and ignore everything else.

Maybe one of the benefits of moving into her current role as captain was that it gave her plenty of practice juggling more than one priority at a time. She grinned as she opened the door onto the fifth floor and was surprised to see Commander Banks standing right in front of her. He held a cigarette in one hand and a yellow plastic lighter in the other. His eyes grew wide when he realized he'd been caught.

"Captain Borelli." His florid face burned even brighter. "I hope you know there was nothing personal in my questions at the hearing. I was doing my job, as I'm sure you understand."

She smiled. "If we don't provide meaningful oversight, we allow the perception of corruption."

"Yes. Precisely."

She noticed his suit jacket had a frayed edge on one sleeve. His tie was too wide for contemporary styles. His shirt's collar looked worn. For a wealthy man, he was looking a little run-down. She wondered if his lavish lifestyle was wearing on his wife's pocketbook.

"Any word on Donnelly's death, sir?"

"Nothing concrete. It may take some time to determine what happened there, and it's out of our hands."

"Yes, of course. Do you think he was working alone, sir?"

Banks gave a poor showing of surprise.

"I've seen no evidence to the contrary. Now, if you don't mind, Captain."

"Of course, sir."

She winked and held the door open for him, and he offered her a grateful smile that faded as he brushed past her and lit the smoke before the door had closed behind him. She masked her expression and went down the hall to find her ex-girlfriend.

Tori's office was two from the corner and faced the Pacific. She grinned, remembering the first time Tori showed it to her. She'd been excited and proud, and Brenda wished she'd been more supportive instead of feeling threatened by the change. If she had it to do over again, she'd buy Tori flowers to brighten up the large, gray space.

It was empty when Brenda knocked, and Tori's assistant Marcus, hurrying back from somewhere, rushed to let her in. They chatted briefly, and then Marcus held out a hand as though warning her of danger.

"May I offer a heads-up, Captain?"

She turned to the lanky thirty-year-old with a quizzical expression. "Sure, what's the deal?"

"It's Commander Young, ma'am. She's, uh, in a mood."

"Ah." She nodded, irritated on Tori's behalf by Marcus's snide sexism. Would he have said the same thing of a male boss? She doubted it.

She thanked him, her tone a few degrees cooler, and waited for him to slip out and close the door. She turned back to face the wide windows that laid out much of Briarwood's downtown and a slice of the sea for her appreciative perusal. Traffic was heavy, despite the late-morning hour, and Brenda wondered what Tori thought when she looked out at the view, if she looked out at all. She had a tendency to develop singular focus too.

The sun shone bright and hot through the glass, and she closed her eyes to savor its warmth on her skin. She had always meant to take Tori to sunny, beautiful places, but they'd done little more in ten years than take a couple of trips to Hawaii and the occasional weekend jaunt to Tahoe or Bodega Bay.

In the sun, with her eyes closed, she could almost imagine she was on some beautiful beach with Tori lying next to her, her wet hair plastered to her head, her skin burnished and sandy, her face relaxed and open. She heard the door open and close behind her but didn't turn around, reluctant to let go of her fantasy. When she felt Tori's arms slip around her waist, at first she could almost think it was part of her daydream. Then she opened her eyes and started to turn. When Tori tightened her grip, Brenda leaned back just a little to nestle into her.

"I—"

"Shhhh." Tori breathed deeply. "You smell good."

She closed her eyes again. "So do you."

"Mmm."

Tori kissed her neck, her ear, her hair. Brenda turned and they faced each other, less than an inch apart. She stroked Tori's soft, warm skin. She stared into Tori's eyes, drunk on their intensity. The electric blues were so bright in the sunlight they almost glowed.

She felt dizzy with desire. All she wanted was to feel Tori's lips. She leaned forward and offered a tiny, chaste peck on Tori's cheek. When Tori didn't resist, she brushed her lips against Tori's and teased her with a tiny kiss. Tori gave a shaky laugh and shook her head. She held Brenda's neck and pulled her in for a hungry snogging that made Brenda's head spin.

Tori's lips were soft and warm and inviting. Brenda felt the rest of the world slip away as she clung to Tori and tasted the mouth she'd been missing for months. She felt Tori's heartbeat, her heat and her immeasurable energy, and she was frantic with the need for more. She clawed at Tori's suit jacket and dragged it off her to drop it on the floor. Then a filmy white blouse was all that stood between her and Tori's bounty of soft, kissable skin. She fumbled with the ridiculously small, ludicrously numerous buttons to finally push it out of the way.

She let her fingers roam lightly over Tori's neck and shoulder and down her arm as the blouse fell. She grasped Tori's hand lightly in hers and moved her kisses to Tori's throat, where her pulse beat in a frantic rhythm.

Suddenly she couldn't breathe. She only saw shadows and felt her pulse exploding inside her every half second. She was dizzy and nauseous. She broke away from Tori and staggered toward the divan. She collapsed onto its unforgiving cushions and held a hand over her eyes.

"Are you okay?"

Tori sounded far away, and she nodded, unable to speak for a few seconds.

"I pushed you," said Tori, who sank down next to her. "I'm sorry."

She shook her head. "No," she finally said. "I just… Suddenly I couldn't breathe."

"Well, you always said I was breathtaking."

She choked, and before she knew it, she and Tori were in each other's arms, this time hooting with laughter like two hysterical schoolgirls. They laughed until her stomach hurt. Finally Tori sobered and shook her head.

"God, I needed that."

"I don't know what to think of this."

Tori shook her head. "Neither do I. Let's come back to it later, okay?"

She searched Tori's eyes but couldn't read what was in them. Finally she nodded agreement.

They parted as something like friends, and she wondered how long that would last. She hoped she wouldn't lose that friendship too. She also hoped she could keep her word and bring Peterson back to his friends, bring Smith back to her young daughter and bring Fortune back to her dealer.

CHAPTER TWELVE

Brenda stopped by her house and then drove to the dark square that housed Briarwood Watchdogs' headquarters. The ominous exterior featured matte black tiles and dark tinted windows. The parking lot was ringed in chain link fence topped with concertina wire. She took a quick survey around the block. Oddly, there seemed to be only a single point of entry on one side of the fortress's perimeter.

An oversized gate featured six uniformed guards standing in a rigid formation that didn't afford them a view of anything but the strip mall across the street. Each of the young men had sweat rings under his arms and on his chest and back, and sweat glistened on each shorn head.

With this little field trip in mind, she'd changed into a black polo shirt and dark gray cargo pants, but quality technical fabric meant the outfit was breathable, lightweight and comfortable in a way the guards' uniforms clearly were not. Her low black boots and short hair would, she hoped, help her blend in without looking too much like she was trying to do so. In the testosterone-heavy world of Dan Miller, one was either a cupcake in a club dress or a pseudo-military wannabe in a uniform.

The Watchdogs compound was supposed to look imposing and authoritative, but it was a showcase of bravado. The militaristic, macho posturing of Dan Miller and his undertrained guards screamed of insecurity and fragile ego, and she suppressed a groan as she approached the guard gate.

Two black-shirted guards walked around her Caliber while a third stood by her open window and held up his hand. His tinted sunglasses and shaved head were meant to look tough, but they only accentuated his protuberant ears and florid razor rash.

"Ma'am, only authorized personnel are permitted on these premises."

She smiled up at the boy with what she hoped was disarming ease. She took off her sunglasses and blinked wide eyes at him, while employing the vocal characteristics of the young lingerie shop employee.

"Sure, totally, sir. It's just that, um, Mr. Miller? That's the boss here, I think? He asked me to come by here today. He's in like China or India or something? And he wanted me to redesign the uniforms. They're kind of itchy, I guess? And they don't breathe, so you guys get super hot. And, uh, not in the sexy way?"

For the first time, the guard showed an inch of humanity. "Really? We been complaining—not that we would, I mean, but, these shirts suck. Ma'am."

"Mr. Miller feels super bad about it, but you know how it is. He can't look weak by admitting they were less than perfect, so he's having me do it while he's in India. You know what I mean?"

The kid pursed his lips and nodded. "But you're not on the list."

"Shoot! That means I can't do my job. I think Mason was supposed to make sure I got on the list. Mason Harding? Do you know him? Is he here today?"

"Oh, man. That's the guy… His girlfriend just died. She was a lady cop."

Blinking at the term, she nodded. "I just feel so bad for him. I don't want him to get in trouble with the boss."

The guard grimaced, and she wondered what Miller was like when he took off his public-relations mask. If this employee's reaction was any indication, Miller was less than charming under pressure. Weak leaders often were.

"But I don't want you to get in trouble either. I don't know what to do!" She threw up her hands as though helpless to come up with a solution.

"Oh, no, don't even worry about me." Youth-fueled bravado kicked in, and the guard nodded as if to reassure himself. One of his gang muttered something at him, but the kid waved him off with a frown. "I got rank on these guys. I'm shift leader. I can take the heat."

"Really? That's so sweet of you. I really appreciate it. Do I need like a badge or anything?"

The young man snapped his fingers at the guard behind him. "Get this lady a badge. Oh, what's your name, ma'am?"

"Sandy, Sandy Watts." She smiled brilliantly at the naïve young guard and watched him fumble with his clipboard while the other undertrained watchman handed her a guest badge.

"There we go." His smile faltered slightly, and she touched his hand with her own.

"And what's your name, sir?"

"Mikey, Michael. Mike. Martinez."

"Oh, Mike, you've been so great. Thank you! Will you be here when I leave?"

"Probably, I guess."

"Then I'll see you on my way out, Mike." She grinned as his unease dissipated, and she toodled her fingers as she cruised slowly past the ineffective guards and into the parking lot.

Guest badge in hand, she left behind the sweat patrol and drove around the side of the building, where she'd noticed the largest concentration of cars. If the employees liked to park there, it probably meant the side entrance was close to the elevator or far from the boss's office.

She parked near the outside end of the second row from the middle and was eyeballing the discreet northern entrance when her phone buzzed a call. She glanced at a number she didn't recognize and took a breath before answering.

Her hello was greeted with a loud exhalation that made her pull the phone away from her ear. She frowned before listening again.

"Captain Borelli? Ma'am?"

"Who is this?"

"Uh, Mason. Mason Harding, do you know who I am?" His deep voice seemed tight with anxiety or tension.

"I'm sorry for your loss, Mr. Harding." She scanned the almost-featureless face of the building in front of her. Anything could happen in there and no one would see it. Was she letting its forbidding façade fool her into thinking Briarwood Watchdogs was more sinister than amateurish? Was Harding looking out at her right now? Why hadn't he returned her calls until she'd shown up at his workplace? She turned slightly in her seat as if she could see into the tinted windows of the monolith.

"Thanks. Uh, can I talk to you? I mean, now?"

She decided to play dumb. "Sure, I'll meet you wherever you like. Where are you?"

His breathing changed, and she heard echoes as in a stairwell. "I'm coming to you. In the Caliber, right?"

"Yes."

"I'll come get in your car, if that's cool."

She turned a bit more and scooted her seat back a few inches before adjusting the passenger seat forward. She was less than thrilled with having him in her car, but she'd wanted to talk to Tami Sheraton's boyfriend for days. If this was what it took, then so be it, but she had to give herself some tactical advantages. She clipped her seat belt behind her and turned a good thirty degrees toward the passenger side. She also changed the angle of her seat so she could fit her arm comfortably between her and the seat back without it getting pinned beside her.

Thirty seconds later a rangy, bespectacled young man slipped out of an unmarked black door and loped toward her. His brutally shorn head, black-rimmed eyeglasses and long, scrawny limbs made him look too young for the uniform that hung on his tall, narrow frame. She blinked in surprise. She'd pictured beautiful Tami Sheraton's boyfriend as an Adonis, muscular and tousle-haired.

She unlocked the car's doors and waited for him to slide in. Her hand hovered near her waistband, and she had to push away unease at being trapped inside her car with someone she didn't know in hostile territory.

He blinked owlishly at her when she extended her hand, and then he pumped it awkwardly across the narrow center console. It was like shaking hands with a giant spider inside a matchbox. His fingers were cold, despite the heat. His grip was weak, his skin dry.

Close up, Mason Harding looked like a refugee from a high school computer camp. He was painfully gaunt and hollow-eyed. While dark with pain, his eyes were clear. His skin was stretched too tightly over jutting cheekbones, but it, too, was clear. His teeth looked expensively perfect.

"Thanks for seeing me," he said in a surprisingly deep, resonant voice. She smiled, thinking Sheraton might have fallen for the rich, sonorous tones he produced. Over the phone he'd merely sounded gravelly. In the acoustic confines of the compact car, he sounded like a movie star from a more glamorous era.

"Right back at you," she said.

"Sorry for not calling you back."

"I imagine you've been focused on just getting through the days and nights."

"Uh, yeah," he laughed, a bitter sound. "Pretty much."

He faced front and made a rueful face, swallowing hard a few times and then glancing around the parking lot like he thought someone might be watching them. His long legs were folded in front of him in the confines of the shortened passenger enclosure, but he made no move to change his seat's position. His knees were inches from his chest, and she realized he wasn't even aware of how restricted his movements were.

"Is this a good place to talk or would someplace else work better?"

"I don't have anything to hide. I just don't normally spend work hours off my post." He laughed. "I'm not a guard, by the way. That's just the way they talk here. I'm a computer geek, as Tam put it. It doesn't matter if they fire me, really. Force of habit to think of it, I guess. I wanted to show her I was a regular guy and I could do a regular job. She was so opposed to moneyed privilege, the idle rich."

Brenda nodded slowly.

"Listen, I wanted to thank you. Tam thought a lot of you." He swallowed again. "She really looked up to you. When you came in the gate, I recognized you right away. We have cameras." He gestured vaguely in several different directions.

She bit her lip. "I wish I'd gotten to know her better. You called her Tam?"

"That's how she introduced herself to me once we were out of costume. Cosplay convention. She was Furiosa, and I basically stalked her for two days. I was Cloud." He rubbed the stubble of his head, knocking his elbow into the window to his right and mumbling an apology. "My hair was longer then."

She didn't know who those characters were, but he smiled at the memory, so she mirrored his expression, taking care not to overdo it.

He again rubbed the top of his head, this time with his left hand. His arm was so long that his elbow came within a few inches of her face, and she stiffened. But he dropped his arm and buried his face in his hands. Loud, ugly sobbing racked his narrow frame, and he hunched over until his forehead, framed by his knees, almost touched the dashboard.

She waited him out for a few seconds before snagging a handful of tissues and shoving them at his arm. Snuffling, he scrubbed at his eyes and blew his nose a few times. Finally he sat back up and held the wad of wet tissues in his upturned palm.

"She was such a good person. Smart, real, beautiful. Compassionate, so warm and so good. The most honest person I ever knew." He sagged helplessly against the back of the seat. "I loved her. I don't know why she loved me back, God knows

I'm not much to look at, and she didn't need my money. But she really did love me back."

She nodded, her expression receptive. She noted his mention of his money. Did he have more family money than Sheraton, or was he unaware of her family's financial resources?

"I miss her every minute. It's like somebody carved out the middle of my chest and left a rock in there. I don't know how to live the rest of my life without her."

She was surprised to find herself blinking away her own incipient tears. "I'm sorry."

The bereft young man closed his eyes and then snapped them open. "Thanks. Thank you. I'm sorry for losing it like that. I've always been a real softie. My whole family's real macho. They think I'm a wuss. Maybe I am."

"She didn't think so," he said. "She thought I was pretty great, actually. But she was the amazing one. We used to talk about everything. I would have done anything for her." He blinked several times and cleared this throat. "She wasn't sure at first—that's why you're here, I guess—about Mark being a crook. She thought maybe she misunderstood."

"She wanted to be sure before she said anything?" She spoke softly. She needed Harding to keep talking.

"Yeah, exactly. She used to make these maps. If this was true, then these five things had to be true too. And she'd look at them, the second tier, she called them. If one of them wasn't true, then she'd have to adjust the first tier. Like that. It was complicated the way she did it. Painstaking. But smart. She thought of things I never would have thought of. Like she could see inside things to what was really there. I used to call her X for x-ray sometimes, to tease her, you know, because of Professor X? Almost psionic. Not really, but sort of."

He laughed and bit his lip and looked down at his big hands, one of which was still clutching a wad of damp tissues. He looked at the white mess as though he didn't recognize what it was, and then he sat silent and still.

"I noticed that," she said, her voice low like she was in church. "She saw patterns where other people didn't. Structures underneath. Sounds like you do something like that too."

"She didn't always tell people what she saw, because they didn't see it too, so they didn't always believe. She had to get proof, she said."

"The camera."

He turned to her, a universe of pain in his dark, shadowed eyes. "She didn't tell me. I wouldn't have wanted her to do it. I would've tried to stop her. I wanted to protect her but she didn't want me to. She started keeping secrets from me so I wouldn't worry. If I hadn't tried to stop her, maybe she would've told me and I could've helped her. You know where I was when she got killed?"

She shook her head, transfixed by his faraway gaze.

"Home. I was cooking Japanese food, 'cause she liked it. It takes forever, chopping all this stuff, and everything has to be fresh. But I learned how to make all kinds of foods she liked. Anything to show her how much I love her. Loved her. She said she'd swing by the liquor store and get some sake. She wasn't even following him that night. She just liked to have theme dinners. We would dress up in costumes, if she wanted to. She didn't drink much. Neither of us does, but she was like that. If we were having tacos, she'd get tequila and play old Spanish love songs and put a flower in her hair. If we were having sushi, she'd get sake and play Japanese folk music and put her hair up and wear red lipstick. Everything was an adventure for her. It was fun. Silly, I guess, but I miss that, the way she made everything into something special. She had this big light inside her, and I couldn't look away." He broke off, chewing his lip and turning away.

She waited him out, swallowing tears she wouldn't allow herself to shed.

"I burned it all, at least what she'd left at my place. Her notes, her maps. All of it. Stupid, I know. But I was real freaked out. Crazy, I guess. Sad, and a little mad. I went kind of crazy for a while. She wasn't even looking for him, at least, I don't think so. I think she was just there to get sake, like she said. I think it was just a coincidence."

He'd confessed to killing Donnelly as much as he would, at least for now, at least without nudging. She could elicit that confession, she was sure. He'd destroyed Sheraton's evidence against Donnelly because he'd decided Donnelly would never go to trial. Some childish part of him was compelled to say he "went kind of crazy for a while." It might even end up being part of his defense, though it was a strategy that rarely worked in a real-life courtroom.

"Mr. Miller talked to me. He said I could have a couple of weeks off for grief. They don't usually give that here. The pay is awful, no benefits. I didn't expect him to be so nice. He treats smart people like they're unfortunate necessities, like he'd rather we were stupid or went away, but he was so nice after she died. He invited me to his house and we went out on his boat. It's huge."

She breathed slowly and quietly next to Harding, blinking a few times. "It sounds like he's been really supportive."

"If we had access, we could have put cameras everywhere and we would have realized Mark was a crook. Maybe Tam would still be alive. Mr. Miller says he and some of his buddies are going to wire up the whole state and help keep everyone safe. Maybe the whole country, one big database, so we can protect everyone. That's part of what I'm working on."

She blinked and kept her expression blank. "And different companies in each metro area, all sharing information, videos, like that."

"Tam thought it was a bad idea, a private corporation having all this footage of people without permission. I get it, but it can be really helpful too. And if you don't have anything to hide, why should you worry?"

"Mark pretended to be supportive of Tam. I never trusted him, but I thought maybe I was just feeling jealous. Tam thought I was just being a silly jerk. She made it sound sweet."

"You must feel so betrayed by him."

"I thought he would help her. Be a mentor or something like that. She trusted him."

"And now he's dead."

He nodded and looked toward the Watchdog building.

She examined him closely. Folded into her small car, with his terrible uniform hanging off his narrow shoulders, he looked to her more child than man. But she firmly believed he had stalked and murdered Mark Donnelly and that he felt little remorse for having done so. The relief in his voice, the way he'd destroyed everything Sheraton gathered on Donnelly, the way he spoke about Sheraton and about Donnelly made it clear. He hadn't returned her calls because he was busy stalking Donnelly.

He was a wind-up toy, all run down now that he'd fulfilled his last mission, avenging the death of his beloved. How much influence Miller had exerted on this grieving man-boy she would never know. He was smart enough to cover for Miller and naïve enough to think it was virtuous to do so. She could push him now, she thought. But he was still clearly under Miller's influence and was loyal enough to believe he owed Miller something.

She couldn't help wondering what he would be like after a stint in prison. For just a moment, some tiny part of her wanted to do nothing about Donnelly's murder. Mason was a decent guy. He would not be interested in killing again for sport or profit or ego. He had loved Tami Sheraton and been driven mad by hurt and grief and outrage.

But he had deliberately killed Mark Donnelly. He could have called the department. He could have called Vallejo or Brenda. He could have done a million things other than kill the man. He had made his choice and would have to accept the consequences of that choice. She wondered if her assumption that Miller had manipulated the kid into killing Mark Donnelly was based on anything real. She pushed this away to focus on Harding.

She could push him, she thought, and get him to confess to the murder. But he wasn't her target, not really. She could come after this kid later. If she got a confession and arrested him now, the crooks might roll up their rugs so she could never find them.

"I have to get back to work," he said, again looking at the big building that loomed over them. "Okay?"

"Sure. Okay if we talk again sometime?"

He nodded and unfolded himself to leave her car. He loped across the parking lot and was swallowed by the black cube.

Had she done the right thing by letting him go for now? Only time would tell. She drove slowly out of the sole point of authorized entry, offering a wooden smile to go with the returned guest badge. She wished she hadn't come to see Harding. Unsure where else to go, she ended up back in Tori's office. She slumped in the chair in front of the desk, waiting while Tori finished a phone call.

"Finally," Tori said, hanging up and reaching into a desk drawer. "Scotch, anyone?"

"God, yes." Brenda smiled. "You always were a mind reader."

Tori came around to sit in the second captain's chair facing her desk and the window, and they sipped decent whiskey out of badge-adorned coffee mugs while they watched the sun set.

"I wonder if Peterson can see it." This was an echo of the question she'd asked herself while watching the last sunset, and she pressed her lips together.

Tori sighed. "I don't know what to think, Bren. It seems really unlikely three people connected to you and Donnelly would randomly disappear at about the same time. But Peterson has been a mess for years, and retirement can be deadly for an alcoholic police officer. And I don't know anything about Staci Smith, and neither do you. Maybe she found a sugar daddy. Maybe she reconciled with her family. Maybe her baby daddy was abusive and he showed up and she's on the run from him. Teresa Fortune is a marginally functional drug addict, according to you. People like her go missing every day."

"You're right."

Tori laughed. "Wow, that was surprisingly easy."

Brenda shook her head. "Fortune? I can see it. She could have taken off for any of a hundred reasons. But why would Smith leave her daughter behind? Have you seen the photos of her apartment? Everything in there says she was a devoted mom."

"I agree."

"That was surprisingly easy."

They shared a quiet laugh. Then Brenda turned to stare into Tori's bright, startled eyes.

"What?"

"What are we gonna do, between us I mean?"

Tori was saved from answering by a sharp trio of knocks on her office door. "Hold that thought."

They both rose to greet Chief Walton, who offered Brenda hearty congratulations on looking well rested and gently broached the subject of her return. She intimated it was forthcoming and left it at that. She let him guide their conversation and hardly heard a word he said. She was abuzz with two warring interests: her desire to figure out where she stood with Tori and her need to focus on resolving the work she'd started because of the death of Tami Sheraton and the disappearance of three innocent victims.

She mindlessly agreed to whatever Walton said and smiled and was, she hoped, reasonably gracious and professional. Tori's physical presence outshone the wordy symphony of nonsense between the three of them as they stood in a loose triangle in the gathering darkness of the fading sunset.

Finally Walton made his goodbyes and strode out, closing the door behind him, and Tori turned to Brenda with a wicked smile. "Did you hear a thing he said?"

Brenda shook her head. "Not a word."

They laughed as quietly as they could out of consideration for their recently departed boss. Within seconds, though, they clung to each other with helpless giddiness and cackled as gleefully as any two crones. They staggered together to the small sofa and collapsed onto it as one. They laughed until Brenda was breathless and sore and utterly drained. She sat pressed to Tori's side, and it was only after several minutes of silence that she looked down and noticed they were holding hands.

Tori was the first to let go. She bumped Brenda's shoulder with her own. "Déjà vu, huh? Let's finish this thing, if we can. Do right by Sheraton and Peterson and the two girlfriends so we can. Is it wrong to say this? Put it behind us?"

"I'm sure there are people who could do both at the same time."

"But you're not one of them." Tori laughed. "Maybe I'm not either. So putting aside our big, messy personal stuff, where do we go from here?"

She shook her head. "I have no clue. Actually I have too many clues and none of them help at all." She kissed Tori's hand, holding it for an extra few seconds just because she could. Then she stood. "For now, let's just say we'll sleep on it and start up again tomorrow."

Tori stayed seated on the sofa. "Could you ever let it go?"

She searched Tori's taut features. "I'm working on it. What happened that day didn't happen in a vacuum. I see that now."

"I am sorry. I wish—anyway, I'm sorry."

She spoke so softly she wasn't sure Tori heard her. "So am I."

Part of her wanted desperately to cross back over to the small divan and lean down and kiss Tori's soft lips and touch her smooth hair and convince her they could make things work a second time. She thought she saw receptiveness in Tori's eyes, in the laxness of her mouth, in the way she seemed to be waiting for Brenda to approach her.

But something held her back and the moment passed. An invisible wall arose from she knew not where, and it was as immutable a barrier as she'd ever encountered. She actually rocked forward on her heels and felt the impassability of the shield as a physical thing.

Part of her thought the notion was fanciful. Still, she could not cross the boundary. Tori watched her, and something like comprehension washed over her features. They said formal goodbyes as if they were and had only ever been friends, and Brenda wondered if she looked as disappointed as Tori did.

Brenda swam into her detachment as she drove slowly home in the cool evening gloom. Something had stopped her from following her impulse to rekindle intimacy with Tori, and she tried to figure out what that something was. Was it fear? Hurt? Bitterness? Anger? Was she giving in to the negative feelings that had been engendered by Tori's adultery? Was she yielding to the guilt she felt over the opportunities she'd missed in their relationship? She wasn't sure. She felt pangs of loss, but she also felt immeasurable relief.

She rolled down her windows as if to escape her thoughts and cold air rushed in. Salty and sweetened by briar-rose greenery, the wind buffeted her hair and face and arms and distracted her from the impossible tangle of her feelings. Briarwood rushed past as she sped along the coastal road, both in a hurry to get home and not.

Tami Sheraton's murder had changed things in a way Brenda could never have anticipated. Arresting Mason Harding was something she would need to do, whether she put the cuffs on him or not, and this would feel very much like another kind of loss. He seemed a basically decent person who'd been overcome by grief and had done the unthinkable.

She'd never met the man before today, but she was heartsick. And now she needed to know who was implicated along with Harding. Without a single scrap of evidence in front of her, she knew he'd killed Donnelly. She would gather the evidence and arrest him. But if someone else was involved, if Harding was someone's puppet, she needed to know that. Miller? Walton? Vallejo? Trimble? One of the commanders? Shay? Tomorrow would be about doing what Harding said Sheraton used to do: map the events that led to the outcome.

She'd survived failures. There had been cases she couldn't solve and suspects she couldn't build a case against. There had been criminal groups whose activities she'd only managed to stunt at the local level. Satan's Lair still haunted her, despite what everyone else seemed to see as a shared victory over its evils.

Friends had left or drifted away or pulled back or become people she couldn't respect. Lauren had died. Tori had left. Peterson had disappeared into a bottle long before he retired and then vanished from the bar. But she'd continued to cling to her fairy-tale version of their enchanted lives in their mythical town, ignoring anything that didn't jibe with her mythos.

Now that mythos was gone, dissipated as quickly as a drop of fresh water in a wide, polluted sea. The world, her world, was a new place, and she grieved for the loss of the old one with a strange neutrality that she supposed was the closest she could get to peace.

"Acceptance," she whispered into the indifferent night, her voice lost even to her own ears. "Acceptance."

CHAPTER THIRTEEN

"Captain Borelli, good morning. I'm so glad to hear from you!" Shay's voice was warm and welcoming. "How are you? I heard you spoke with Mason."

"He called you?"

"Listen, Captain Borelli, could we meet for lunch? Today?"

"Uhhh, yes, sure. Would one thirty be too late for you?"

"No, of course not. There'll be a big food-truck thing at Livingston Plaza today. Do you know it?"

She swallowed questions about the unusual choice. "Across from the boardwalk, right?"

"Exactly. I can show you part of what I do for a living. See you then."

She hung up and called Andi, hoping the midmorning hour was a relatively slow period for the bakery and café.

"Come on by. I want to talk to you."

The tension in Andi's voice propelled Brenda to drive more quickly than she might otherwise have done, and after circling the sand-dusted beachside public lot for several minutes, she was squeezing into the last parking space at the far end of the last row. She trotted double time across the lot, glad the food trucks at Livingston Plaza had drawn large crowds that spilled over onto the boardwalk across the street.

Two dozen restaurants-on-wheels crowded the shopping center across from the beach and boardwalk, and the smells of foods and spices from around the globe danced on the fresh seaside breeze like olfactory siren songs.

She sniffed curries, garlics, onions and a hundred other scents as she headed toward the homier fragrances of Andi's place. The café bulged with hungry visitors. Five aproned employees rushed to tend the customers, and Andi directed them with the cool confidence of a gifted maestro. She glided away from the controlled chaos and with a quick gesture disappeared into the back room. Brenda obeyed the wordless command and followed, ignoring the stares of the curious.

As they hugged behind the swinging door, Brenda frowned. "Are you okay?"

"I'm fine. Sorry if I scared you. I was just busy."

"I'm a little sensitive to crisis these days."

"No word on Jonas, still?"

Brenda shook her head. "I'll let you know as soon as I know anything. But now that I see you, I know you're better than okay. So what gives?"

Andi was glowing. Her dark eyes shone with good humor, and her wide mouth seemed determined to smile despite her best efforts to frown. "The kids have it under control, and I wanted to see you. We'll be completely swamped for the next three days, so this is actually the best time to see for myself that you're okay."

She shrugged. "What's up?"

Andi giggled. "Diane and I are actually going on a date. Not until Monday, because things are so crazy here right now, but we've been talking on the phone, and texting, and I feel like I'm seventeen." She shook her head, sobering. "Like there's this whole part of me that just went dormant when Lauren got sick. And it's coming back alive."

She grabbed Andi for another long hug. "I'm so glad. I'm proud of you for being brave."

"Okay. Thanks, love. Get out of here now. Things are crazy." She laughed. "Okay. Call me if you need anything and have fun. Does everybody come here for dessert after they eat all the spicy stuff across the street?"

"Here and the ice cream place. They're shopping too. Even the locals are spending money on sunglasses, hats, whatever. This is turning out to be great for everybody's business."

"Rolling with the times, right?"

"You got it. Stay with it or get out of the way. Sugar, I really appreciate you coming by. I know you're worried about Jonas."

"Am I crazy for thinking he didn't just take off? I know he's been drinking a lot. I just don't think he'd leave without a word. And it's too strange, three people disappearing."

"You're not crazy. You know him. The other two, I can't say. But Jonas adores you. He would never leave you hanging like that. So you won't leave him hanging either."

She wanted to ask for reassurance that Peterson was still alive, but she couldn't bring up the possibility of his death without taking the shine from Andi's eyes, so she stifled the question.

Releasing Andi from a final hug, trying to mirror her friend's delight, she escaped from the crowded bakery and stood at the boardwalk railing to stare out at the gently rolling waves. Seeing how happy Andi was, how thrilled she was to be engaged in something other than a caregiving role, was a gift. She would like very much to see Peterson safe and happy too. Did he even know how to be happy anymore? She wanted him to have the chance to try. She wiped away tears, unsure if they were grief or joy, and strode resolutely toward the food trucks.

As she approached the crosswalk, she saw three Watchdog guards huddled around an unbathed, ragged teen. The undernourished, wan-faced blonde was crying and hugging herself.

One of the guards reached out and snagged her backpack off her shoulder, pulling her hair in the process. She cried out, and the guards edged in even closer, boxing in the diminutive girl with their combined girth.

She quickened her pace, reaching for her badge and opening her mouth to announce herself. Just as she reached earshot of the trio of costumed thugs, they broke up their circle and dispersed. Two dashed out into traffic against the light, nearly causing a collision. The other flung the appropriated backpack at the girl behind him as he scurried away toward the shore side of the boardwalk, disappearing from sight within seconds. The shaken teen stood staring at Brenda, her eyes wide and damp.

"Thank you, oh my fuck, they were hella scary! What the fuck? I didn't even do anything. Those assholes!" The kid looked maybe fourteen or fifteen, with her heavy makeup smeared by tears and her mouth drawn dark except where she'd chewed off the lipstick. "Fuck! I seriously didn't do shit. I swear to Bob!"

Brenda hid a smile at the girl's apparent aversion to taking the Lord's name in vain even as she tried out other curse words.

"You okay?"

"Fuck, yeah. I guess so."

"Where do you stay? Do you have a place?"

"Yeah, yeah, sure." No more willing to trust Brenda than any other unknown adult, the girl sidled away. "Anyway, thanks. Those guys are motherfuckers, you know."

"Hey, I'm not trying to hassle you, but I am a little worried about what those guys are up to. Can I buy you a cup of coffee?"

"Nah. I mean, I just got to town and all, so—bye!" The girl turned and broke into an awkward run, escaping up the street and into the crowd headed toward the food trucks.

A good twenty minutes early for her meeting with Shay Sheraton, she did a quick circuit around the perimeter of the chuck-wagon convention. In addition to the food trucks there were other vendors hawking everything from handmade jewelry to seascape paintings to hand-carved wooden toys. Alongside these were booths advertising financial institutions, cell phone service providers and insurance companies. Local produce vendors had gotten in on the act too, and it looked like half the town was milling around Livingston Plaza.

For a moment she was not a police officer but a civilian, strolling around a fun event in her favorite city. She listened to the overlapping voices around her. They spoke a dozen languages and all sounded excited and convivial.

"Isn't it amazing?"

She turned to see Shay smiling back at her, her dark eyes shining with good humor and her strawberry-blond hair golden in the sunlight that snuck through the clouds. Even in a severe gray suit and clunky platform loafers, the attorney looked like a kid at her first county fair.

"I've been standing here sniffing the air like a puppy for an embarrassingly long time," Brenda said. "This is incredible. I didn't know we had something like this in Briarwood."

"That's because it's the first one," crowed Shay. She came to stand right in front of Brenda and was bumped by an eager passerby. Her hands flew up reflexively, and Brenda steadied her with care. They grinned at each other for a few extra seconds, the air between them electric with energy Brenda decided not to examine too closely. The objective was to find out whether or not Shay had conspired with Harding to kill Donnelly.

"Tami would've loved this."

"Harding said she made everything into an event."

"She did. That's a great way to put it." Shay smiled. "Costumes, music, the whole thing. She was fuller of life than anyone I've ever known."

Falling into silence, they let themselves be propelled forward and jostled closer together. Just when it seemed they were going to get carried along indefinitely as if by a tide, Shay grabbed Brenda's hand and pulled her to the side, into a narrow passageway between two booths.

"Thanks." Brenda let go of Shay's hand. "This was a great idea."

"You're welcome. It's great, isn't it? I set this up, you know. I mean, not myself, of course, but the city council was dead set against it. I had to negotiate for the last six months just to get the permits. Your department was more than a little opposed to it too."

She scanned the crowd from the relative peace of their little alleyway. "I don't see any officers."

"That's one of the concessions we had to make. My firm had to get the coalition of investors to agree to pay for security. Dan Miller's guys, Watchdogs, are providing the security for a pretty hefty fee."

She wasn't able to hide her distaste.

Shay laughed and made her own rueful face. "I know. It's hardly optimal. But we just had to make money this one time, and then the city will go along with the next one. They've already made more than enough to justify the expense of police patrols, and we're negotiating the funding distribution next week. I'd like to make it a yearly thing, maybe even quarterly."

"This is incredible. And I was over at the boardwalk earlier. They're crowded too."

"That's exactly what we were hoping would happen. Once people are down here, at least some of them will stay to shop. I'd like to set up shuttles so people don't have to worry about parking, and I'd like to do it on weekends, when people don't have to hurry back to work and they can bring their kids. I really think Briarwood is ready for this."

"I agree." She looked around and grinned. "If this is your baby she's a beauty."

Shay laughed. "Thanks. I'm just a cog mover in a very large machine, but I do feel proud of this. Briarwood's old guard gets a little stodgy sometimes. It's time to push past that resistance and really celebrate what this community can be."

"Ms. Sheraton, you are a visionary."

"Thanks. What looks good to you?"

They spent a good ninety minutes walking around and sampling bits of this and that. They shared fruit kabobs, a spicy Thai peanut butter roll, lobster puffs and so many other treats Brenda thought she might slip into a coma from the effort of digesting. Shay seemed to know all the vendors and chatted up many of them as they went along.

Finally the two women found a bench at a quiet table near the edge of the festival. The happy music of the chattering crowd played accompaniment to their quiet conversation.

"Thanks for meeting me here, Captain Brenda Borelli."

She let silence fill the pause. She wasn't yet ready to invite Shay to call her Brenda, certainly not while she was trying to find out whether she was involved in Donnelly's death. She resisted the notion Shay could be party to Peterson's disappearance, though anything was possible.

They sat side by side, inches apart, while both scanned the crowd. She was surprised by the intimacy she felt just sitting next to Tami Sheraton's big sister. Was their shared grief the reason she felt close to this woman she barely knew?

Shay took off her sunglasses, and she reflexively took off hers too. They exchanged a long, silent look that felt more intimate than any conversation. Shay's big, dark eyes were wet with tears. As they rolled down her cheeks, she swallowed.

"You've been very kind to me. As you were kind to Tami."

"Your sister was a good kid," Brenda said.

"Yes. She was."

"I'm sorry she was killed. I wish—I'm sorry she was killed."

"Thank you. Do you think it'll be over soon?" Shay put her sunglasses on.

"Not sure." Brenda put her shades on too.

"You know more than you're telling me."

"I'm afraid that's how it has to be for now." She bit back the question of whether Shay knew more than she was telling her.

Shay nodded. "I understand."

"I don't think she was following Donnelly," said Brenda. "She was just going to the store, and he happened to be there. Mason said she was going to get sake. And the store owner said she shopped there regularly. He had her come to the back door because in that neighborhood, police make people nervous. I think it was a coincidence."

Shay gaped at her. "Seriously?" She grimaced. "That's—oh, my God. I don't even know what to think of that. Thank you for telling me. Somehow that's better, I think. It was random. I couldn't have done anything to stop it."

"You know Mark Donnelly is dead."

Shay nodded.

"Do you think someone killed him?"

Shay shook her head. "You would know more than I. I'm not really watching the news these days. It's mostly pretty terrible news, and I'm more sensitive to that now."

"That's not hard to understand."

"You think someone killed him. You don't think it was suicide."

She shrugged. "I don't know enough to say anything definitively."

"Prison would have been better." Shay sighed. "He's dead and will never have to face up to what he did. A nice, long prison sentence would have meant decades of suffering, and I would have preferred that. Does that sound terrible?"

"No," She wondered if Shay had anticipated her suspicions and said what she did to allay those suspicions. She didn't think so but had to wonder if her attraction to Shay was interfering with her perceptions.

She stood, and without thinking, offered a hand to Shay, who took it and stood gracefully without actually needing the help. It was another oddly intimate moment with a near-stranger who was the sister of a victim, and Brenda stiffened. She'd always been a stickler for propriety and was unwilling to relinquish her integrity for a momentary connection. Still, she felt the warmth and softness of Shay's hand long after she'd released it. They walked back toward the center of the dissipating fray in silence for a few seconds.

"The crowd's thinned a lot."

She looked around. "It has. People were mostly on their lunch hour, I guess."

"It was supposed to be over by now. We didn't expect this many people to show up, so everyone will be happy."

"Congratulations." She looked at the sky and shivered. "Weather's turning. That might end things now."

Shay laughed. "That's okay. We've already exceeded everyone's expectations. Next time, I'd like it to last longer. I suggested a real festival, pony rides, face painting, live music, all of it. Your friend Andrea suggested we have local folks sign up for time slots on a stage. Kids could do their dance routines, folks could sing, read poetry, all of it. Spring Festival or something."

"Andi always wants to give people a chance to be heard." Shay smiled. "She could rule the world if she wanted to."

She laughed. "Yes, she could."

"So, you'd be interested? In an expanded carnival or festival? You think it's a good idea?"

"I do. The logistics will take some work, but Briarwood's ready for some fun events that allow it to come together as a community. Why not a carnival?" She thought of what Peterson would say and made a face. "Minus the carnies."

"Yes," Shay said, laughter in her voice, "minus the carnies."

"Thanks for meeting me here. I'm glad we got to experience this."

"I know you wanted to meet with me for a couple of reasons."

"Oh?"

"You like me back. But you also wanted to see if there was anything I knew that would help you figure out who else besides Mark Donnelly was responsible for killing Tami."

She didn't say anything.

"If I knew anything, I would tell you."

"Thanks."

"I know you can't reciprocate and I understand that. If there's anything I can do to help, let me know, okay?"

"I may take you up on that sooner rather than later. I have a few ideas but not enough proof to act on them yet."

"Call me anytime and I will help you. When this is all done," Shay said. Then she stopped and looked away.

"Yes?"

Shay shrugged. "For now, I will call you Captain Borelli and not ask you if I can call you Brenda. I will step back because for you I'm off-limits until this case is resolved."

She opened her mouth and closed it again.

"And I'll back off because I can't tell if you and Tori are still a thing or not. I will allow this formality between us because I'm the sister of a victim. So there's all this stuff between us. This wall of propriety. And that's fine for now. But at some point this will be resolved, and you and Tori—who's lovely and brilliant and one hell of a golfer—will either be together or not, and whoever you may need to arrest will be in prison. It will be done."

Brenda nodded slowly. "And then?"

"That's the question, isn't it? Because I like you. You like me. At some point I'll want to know if you're willing to see where that could take us."

She twitched her mouth.

"No, don't answer me now. Think it over. You will meet your obligations and fulfill your ethical duty and keep your side of the street clean. I respect that. But at some point, when all of this ugliness is cleaned up, then I'll ask you again, and I'll expect some kind of yes or no. I'm hoping it's yes."

With that, Shay touched her lightly on the arm and walked away, her eyes again shielded by designer sunglasses. Everything about Shay was contained beauty: her hair in a low, tight bun, her lush figure imprisoned in its tailored gray suit, her feet encased in their weighty leather prisons. She waggled her fingers over her shoulder without looking back, and Brenda could only watch her walk away with a mix of hope, fear, regret and longing.

She was inclined to believe Shay had not influenced or assisted Harding in murdering Mark Donnelly. So at least she'd accomplished that much. It seemed a small thing, compared to what she still had to do.

She needed to find Peterson, Smith, and Fortune. She needed to figure out whether Harding worked alone to kill Donnelly. She needed to determine which, if any, members of her department were corrupt and dangerous. Things were about to get very hairy. Whatever happened next, it would be less enticing and much less complicated than getting involved with Shay Sheraton.

CHAPTER FOURTEEN

She swung by Andi's bakery and saw a crowd gathered in what loosely approximated a line snaking out of the front door. She strode to her car with a renewed sense of purpose.

In the relative quiet of the Caliber, she examined the myriad things she needed to resolve with her missing partner and the two vanished women at the top of that list. Some speck of insight glimmered on her mind's periphery. She felt she had been chasing mental clarity for days. Now she realized she needed to stop chasing it and let it come to her.

Having had this thought, she found herself listening for her phone, as though her decision to wait for the answers would summon them. When a full thirty seconds went by with no ping or vibration, she laughed at herself for waiting. Then she checked her phone. Darius had emailed her, and she read the material he'd sent before calling him.

"Brown, you're a genius!"

"Borelli, you're easily impressed."

"How did you get the financial information?"

"What I've sent you is all part of the public record. I wouldn't give you something you couldn't use, obviously."

"I had no idea how complicated this all is. These guys are bigwigs. How can they be in this much trouble without anyone knowing it?"

"People see what they want to, I guess. If you think somebody's rich, you ignore anything that contradicts that, especially if they're working hard to maintain the illusion of wealth. The rich are sharks, and they smell blood in the water faster than you or I would."

They chatted briefly before he had to ring off to attend a meeting. Then she focused on absorbing the wealth of material he'd sent. Both Marty Banks and Captain Walton were living a lie. They resided in mansions, drove expensive vehicles, dined out in style and displayed daily sartorial splendor. Meanwhile, they were both drowning in debt. Were they both corrupt? She wasn't sure, but at least she could focus on two department men instead of dozens.

She needed to send Brown a gift, she knew, something the whole family would enjoy. She would figure out what after this was all resolved. With his help, it soon would be, she thought.

She started the car and put it in reverse, and then the phone rang. Dan Miller's name flashed, and she sobered, putting the car back in park.

"Mr. Miller, thank you for calling."

"Sorry for the delay, Captain Borelli."

"Are you here in Briarwood, sir? I'd like to meet in person."

"Well—"

"How do you know Jessica's not yours?"

"What?" There was loud, fast breathing on the other end of the line, and Brenda smiled grimly.

"Mason Harding works for you, right? Some kind of computer genius?"

"Yes, but—"

"You've been trying to woo me to the private sector for as long as I've known you. Are you still interested?"

"Of course I'm interested. You'd be a valuable asset—"

"How about Dave's Diner at seven?"

"Captain Borelli, I've just arrived after a grueling travel day. I—"

"Of course, how about tomorrow evening at seven? I'm sorry to press on you. I just want to be able to wrap things up with a nice, neat bow and move on."

There was silence. Brenda counted to fourteen. She worried she'd been too obvious.

"Well, I'm embarrassed. I got caught being a wimp by someone I admire. Why don't we go ahead and meet tonight? I mean, I'll never sleep tonight anyway, right?" The salesman in Miller seemed to rouse himself. "I'm so glad you called, Brenda. I look forward to the chance to really talk with you."

"And I with you. Thank you for meeting with me on such short notice. A good meal and some interesting conversation may help you through your jet lag. I'll see you there and will try to make it worth your while."

She rang off and drove home to go over her notes one last time. She wanted to find out whether Miller pushed or helped Harding to kill Donnelly. She also needed to know whether his many cameras had ever shown Donnelly's activities and what if anything Miller might have done with that. There were a few other things she would explore, and those gave her the shivers despite the hot water. When her chest started to tighten, she forced herself to breathe easily and slowly. She had a long list of things to do before seven o'clock.

By five thirty she had arranged everything. She went over her plan with careful attention to detail and hoped she'd anticipated every possible potential outcome. She'd moved the pieces into place on the chessboard of her choice, which was about the best she could hope for.

Eleven phone calls, nine purchases, two outright lies and a handful of omissions all added up to one big, fat snare. What exactly that would catch she would soon learn. Now it was time to get into her costume and begin her brief and hopefully successful acting career.

By six forty she was standing on the deck outside of Dave's and staring out at the churning sea. The clouds she'd watched blow into the harbor that afternoon framed the setting sun and gave the dappled seascape an ominous air.

With a sigh she turned to circle the restaurant. Her gaze wandered to allow her peripheral vision to give her a view inside the eatery. By the time she reached the entrance that faced the parking lot, she had reviewed her mental map of the room and her plan for the evening.

She heard Dan Miller come in behind her but pretended not to notice. He stood watching her for a second and then circled around her, leaving too little space between them. She faked pleasure at seeing him, and he stuck out his hand to shake hers. As before, she was prepared for his squeeze and yank. This time, she let him crush her fingers and strain her shoulder.

"I'm sorry for not being available to you earlier. It's just one of those things. The world is changing fast, and I want us to be bleeding edge. They'll leave us behind if we let them. Believe me, I know the truth, and if you stick with me, you will too."

She nodded and smiled blithely.

They were seated at the best table in the crow's-nest section and given their drinks—beer for him, iced tea for her. Without asking, Miller ordered the seafood special for both of them, and Brenda let him. She exclaimed over the good table and let him feel like a big shot.

"Wait'll you see this dinner. You'll love it. I only get the special. It's the best. It's amazing, and you won't believe it. Yes, it's expensive, but I've earned it and I want to share the wealth."

She listened with half an ear and a doubled smile. Miller had decided to take the lead and establish dominance. She had anticipated it and planned to let him do so until it was time to make a change. She played the polite, easily manipulated dupe as well as she could, smiling too much and paying rapt attention to his carefully constructed sales pitch.

He was, as always, the hero of his own stories, the long-suffering good guy who overcame endless trials and tribulations to stumble haplessly into immeasurable success.

Brenda drew him out, offering a sympathetic ear and a noncritical audience for his self-serving narrative. She wanted to see how long it would take before he realized he was self-aggrandizing, but he went on and on without appearing to discern how ridiculously adolescent he sounded. She leaned forward, her eyes wide and blank and fixed on his endlessly spewing mouth.

If she were a con artist, she'd zero in on Dan Miller. He was all hot air and ego, too self-absorbed to assess other people with clarity. He was, to all appearances, successfully building up his business to an ambitious degree. It didn't take too close an examination to find cracks in the foundation.

He was insufficiently astute to anticipate market needs, too shortsighted to build his most important asset—his personnel—out of quality candidates. He hired the cheapest muscle-bound idiots he could find, instead of paying fifteen percent more to get experienced, well-trained veterans. He saturated the relatively limited home and business security markets with enticingly low-priced introductory contracts that expired after a year.

A customer who wanted to renew that contract found himself paying more for each subsequent year. Having paid for the installation of the equipment, clients were unlikely to drop the contract for the first few renewals. It all seemed like a sound plan for rooking people out of their hard-earned dollars. But from what Darius Brown had found, customers tended to drop his service in the fourth or fifth year, by which time they were paying nearly thirty percent more than in the first year. Then they would never do business with him again.

It didn't seem like a formula that would lead to long-term success, but maybe Miller would move on to another new field when he'd burned all his bridges in this one. He'd done that several times before. She was far less interested in the shelf life of his doomed business venture than what inroads he'd made in her city's government and police department. She was also interested in his expenditures, as uncovered by Darius Brown. Who was on his payroll? Who was his lackey in the Briarwood Police Department?

He had not one but two yachts, one berthed at Green Hand Marina and one at his mansion's private dock off the northern point known locally and colloquially as Snob Hill. The smaller of his oversized crafts was large enough to sail around the world. She had to wonder why he needed a floating city berthed by his palatial home. Miller owned several strip clubs in Briarwood. Could he be hosting parties at which the exotic dancers were expected to accommodate the desires of his male guests?

Finally, after a particularly long exposition on his own brilliance, he seemed to run out of air. He gulped half his beer and looked restlessly around the room. He'd bored himself, she realized.

"Wow," she said, grinning idiotically at her dinner companion, "I'm in awe. You've really thought this through."

Cocking his head at her, he puffed up like a preening rooster. "I've always been good at seeing the big picture," he bragged. "Most people can't do that."

"It's true," she murmured. "Can I ask a question?"

"Sure, sure," he said blithely. "Whatever you want, ask."

"What percentage of your budget do you spend on personnel?"

He narrowed his eyes. "Why are you asking me that?"

She widened her eyes, lifted her voice to a girlish whisper. "I just feel like in the department, I'm constantly running up against budget constraints. I can't help but notice we spend so much of our budget on things the unions demand."

This launched him into a diatribe against unions, labor and the greed and laziness of the officers and people in general.

"They don't appreciate what they've got," she said in a sympathetic tone.

"They're leeches, every one of them," he announced, his tone strident and his pitch awkwardly high. He was red and splotchy, his eyes snapping. He slammed his beer bottle on the table with a too-loud bang. "The city won't listen to me, even though I'm the expert here. My taxes—I make more money than anybody in this little town, and it's my money they're spending. They could save a lot of my hard-earned money if they didn't have to coddle all these so-called public servants and—"

"But we need police officers, firefighters, teachers—"

"Sure, sure, sure, but I could do all of it for half the cost, less, and save taxpayers like me millions! Then there's a whole huge amount of the population that's useless. They just sit on their asses and leech off the money you and I pay in taxes. You know that? Welfare queens, drug addicts, immigrants, convicted felons, all them—they won't work hard, so they can't make it, so they just sit back and roll in our money, and we let them! We pay them to be useless! I don't have kids, but my money pays for schools. Why should I pay for that? I don't take drugs, but my money pays for drug rehab for junkies. I don't need birth control, so why should I pay for it? Why should I pay a single dollar for something people chose?"

"You feel used," she said gently, her tone and expression sympathetic and encouraging.

"Damned right I feel used! And so should you! There're maybe a hundred, maybe two hundred people in this whole town who are worth anything. The rest are illegals, criminals, homeless, fat, lazy, worthless. They just sit back and enjoy the good life on our dime, and the decent people break our backs trying to help them. What for? What do we owe them? Nothing."

"How would you make it better? If you could change how things are?"

He nodded, steepling his hands in front of him and staring at her with an evangelical light in his eyes.

"Look at my company," he said, his tone suddenly dropping into what she guessed he thought was professorial register. "I took my money that I earned from the sweat of my brow, and I invested it. American dream, that's me. I was smart about it. I've always been smarter than other people, and that's just how it is. You know, you're smarter than other people. You're almost as smart as me, which is saying something, believe me."

She manufactured a blush and nodded at him to continue. She knew the money he referred to was comprised of his father's loans, gifts, and estate.

"Once I had enough capital and a few investors, I moved forward."

"How did you find investors?"

"They approached me. Said they heard I was some kind of financial genius. I had other things I was doing. People wanted me to be a professional athlete, an actor, a movie producer. I almost ran for office. I had a million options, but these guys needed somebody like me. They said I was the only one who could do it."

"Wow," she said. Thanks to Darius Brown, she knew he'd squandered over twenty million dollars the first decade after his father's death.

Then he teamed with another huckster to form a pyramid scheme that bilked elderly investors out of their money. His old partner fled the country under the cloud of a dozen warrants. Miller made some kind of deal, and a handful of his employees went to federal prison in his stead. Darius thought part of the deal was Miller had to stay out of banking, finance, and real estate. It was then he started up Watchdogs.

He offered a modest grin. "I have so much money, believe me, it's amazing. I was still trying to decide what I wanted to do with my capital. And one of the guys—these guys were eating out of my palm, okay?—one of the guys suggested I buy this little security firm. It was maybe ten guys, working a few little contracts, and their boss ran it into the ground. I rescued them. I mean, at the time it was an act of charity. I hated to see these guys out of work. Veterans, you know? Once you've been on the front line, you have a bond."

She knew he'd spent two years at military school as an adolescent but had never served his country in any branch of the military. She also knew the original owner of Watchdogs, Tim Lancaster, was a retired police officer. He paid good wages and kept overhead to a minimum. Then Lancaster's wife got pancreatic cancer and he gutted his business trying to save her.

When Lancaster was desperate, when he was flying all over the world trying to find a way to save his wife, Miller came in and took advantage of his desperation. Miller was a parasite and he had the audacity to play the hero. She masked her disgust and listened to him boast about rescuing the floundering former owner.

"So, you really saved the company," she murmured.

"Oh, yeah. I mean, I didn't even want it, but then I had to help the guy out."

"So kind," she said, her tone low and admiring.

The idiot blushed and offered a shy grin. Had his hair been long enough, he'd have tugged on a forelock.

"So I'm pretty savvy. I know what I'm doing, you know, and I built it up great. Now it's practically an empire. You've seen it. We're everywhere!"

She nodded, her smile vacuous and her eyes reflecting nothing but admiration. "It's really impressive," she said. "I don't know how to ask this, but I do have a question."

Like every con man, he was overconfident and therefore both cynical and naïve. He fell for this bit of manipulation without a fight.

"I bet you have a few questions."

They shared a laugh, as though the moron had said something clever. He snapped his fingers at the waiter and demanded another beer for himself. "And the lady will switch to white wine."

She grinned as if she liked his imperious manner. "Thank you."

He gave a lordly nod. "So, first of all, yes, I am the brains behind this operation. Yes, I really am as rich as I seem. Yes, I really do run the business myself. People tell me," he said, leaning forward and tapping the table with his index finger, "I am the heart of the operation. The men look to me for guidance on everything. I can't be weak or indecisive or, or, or anything like that." He sat back. "It's a burden, honestly. It weighs on me."

She made a sympathetic face and waited him out.

"It's just the beginning, you know. I mean, sure, I've been successful here, obviously. We've done great. A lot of men would be happy with achieving what I have. A lot of men."

"But you're not a lot of men."

He laughed, throwing his head back. He was giddy with glee over her attention, and for a moment she felt sorry for him. He was so easily manipulated that she felt predatory playing with him. Then she remembered why she was doing this. She needed him to let down his guard so she could learn about his possible involvement with Donnelly's death.

He pointed at her, nearly knocking over the wineglass the waiter was just setting down. "You see it. You get it. That's why I've always been interested in bringing you over to my side. You get it."

She smiled and lowered her eyes demurely, thinking as she did so that straight women had it easy in at least one way. A lot of men were astoundingly gullible.

Michael Morgan glided up to their table on cue, his dark hair shining in the soft glow of the restaurant he'd made over.

"Michael," said Miller expansively, "allow me to introduce Captain Brenda Borelli."

His expression untroubled, Michael nodded and shook her hand. They exchanged a quick look and she knew he'd play along.

"Always a pleasure to meet one of Mr. Miller's friends. I hope your dinner is perfection. If it's not, please alert me right away, and please, enjoy dessert on me, will you? Mr. Miller, I see you're looking a little thirsty. Someone will be right here. Enjoy your evening."

As Michael eased away, Miller beamed and examined her expression.

"You'll get used to it. Wherever I go, people always suck up to me. I don't ask for that kind of thing. I don't need it, but people can smell power. They naturally try to get me to like 'em, and I don't mind it."

She made sure to look dazzled, and the Watchdogs CEO seemed satisfied.

"You know everyone," she murmured. "And they all know you."

"You're right. I can get this company in place to take over law enforcement, code enforcement, fire patrol, hell, why not the parks too? Get a few girls in, take over city hall, the schools too—millions, billions of dollars. But it's bigger than that. Why not change the way the whole state does business? California has a huge economy, enormous amounts of money. Believe me, if we could stop paying these damned lazy public employees their ridiculous salaries, we could save taxpayers billions every year!"

"Wow!" Brenda whispered the word.

"Right? And why not the whole country? People like you and me, we're special, Brenda—we're the engine that moves this country. We need to decide we're tired of taking their shit. We deserve to be successful. The reality is, they need us to guide them. A lot of people tell me I should drive this train."

Brenda gaped at Miller.

"I mean it. They're sheep. Do you let sheep run wild in the, the wilderness? No, you get a sheep herder to tell them where to go. They're happier like that. They need someone to guide them. You and I are sheep herders. And we deserve to profit from that. Don't we?"

She allowed a hint of skepticism to show on her face.

"I know, I know." He sat back, gazing fondly at her. "You feel sorry for 'em. I get it. I used to feel sorry for them too. But if you look at them, they're idiots. Take my guys you tricked into letting you in to Watchdogs."

She had the grace to look embarrassed. "Yeah, about that—"

"No, no," he said, waving off what he clearly assumed was an impending apology. "I get it. You used your superior intellect to manipulate them into doing what you wanted. You had a job to do, and that's that."

The air was thick with his ego and his cynicism, and Brenda hid her relief when the waiter brought the seafood specials to their table. He suspended his asseveration to smack his lips and exclaim over the bounty of the sea. She hid her revulsion and moved things around on her giant platter as he gobbled shrimp and scallions and lobster. He smacked his lips, drooled on his chin, spewed bits of mussel and cod and rice and crab. He caught her watching him and grinned broadly, displaying bits of food in his teeth and clinging to his lips. He was shiny with grease from his fleshy cheekbones to his tight collar.

"It's amazing, right? I bet you could never afford to get this kind of thing on a cop's salary. But it's my treat. Go ahead, enjoy!"

"Thank you. I suppose you know why I met with Mason Harding?"

"I assume it's normal procedure. I know a lot about police work, of course. I have a certain background. I can't talk about it, naturally. I can only say I've served my country in ways they don't give medals for."

She smiled and forked a tiny amount of rice, wondering if she'd ever be able to eat seafood again without seeing his oily, gaping maw. Did he really imagine she'd believe he was some kind of super spy?

After several minutes of noisy, messy grubbing, he gave a loud cry of triumph and pushed his platter away, displacing the tablecloth and nearly knocking her wineglass onto her lap. She caught it in time and pretended to take a sip.

"Never overeat," he said, flicking his greasy hand at his half-empty plate. "That's the key. Enjoy, savor, all of that, but know when to stop."

She smiled again. "Good advice."

She laid down her fork and blotted her lips.

"You've told me things need to change. But how do we make it better? What can we do?" She leaned forward, her eyes fixed on his florid, sweaty face.

"That's it, right? That's the key. That's what makes us different from the animals. The answer is, we work together. We go behind the scenes and pull the strings without advertising what we're doing."

"But how do you know who to trust?"

Miller clapped his hands three times, pausing between each clap. "So that's where I come in. I have two gifts. One is, I know people. It's a gift. It's just always been like that. I know when somebody's worth my time and when he's not. You notice I'm not asking John Vallejo to dinner. I asked you. Why? Because I know you're worth my time. My time is valuable. You wouldn't believe how much I'm worth."

She smiled again, wondering if she looked as mechanical as she felt.

"Plus, I use the latest in technology. Bleeding edge, all the way. I have cameras everywhere in this town. I know how to hire the best, only the best people. I watch everything that happens in this town. I know who goes where and when, and why. I look to see who's cheating on the wife in the wrong part of town, women, drugs. I know all the secrets. And if I have to push on people a little, I do it for the good of the city."

"I have a question, but I'm not sure if it's okay to ask."

"Anything," he said, with a magnanimous smile. "Anything at all."

"Did anyone notice what Donnelly was doing? The extortion?"

"No."

"When he was leaving Briarwood, do you have any footage of that?"

"No."

"Do you think he died by suicide, accident or murder?"

Miller shifted in his seat and shrugged.

"He murdered Tami Sheraton, who was an innocent. His death was no great loss to society."

"Why are you asking me about this?"

"We're talking about how your company can make Briarwood safer. Using recent crimes seems like a reasonable test of that theory. If you were already doing the police work, would this all have happened?"

"I see what you're doing!" Miller laughed raucously. "I said you were smart. You're right, none of this would've happened on my watch. I assume everyone's a crook. That way, I can watch them all. Everyone's watching everyone else, and they all report to me. I'm the top of this heap, and I can shape the world the way it should be. Things have changed for the worse, and I can turn back the clock and make this town what it used to be."

"Can you really do that, turn back the clock?"

"Your department is full of men with secrets, and so is city hall. The state legislature is full of crooks and cheaters and gamblers and drug addicts. You'd be amazed at the things I know. And I use that power to make things better for people. That's all I do, try to make things right."

"Wow."

"I have plans for you. I want you to stay where you are. Trust me, there's gonna be some big, big shakeups. I want someone I can trust at the top of the heap when it all shakes out. I want you to be our first female police chief."

"Can you really make all of that happen? I mean, I don't mean to sound—"

"Yes." Miller stared hard at her. "I can make you the new chief. But I need to know you'll play ball with me. I need to know you'll remember who your friends are."

She nodded. "Why me? Why not Tori?"

"I thought about her. But I don't trust her like you."

"You have no reason to trust me."

He grinned widely. "Remember what I said? You have to listen. I have the gift. I can see into people. Tori Young is pretty and smart and sexy and slick. But she looks out for herself first. I need someone who can come in, lead the way, and remember who her friends are. I know I can count on you to keep your promises."

She sat back. "You've given me a lot to think about."

He nodded vigorously. "I'll give you two days to think it over. Then we'll meet for dinner again and I'll expect an answer. My house, you been there? No, no, you'll love it. It's the best house in town. Needless to say, this discussion stays between the two of us. Our little secret, right?"

She echoed his nodding. "I want to thank you, Mr. Miller. You've given me a great compliment."

He smiled expansively. "You're right. You're definitely right. I told you. I know people!"

"One quick thing," she said, smiling coquettishly at the man across from her, "I need to know."

"Anything," said Miller, with only a trace of doubt in his booming voice.

"Just like you need to trust me, I need to trust you and the other people on our team. So who is on our team?"

Miller narrowed his eyes. "You don't need to know that."

"I disagree. If you want me to lead this department, I need to know who my friends are. Who our friends are."

"I'll tell you, that's what I like. You're a straight shooter." Miller shrugged. "What the hell? Two of the commissioners. One of the other captains. The chief. Two city council guys. The mayor. Both guys in Sacramento. All mine."

"Names." She stared at his bloodshot eyes until he broke contact. "You said not Tori. Give me two others that aren't yours. If I can't figure out which commissioners you own, you shouldn't hire me."

He straightened his collar with a wry grin. "Olivares is not one of mine. Neither is Banks."

"Okay. When I come to dinner I'll name the two you recruited."

"Well, then, we're halfway to the altar, you and me!" He yanked out his wallet and threw a handful of twenty-dollar bills on the table, winking at her. He stood and watched her rise.

"Thanks for the compliment and for dinner," she said.

He gestured at her to lead the way to the entrance. As she moved forward, he pulled out his phone and, staring at it, pushed past her. He stopped short, blocking the doorway. She stifled her irritation and waited as he jabbed at his screen.

"I'm happy to share the wealth, Brenda, just remember that. As long as you play nice with me, I'll play nice with you." And finally he was gone.

She trailed out of the front door after him and watched him yell into his phone as he roared off in his Land Rover, nearly running down a pair of elderly women on the way.

She escaped to her car, head pounding and stomach churning. She sat in the stillness of the Caliber for a few minutes to clear her head. She peered up at the night sky and saw only gloom. Thick clouds obscured her view of the moon and stars, and somehow that seemed to her fitting. She felt obscured by a cloud of revulsion. Then she took the short way home and, sick with disgust, yanked off her clothes by the hamper so she could drop them directly into it.

Their very fabric seemed stained by exposure to her noxious dinner companion. She took a quick shower to clean the evening off her skin and clear her head. She'd barely made it back to the master bedroom when her phone vibrated.

"You little slut!" Tori's voice was high with laughter. "Michael called me. He said you practically humped Miller on the table. What are you up to?"

"He's easy to play," she said, allowing herself a small smile. "But this isn't over yet."

"No, I know, but it will be soon. And then—"

"And then we'll see." She chewed her lip. "One thing at a time, okay?"

"Yeah." Tori sounded subdued now. "Of course."

"Thanks. For your help and your patience. I know I'm not always easy to deal with."

There was a long silence and then Tori laughed. "Nobody interesting is."

CHAPTER FIFTEEN

The texts and emails poured in over the next few hours. Peterson's diner pals had put together a dossier on each of the city leaders and department brass, providing surprisingly thorough details of their financial and social obligations and resources. She was stunned to find out how many of the city's movers and shakers were overextended. The recession had hit many of them harder than appearances suggested.

Unlike many other city leaders, the mayor was reassuringly solvent. He had a fat portfolio of blue chip stocks and only a miniscule percentage of his investments were even moderately risky. He also came from an old money family not unlike Shay's. The Sheratons were also in excellent shape, having used the recession to snap up both real estate and stocks at bargain prices. Three of the city council members, including the chair, were similarly well situated.

Several individuals of consequence in the district attorney's office, the police department, the planning office, and the big-money circle were of much greater interest. They were, almost to a man, on far shakier ground. Illicit affairs with rather desperate women and men, gambling debts, drug abuse, shady business practices and scores of secrets—it was an embarrassing wealth of evidence.

Staggered by the amount of data, she created a spreadsheet to quantify the strengths and weaknesses of the town's elite. Even in politically and socially moderate Northern California, the power structure excluded women almost entirely. There were two women on the city council, but there was no evidence they had any particular sources of weakness. One of them had a teenage son with a drug problem, but it had not yet reached the stage of catastrophic consequences. The other drank too much, but she was still functioning successfully.

Miller had not exaggerated the vulnerability of Briarwood's leaders. Between the sex scandals, shady deals, gambling debts, poor investments, drug and alcohol abuse and shortsighted spending habits, the city's elite were practically begging to be blackmailed and extorted. She assigned each vulnerability a numerical value, based on how damaging public disclosure would be. Given the wealth of secrets delineated before her, she had to do a lot of math.

She was stunned by the amount of information the diner crew had collected. For nearly every rumor, tidbit of family history and conjecture, there was a body of documentation to back it up. She shook her head and laughed. She'd assumed Peterson's pals would offer unsubstantiated gossip, but she'd underestimated the men badly. To be sure, she fact-checked the more important data, and it was consistently reliable.

Reviewing her conversation with Miller, she tried to decide which of the commissioners he'd insisted did not dance to his tune. One of them was likely to be crooked, she thought, based on the salesman's limited intellect. She examined their columns on her spreadsheet. Olivares was cheating on his wife and had put a second mortgage on his house to finance his twins' college tuitions. But for many years he'd stolidly saved his money, paid his bills on time and lived his upper-middle-class life with care. His vulnerability score was three.

Walton was cheating on his wife with a woman young enough to be his daughter, and he lived well beyond his means. He'd done so for decades and had somehow managed every several years to pay off his considerable debts with a sudden and generous infusion of cash from ill-defined sources. He gambled via the stock market, and it was entirely possible some of his higher-risk investments had actually paid off. She gave Walton a vulnerability score of eight.

Banks's bad habits were numerous: driving expensive cars recklessly, engaging in multiple adulterous affairs with dangerously young women, spending too much on bespoke suits, overpriced clothes, gobbling great quantities of rich food, and falling for get-rich-quick schemes. Worst of all, he continued to tunnel further and further in debt by trying to hide the fact his long-suffering wife had essentially cut him off financially some years back. Her family's substantial money and holdings were held in trust for her and for their children, and good old Marty got only a modest stipend for the rest of his working life.

Once he retired, he'd be stuck with his pension and whatever money he'd managed to acquire on his own. If the couple divorced, he got nothing. If his wife predeceased him, he got nothing. Yet he'd saved nothing. He'd spent, lost and failed to capitalize on truckloads of money. Banks had a vulnerability score of eleven.

And on it went. By midnight she had nine good suspects, three of them inside the department. She continued to assess each one, examining the behavioral patterns with care. She looked at each of them as an opportunist might. If she wanted to corrupt the department, if she wanted to burrow inside the power structure of the city that was already straining under its burgeoning growth, how would she do it?

An image came to her then of an innocent-looking cotton boll taken over from the inside by weevil larvae. The burrowing pests were protected from insecticides and predators by the cotton's own structural integrity. There would be a mark somewhere on the outer layers of the boll, small but visible to the keen eye. As she eyeballed the spreadsheet on which she'd recorded the information and her evaluation thereof, she felt like an exterminator examining a cotton boll. A healthy boll would be most appealing because the cotton fibers would provide food for the larvae. How did the weevil know which boll was best? She wouldn't go where another mother had already been. She would not choose one likely to attract predators.

"Okay, little cotton bolls, which one did this weevil pick? Or which ones, maybe."

She put herself in the place of each individual and imagined all the ways things might have happened. She sat on the sofa with her legs stretched out under the coffee table, her cell phone plugged in and resting beside her hand. It was closing time at the local bars when she gave in to her exhaustion, leaned her head back and closed her eyes.

She awoke as the morning's first thin rays started peeking through the heavy clouds. She checked her phone but saw no missed calls. That was a good sign. It meant no one had encountered one of the troublesome contradictions she had anticipated might arise.

She felt surprisingly well rested and hoped that was a sign she'd done enough to prepare for the day. It was going to be a busy one, and if she was mistaken it would be busy for no good reason. An hour later she was in her disguise, with a backpack full of kit on the passenger seat. She called Andi to ask a favor and then drove to the boardwalk.

She borrowed Lauren's old Volvo, which Andi kept parked at the public lot in case of emergencies. A quick thank-you text later, she began surveillance on her first subject. She made meticulous notes, going over and over her theory to ensure she wasn't missing anything.

She sat in the Volvo in front of Nic's Knacks, a tourist trap a few doors down from Dave's Bistro. She'd chosen the spot because the owner of the kitsch shop updated her website weekly, and Brenda knew what day she spent compiling the new photographs. She figured the retailer was too busy on this particular morning taking pictures of the current wares to notice the salt-pitted sedan parked in front of her store. A blond wig, bright pink lipstick, and oversized sunglasses were enough to disguise her identity. She fit in with the other window shoppers as she examined the overstuffed display from the sidewalk.

The thickening clouds made using the window reflections tricky, but she took her time and eyed each passerby. Still, she was able to see no one she was looking for. Glancing up, she wondered if the coming rain would interfere with her plan. A short circuit up and down tourist row netted her an overpriced bag of peanuts and a view of her quarry entering Dave's. Without reacting to the sight, she ambled back to her car and ate peanuts while feigning interest in something on her phone.

When her subject finally exited the popular eatery two hours later, she smiled to see his companion. Dave's Saturday morning brunch was always booked well in advance, especially this time of year when the weather was usually fine. That thought made her look up to see the storm she'd smelled was just starting to coalesce. The air was heavy and thick under the ominous daytime gloom.

The brunch companions shook hands and parted ways, and she followed her new subject's very nice car to Livingston Plaza, only a quarter mile away. The crowd was even bigger than usual at the plaza's weekly farmers market and at the nearby boardwalk on this late Saturday morning, despite the turbulent weather. She wondered if locals had been inspired to visit the fun parts of town by the food truck festival.

A few sprinkles dropped here and there, and at a gust of wind dozens of faces turned up to examine the clouds. There were umbrellas over many arms, she was glad to see, and someone had erected a series of large open-air tents over the benches and picnic tables. The wind was just beginning to whip the flapping canvas. A particularly strong gust rocked the Volvo back and forth, and she hoped the weather wouldn't overcome her timeline.

The call she was waiting for came after several minutes sitting, parked and impatient, in Andi's merchant spot. The darkened sky and low-hanging mist helped render her nearly invisible, and she watched her caller while she answered his phone call.

"Brenda Borelli speaking," she said, her tone light.

"Do you know who this is?"

"What can I do for you, Commander?"

"I'd like to see you on the QT."

"Sure, of course," she said, trying not to smile. "What'd you have in mind?"

"I have a boat," said Banks, his voice too casual. Wind blasted the microphone of his cell phone, and she squinted at the intrusive sound. He ran his fingers through his thinning hair when the wind ruffled it again. He looked up at the sky in what appeared to be consternation. His jowls shook as if in outrage.

"In this weather?"

"Don't tell me you're worried about a little rain?"

"Nooo," she said, drawing the word out to demonstrate uncertainty.

"Good, good," he said, loudly jovial. "In an hour?"

"Okay, where?"

"Green Hand."

"Right." She was all too familiar with the north end of the docks, the exclusive area named for a jutting rock formation painted by a verdant crop of algae and ice plant. Everyone in the upscale sailing club known as Wharf Rats had a berth in Green Hand Marina, with proximity to the slimy rock a strange status marker.

"Berth 16. Prestige. *Blue Skies.*"

"Yes, sir. I'm intrigued."

"Good." Whatever else he said was swallowed by the flapping of tent fabric near him, and she watched him stuff his phone back in his pocket and hustle toward his Mercedes, parked in one of six blue-painted spots near the entrance to Livingston Plaza. She knew he had no placard, and neither did his wife.

She disconnected and took a deep breath. Only a few more moves and this chess game would be over. Reaching into her backpack, she pulled out two keys on a leather cord. She'd put the keys on a red ribbon in a gift box seven months earlier for Tori's birthday gift. Earlier that morning she'd taken the keys off the pretty red ribbon and replaced it with a black leather cord. She slipped the aborted gift on her neck and zipped her jacket over the adornment. The keys were cold through her shirt, and she swallowed hard.

"Suck it up, cupcake," she admonished herself. "Moving on." She called Big Henry. "Any joy, sir?"

"I emailed you another file. The fellas are pretty pleased with themselves. We all are. I think we got what you need."

"How? I mean, thanks. The info from last night was very helpful. I'm going to have to know where it came from at some point." She put him on speakerphone and opened the email.

"Stan's little brother is a judge. We ran our methodology past him, to be sure we were clean. It all had to be from verifiable, legal, publicly available sources. We put it in a story, like you said. Just Henry followed the money, like you said. You're very good at this. Peterson—he always said you were a sharp cookie."

"Thanks. Let's hope we can hear him say it in person again soon. I'll check in when it's all done. My thanks to the guys."

When her phone vibrated in her hand as she disconnected, she saw Shay Sheraton had texted her a picture taken from under one of the big tents across the street. The temporary midway was still open, but the photo showed vendors shuttering their trucks and taking down their booths on the banks of a river of attendees fleeing for their cars.

Timing is everything, right?

She smiled wryly and sent a text congratulating Shay on the festival beating the storm. Without letting herself think about it too much, she added an invitation to dinner for the following Friday night.

I'd love to.

She sat staring down at the screen for a good ten seconds before she promised to call Shay later in the day to nail down the details. Would this really all be resolved by then? Would Peterson be back with his friends for daily breakfast at the diner? Would Staci Smith be home with her daughter? And Teresa Fortune, would she get back to her life? When her phone rang, she knew it was Tori.

"The fish is nibbling."

"Already?"

"Greed is impatient, I guess."

Tori snorted. "True enough. Anything I should know?"

"Go to your office and be near the phone."

"Really? Shall I bake you a cake while I'm waiting for you to do the heavy lifting?"

"You should be the one to take the call."

"Where will you be?"

"Green Hand. You know it, I assume. Don't come here unless I tell you, and don't send anyone here. This will only work if everything goes perfectly."

"You always hated the idea of getting a boat and joining Wharf Rats. Now here you are, traipsing off to Green Hand like the fancy folk."

"Just do it, okay? Stay in your office. Don't even go to the restroom. Trust me, you'll be glad."

"Okay. I promise." Tori laughed. "I need specifics if I'm going to help you."

She thought about that. "You'll need to testify that you didn't know anything. You were humoring me, out of consideration for the many years of good service I have given Briarwood. Anyway, thanks for your help. I've really leaned on you, and you've been incredible."

"I don't like that you won't let me—"

"I need you in your office. I can handle what I need to, but I need you to keep that Crisis Response Team at least a block or two away until I say it's time. Please."

Tori said something more, but a series of monstrous gusts ripped through the air, and the call was lost. She grimaced and glanced at Livingston Plaza. Though it had only been a few minutes, the crowd had dispersed and flooded the parking lots. The food trucks were already closed and forming a line near the south exit. Vendors and volunteers worked frantically to tear down the remaining tents and booths.

As she watched, a williwaw tore one of the large tents free of its moorings and yanked it. The huge bundle of vinyl and about half of its poles flew over Wave Street toward the boardwalk.

There were a few screams, and several drivers skidded to a panicked stop. The kiting vinyl had already changed direction. It dove toward one of the departing food trucks and then puffed up and drifted almost gently to the ground in a crumpled heap.

Workers scrambled to disassemble the wayward tent and bundle it up. As she watched, she debated jogging around the boardwalk to check on Andi. The impulse tugged at her, but she knew the steel storm shutters Lauren had installed would protect her better than Brenda could. She ducked back into the Volvo, straightened her wig and zipped past the impending traffic snarl.

Shay would be one of the last to leave Livingston Plaza, but that wasn't something she could worry about. Shay had been driving on her own for many years without Brenda to check up on her. The woman had sailed around Australia or something like that and could surely handle a little storm in Briarwood without her help. She had to get to Green Hand before Banks.

After a slow, lurching ramble up Wave Street, she parked in the elevated employee lot of the Wharf Rats country club, which was an inconvenient distance from the docks but which was sheltered by several overgrown oaks and had, she noticed as she pushed her way out of the wind-rocked Volvo for the second time in minutes, one of the best views in Briarwood.

She grinned to herself as she looked down in wonder at the vista enjoyed by the dishwashers, servers, janitors, bartenders, gift-shop cashiers, and office personnel who catered to the sailing-club snobs whose luxury vehicles were parked down behind the upscale sailing club near the Dumpsters. She eyed the lower, closer, more crowded lot. Midday on Saturday was a busy time at the sailing club, and that would help her.

Evading the customer lot, she ducked down the sandy trail on the other side of the Dumpsters. The trail was used by the workers and ran between overgrown oleanders and utility sheds. She grinned at a hopping sparrow that cocked its head at her before disappearing into the hedge.

She hurried down the damp hill, sliding here and there. As the sand yielded to a rough concrete walkway, she jogged toward the service entrance of the club's bar, Rats' Nest, whose cedar shingles rattled and screamed in the wind as the first real raindrops swatted everything in sight.

Hurrying toward the humble service corridor in a black-hooded raincoat, she was rendered invisible by both perceived station and by her head-to-thigh waterproof. She paused to see no one was watching before she scurried surreptitiously under the pier that held aloft The Nest, as the highbrow members called it. The surf was higher here, where the shoreline started curving west toward the mouth of the bay, and she crossed under the pier with waves knocking into her legs.

She was soaked from spray, even under her rain jacket, by the time she reached the underside of the pier. She crept, dripping and shivering, down the sandy slope away from the surf and toward open sky, where fat drops plopped loudly on the beach and her slicker.

She stuffed her dripping, ruined wig in her jacket pocket and pushed her self-examination aside. She snaked along under the porch of The Nest, her back to the exterior of the clubhouse, and slowed her breathing. She would have to be quick and invisible now.

She could hear music above and behind her and hoped the privileged patrons were following their tippling tradition. An inebriated crowd listening to loud music was unlikely to notice her. She was just starting to feel confident of her inconspicuousness when a man in a dark green rain suit came around the corner she'd just turned herself. She gaped up at him as he trudged toward her. His features were hidden by his anorak's hood and by a bushy gray-brown beard.

She felt her nostrils flare and her muscles tense, and she turned slightly to a more advantageous angle, shifting her weight and easing up her jacket so she could reach her weapon more easily. Then she relaxed and grinned.

"Jorge?"

"Miss Borelli, are you okay?' Maggie's husband gaped at her. "I saw you go around, and I didn't know who you were. I thought you might need help."

She put her finger to her lips and winked at Jorge, and he raised his bushy eyebrows. She grinned at him until he shrugged and strode past her as if she weren't there. Say what you will, she thought, the man can take a hint.

After Jorge went on his way, she saw no one. Boats scraped and banged against the docks as they danced on the surging, dipping, frothy waters. Buffeted by sea and gale, the pier creaked and groaned. To reassure herself, she placed a hand numb with cold against one of the thick, weathered pilings. It felt solid, but she wasn't thrilled with what she now had to do.

North of the pier was Green Hand Marina, where Banks moored his fifty-foot yacht, *Blue Skies*, a mere twenty yards from where her more humble cruiser, *Bernice*, had sat ignored for the last seven months.

Between her and Banks's luxury craft was a universe of crashing waves, blowing debris, bouncing boats and seesawing shrubbery. The denizens of the clubhouse were no doubt watching the churning surf and keeping an eye on their pricey watercraft, and she would have to get past all of them unnoticed.

She eyeballed the route, adjusting and refining until she could see the best way to go unnoticed. The four finger slips were several yards apart, ranged along the gently curving shoreline north of the clubhouse. She took a deep breath, glanced around at the darkened recesses of the pier's bottom and darted across the beach, almost immediately falling when a williwaw knocked her over as easily as if she were made of paper. Cursing softly, she crouched down and staggered along the wet, firm sand nearer the waterline.

The storm buffeted her as she pushed along on the churning shoreline, past the deserted finger piers to the last one. At the locked gate she fumbled to unzip her jacket with her cold, wet, unfeeling hands. Then it took painfully long seconds to grasp the gate key and force her shaking fingers to find the lock and jam the rarely used key into it. The gate, once unlocked, swung wide when caught by the next gust of wind, and she glanced toward the clubhouse.

The power was out, she realized, not only at The Nest but all along the coast. In the gloom of the storm, with mist and low clouds and falling rain obscuring the world, an electrical outage would slow down the whole city. People would look outside, left and right and up and down. It was a natural impulse, and it put her plan at risk. She yanked at the tall iron gate and forced it shut it behind her. Crouching low despite the protests of her knees and hips, she raced as quickly as she could on wet, frozen feet toward her goal.

Seven minutes later she was done with her preparations and back at the gate. She locked it behind her and scrambled over the pebbled patch that led to the shortcut she'd discovered earlier. Between the oleanders and the storage sheds, back to her car she went, struggling up the hill against streaming rivulets that threatened her footing. Finally she was back at Lauren's old car, stripping down there in the windblown parking lot and tossing her sodden clothes into a trash bag she pitched toward the backseat.

She crawled in, pulling the hatchback down as she kneeled in the back of the car. She toweled off and threw on her next costume, including an expensive purse she'd never used. She texted Tori and said a prayer her plan would work. If it didn't, she would end up in a pretty bad spot and would fail to save Peterson and the two women who'd been kidnapped.

She was four minutes late for her meeting with Banks when she parked next to his Mercedes in the customer parking lot of The Nest. He was in his car, obviously waiting for her. She slipped from the Volvo into the passenger seat of his Mercedes, turning to smile at him.

Her hair was wet and her cheeks flushed, but she was dressed better and smiling more broadly than he'd likely ever seen. She saw his attraction to her and was glad she'd taken the time to dig out her priciest red blouse and tailored trousers. Her bra had been too wet to wear, so she'd taken it off, and she saw him notice that too. She needed every advantage.

"Commander Banks," she said in a warm tone, extending a frozen hand.

Florid and bright-eyed, Banks crushed her hand and leaned forward to buss her icy cheek. She hid her shock and tilted her head to smile again.

"I'm late," she said, pulling away and making a rueful face. "Please forgive me?"

"I'm amazed you're here at all." His breath was hot with whiskey. "This storm is a nightmare. The traffic must have been terrible!"

She nodded. "Thanks for understanding. The lights are out all the way down. And you know people can't drive in the rain. Anyway, thanks for your call. I'm very curious about what you want to talk about."

"Are you okay with meeting on my boat? She's pretty large, so it should be fine. But if you're nervous—I'd just like to speak privately, and the car isn't very comfortable for a chat."

Feigning naiveté, she nodded. "I trust your judgment."

"Good, then let's hurry."

He led the way as they dashed along the protected north-side decking toward the pier. At the steep staircase that led to the beach, Banks hesitated. He turned to look down at her feet.

"Those aren't too spiky to go on the beach, are they?" His voice sounded small and thin in the roaring wind, and she shook her head rather than answering verbally.

He spun around and lurched down the stairs on what looked like stiff knees. His large body was top-heavy and his long gray coat was too tight across his shoulders and hips. He couldn't button it, she realized. It flapped around him like the ruffled feathers of a pigeon.

She took her time picking her way down, wanting to give the impression of feminine delicacy. Despite knowing her for two decades, he seemed ready to accept her seeming helplessness and daintiness. She finally reached the creaking bottom and took his arm.

"If you don't mind," she said, looking up at him in what she hoped looked like trust.

Whatever he said was lost in the wind, but she tightened her grip on his right arm and let him lead her toward the slip row. They stuck to the stone path, so she repeated the same trip she'd made only minute before with much greater ease. Back to the locked gate, back down the berth pier, all the way back to his luxury yacht.

Blue Skies looked like a toy in a bathtub, despite its length and weight. He nearly fell embarking but steadied himself after a moment's struggle. Looking apoplectic with effort, he nonetheless held out a gallant hand to escort her on board.

They slid across the wide, slippery aft deck to the cabin door. He yanked on it and hustled inside with Brenda right behind him. They huffed about the brutal weather and hung their coats on hooks.

"Whew!"

"Drink, Captain?"

"Please. Whatever you're having." She pushed her dripping hair off her face, thinking she might have skipped the two minutes she spent drying the droplets she'd shed during her solo trip to Banks's yacht. "Sorry, I'm making a mess of your floor."

"What can we do?" He laughed. "I did ask you to come out here during a monsoon."

"You don't lock this beautiful boat?"

He laughed and gestured toward one of the white leather benches as he pulled down the bar tray. "Usually I do, but I was out here this morning. Who's going to break in during a storm, anyway?"

"Good point," she conceded. "Wow, this is gorgeous!"

He beamed with pride and handed her a double whiskey in a beautiful cut-crystal highball glass. He sloshed a triple into his own glass and sipped at it delicately.

"She's my pride and joy," he said. "Someday I'll retire from this rat race and sail her around the world."

"Good for you," she said, eyeing the beautifully appointed lounge and galley. Even the second-highest officer in the department shouldn't have been able to afford such a craft. It had to cost at least ten times what she'd paid for her vessel. No wonder the man was drowning in debt. She let none of her thoughts show on her face and tried to look receptive and pleasant and nothing more.

He bragged about *Blue Skies* for a good ten minutes, showing off the carved fruitwood counters and tables, the plush cushioning on the benches and chairs, the fancy sonar and GPS and ergonomic instrument panel, the custom captain's chair and tinted windows. She murmured approvingly and let him ramble on. Finally, looming over her, he looked down at her upturned face and shook his jowls.

"I know what you must be wondering."

"I don't want to pry."

"My wife's family has some money, and she loves me very much. As I love her," he rushed to add. "We've been married twenty-seven years. Did you know that?"

"Wow, congratulations," she said, nodding.

"And I've always been very good with investments and so forth."

"Good for you." She grinned brainlessly. "It's important to be financially savvy."

"Indeed, it is." He drained his glass. "Which brings me to why I asked you here today."

She nodded and sobered. "Commander, I'm all ears."

"You and I haven't ever gotten close," he said. "I regret that. I'm afraid recent events may have driven a wedge between us."

She shook her head. "All you and I have ever done is our duty. We try to serve the people of this town as well as we can. Sometimes well-intentioned people see things differently, that's all. As I said before, I don't take it personally."

He nodded. "Good, that's the attitude. I'm glad to hear you feel that way."

She waited, sipping the smooth whiskey. The boat dipped starboard as a huge wave rocked it.

"Well, I'll get to it before we end up in San Diego." He laughed. "The world is changing, Captain Borelli."

"Brenda, please."

"Brenda. Personally I like the old way. I prefer the police department continue to serve the community, just like you were saying, and we maintain the high standard we've been setting all along. But that's not the way things are going. So we can lie back and get left behind, or we can get in on the ground floor of the changes and try to make things as good as possible for the civilians."

She tilted her head in a pantomime of curiosity.

He frowned at her. "You know Dan Miller, right?"

"Yes, in fact, I had dinner with him last night."

He nodded. "He likes you. I like you. We all do. And we'd like you to be Briarwood's next chief."

"He said, I'm sorry, but—he said you didn't work with him."

"Dan's cautious, as you might understand."

"I do." She swirled the whiskey in her glass and stared down at it. "What about Chief Walton?"

He stepped over to the bar tray, pouring himself another triple shot. He was surprisingly steady on his feet for a drunken man on a rocking boat.

"Walton is a politician. He was never real police. Not one of us. You've noticed it, haven't you? He knows how to say the right thing, how to play both sides against the middle. But he's not one of us."

She nodded in concession and waited him out.

"He also has some, ah, personal issues."

She frowned to hide any involuntary humor in her eyes at the irony of this man talking about someone else's personal issues. Walton was having an affair with a woman in her twenties, but otherwise appeared to be unblemished. In comparison to Banks and a startling number of his fellows, Walton was a choirboy.

"They may come to light or he might decide to retire. Either way, he'll be gone in the next year or two. I want you to take his place."

"Why me? Why not you or Tori or any of the other commanders?"

He waved his glass, spilling several drops of whiskey on the sofa and on Brenda. He loomed over her again, and she fought the impulse to back away when he leaned down to stare into her eyes. He was sweaty and flushed and glassy-eyed.

"You don't have to worry about that. All you have to do is your job. Look out for your friends. That's all. Can you do that?"

She nodded slowly, and he fell heavily onto the bench next to her when the boat tipped to starboard again. It was a smooth move, one that almost looked like an accident. When his hot hand landed on her knee, he left it there for several seconds before lifting it with a mischievous look.

"I wouldn't expect you to do anything illegal or immoral, of course." He laughed, the grimmest sound she had ever heard. She felt a stab of pity for the corrupt fool pressed against her side.

"I'm not making some kind of Faustian deal, right?"

"No, no, no, no!" He released his terrible laugh again, and she swallowed hard. It wasn't warm in the cabin of the boat, but she was uncomfortably hot anyway. He radiated heat and was pushed up against her and panting into her ear. "Of course not."

She grew tired of dancing around with the man whose hand had found its way back to her knee and whose spittle dotted her ear and check and neck.

"I'd feel more comfortable with more information, Commander, but I don't—"

"That's the thing, Captain. Brenda. Dan told you I don't work with him. But that's not strictly true. He's a cautious man. Like I said. As am I." His hand rubbed her thigh as if of its own accord.

She nodded and pretended she didn't want to punch him in the throat.

"Was that why Peterson had to get out of the way?"

For the first time, Banks looked worried. "I know he's important to you."

"Loyalty is very important, as I'm sure you'd agree. Still, I'm a realist," she said slowly. "Is he part of the team? Is he alive?"

"He shouldn't have been driving," he said. "He left himself vulnerable and then wanted to play coy. It was just one thing, a little thing, and he wouldn't do it. He's a fool."

His gaze drifted north, toward Miller's house and yacht, and she pretended not to notice he'd given away Peterson's location. Whether Miller was still keeping him and the other victims there or not, at some point they'd been in Miller's house or on his big luxury craft.

"Not everyone can adapt," she said, adopting a rueful expression.

"Adapt. Yes. Every piece has to be separate. You just have to do your job, and once in a while you'll be asked to take one position on an issue over another. Nothing big. Nothing ethically questionable, just opinion type of stuff. And you'll take the position you're supposed to take. Nothing bad will happen. You'll never be in a bad position, criminal, any of that. Just play ball, that's all. That doesn't sound so terrible, does it?"

"No," she mumbled. "I guess I'm not entirely clear about what kind of positions, what kind of opinions." She removed his hand from her hip, placed it on his thigh and patted it. "I imagine you had the same kinds of questions when you were approached."

"I did." He struggled to his feet and drained his glass for the second time. He looked at it for a second before shrugging and refilling it.

"I wouldn't want to kill someone."

Banks stared at her. "What do you mean?"

"Someone killed Donnelly. I know it. Was it you?"

Banks snorted. "Miller thinks it was the boyfriend. Marvin? Max?"

"Mason Harding." She sighed. "Did Miller point him at Donnelly?"

"I have no idea. Listen, this isn't some gangster bullshit. It's business, that's all. We're not criminals, Brenda. It's a matter of working with allies instead of alone. It just makes you more effective."

"To do what, exactly? I'm interested in working with friends and of course in being Briarwood's first female chief. And I definitely want to move with the times, but I need to know the plan before I sign the contact."

"Fix what's broken, that's all. Make things smoother for business. Once we pave the way for the job creators, the jobs will come pouring in. They want to hire people. They want to make money and contribute to this community. Rising tide, and all that. We just need to make it easier for them to pick Briarwood over some nowhere little city in Nevada or Arizona. Compensate for the higher taxes they'll pay in California.

Nobody will get hurt. Nobody loses out except the bums and illegals getting free government money. More for you and me and people like us who've paid our dues."

She shook her head. "I'm sorry, Commander, that's not good enough. I need an actual answer before I commit to anything. You and Miller give the same speech, but neither of you spelled it out for me. What exactly is the plan? What's my role, really? What are you really asking me to do?"

His sunny expression soured, and he smacked the edge of the sofa with the flat of his hand. The loud sound startled her, and she frowned up at her host.

"Why do you always make everything harder than it needs to be?"

She stared. He hit the nail on the head, she thought. That is exactly what I do.

"Either you play ball or you're in the way. Do you know what happens when you're in the way?"

She shifted in her seat as if to face Banks, who'd lurched toward the galley. When he turned to retrieve his Ruger from the first cupboard, she snagged her duty weapon from her waistband where it was hard to see under the lovely red blouse he admired so attentively.

When he turned around with the pistol in his hand, he seemed startled she had her own gun drawn.

"This is why the women should stay out of it," he said with a sneer. "What are the choices? We get the blond bimbo or the bitchy dyke? You ruin everything!"

He lunged toward her, pulling the trigger once, twice, three times before noticing the clip had been removed. He raised the revolver like a club as if to brain her, and she pointed her own weapon at his groin.

"Stop," she said in a low, loud voice. "Before I have to blow a hole in your lovely boat through you."

He tried to stop himself, but a wave tilted the boat starboard. He hollered as he tumbled and was at her knees, gasping, a second later. She kicked the revolver out of his hand and stood over him.

"Now," she said, her weapon trained on his red, sweaty face. He stared at her, puzzled, and she shook her head. "I wasn't talking to you."

She gestured with her other hand, and he gaped, apparently noticing for the first time the small camera and microphone she'd affixed to the bulkhead.

"You don't—you can't! I'm a commander!" He sobbed.

She gestured again.

"Warrant," she said. "You made it easy. You spend money like you're allergic to it. Your wife cut you off years ago. You can't even kill her for money. You'll never pay off your debts, no matter how many dirty deals you make."

His features crumpled, and he collapsed bawling on the floor of the stateroom, his voice a hoarse, childish bellow of surprise and protest.

It wasn't until she'd handcuffed his meaty hands behind his back and searched him that she looked up at the second camera, which she'd placed above the captain's chair. She stood over him and ignored his blubbering and inarticulate arguments for his freedom.

She glanced to her right at the digital clock on the instrument panel. It took nine minutes for the Crisis Response Team to arrive, and by the time the first black-clad, helmeted officer approached aft, she was exhausted.

She relinquished control of the prisoner and let a pair of young officers assist her from the yacht to their large, high-tech vehicle. They asked no questions but handed her a blanket. She wrapped herself in it and only then realized how cold she'd grown. Her muscles were stiff and her limbs heavy, and she shivered uncontrollably as she leaned back against the hard seat in the far end of the tactical van.

She leaned back and let the unit do its work without her for a few minutes. Then she shook her head.

Digging through her dripping purse, she pulled her cell phone out of its zippered baggie and found it dry.

"Tori," she said, unable to raise her voice above a whisper. "There's a boat. Snob Hill, at Miller's place. It's—"

"I know it," Tori cut in. "What's on the boat?"

"Not what, who. Peterson, Smith, Fortune. I'm sure of it."

There was a pause, and Tori grunted. "If they're alive."

"Yes." She closed her eyes. "If they're alive, that's where they are. We need a warrant. Banks—that should help. And Judge Fuller likes you."

"I'll let you know."

And she was gone. She thanked each of the men and looked around. The officers needed her to leave but didn't know how to ask, so she gathered the itchy blanket and held it aloft as she navigated out.

"Great work, you guys, thanks," she said over her shoulder. She hustled to what had once been Lauren's Volvo and sat for a moment staring at the sky. The storm was moving out. The rain had mostly stopped, the lights were back on, and the clouds were thinning. In an hour or two the afternoon would be as bright as if the violent, blinding storm had never come.

She knew what to do and realized she had very little time in which to do it. She snagged her backpack and purse and ran to the dock. An officer stepped in her path as she headed toward the finger piers, and she yanked out her badge to show him.

She cut left and went down the third row of berths to *Bernice*. She'd bought deck shoes and a captain's hat for Tori, back when she bought the boat. Thankful she and Tori wore the same shoe size, she kicked off the hobbling heels she'd donned for her excursion onto Banks's boat, shucked on the Sebagos, and eyed the ignition. She'd never taken the cruiser out, and she muttered an inarticulate prayer as she turned the key. The cold engine turned over, and she let her long-dormant muscle memory take over. The refurbished craft with the new motor was thirty-four feet long and moved smoothly despite the chop. She eased out of the berth and into the channel, the only boat moving for now.

She eyed the sky for what felt like the tenth time that day. The clouds were indeed thinning, and she cursed. Other folks would come out, if only to check on their boats. She'd have to skirt the shoreline instead of cutting across the open water.

She headed north. As she zipped along, she could smell her own fear. She was cold and tired and brittle with adrenaline. What if she failed? What if they were already dead? What if she was wrong, and they weren't being held on the boat?

"Suck it up, cupcake," she told herself for the second time that day. She shook off her fears and thought about how she'd get on the yacht without being detected. It took eighteen agonizing minutes to cruise the shoreline and get within sight of the gigantic yacht, and by then she knew what she'd have to do.

Snob Hill, as Briarwood's northernmost point was called, was an isolated enclave left to forest but for six far-flung mansions, and Dan Miller's behemoth domicile was the first of these. She dropped anchor just before sailing into his potential line of sight.

She eyed the tender she'd protested having to buy when she berthed at Green Hand Marina. The harbormaster had insisted, stating the regulations dictated every craft at Green Hand have a working lifeboat of some kind. She'd grumbled about it but had bought the cheapest aluminum dinghy available through the harbormaster's cousin.

She'd never even checked its seaworthiness, so when she dropped it in the water she held her breath. The small boat sat low in the water and barely had room for her and the attached oars, but it floated.

She eased down off the port side, backpack on and feet pressed against the far end of the tender. She hadn't rowed a boat in ten years or more, and her body was already sore from her earlier exertions. Nonetheless, she grabbed an oar in each hand and blew out air to clear her head.

"Slow and easy, now." She started gently, drawing the lightweight paddles through the water. The waves she'd sliced through on *Bernice* were hurdles the dinghy had to scramble over one by one. She fixed her gaze on Miller's long, tall yacht, too big and too fancy for this small city. Then she worked one paddle to turn a one-eighty. She eyeballed a cell-phone tower that had been made to look like a conifer and checked over her shoulder to make sure of her geometry.

Then came the hard part. She rowed back toward his floating obscenity with her eyes focused on the ugly signal tower. It reminded her of the fake roses on his plastic signs. She focused on that ugly fake tree and how it reminded her of his ugly fake flowers and let her disgust fuel her. Her shoulders were screaming within the first minute, and her entire torso joined the chorus only seconds later.

"Oh, I'm outta shape," she muttered as she made her snail's progress to the yacht. The clouds thinned more as the minutes ticked by, and she saw a few persistent rays of sunlight break through as the storm moved east. Soon, she had no idea how far she'd gone or how long she'd been rowing. She squinted at the cell tower and adjusted slightly.

"Well, if I see his house in front of me, then I've gone too far."

She laughed, a low sound that to her ears seemed more hysterical than ironic. But she was committed now. She would row until she reached that damned yacht if it killed her. She couldn't live with the alternative of leaving three innocent people to die, especially when one of them was her former partner and one had a little girl depending on her. She started counting up all of the time she'd taken to figure things out, all of the time she'd wasted because she was distracted by Tori, by Shay, by her own emotions. Every minute of sleep, of driving, of losing focus was a blot on her soul. What if she was too late? What if Miller had them all killed yesterday, this morning, ten minutes ago? She shook her head and focused on the work.

She couldn't feel her hands anymore, but the rowing took over. She pictured herself as part of a toy boat, a robot woman whose movement was driven by motor rather than muscle. That helped. She felt the pain, the cold, the exhaustion, the despair. But it didn't matter.

When she backed into the tall, wide stern of Miller's huge yacht, she was startled out of her nearly somnolent state. She drew around to the port side, away from the house, and looked up. *The Biggest* was so tall she couldn't see at first how to board her. But a rope ladder hung only feet from her, and she blinked at it for a moment as if trying to remember how to climb such a thing.

Finally she managed to break out of her reverie and shift. She tied the tender to the bottom of the rope ladder and pulled out her phone. Tori had texted a brief message: *Warrant signed. Boat only.*

She took out her old Smith and Wesson .38 revolver, the one she'd had since her first years in Briarwood. Her duty weapon was in the hands of the Crisis Response Team, and she hadn't brought anything bigger. She couldn't have it in hand while going up the ladder, so she stuck it in the ankle holster she'd slipped on just in case.

After taking a moment to catch her breath, she pulled herself up to hang off the ladder's bottom rung. Her arms were shaking and her legs leaden. It was several seconds before she could compel herself to reach higher. Overtired and shaky with adrenaline, she missed with her first attempt at swinging up her right foot and almost fell into the water. She cursed softly and shook her head to clear it.

Peterson would find you and save you, she told herself. He would never give up on you. Don't you dare give up on him. And don't forget little Jessica, stuck in foster care until she gets her mommy back. She thought about Teresa Fortune and her dreary life and blinked hard. It might not be much of a life, she thought, but Fortune has a right to live it.

That was enough to make her take a deep breath and try again. This time her foot found purchase, and she hauled herself up. Both feet on the bottom rung and her sore hands barely gripping the sides of the rope ladder, she was able to talk herself into going up to the next one. That was much easier, and the next rung was even easier. She was up at the edge of the platform in a matter of a couple of minutes, and she eyeballed his peach-colored mansion as she rested for a moment before taking on the task of pulling herself from ladder to deck. Her head was only a couple of inches above the rail's edge, and she prayed no one noticed her.

What she expected to see, she couldn't have said. Giant topiary animals bordered wide twin lawns and matching fountains. They weren't playful giraffes or elephants, though. The greenery had been carved into the shapes of verdant predators. Pouncing tigers, roaring lions and looming bears threatened anyone who looked at his home. She got the giggles then, unable to rid her mind of the picture of him as a belligerent, frightened child who needed the promise of protection the brutally shaped bushes offered.

Fear makes men dangerous, she thought. Taking a couple of deep breaths, she forced her body to make the last great effort to scramble from the ladder to the deck quickly and quietly. It wasn't graceful, she was sure, but she managed to find herself flat on the wide, flat diving platform that was unusable in relatively shallow Briarwood Bay. She could have kissed its dirt-spattered surface. Instead, she sat up and pulled her revolver out of her ankle holster.

She gave herself twenty seconds to rest. Then she crawled forward and sat up when she was sure no one could see her. Catching her breath for another few seconds, she looked around. As far as she could tell, no one was aboveboard on the luxury yacht. She crouched and snuck along the port side, ensuring she could see no one on the boat and no one could see her.

Finally, crouched low, she entered the saloon. The expansive interior was lavishly appointed but featured a variety of broken glasses and bottles, trash strewn on the floor and benches and a few broken branches and pebbles.

Even given the recent storm, it was a lot of debris for a large, mostly sheltered space. Finally she saw a torn plastic trash bag hooked on a window blind. The back of the main saloon was open to the aft deck, and she could almost picture the gusting wind thrusting a bag of garbage up to where a fixed window blind cut it open.

She examined the trash. Water bottles, browned apple cores, greasy burger wrappers and an empty strawberry-scented pink lip balm tube told the story. At least one woman, at least one or two prisoners kept on the yacht for several days. This made sense if her theory was correct. She again took her phone out of the zippered baggie and ensured the sunlight had strengthened enough that she didn't need to use her flash. She took several photographs, ensuring at least two included the lip balm. She texted them to Tori in case something happened to her or her phone.

Past the main saloon were a second large stateroom and a good-sized galley. Still crouching, she threaded her way forward. The galley was split in equal halves by a tall, wide hatch adorned with a lock as big as her fist. She eyed it balefully and wondered if she'd have to force it off the door.

She looked in the drawer nearest the hatch and rolled her eyes when she found in it an oversized key. She pocketed the key after removing the heavy lock, wondering if this was all too easy. Had Banks had time to somehow warn Miller? Had her reckless plan spurred him to kill the kidnapped trio? She steadied her breathing. If she might face foes on the other side of the hatch, she'd better be ready. She felt reassured by the solid feel of her reliable old .38 revolver that never misfired and rarely missed.

She eased back and waited, bunched on her aching ankles with her weapon her only friend—and listened. She heard birds singing on Snob Hill and a few truck engines laboring up the frontage road just north of Green Hand Marina. She heard the waves, calmer now and lapping at the yacht and its dock. She heard no movement on the dock and no movement on the luxury watercraft, but she waited an extra thirty seconds anyway.

She took a last look around before finally moving forward and stepping through the hatch. She went down two steps and eased the hatch shut behind her. She crouched to take in the dim view. Again she waited, letting her eyes adjust to the gloom, and tiptoed down to the lower level, her legs bent nearly in half as she led with her weapon as much as she could.

It was oddly silent in the narrow passageway belowdecks, and she listened in vain for movement. The sound of the waves was deafening. Ah, she thought, natural soundproofing. White noise from the water. There was a large stateroom dead ahead, its pocket door open. She passed two doors on each side, each with a locked deadbolt on the outside.

The oversized captain's quarters extended all the way to the prow. Red, gold, and white furnishings and a quartet of portholes on each side made it bright and cheery. It was also empty. She cleared the head, just in case, and headed aft to check the head under the galley. That, too, was empty, and she eyeballed the cabins on either side of the corridor.

She picked the port side to open first. She crouched low before she opened the deadbolt and swung the door open.

Peterson lay curled on his side on a short bench. He glared at the open door and then saw her. His eyes flew open, and she put a finger to her lips. He'd lost weight, and he looked about a decade older than he had just days before, but he was alive. He wore a stained white undershirt and track pants too short for his long legs. His beard was patchy and nearly white, but the spark in his sunken eyes was bright. She motioned at him to stay put and be quiet, and he nodded his understanding, pressing his thin lips together.

She made a questioning face and he pointed. She nodded and eased back out. A minute later she'd opened both starboard doors and signaled to Staci Smith to stay quiet. Smith had lost weight too and had dark circles under her eyes. Her hair was lank and limp, and her skin was sallow. She wore a black tank top and fuzzy pink pajama pants. She gaped at Brenda and teared up, covering her mouth with both hands.

The third cabin was empty and smelled of vomit and feces and bleach. The fourth was empty save a built-in cot and cupboard. She gestured in the doorway of the occupied cabins and looked up at the hatch. If someone came along, she had no real plan to get out other than shooting at anyone who came down.

By now the two prisoners were behind her, and she whispered to Peterson. "Fortune?"

"Dead," he said. "Junkie, only lasted three days."

She handed her cell phone to Smith. "Text Tori. Name's right there. Tell her two urgent packages. Move on the second warrant."

"What?"

"She'll know what it means."

They had to wait nearly eleven minutes, with Brenda stationed in the narrow hall. She convinced Peterson and Smith to hide inside Teresa Fortune's former cell, since due to its aft position it was the one hardest to hit with gunfire from the hatch.

By the time the Crisis Response Team sent its first scout onto the yacht, her arm was shaking, and the tip of her Smith and Wesson was dancing. She ascertained the new arrival was a member of the department and that the rest of the team was behind and around him, and then she let her hand slowly drift downward. She handed her revolver over to the next man down the stairs, and for the second time that day she let the Crisis Response Team take over.

Everyone around her was talking, moving, asking her questions, and she just wanted to get Peterson and Smith out of their nightmare.

"Listen, fellas," she said, "I gotta get off this bucket. I fucking hate boats."

They laughed as if she'd made a joke, and she smiled to let them pretend.

"You'll never hear the end of that one," Peterson said in his low growl. He laughed, and she was startled into giggling. By the time they disembarked they were clinging to each other, howling with laughter. She tried to ignore how gaunt he was, and how even with the nightmare he'd been through he looked better than before, because by now he'd been sober for days.

"We need to get you to Joe's as soon as possible," she said when she could talk again. "Sop up some of that grease with your buddies."

He nodded, his mouth screwed up tight because a man doesn't cry in front of other people. That's what she knew he thought, and she rubbed his bony back to give him the love he didn't want to admit he needed.

"It was my fault," he said. "I got pissed over them dragging you into that damned hearing. The little gal there loved him, but he had to be working for somebody smarter. I talked to Vallejo one night at The Hole, and I said too much. I don't know if he said something or if somebody overheard me."

"Peterson," she started.

"I asked Vallejo who was important to Donnelly, Borelli. I got him to tell me all about the little gal and the other, the junkie. All I got was their names, and I musta been talking too much, I don't remember. I'm so sorry."

She shook her head. "Not your fault. I should never have gone out on my own like that. They must've panicked."

"They were going to kill us tomorrow. That little gal talked about her baby all the time."

She looked up at his expressionless face and realized he'd accepted his own impending death but hadn't been able to accept Smith's.

"I should've put it together sooner," she said.

He laughed. "You always were a little slow on the uptake."

She laughed and hugged him. "When everything settles down, you and I need to talk about Dottie's boyfriend."

"Aye-aye, Captain," he said, sputtering with laughter when she flipped him off.

Tori was on the dock, running toward her. She broke off from Peterson and smiled so Tori would know everything was okay. They hugged, and she felt Tori pull Peterson in to join them. When Smith sat on the dock and started crying, Brenda pointed.

"Let her call her daughter. Let the baby hear her voice."

Tori pulled away and called the social worker, who called the foster mother, and the three of them shamelessly eavesdropped while Smith told Jessica that everything was going to be okay. They'd be together again soon, home again soon.

Then it was a trip to the hospital and hours of debriefing and Peterson's friends showing up with their big smiles and back-slapping and teasing, once they saw Peterson was all right. They all stood around to watch Smith's tearful reunion with her daughter, and at one point Tori joked there better not be any crime in Briarwood because half the department was at the hospital. Then it was back to the station and more debriefing.

By the time everything was done, she was giddy with weariness. She let Tori drive her home and slumped in the Mustang's passenger seat with her eyelids half-closed.

"Hey, we're here." Tori's voice was soft. "Want me to help you in?"

"I'm okay." She couldn't make herself move. "Thank you. Will it all stand?"

"Oh, yeah, definitely. Banks is singing like a little bird. They can't get him to shut up. Miller's done. The whole network is unraveling. Walton's already given a press conference. You could have been the hero of the story, but he's respecting your wishes. You're just an unnamed officer, for now. When it all goes to court, it'll be different. Shay called to ask if we needed help, if you were okay, if everyone made it."

"Mason Harding?"

"Arrested without incident. Shay hired him a bigshot lawyer. She's going to help him negotiate a plea deal."

"I don't think he's a bad guy. I think he was a little crazy with grief, and Miller played on that."

"I assume the lawyer will say something like that. And Harding had access to a lot of Miller's information. He built the server it was all stored on. I get the impression he has a lot to offer the DA, which will help."

"Good. Thanks."

Tori nodded in acknowledgment. "You did a great job. How did you get—I saw a little rowboat. How did you get that?"

"I bought you a boat. For your birthday."

"What? Where have you—Jesus, Brenda, why didn't you tell me?"

"Green Hand Marina. The boat is *Bernice*." The other question she ignored.

"For Bernice Bing, of course. And you took the boat as far as you could and then rowed the little one over so he couldn't see you."

"Uh-huh." She sat up and looked Tori in the eye.

"You knew they'd been taken. I didn't believe it. I'm sorry."

"Don't apologize. You had no reason to believe it."

"They took them because you talked to them, just like you said."

"Peterson mouthed off about Donnelly not being smart enough to organize this whole thing. He doesn't know who overheard him or if Vallejo told Banks or what."

"Miller panicked, from what I heard. He got some of his less-scrupulous guards to kidnap these people, and then he didn't know what to do with them. There's a crowd of his employees begging to flip on him. Bren, you did it."

"Thanks for being a lifeline. You really came through with the warrants, with the teams. This wouldn't have been possible without your help. I don't think I ever realized how good you are at your job. You're a good cop. I'm sorry I never really recognized that before."

Tori looked stricken. She screwed up her face, looked away and swallowed hard, and finally looked back at her with damp eyes.

It was just dawn, and the first rays of the new day were poking over the horizon. They lit Tori with the golden light of hope and renewal, and she thought for a moment of just leaning forward and kissing her longtime lover, her would-be wife.

They could rekindle the love they'd shared. Tori could move back in, or they could buy a new house. They could take all those trips they talked about. They could get married at long last. They could adopt a child. They could get a dog. They could live the dream. Part of her yearned for the life they'd once imagined living together. Once upon a time, they were good together and could have built that life they both wanted. And now they were both wiser. They were both more grateful and more accepting. It would be easy to start over. They would do a better job this time, both of them.

But she didn't do it. She couldn't have explained why, but just like in Tori's office there was a wall between them. She smiled and thanked her again. She dug in her backpack for the leather string with the keys to the Green Hand slip row gate and the *Bernice*.

"She was a gift to you. You should have her. Berth Twenty is her home. She's anchored just east of Snob Hill, just about in line with Tremont Parkway."

Tori shook her head even as she took the key. "But—"

"I'll get the paperwork to you next week sometime. You can take over the berthing fees next month. They're monstrous."

"You're getting rid of me," Tori said, frowning. "This is your way of getting rid of me."

She laughed. "You know what? I don't know where we stand. I'm sorry. It's not that I don't care, I just don't have the energy to think about it right now."

"Of course not. You're exhausted." Tori's bright blue eyes searched her face. "And maybe Shay has something to do with it."

She blinked. "I don't know."

"Yeah." Tori laughed. "If you say so, Bren."

"I love you. I always will. If you need me, I'll be there, no questions asked. Beyond that, I don't know."

Tori turned to face the steering wheel again. "Okay."

"I do know one thing."

"What?"

"I really do hate boats."

Bella Books, Inc.

Women. Books. Even Better Together.

P.O. Box 10543
Tallahassee, FL 32302

Phone: 800-729-4992
www.bellabooks.com